James Phelps is an award-winning senior reporter for Sydney's *The Daily Telegraph* and *The Sunday Telegraph*. He began as an overnight police-rounds reporter before moving into sport, where he became one of Australia's best news-breaking rugby league journalists. James was then appointed News Corp Australia's Chief National Motorsports Writer and travelled the world chasing Formula 1 stories, as well as covering Australia's V8 Supercar races. As well as writing bestselling and critically acclaimed biographies of Dick Johnson and Johnathan Thurston, James established himself as Australia's number-one true crime writer with his bestselling prison series, including *Australia's Hardest Prison*, *Australia's Most Murderous Prison*, and *Australia's Toughest Prisons*. His most recent books are *Australian Heist* (2018), a dramatic retelling of the true story behind Australia's largest gold robbery, and *Australian Code Breakers* (2020), a gripping account of how Australian cryptographers helped bring about the most vital Allied naval victory of World War I.

Also by James Phelps:

JAMES PHELPS

THE INSIDE MAN

HarperCollins*Publishers*

HarperCollins*Publishers*

Australia • Brazil • Canada • France • Germany • Holland • India
Italy • Japan • Mexico • New Zealand • Poland • Spain • Sweden
Switzerland • United Kingdom • United States of America

First published in Australia in 2021
by HarperCollins*Publishers* Australia Pty Limited
Level 13, 201 Elizabeth Street, Sydney NSW 2000
ABN 36 009 913 517
harpercollins.com.au

A catalogue record for this book is available from the National Library of Australia

ISBN: 978 1 4607 5864 9 (paperback)
ISBN: 978 1 4607 1241 2 (ebook)
ISBN: 978 1 4607 8640 6 (audiobook)

Cover design by Luke Causby, Blue Cork
Cover images by istockphoto.com
Typeset in Sabon LT Std by Kirby Jones
Printed and bound by CPI Group (UK) Ltd, Croydon, CR0 4YY

PROLOGUE

Holsworthy Army Base, Sydney, NSW, Australia

RILEY Jax woke up with a gun in his hand and a body on his floor.

Bee-beep. Bee-beep. Bee-beep.

He turned off the alarm on his wristwatch.

6 am. A Monday.

There was a sharp, unfamiliar metallic taste in his mouth, his head was fuzzy and he was coated in a fine sheen of cold sweat. He eased himself up out of his military cot bed and forced himself to study the body on the floor.

It was a clean kill: the dead man had taken one bullet to the brain and another to the heart, at close range. He was dressed like a civilian, but could have been ex-military from his build, his buzzcut, his neatly pressed clothing and his shiny boots. Jax had never laid eyes on him before – he knew that for sure because he never forgot a face. Never.

Jax tried to recall the events of the previous night, but the thread was broken – he had lost almost ten hours. He couldn't remember anything after 8.14 pm.

Nothing. Not a thing. Everything black.

He remembered leaving the mess hall after dinner at 7.04 pm. It had been a balmy evening, the temperature still high after the heat of the day. A couple of the guys had been sitting around outside. He'd stopped and chatted with them for a few minutes, not because he wanted to but because it was expected.

After that he'd walked into his army-issue apartment – little more than an oversized bedroom with a small adjoining bathroom containing just a toilet and basin – grabbed a towel, his toiletry bag and his thongs before walking back out. The floodlights had been on but not yet needed.

The base, a haphazard assortment of buildings bedded on concrete and bordered by barbed wire and bush, had been quiet. It always was on a Sunday night, the last night of freedom before the week's first crack-of-dawn roll call; most of the soldiers would have been at the pub. They wouldn't start stumbling in until 10 pm. Some wouldn't be back then. They would have just enough time to change out of their perfume-soaked civvies and make muster.

Jax had only walked past two men on his way to the shower block. He'd nodded at them before entering and showering on his own. Towel tied around his waist, thongs squeaking as they were worked by wet feet, he saw nobody after his shit, shower and shave.

His memory became clouded after that, though he did remember returning to his room. He recalled pulling on boxer shorts and a singlet, checking his phone to find out if Nikki had called and, seeing she hadn't, grabbing a book – *A Theory of Human Motivation* by Abraham Maslow – and collapsing into his cot for an early night. And that's where his memory stopped, at 8.14 pm.

Since then: nothing. *Not a thing. Everything black.*

Instead of the Maslow, he was now gripping a Glock. His

Glock. Two rounds short of being fully loaded. He had no memory of firing his gun. He had no memory of loading it. He had no memory of even signing it out. The book he had gone to bed with was back on the shelf. He noted that it was sitting next to another title by the same author.

The fuzziness he'd felt on waking had been replaced by a hangover-like headache. The metallic taste in his mouth remained: more bile than blood, he noted, as he turned his attention back to the body. To the dead man on his floor.

Clean-shaven with a square jaw chiselled as if from rock, the deceased male was partially propped up against the wall opposite where Jax slept. The hole in the plasterboard above the body was the size and shape of his head. Eyes open and pupils enlarged, the dead man sat in a pool of blood. His fingers were splayed and stiff. *Rigor mortis. Dead for at least four hours.*

Jax scanned his room. *One entry and exit point.* He then looked at the body. He considered the victim's path. He considered the killer's path. He stood and shuffled left, stopping when he reached the adjacent wall. He hugged the plasterboard as he tiptoed along the carpet. Keeping to the base of the wall to avoid contaminating the scene, he was soon close enough to touch the body. He extended his arm and placed the back of his index finger on the victim's neck.

The man was cold – but still warmer than the room. *Dead for at least four hours but no more than eight.* He looked at the man's eyes. He did not have a flashlight but knew the oversized pupils would not react if he did. It was, however, bright enough for him to note the whites were lightly bloodshot and slightly yellow in the corner. *The Kevorkian sign.* He had only read about it once, but that was enough for him to remember it. He would need a thermometer and access to the man's anus to establish the exact time of death, but the rigor mortis, his touch test and the opacity of the eyes told him that the man had expired sometime between 10 pm and 4 am. He retraced his steps and returned to the bed.

Jax turned his attention to the blood spatter. Gun still in his hand, standing beside his bed, he studied his walls and then his ceiling. He did the maths, taking into account the man's size, what he knew about speed and impact – which was more than most – and the specs of the only weapon in the room.

It all added up.

The size of the hole in the wall, the blood spatter, the position of the body and the time of death all indicated the man had been killed right here, in this room. The numbers did not lie. While blood could be flicked and bodies could be repositioned, figures could not be fudged.

The dead man had been standing in the centre of Jax's room when the first round had been fired into his skull. The blood spatter on the ceiling and the entry wounds on the corpse indicated the round had struck with force, the impact of the kill-shot snapping the man's head back and to the left. He'd been falling when the second round had hit him in the heart. Thumping into the left side of his chest, the force of that shot changed the body's path – sending it slightly to the right. The wall broke his fall and left him propped up. Sitting. The blood spatter on the wall above the victim's head had come from the exit wound caused by that second bullet. Detectives would find one bullet lodged in the wall behind the body and the other in the back of the corpse's brain.

Jax looked back at his gun. His Glock.

At the murder weapon.

He suddenly felt cold. Numb. His mind went quiet. He began to sway as he looked at the ground. His boots snapped him out of the trance. They were shined to perfection and tied tight, but he could not remember putting them on. Book in hand, he had flicked off his thongs and swung his bare feet onto the bed.

Jax slapped himself in the face. It didn't help. He still couldn't remember putting his boots on. Nor could he remember killing a man. And that was impossible. For Riley Jax remembered everything. He had never forgotten a thing in his life.

Until now.

CHAPTER 1

Saint-Étienne-du-Rouvray, Normandy, France

'*ALHAMDULILLAH,*' he said before ending the call.

The bald man scanned the green grass and the cobblestone path that divided it before turning his attention back to his phone. Holding the phone with his left hand, he used his right hand to stick a paperclip-like tool into its side. A small black tray popped out. He lifted the SIM card from its cradle before dropping the phone onto the stone path. With a violent thrust of his hip, he jammed his foot onto the phone, then stomped on it over and over and over until the screen was smashed to shards.

Satisfied the phone was destroyed, he put the SIM card between his teeth and bit down. He had to wriggle and twist it to rip the toughened plastic. Once he'd finally torn it in two, he examined the metallic markings – the electronic chip that held all the information – to make sure they were severed, before putting the pieces back in his mouth. Then he swallowed.

He thought it was pointless. The SIM would be destroyed if he succeeded in his mission. And he would not fail. But he'd been told to do it. So he did. He never questioned the Mahdi. No one questioned him.

He unzipped his backpack, reached in and pulled out a two-litre container that he had filled with liquid. He twisted the lid off, picked up the shattered phone and dropped it in. He screwed the lid back on and put the container – with the useless iPhone now at the bottom – back into his bag.

'What about the pills?' his companion asked. 'He said we had to take the pills. It will make it easier.'

The man reached into his pocket and pulled out a white plastic pill bottle.

CONTROLLED DRUG – POSSESSION WITHOUT AUTHORITY ILLEGAL
DEXTROAMPHETAMINE SULFATE 5mg
TAKE ONE A DAY

They both swallowed five before removing their black hoods.

DESPITE the sixteenth-century Church of Saint Étienne being the oldest Catholic institution in the small suburban town of Saint-Étienne-du-Rouvray in northern Normandy (home to 30,000 people), waning attendance at mass had been a problem for years and the church was generally only well attended for the occasional funeral or wedding. But Father Bisset had managed to draw a full house for mass on this bright May day, largely due to the changes he'd been making to the service over recent months. With permission from the local diocese, Bisset had scrapped the traditional Latin Mass and replaced it with a French-spoken, more family-friendly service. A number of the older parishioners had resisted the changes, but Bisset had been adamant that the church had to adapt to stay relevant and survive, and the parishioners came around when they started to see the pews filling.

Bisset looked out at the congregation – children, young

mothers and fathers, the future, in other words – then left the sacristy and made his way to the altar. He noticed a couple of men he didn't recognise sitting close to the aisle in the very last row of pews. He may not have even spotted them had it not been for the morning sun streaming through the oversized stained-glass windows and lighting up the pair's closely shaved scalps like light bulbs.

White robes flowing, modernised missal in hand, Father Bisset climbed the three steps to the altar, the congregation quietening down as he did so. He paused for a moment of silent prayer when he reached the predella, and then turned to face his people.

Father Bisset's brow furrowed when he saw that the bald men, the newcomers, were no longer sitting in their pew, but had moved to the doors of the main entrance, where one of them was wrestling with what appeared to be a length of chain. Usually wide open and welcoming, the oversized oak entrance doors that were as old as the church itself had been shut. Bemused at first, the priest studied the men, a few of the congregation also turning in their seats to see what the commotion was.

'Excuse me,' Bisset called loudly. 'What are you doing?' Though murmurs rose from the congregation, the men said nothing and carried on as though they hadn't heard the priest at all.

'Excuse me! Excuse me!' the priest shouted more loudly. 'Who are you and what are you doing back there?'

The men looked up this time, but still didn't respond. Instead, one took up a position in front of the closed doors as if guarding them, while the other stepped forward into the aisle, reaching into a backpack as he did so.

The priest's stomach turned when he saw the gun. 'No!' Father Bisset boomed, dropping his missal, the holy book forgotten as the word 'gun' swept through the congregation and terrified cries began to erupt from the pews.

'Silence!' the man yelled in French as he waved his gun. He was holding a hunting knife in his other hand.

As the priest strode down the aisle, one arm outstretched in an attempt to pacify him, the intruder raised his gun and aimed. 'Shut up! Or I will shoot,' he screamed, pointing the scratched and scuffed weapon at the priest's chest.

Time slowed right down and silence returned while the congregation took in the scene. As he closed the distance between them, Bisset could see that the gunman had shaved more than his head. He had no eyebrows, no eyelashes. No hair at all.

THE GUNMAN was soaked in sweat. His heart was pounding, his pulse racing: the dextroamphetamine – a pharmaceutical-grade amphetamine, usually prescribed to narcolepsy sufferers – had kicked in. He felt euphoric. Gun in one hand, knife in the other, he was doing Allah's work.

'Get back, get back!' he roared, stalking towards the priest, his adrenaline pumping, almost feeling like a god himself.

The priest backed up, stumbling on the steps as he reached the altar, before retreating as far as he could.

'Don't move,' the gunman said, gesturing to his gun as he made it to the altar and then swivelled to face the people.

The cries started up again, some parishioners cowering in their seats, others frantically scanning the nave for a means of escape or defence.

'Shut up!' the attacker shouted, this time in English, as he fired a round into the ceiling. 'Sit down and shut up, or die!' He turned back to the priest. 'Tell them!' he demanded in English. 'You understand what I am saying?'

The priest nodded and stepped nervously forward and into the light. 'My people,' he said, clearing his throat. 'Be calm, my people, God is with us.' The crying and wailing slowly died down but the church was not silent. Some sobbed. Some whimpered. A lone baby somewhere up the back was crying.

'Pray to the Lord our saviour now.' The priest looked to the gunman and nodded. 'And do what this man says. Pray for this man that the Lord comes to him. The Lord will protect us, he is watching over us now, as ever.' Bisset made the sign of the cross and many of the parishioners followed him, crossing themselves silently and mouthing soundless prayers.

The gunman walked behind Father Bisset and pulled him into a headlock with the arm holding the Beretta. The blade glinted as he held it to the holy man's throat, drawing a small amount of blood as he pushed it into the priest's plump skin.

'*Arrêtez-vous!*' boomed a voice from the mass, as a lone male parishioner in his forties pushed through a pew of people and started down the centre aisle. 'Stop right now!' he bellowed in heavily accented English.

The gunman regarded him, surprised, and a small smile played on his lips – just before he shouted, '*Allahu Akbar!*', and slit the priest's throat.

Blood gushed onto the altar.

The assassin didn't bother pointing his gun at the snarling hero who was still charging towards him, his fists raised and ready to strike. Though he was only a couple of steps away, the gunman was sure he would never reach him. And it didn't matter if he did: they would both die anyway.

He dropped his gun and smiled at the hero as he closed in.

'*Allahu Akbar!*' the man at the back echoed, as he detonated the bomb.

CHAPTER 2

Long Bay Correctional Complex, Sydney, NSW, Australia

JAX looked up as the bus came to a shuddering halt. He'd spent the entire trip with his head down, eyes boring into the floor or staring at the scuffed boots he'd worn to court. He'd been wearing the same boots when he'd killed the man in his room. If he'd killed him. His memory had not returned.

Jax hadn't dared make eye contact with anyone since he'd been hustled onto the bus. He was one of fourteen cuffed and chained men who'd boarded at Sydney's Downing Centre in the middle of the city forty-five minutes earlier. Each had been escorted by a guard to a single seat within a padlocked cage-like frame, the heavily customised functioning as a high-security prison on wheels.

He was under no illusions about who his companions on this journey were. Shaved heads, neck tattoos, bulging biceps, scars, noses that had been broken too many times – these were hardened men who had committed crimes serious enough to warrant a stay in Long Bay.

And he was one of them.

He fixed his gaze out the window and tried not to think about Nikki, and the look on her face when his sentence had been handed down. Ten years on the bottom, twelve on top. She'd been so shocked that all she'd done was let out a small cry before collapsing back into her chair in the gallery, her head in her hands. Nikki hadn't believed it would come to this, but he had known it would. A man with no memory cannot mount a defence. And like everyone else, Jax saw the evidence. All the evidence …

Jax heard the doors of the bus open and the driver shuffling out of his seat. He kept his eyes trained on the window, observing the man's movements in the reflection. His instincts told him to always be aware of his surroundings. To study every detail. Assess every risk. But he had to be careful here. He didn't want to draw attention to himself – he knew where that would lead.

As his fellow passengers started shifting in their chains, a few of them making incoherent grunts, Jax took the opportunity to glance around very quickly and take a mental snapshot of his new home. It was grim. What was left of the day had been swallowed by a towering sandstone wall, medieval and menacing, almost ten metres high and topped with loops of razor-wire. The sandstone looked as though it could withstand a nuclear blast. The fact that it had been built to keep people in – and not out – was a stark reminder of everything that Jax had lost.

'Hey, shitbags,' shouted the bus driver. 'Welcome to Long Bay. She's a fuckin' palace, ain't she?'

The driver stepped off the bus and passed an untidy bundle of papers through a slot in a glass window to a guard in a small brick station by the gate.

'Clear,' the gatekeeper hollered a few minutes later, after examining the paperwork.

As he climbed back aboard, the driver studied his cargo and his face broke into a smile. 'Marsh, huh,' he said, looking directly at a big man seated in front of Jax. 'It's welcome home for you, isn't it, mate?' He chuckled as he got back behind the wheel and shook his head as the engine burst into life.

The iron gate, its pitted metal covered by a fresh coat of olive-green paint, began to open. The noise was horrendous: two five-inch-thick slabs of metal being dragged across concrete, all grind and groan, a heavy-metal version of fingernails on a blackboard. The driver grabbed a gear and gave it some gas, the diesel explosion rocking the bus floor and bouncing the chains they all wore on their ankles.

No longer able to stop himself, Jax peered around and quickly took in his surroundings, almost subconsciously cataloguing and committing the details to memory. *Three guards talking in a group not far beyond the checkpoint we just stopped at.* He ducked his head a little lower and observed the scene beyond the bus's wide front windscreen. *Approximately 50 metres of road leading to another set of gates flanked by another small brick gatehouse.*

The bus threatened to stall as it slowly rumbled down the road. *Another guard, four in total, stationed along the road.* He squinted into the setting sun crossing his vision. Just inside the first gate, he saw a low, squat brick building, no more than two floors, with four east-facing windows per floor. *The reception block.*

'The birdcage,' said the big man the driver had addressed as Marsh, who had turned round and was now looking Jax straight in the eye, one pointed finger jabbing the air. 'That's what they call it. Just a stretch of road between two gates. They shut one gate before the other opens, so none of the animals get out.'

Jax said nothing and looked down. There was a moment of silence. When Jax looked back up, the man's face was contorted with rage. He was menacing: clad in muscle and with a face punctured by scars. Probably about forty years old from what Jax could tell.

'Don't you fucken ignore me, ya young cunt. When I talk to ya, ya fucken listen, okay,' he snarled.

Time suddenly slowed as Jax considered his response. Usually, Jax could process in seconds what others would take minutes to fathom. But right now he couldn't make a decision. He didn't have enough information. He went to say something but stopped himself.

Fear was clouding his mind.

Killers wore a warning in their eyes. Jax had seen it in the army and he was seeing it now. The cuffs, the chains and the fact that the man called Marsh was on his way to a maximum-security prison obviously marked him out as dangerous, but it was his eyes that offered the starkest warning. They were cold and cruel. Vacant. Dead.

Jax didn't know what to say, so he simply nodded before returning his gaze to the floor. He tried to shake off the dread. He told himself that there was nothing to worry about. It was just tough-guy talk. He had hardly been antagonistic – the only thing he had done was look down. Surely this Marsh would not seek retribution for such a non-event? Merely looking away couldn't make him a target. Could it?

Jax shuddered internally. He no longer had all the answers. Not in here. Not in a place where the rules of the real world no longer applied. Not here in Hell.

He retrieved an image of Marsh from his mind. He hadn't had the time to study him during the short exchange, but he could picture the man's face clearly now. It was the face of a fighter. Nose broken at least three times and never properly reset, skin pockmarked with scars, cauliflower ears – Marsh wore his violent history on his head. Jax paid close attention to the scars, all different colours, suggesting they had been sustained in not one incident, but over many years. In many fights.

Jax had only ever had two fights, and not in dark alleys or in nightclubs, but in the schoolyard as a boy. And neither of his opponents had been anything like Marsh. Jax decided to look up as soon as he thought it was safe. Compelled to continue scanning for threats, to assess this foreign, frightening world, he dragged his eyes from the floor. He was counting on Marsh having lost interest in him. But as soon as Jax lifted his head, Marsh smiled.

And then he winked.

JAX's mind raced as the bus slowed at the second gate. He couldn't be got at. Not yet. Not while he was locked in his one-man cage on the armour-plated bus. It was later he was worried about. When he was alone.

He recalled the conversation he'd had with his defence lawyer after they'd learned his sentence would be served in Long Bay. Still thinking about Nikki and her spine-tingling gasp, Jax had been distracted but he'd nevertheless taken in what was said. He closed his eyes briefly and the man's words of caution echoed in his mind.

'It's a tough break, Jax,' his lawyer had said, his voice grave. 'I was certain you'd end up on a farm. Somewhere like Lithgow. Not a maximum-security prison. Certainly not Long Bay. There's no sugar-coating it, Long Bay is a nightmare. They'll tear you apart, a young clean-cut guy like you. You're going to have to ask for protection. Are you listening? I'm trying to save your life. You are going to have to tell them you are scared, that you can't defend yourself. Tell them you have enemies. Tell them that and they'll have to put you into protective custody. And you'll need it – it's the only way you'll survive.'

He'd levelled with Jax because he felt bad. With Jax insistent on entering a guilty plea, the lawyer had only one objective: a minimal sentence in a low-security jail. And he'd failed.

'Do not refuse protection. If you do, they will come for you. They will come for your possessions, they will come for your food, they will come at you just because you are young and white. It will never be one on one. You'll have ten of them on you. They will bash you. Stab you. Might even rape you. You will be bashed, fucked or murdered. Maybe all three. And it won't stop until you do what they want. Or until you are dead.'

Jax shivered as he pondered the lawyer's final declaration. Even though Jax thought he could handle himself, he knew he'd be a fool to dismiss the warning. He knew there was some truth to it – he was entering no-man's-land now.

The driver interrupted Jax's thoughts. 'Home sweet home,' he called out as the bus shuddered to a stop. 'Her Majesty's palace. Sit tight. A guard will be along shortly.'

Jax kept his eyes down but listened hard. The pneumatic bus door whooshed open. Boots stomped and keys rattled. Five guards. They made their way down the central aisle, calling names and cracking cages. Last name first. First name last. Then a script of instructions issued matter-of-factly. The heavy-duty locks thudded as they sprang back into their metal recesses; the cage doors squealed as they were dragged open.

'Marshy,' Jax heard one of the guards rasp. 'Heard you were coming back.'

A departure from the script. Jax resisted the urge to look.

'Dodge,' came the reply. 'Looks like you've been in a good paddock. I might have to cut your rations. You get a cell sorted for me?'

'All the bells and whistles, mate.'

Jax heard a cage door screech shut and stole a glance as the pair's voices became muffled, more distant.

Marsh looked even bigger now that he was standing up – about six foot four – and his slightly hunched shoulders were broad and thick with muscle. He was wearing a T-shirt with a graffiti print, loose-fitting sports shorts and shoes without socks. There would have been nothing remarkable about his attire had he not just come from court. He hadn't made the slightest effort to look respectable for his sentencing.

The guard was far less imposing, at least from behind. Short and overweight, he lumbered his way down the aisle, continuing the banter as he escorted Marsh from the bus.

'Jax,' yelled the guard who was suddenly standing in front of his cage. 'Jax, Riley.'

'Yes, sir.'

'Officer,' the guard barked. 'Not sir. You will address me as Officer.'

'Yes, Officer,' Jax said.

'Stand up and place your hands on the bar,' he commanded, repeating an order Jax had heard the other guards issue. 'Leave them there until I say otherwise. Understand?'

'Yes, Officer.' Jax stood and faced forward, reached up to the bar in front of him.

'Okay, turn and face me,' came the command.

The man was huge, head glancing the roof, chest the width of the heavy cage door he was effortlessly pulling open. He had to be six foot eight. He was clean-cut and sharply dressed, in well-cut navy-blue trousers and a sky-blue button-up shirt that was snug enough to showcase the athletic torso beneath it. Jax, who stood six foot two, suddenly felt small.

He had read about the 'reception biff' shortly after he'd decided to plead guilty to the murder he didn't know if he'd committed. A prison stint assured, he'd bought every non-fiction prison book he could find in preparation for his sentence and speed-read the lot, scanning for salient details. A number of accounts said that the reception biff – the practice of guards viciously assaulting newly arrived prisoners in a bid to establish a position of power – was once commonplace. Once. Jax told himself not to worry.

'Exit the cage,' the guard boomed. 'Walk. Exit the bus and turn left.'

Jax complied, his chains clinking, clunking and clattering with every shuffled step. He stopped himself from raising his head after negotiating the steps. He didn't want to look up. Didn't want to lock eyes with Marsh again.

'Move,' the officer demanded. 'To the yellow line.'

Looking only at legs and the line, Jax moved to his spot in the line-up.

'I'm Officer Turner, and I am in charge of getting you all admitted and processed without incident. You will all now be placed in a holding cell,' the big man said after the bus was emptied. 'You will be separated into two groups, seven in each cell.'

Jax thought of the wink. Of being locked in a cell with Marsh.

'You will wait in that cell until your name is called. If you do not cooperate, we have the right to use force, including Taser force,' he continued. 'Once called, you will be processed by a reception officer.'

The giant walked over to Marsh. Got right up in his face. 'I meant what I said. No fucking around, Marsh,' he spat. 'No fighting, no shit. Or I won't just Taser you, I'll put you in with the Lebs.'

JAX could feel him staring. The last of the seven to be put into the first holding cell, Jax had felt his heart rate spike the moment he'd spotted Marsh sitting on a bench on the right side of the cell, his arms crossed and his back against the concrete wall.

So Jax went left, towards an underweight middle-aged man covered in sores. He ignored the smell – a cocktail of stale sweat, piss and Rexona roll-on – and took a seat next to the drug addict.

The man's stench was nauseating, but Jax was more concerned about Marsh. As Jax discreetly sized up his other cell companions, the junkie started fidgeting. Moving. Squirming.

Then he raised his knees and shoved a hand down the front of his pants.

He wriggled and groaned. The smell of shit now overpowered all the other odours. The junkie pulled his fist from his pants, pushed it towards Jax's face and partially opened his hand. 'Do us a favour, mate?' he pleaded, his whispered voice hoarse. 'Take this in for us? I've been done before. But they won't be looking at a clean fella like you.'

Jax looked at the junkie's shit-smeared palm. Then at the metal mint container – spearmint Eclipse – sheathed in cling wrap and coated in spittle. He politely shook his head.

'Argh, come on, man,' the addict said. 'Help a fella out. I'll give ya half if you get it in. They won't even search you.'

'Oi, smackhead,' a voice from across the room boomed. 'Fuck off. Go on. Fuck off. Leave me little mate alone.' Jax looked up to see Marsh stalking across the cell, pointing at the man next to Jax. 'Get up, cunt,' he continued. 'MOVE. Take your hepatitis and fuck off over there.'

The man jumped up and scurried off. Jax glanced at the now empty bench beside him. He clenched his teeth as he summed up the situation. *Six prisoners. No guards. Two cameras.* While the addict and another two prisoners lacked the physical capabilities to inflict any significant damage, aside from Marsh there were three other men in the room with enough bulk to present a threat.

'Fucking smackies,' Marsh said as he sat down heavily next to Jax. 'Place is full of the useless cunts. They would sell their mums' pussies for a hit. Don't go near 'em and certainly don't fuck 'em … They've all got fucking AIDS.'

Jax didn't respond. It was clear that Marsh was a bikie. A white Anglo-Saxon, covered in ink and powered by steroids. A man two guards had known by name. All he was missing was his leathers and patch. A Comanchero or maybe a Rebel, Jax figured. Marsh slid along the bench.

Closer to Jax.

Marsh stopped when he could move no more, his left thigh firmly pressed into Jax's right leg. Too close. Marsh placed his left arm around Jax's shoulders and pulled him in roughly.

'But you don't have to worry about 'em,' Marsh said into his ear. 'None of 'em. Not the junkies. Not the Lebs. Not the FOBs. Not the gooks. None of them. No one will fuck with you if you're one of my boys.'

His grip, loose at first, tightened.

'You're my boy, right?' Marsh asked as he flexed and squeezed.

Survival instinct kicking in, Jax gave a barely perceptible nod. It was a reflex, not a decision.

'Good,' Marsh relaxed his grip. 'You're gonna be just fine. Leave it to me. I'll make all the arrangements.'

'Marsh,' a guard shouted. 'Daniel Marsh.'

'Yep,' Marsh said as he released Jax. He stood up and crossed the cell. As the guard appeared at the cell door with a set of keys, Marsh stopped and turned back to Jax. 'I'll make the arrangements,' Marsh said again, baring his teeth in a wide grin. 'And I'll catch up with ya soon.'

Jax exhaled when Marsh was finally gone. He wanted to chase after him and tackle him. Probably would have if he'd been given another minute, but fear had temporarily paralysed him, forced him to make an unconsidered decision. And although it was nothing more than a nod, he knew his mistake could determine his standing in prison. Even cost him his life.

Still, right now Jax had a more immediate concern. The herd was thinning, with only a couple of men left in the cage, and he would soon be called and taken to another room where he would be stripped and searched. Jax wasn't overly concerned about the humiliation – dignity had long ago deserted him. He was, however, dreading the possibility of a cavity search. He was also no longer so sure that the reception biff was a practice of the past. Minutes ticked by.

'Let's go.' The guard didn't even need to call his name – there was no one else left in the cell.

Jax pushed himself to his feet and followed the guard. It was the out-of-shape officer Marsh had called Dodge. No other inmates around, Jax took the opportunity to carefully examine his surroundings. There wasn't much to see. The only thing that was of any interest in the hallway was the camera. The little red flashing light was a comfort as he followed the guard across the filthy linoleum towards a double set of sliding doors. The second set did not open until the first was shut. *Two guards. Both with batons. Another behind the counter.* Jax continued his scan. *Two cameras. One blind spot. Fuck.*

'Riley Jax,' Dodge grunted as he and Jax approached a scruffy-looking guard behind the counter – a surfer, judging from the tan and salt-matted sun-bleached hair. 'No MIN.'

The young guard got straight to it. 'Strip,' he said flatly. 'Everything off.'

'Here?' Jax asked.

'Yep.'

Jax removed his boots first, then his long black socks, each of which he rolled into a ball and stuffed inside a shoe. He placed the boots on the counter. His suit jacket slid easily off his shoulders – he'd lost weight since the arrest. His nan had brought the only suit Jax had ever owned to the courthouse on the first day of his trial, and back then he'd struggled to get the jacket on. She'd delivered that suit to Jax for every court appearance for eight months, taking it back home at the end of each day, hanging, pressing and spot-cleaning it with care. He winced at the thought of her and of the now bare cupboard where the suit had once hung.

Tie and shirt next, then he removed his belt, his pants and finally his underwear. He placed the last of his clothes on the countertop and waited for further instruction.

'I said everything.'

The kid did not even look up from the form he was filling out.

Jax looked at his wrist. 'The watch?' he asked.

'Unless it's a knock-off,' the guard said. 'Nothing worth more than fifty bucks is allowed in.'

Jax looked for the logic.

'It's so you don't get rolled,' the guard offered before he had time to figure it out.

His Casio G-Shock, bought for its military accuracy, was no fake. He figured someone would try to steal it even if it was. He took it off and gave it to the guard.

Jax stood silently as his clothes were catalogued.

'Can you can confirm everything has been accounted for?' the guard asked as he pushed a form towards Jax before handing him a pen.

Jax signed his name on the dotted line and then looked on while every single item he'd brought with him was taken away. Wrapped in plastic and placed in a tub, not to be seen for at least eight years. Maybe ten. Maybe never.

'Rogers,' the young guard shouted to Dodge. 'All done.'

Rogers took a few minutes before returning and directing Jax towards the two other guards.

'Move to the yellow line,' one of them ordered.

Jax kept his head up as he walked.

'Legs apart and bend over,' the guard ordered.

Jax widened his legs, bent at the waist and waited, trying to squash the acute humiliation rising in his chest.

'Balls up,' the guard barked. 'I said balls up. Lift your nuts. Your testicles.'

Wincing, Jax complied.

'Okay,' the guard said, satisfied he had nothing taped, stuck or strapped to his scrotum. 'Now spread your cheeks.'

Jax gritted his teeth and did as commanded. His cheeks burned. The fluorescent light above him hummed.

'Wider,' the guard said. 'Open it right up. A big stretch.'

Rogers, who was off to the side witnessing the search, chuckled and said, 'She won't be that tight after a night with Marshy.'

'Wider,' the examiner demanded.

Jax took a deep breath and swallowed. He tasted bile as he did as the guard said.

'Good,' the guard said. 'Now stand up and spin around.'

Jax complied.

'Faster,' the guard said.

Jax spun faster.

'Now bend over again and spread 'em,' the guard said. 'Nice and wide like before.'

Seemingly satisfied and ignoring another wisecrack from Rogers, the guard walked to a bench and set down his torch. Jax watched as he pulled out a rubber glove from a tissue box–like packet. Then another. White and coated in a light lubricating powder. He put them on, one at a time, tugging at the ribbing near the wrist to ensure they were tight. The snapping sound of the rubber made Jax shudder, and a sickening nausea rose in his throat.

Gloved and good to go, the officer turned back to face Jax, who was still hunched over and now fearing the worst. The guard pulled his fingers into fists and then spread them wide, stretching and straightening. Jax closed his eyes. Braced himself as best he could. His knees shook as he waited for the inevitable.

'Stand straight,' the guard ordered, now placing himself directly in front of Jax. 'Look straight ahead and stay still.' The guard combed his gloved fingers through Jax's thick blonde hair. Jax exhaled with relief.

The guard then pulled back Jax's ears and looked into

them before lifting his eyelids. 'Open your mouth,' the officer ordered. 'Wide as you can.' The guard lifted Jax's top lip and traced his upper gums with a rough gloved finger, before moving on to the bottom gum. He finished by fish-hooking the corners of Jax's mouth.

'Clear,' the guard said.

Still naked, Jax was sent back to the young surfer dude, who was checking two oversized plastic tubs on the countertop.

'Everything you own is to be kept in these two tubs,' the kid said. 'And if you can't fit it in the tubs, you can't have it. The only thing we will not take and destroy should you break this rule is legal papers. There is no limit on legal papers.'

He handed Jax a list.

'By law I am required to offer you an opportunity to check that all the items listed on this form are present and accounted for,' he said. 'Would you like to take that opportunity?'

Jax nodded. He was instructed to open the first tub and check the items against the list.

T-shirts: 4.

Check.

Fleecy tracksuit tops: 2.

Check.

Fleecy tracksuit pants: 2.

Check.

Shorts: 2.

Check.

Singlets: 4.

Check.

Underpants: 7.

Check.

Socks: 7 pairs.

Check.

Shoes: 1 pair.

Check.

Washbags: 1.

Check.

With the exception of the underpants and socks, everything was green. No logos. No patterns. No print. Solid avocado.

Jax moved on to the second tub and found his bedding. Dark blue with white stripes, the sheets brittle from bleach. One of the two solid-blue pillowcases was heavily stained. *Blood?* The blanket was covered with lint balls, more sandpaper than soft.

Then came the toiletries: toothpaste, toothbrush, toilet paper, soap and a roll-on deodorant. He checked off a plate, a bowl, a cup and some cutlery – all plastic – in the bottom of the tub, along with a number of small sachets of detergent and washing powder.

Jax confirmed that all the items on the list were present. He was then ordered to dress. Underwear and socks first – the only whites – then the tracksuit pants. They were baggy and a little short in the leg, but he doubted the prison had a tailor.

Jax grabbed the first T-shirt from the pile he'd made on the countertop and slipped it on. He noticed that none of the four T-shirts were the same shade of green. All faded to differing degrees. All second-hand. He wondered who had worn the shirts before him. A serial killer? At least the underwear appeared new.

Jax completed the all-green ensemble with a pair of custom-made prison shoes – green of course. A pair of joggers made by Dunlop, vinyl not leather, with a ribbed rubber sole, the shoes were secured with Velcro straps instead of laces. So that was true.

Jax came to a sobering realisation: his entire life had been reduced to green garb, plastic cutlery and blue-and-white sheets. A numbness descended. Jax returned the remaining items back to the tubs, which the kid told him would be delivered to his cell.

Rogers strolled in and snatched up a file before nodding Jax towards a set of double sliding doors at the rear of the room. 'Move to the yellow line,' he barked once they had whooshed open.

Jax walked into a large open space that smelled of bleach and was completely bare, except for a few faded posters tacked to the wall. 'You Are Under Video Surveillance' and 'Do You Have an Infectious Disease?' they read.

A heavy security door on the eastern wall opened and a man who looked more like an accountant than a law-enforcement official stepped through it. He waited for Rogers to walk over and hand him the file, and then took a moment to study the first page.

'Riley Jax,' he said. 'This is the last of it. Come through and take a seat.'

Short, thin and bald except for a swath of close-cropped grey hair above his ears, the man ushered Jax into an office. As the door banged heavily behind them, the man gestured to Jax to take a seat in a metal chair that had been fixed to the ground in front of a cluttered steel desk, also bolted to the floor. Jax noted two D clips, one on the floor at the base of the chair and one at the front of the seat. Anchor points for cuffs. He was obviously considered low-risk given that he hadn't been cuffed. There was also a red emergency call button on the far wall.

'All a bit strange,' the bespectacled officer said as he shuffled his way round the desk and took his seat. 'Especially for the first time. I'll try and make this as painless as possible. I am here to give you all the information you need.' He took another moment to flick through the file. 'Nineteen,' he said, with a small shake of his head. He didn't look up, so Jax assumed it was a statement not a question. 'Still a boy.' He spent a few minutes skim-reading before pulling an information booklet from the top of a pile on his desk.

Jax remained silent as the admission officer shot information across the desk, rapid-fire. He was told about muster, the mess, the timetable, ID cards, cell cards, phone privileges, mail, visiting days, the medical clinic, the pastoral program, the library and how to purchase goods, which he referred to as 'buy-ups'.

'Are you getting all this?' the officer asked.

Over the years, Jax had often asked questions to fit in. To look normal. He knew that most first-timers would have stopped, asked and argued, but he no longer felt obliged to act.

'Yes,' Jax said. 'All understood.'

'Well, please listen carefully to what I say next because I am about to ask you some very important questions. Your answers will determine where you will be housed. Do you understand?'

Jax nodded.

'Do you have any enemies or suspect that you could have enemies incarcerated in this prison?'

Decision made, Jax shook his head.

'Do you fear for your own safety?'

Jax shook his head.

'Do you feel that you are capable of protecting yourself should you need to?'

Jax nodded.

'Would you like to be put into protective custody and, if so, please state your reason?'

Jax shook his head.

'Would you like to be put into protective custody and if so please state your reason?' he asked again, slower this time and nodding while he spoke.

'No,' Jax said. 'I do not want to be put into protective custody.'

The officer sighed.

'I can't force you, but I am going to highly recommend it. Given your age, your ethnicity and your appearance, I believe placing you in the general population would be a significant risk. You do understand that your safety cannot be assured if you do not agree to protection?'

Jax was under no illusions about how tough life without protection would be. He had no doubt that they would come for him. For his shoes, for his food or just for fun. But there was no point trying to run from it. He was here for the best part of a decade at least – he needed to accept that reality, adjust to his new world and get on with it. He couldn't hide forever.

He also knew the protection wing was populated by rapists and paedophiles – the kinds of criminals other prisoners would knock around if they weren't separated from the pack. He would be able to deal with the other residents – the Marshes, the bullies – but the thought of sharing a cell with a child abuser frightened the hell out of him. Not just because of the disgust he would feel, but because he didn't know what he might be capable of doing to such a man, given half a chance.

'I am only going to ask one more time,' the officer said. 'Would you like to be put into protective custody?'

Jax looked the man directly in the eyes and held his gaze – the first time he'd looked at anyone this way since getting on that bus that morning.

'No.'

The older man pulled a card from a folder and drove a stamp onto it: 'MAXIMUM SECURITY'.

'Don't say I didn't try,' he muttered as he filled in the rest of the card by hand.

Jax read the words as the man wrote them: 'Jax Riley. D-Block. Cell No. 7. One-out. MIN: 60079.' He made a duplicate of the first card before pushing them both across the desk.

'One to be displayed outside your cell,' the officer said. 'The other to be kept on you at all times. Any questions?'

'What does MIN stand for?' Jax asked, finally stumped.

'Master Index Number,' the officer said. 'And you'd better learn it fast because it is your new name. From here on in, you are no longer Riley Jax.'

Now he had truly lost everything.

ROGERS led Jax down another fluorescent-lit corridor, through a steel cage attached to the external wall of the block and into an open-air concrete courtyard that was hemmed in by brick buildings. He looked up at the sky. A cloudless night, the full moon was directly above. *Midnight.*

Jax bounced on his toes to warm up as he waited for the guard to unlock the next reinforced gate. It was cold and his two green fleecy tracksuit tops were back in the tub. Through the gate, they moved along a path towards a red-brick building. Once inside, Rogers' boots echoed as he strode down the linoleum-covered entrance. The fresh rubber on Jax's Dunlops squelched and occasionally squeaked as they walked.

They came to a stop when they reached another grim double steel door. *Stride (82 centimetres) x steps (552) = 452 metres* – the distance between the reception block and the ominous entrance to his wing.

D-BLOCK
WARNING: HIGH-RISK INMATES
AUTHORISED DOCS PERSONEL ONLY

The black letters, stencilled on a coat of grey, were unmissable. Jax sucked in a big gulp of air and steeled himself for whatever he was about to face. He could not show fear. He could not look weak.

Rogers ordered Jax to step into a yellow-painted grilled contraption a little reminiscent of a small elevator. As he did, Jax clocked the archaic surveillance camera mounted on the wall to his right. Its body was the size of a shoe box and its lens looked like an aerosol can – Jax was almost certain the model was too old to even record in colour, let alone capture audio.

After locking Jax into the box, Rogers moved out of sight briefly, then back into view as he waved an electronic key in front of an electronic lock in a side door. The red light above the keypad turned green, but the doors did not open. Double authentication. Jax paid close attention as Rogers extended his index finger and prodded the keypad. Jax squinted, trying to make out the slight movements of then guard's finger: *4-5-3-9-8-7*. The green light began to flash.

Rogers disappeared through the door before reappearing a few moments later on the other side of Jax's box and releasing him. Jax stepped into an aircraft hangar–sized space, which was silent and still. He held his breath and braced as they set off.

It was almost a let-down. There were no reaching arms or cat calls, as there always are in the movies. No tin cups clanking against bars. In fact, there were no bars at all. No inmates either – the wing was all closed doors and concrete. It was also dark. The corridor was only lit every six metres by a lightbulb inside a metal cage. Each bulb only threw the light a few feet. Jax could not see far enough to even count all the steel doors, each of which he presumed led to a cell. He could only just make out the stairwell in the middle of the corridor, which led up to another floor. As far as he could make out in the dim light, it was a mirror image of the ground floor: the cells stacked like shipping containers – one up, one down. Jax couldn't make out any colours; everything was a shade of grey.

'Right,' Rogers said after taking a fresh look at Jax's cell card, 'follow me.'

Jax breathed only through his mouth as he followed Rogers into the darkness – ammonia hung in the air and the wing smelled a little like a hospital. And the chemical smell masked something more acrid, an odour Jax couldn't quite put his finger on. He was no stranger to close quarters – army barracks always imparted an odour that you couldn't seem to get rid of no matter how hard you scrubbed. This was worse.

Rogers stopped in front of a door on the left. 'One-out,' he said after opening the cell door. 'Someone must have liked you ... Well, in ya get. Judge has already written ya a fucking invitation.'

Jax's heart dropped to his stomach as soon as he stepped into the cell, a freezing concrete box with a single bed and a stainless-steel toilet without a seat, measuring about three metres by one and a half metres. The walls were covered in graffiti. No hanging points. The only other furniture a desk, a chair and a small unit containing box-like shelves. No storage tubs. And his mattress was a urine-stained slither of foam.

He turned to ask about the two missing tubs, only to have the door slammed in his face. He remained still and slightly stunned as he was locked in, the lock first buzzing and then snapping. Then he listened to Rogers' footfall. Light. Lighter. Gone. Then nothing.

Jax was astonished by the silence. He had expected a ruckus, shouting and screaming. He listened hard. No voices. He listened harder. No passing cars. He was hoping to at least hear a cricket chirp.

Dead silence.

He suddenly felt completely alone.

And then the lights went out.

CHAPTER 3

Supermax, Goulburn Correctional Centre, Goulburn, NSW, Australia

HE slowly ran his flattened palm across the concrete. It was pitch black in his windowless Supermax cell, so he had to feel his way along the wall. Holding a sharpened plastic knife in his right hand, he smiled as his recognised the outline of a recent carving beneath his fingers: a star chart, Galileo's. He was close. He brushed past the Italian script and found a smooth section of wall, untouched – a blank canvas.

He withdrew his hand and placed it on his naked body, every inch of which was covered in script and symbols. His skin was a patchwork of professional and home-job tattoos, and he had also cut, burned and branded himself to create a terrible topography all over his body, encompassing biblical passages inked in perfect twelve-point lettering and even a scale keloid replica of Mount Hira. He had used every inch of skin.

Exhaling, he closed his eyes and pushed his palm down his torso.

He began the ritual.

Nothing.

He kept going. Minutes passed.

Still nothing.

He persisted.

It would come.

Just as he was beginning to doubt, there it was.

The revelation.

He pressed the sharpened knife into the wall and scraped, scratched and dug. His guttural cry pierced the silence and he entered an almost trance-like state as the visions came – as if he were merely acting as a scribe for some higher power. Sometimes he was lucid enough to recognise whether he was producing charts, words or maps and sense the language: mostly English, often Latin, but sometimes an unknown tongue that was yet to exist in the realm of men. Today the script was cursive: flowing lines and linked loops, topped with dots and dashes. Arabic.

The Serpent dragged filthy fingers across the carving when he was finished.

'And he shall rise,' he said.

CHAPTER 4

Long Bay Correctional Complex, Sydney, NSW, Australia

FOUR steps from wall to wall, back and forth he went. Over and over and over again. Mind racing and adrenaline pumping, Jax spent the first couple of hours pacing around his cell, processing the events of the day.

He thought back to the bus and his encounter with Marsh.

Bashed, fucked or murdered. Maybe all three. The lawyer's voice haunted him, the seven words bouncing about his brain. He wished he could wipe the conversation from his mind, but he couldn't. Jax did not forget things. He remembered them. Everything. Except for the murder.

He thought back to the holding cell. To the drug addict. Then to Marsh. What he'd said. *I'll make all the arrangements.*

His original plan had been to remain unseen – to go under the radar. Too late. He shuddered when he realised Marsh might not even be the worst. Some might be meaner, tougher, bigger.

Jax was exhausted. He needed sleep. But the temperature in his cell could not have been more than five degrees. Without bedding or a jumper, the back-and-forth calories that he was burning were the only thing protecting him from the cold.

Eventually he reasoned that while the cold would not kill him, a sleep-deprived misjudgement made in the morning might. So he swung himself onto the slim single cot, sat back against the wall, pulled his arms through his T-shirt sleeves and stretched the shirt over his tucked-up knees. A ball on his bed, he rocked as he hugged himself hard and tried to quieten his mind, despite knowing it was impossible. His mind always raced.

JAX woke up shivering. His teeth chattered and his body shook. He jumped from the bed and began running on the spot. He groaned and grunted while he pumped his arms and legs, a cloud of condensation forming with each breath.

His face, toes and fingers were numb and the air filling his lungs felt like liquid nitrogen; he hadn't been this cold since an ambush in Afghanistan had forced him to spend two nights in a mountain cave. Swapping the on-the-spot running for star-jumps, Jax could feel himself starting to thaw as he bounced up and down. He stopped shivering midway through a set of sit-ups then, to his surprise, noticed he was sweating following a round of shadow boxing.

The threat of hypothermia had passed.

Jax stood still, and, although he knew his watch wasn't there, he still looked down at his wrist expecting to find the time. He didn't know how long he had been asleep. All he knew was that it had been a long night that he would like to forget, but wouldn't. Couldn't. The best he could do was watch it end.

He had to stand on the desk to see out the shoebox-sized slot in the wall, the standard government-regulated window found in each cell. Its hardened clear plastic was permanently foggy, and even though a toddler would struggle to squeeze through it, rusted vertical bars ensured it couldn't be breached.

Jax craned his neck to glimpse the outside world. He could not see the moon, but he knew it was still there – somewhere in the sky, unseen, dancing in the dark. The absent moon made Jax think of his ten-hour blank: there but unseen. Dancing in the dark.

He stood and watched as the patch of sky changed, a deep purple first spilling into the black, followed by an overcrowded palette of colours: pink, red, orange and yellow. The sun finally revealed herself with a blazing burst of white that bled blue. Jax smiled as he felt its warmth radiate through the window.

As morning sunlight slowly illuminated his cell, Jax lowered himself to the ground again, and for the first time noticed the years of graffiti scratched into the desk he'd been standing on. It was juvenile stuff, the kind of thing you'd expect to find on a school desk, and there was nothing of note in the messages. He took a moment to study the initials, names and styles – a short history of the cell and its inhabitants. While he was no handwriting expert, Jax could made out a dozen different names and sixteen different scripts pretty easily. He sat back on the bed and wondered about them. Who they were and what they had done. Were they murderers like him? Maybe they hadn't known either.

THE first cell was cracked at around 7 am. Jax did not have a watch, but he'd read a sunrise chart a few years back and could recall the numbers. He had kept an unconscious count since first light.

As he was only four cells from the beginning of the block, Jax did not have to wait long for the guard to get to him.

'You're keen,' a new face said, surprised to be confronted by the fully awake and fully dressed prisoner. Not that he'd had a choice – the rest of his clothing was yet to be delivered to his cell.

Jax studied the guard without staring. Mid-twenties, pock-marked cheeks, short back and sides, he looked like a soldier he knew.

'And young,' he continued. 'Shit, you even eighteen?'

Jax nodded. 'Blessed with a baby face.'

'No blessing in here. Where's your bedding?'

'Not sure, mate. It didn't arrive.'

'Why didn't you knock up?' he pointed to the one-way intercom beside the open cell door.

'I didn't think it classified as an emergency.'

The guard laughed. 'Mate, some of these shit-bags knock up just to ask for the time. Had one bloke ask for a large Big Mac meal once, thought he was in a McDonald's drive-through. Use it if you need it. I'll chase up your kit. You've got fifteen minutes until muster. Chuck a left and keep on going until you find the yard. And keep your head down, babyface.'

THE central section of D-Block was now bathed in light. UV poured through a gigantic sunroof, straight through the metal mesh landing that separated the ground floor from the first. Jax squinted at the sun reflecting off the linoleum floor and onto his face.

There were now details where last night there had only been shadows. The walls were cream, the cell doors light blue. A quick audit revealed a total of eighty cells in the wing. Forty down and forty up. Jax didn't have to count the prisoners to know there were more than eighty. They straggled out of cells and onto the landing and into the wing in twos, threes and even the odd group of four. He realised his one-out cell was an anomaly.

He stood in his open doorway and watched as the crowd flowed past. Some stretched and yawned, others, wide awake, jostled and joked. They were all decked out in green. From either end of the upper floor, they spilled down two staircases, the metal steps rumbling beneath the tide of men. Jax could see that they were mostly aged between twenty-five and forty, heavily tattooed and Caucasian. Guards of varying ages and sizes were dotted throughout the wing, some standing silently observing, others calling out here and there to one or another inmate. No sign of Rogers. No sign of Marsh.

Jax could not see anyone who looked younger than him, or anyone less physically developed. Although he was taller than most, he was a lightweight. Seventy-seven kilograms last time he checked. He suddenly wanted to retreat to the safety of his cell. Go back to his wafer-like mattress and never come out.

He left it as long as he could before joining the fray. Besides needing time to regain his nerve, he also thought waiting for the wing to clear would minimise risk. He wanted as few inmates to see him as possible. So, he waited, waited and waited – and finally he moved.

Just as he was starting to get into his stride, Jax heard a cell door screech behind him, followed by a heavy footfall echoing closer and closer. He didn't dare turn back to look, but judging by the loud noise the rubber soles made as they smacked the tiles, he was a big man. Over 100 kilograms, Jax estimated. But even though the man's pace was steady and quick, he was dragging one of his legs. A limp.

Jax walked as if expecting a blow: head down and body tensed. He was waiting to be tripped, or maybe slapped on the back of the head – the sort of thing the bullies used to do to him at school. But he made it to the yard unscathed and intact.

The inmates had already formed themselves into crude lines. They were facing a severely outnumbered guard armed with only a clipboard. Jax plugged himself into a gap and put his head down.

'50387,' the guard called.

'Here,' came the reply.

Jax noted the number but could not see the man, as he was evidently on the far side of the pack.

'56758,' the guard called.

'Present,' came the reply.

Jax couldn't see 56758 either.

'49845,' the guard called.

'Here,' came the reply.

The 'here' came from a man standing to his left. Jax snatched a glance, and quickly assembled a profile. Prisoner number 49845 was a senior citizen. At least sixty.

The age of the man told Jax something about the MIN number system – he had found a hack. Learning each man's number would be a shortcut to establishing how long the inmates had been inside.

'60077,' the guard yelled.

Nothing. No reply.

'60077,' the guard yelled again, louder this time.

Nothing.

'Overton,' the guard yelled instead. 'Paul Overton.'

'Yeah,' came the softly spoken reply.

The entire yard turned to look at this Overton. This inmate that didn't know his MIN. This inmate who had a number that started with six. An inmate just two admissions fresher than Jax.

'50182,' the guard called as the mob returned its focus to the front.

'Here,' came the reply.

A low number. A prison veteran. Someone to watch.

'59999,' the guard yelled.

'Yeah.'

Jax snuck a look at the lightly built man with shoulder-length straggly hair who'd replied sheepishly. His number indicated he hadn't been in prison long either, but his black eye and swollen nose suggested it had been long enough.

'60079,' the guard called.

'Here,' Jax said, lifting his head only to answer.

The whole yard turned.

* * *

JAX did an about-face and powered his way back to his cell the moment roll call was complete. Joining the back of the muster had allowed him to avoid most of the men on the way out. But now he had to brace for breakfast – and finalise his strategy. It would be served in the mess hall, a factory-sized room adjoining the wing. Having attracted the attention of everyone in the yard as new inmate 60079, he knew there would be no hiding at the back of the pack this time.

Jax considered skipping the morning meal altogether, going hungry initially seeming preferable to exposing himself to the mob. But it was only a fleeting thought. He had already been noticed. Not only by Marsh, but now by the rest of the yard. Others would be aware of the MIN sequence. To apex predators especially, the sound of a high number being read out would be like the cry of a wounded animal. Their first chance to size him up would come at breakfast. They would be waiting, they would be watching and they would notice if he did not show. Weak. Scared. Theirs. They wouldn't even have to circle to confirm that he was ripe for the kill.

Jax walked into the mess hall late but with cool confidence. His tardiness was again tactical. With most already self-served and seated when he walked in, he could choose his table mates. The fact that they were all focused on their food, scoffing and slurping as he strode down the centre of the aisle with his head held high, was a bonus.

He was relieved to see the familiarity of a mess hall during mealtime. He had been eating in mess halls since the day he turned sixteen, the minimum age for an army recruit. He didn't have to ask how it worked, what he could take, or where he could sit. He wouldn't stink of rookie like 60077, who was still trying to find a plate.

He joined the end of the short, fast-moving line and started to pile food on his tray. Leaving the bain-marie with an empty plate was a sign of weakness: you had to take everything you could get. He turned and started heading to the seat he had selected as soon as he'd walked into the room. He walked past 60077, who was still wandering about near the food. The poor bugger had no idea he was standing centre stage, virtually auditioning for a part in his own beating.

Jax made a beeline for the least populated table in the mess hall and took a seat, ensuring there were three empty spaces between him and his nearest fellow diner. There was also a guard standing directly behind him and the table was at the edge of the group, giving him an almost unobstructed view of the whole space. Jax spoke to no one and to his surprise, no one spoke to him. Not a word.

He snuck a look at the room after buttering his cold toast with a plastic knife. Fifteen tables with twelve seats, full but for a few empty seats on each table. He snuck another look after heaping on a slushy serving of scrambled egg. Ten cameras. After his third look, he had a complete picture of the room: 138 inmates, ten guards. But as most had their backs turned, he couldn't begin profiling them. He couldn't see Marsh either, which was a setback, as he needed to know as soon as possible where he fitted into the pack. He stole another look at the room while he peeled his banana, his eyes darting from table to table. Still no Marsh.

Although he couldn't see all the faces in the room, he had seen enough to know he was in a racially segregated block. He'd also heard enough – 'I'll put you in the Lebo yard' – to suggest that the other wings were too. The rules might not be hard and fast – facial structures and colouring suggested some in this room might be Slavic or Mediterranean – but the overwhelming majority looked at least three generations white.

Jax turned his attention to the six men on his half-empty table. All thin, with lightly loaded plates, two of them completely forgoing food – he didn't have to see track marks to know that these men were addicts. But even though most of them were underweight, sickly and unlikely to be concerned with prison politics, Jax knew they still posed a threat. Addicts were dangerous: volatile, malleable and often psychotic, there was nothing they wouldn't do for a hit. Right now, though – having been medicated, he presumed – they were placid, docile and ignorant of the new clean-cut kid.

One of them, all grey hair and long brittle beard, caught Jax's eye, not because of the way he looked but because of what he was doing: flattening a carton that, until recently, had contained milk.

'Mate, this is gunna be good,' he said as he compacted the finished 300-millilitre single-serve carton. 'The filthy flog is gunna get it.'

The man lifted his jumper and pushed the flattened container into his waistband.

'Shit yeah,' said another as he unfolded then flattened another carton. 'Can't believe he got away with it for so long. How many of 'em did he rape? All on the set, right?'

At first Jax thought the milk containers had nothing to do with the conversation. A drug thing? But then he noticed that the carton-flattening was not restricted to the addicts at his table. Behind glazed eyes, he tuned in to the chatter from another table nearby, all the while hoping he appeared uninterested.

'Used to be my favourite show,' he heard. 'He was like the dad I never had. Makes me feel fucking sick now. I'm going to kill the cunt if I get a chance.'

'Yeah, I'd rape him first,' another man joined in, while pouring the last of his milk onto his plate. 'Give him a taste of his own medicine.' He corrected himself when his declaration turned heads. 'Na, not with me schlong, ya fuckwits. I'm no queer. I'd bend him over and throw a shotty up his arse. I'd jam it in there, all the way, as far as I could, and then I'd let him have it.' The man held up an imaginary shotgun and pulled the trigger. 'Boom.'

By now Jax had worked out which inmate they were discussing – a well-known actor who had raped three children. But he was still wondering what the cartons had to do with him. Whatever it was, the guards didn't seem to mind. They even contributed, walking around the room handing out second servings of milk.

Breakfast was followed by free time. After going back to his cell and realising he couldn't lock himself in, Jax decided that the yard, watched by both cameras and guards, was his safest option. He took a moment to steel himself before walking back through the wing to the oversized opening that led to the yard. He was surprised to find he was one of the first there: so far, only a few inmates had congregated in front of the ten-foot wire fence on the far side.

The D-Block yard was one of four located in the prison's gigantic central quadrangle, which was bounded by the sandstone walls of the four original wings. At some point, wire fencing and walkways had been erected to divide this space into quarters. It had been one of these fenced-in walkways he'd been led down the night before, but it had been too dark for him to make out much detail.

Jax figured the prison yard would be a lot like the school yard he had disliked so much as a child. Each section of the concrete quadrangle would be marked by invisible stakes. He knew stepping into the wrong area could be deadly, so he made his way to the darkest and coldest corner of the yard, figuring that the worst real-estate would likely be the least popular.

He ignored the empty aluminium bench seats, the type he'd sat on at school – alone while the others played – and lowered himself onto the cold concrete ground. He leant back against the wall, which had been decorated with murals: a surfer riding a wave, an Australian flag, and, of all things, a pink flower – what looked like a waratah gone wrong.

Scanning the yard from his frigid spot on the ground, Jax raised a brow when the groups he had anticipated failed to form. Instead, as men spilled from the wing, they joined a single moving mass, all back-slapping and excited, a mob heading for the far fence.

Jax sighed knowingly when he spotted what they were holding: the milk cartons, now reconstructed and apparently full.

He continued to watch from a distance as the famous actor who'd been the subject of discussion at breakfast that morning stepped from the shadows and into a sunlit walkway on the other side of the ten-foot-high wire cyclone fence.

'He's here,' came the cry. 'It's him!'

'Cop this, you fucking scumbag,' another inmate screamed.

The shit slapped against the side of the actor's face before he'd even turned to see who had yelled, the faeces hitting him with force. Jax saw the man stop and turn back, start to head back to where he'd come from, but a guard pushed him forward as the group of inmates roared their approval. From where he was sitting, Jax couldn't see the whole scene, but he thought it looked like the actor was trying to negotiate with the guard – his hands were gesticulating dramatically. Jax figured once you'd been a performer, it was hard not to continue to play the part.

The guard pointed towards the maximum-security prisoners, now a heaving, unruly mass of limbs and flesh whaling on the fence. Some seemed to be attempting to scale it, even though they would get no higher than the razor-wire. Others tried in vain to reach through the gaps, their fingers outstretched, nails ready to scratch. The man remained beyond their reach, but the wire fence didn't prevent them from ejecting the urine they'd collected in their empty milk cartons into his face or at his torso, nor did it prevent them hurling cartons of excrement over the fence and onto his head.

Jax was certain that this was against regulations, that confrontations such as these were supposed to be avoided. It was clearly a set-up, he realised, as he watched the rest of the guards – both on the path and in the yard – stand back and watch as the hive of men erupted with bloodlust. The officers had done more than just manufacture the scheduling clash, Jax mused. They must have also told a couple of D-Block heavies that the famous actor – now a convicted paedophile – would be escorted across the yard at 9 am on that very morning.

The actor was shouting inaudibly and shielding his head as a urine-filled milk carton crashed into his shoulder and burst, splashing the liquid all over his face.

'Fucking paedo,' screamed the inmate who'd hurled the carton over the fence. 'Welcome to Long Bay, ya cunt.'

The officer gave the sex offender a shove after copping some stray urine himself. 'Go,' he shouted. 'Run, you stupid fuck. Get away from me.'

So the actor ran, holding his hands over his head as he weathered the incoming storm. A couple of heavier objects were thrown over the fence – a full can of food sailed high and then dropped fast, missing the man by inches. A rock hit him hard in the back, and he stumbled, falling to his knees, as the assembled crush of men bayed for more.

Soon, however, he was out of range and then out of sight, inside a fenced-off recreation yard on the other side of the prison. The madness – the hurling, shouting and fence-shaking – had only lasted a couple of minutes. The 138 prisoners that Jax had counted in the yard had had their fun and started turning away from the fence. Moving in small groups, apart from a few loners, they slowly dispersed across their own yard.

HAVING watched the ruckus from start to finish from his cold corner, Jax felt a little better about refusing protection. That could have been him doing the perp walk, or even worse, the man who'd been attacked could have been his cellmate. The paedophile had got what was coming to him, Jax supposed. But Jax wasn't there to deal out retribution – and who was he to play judge anyway? He'd killed a man he'd never laid eyes on, for a reason he couldn't remember.

Jax did his best to discreetly study the groups in the yard when they finally formed, sneaking a look when he was sure they weren't looking at him. He noted the size of each cluster, the racial make-up, who was doing the talking, who was doing the listening.

The biggest group would most likely be the strongest, the gang that ran the yard; the next biggest group would be the next strongest; and so on. But group size wasn't the only factor influencing power: a smaller group could be stronger if they had access to phones or drugs. But he didn't have that information. Not yet.

Jax counted the groups, the numbers in each group, and came up with a hierarchy based on the visual information. He would rearrange that order as he learned more, if need be.

He could tell a lot about the dynamics within a group based on their interactions, their body language. He was only close enough to overhear one of the group conversations. Well down the pecking order, a gang of just four, they appeared more user than dealer.

'I got the cunt right in the face with the biggest piece of shit you've ever seen,' one of them said. 'Seriously you should have seen the size of my shit. I almost ripped my arsehole pushing out the fucker. Dead-set. It was like I was giving birth.'

'Ah, I did better than that, mate,' said another one. 'I had the squirts, been spray-painting the bowl all week. I hit him with half a litre of diarrhoea. You can't beat that, mate.'

The first man didn't respond.

Even from an exchange as short as that, Jax could tell which man was in charge.

Jax scanned the yard again. One of the groups – only a midsize pack – had already descended upon 60077. Jax couldn't hear them, but judging from the rookie's reaction, they hadn't approached him for a friendly chat.

As impatient as he was, Jax didn't have sufficient time or a clear enough vantage point from which to observe the rest of the groups right now, nor did he yet have the courage to move from his wall. He hadn't been singled out. But he knew it was just a matter of time.

CHAPTER 5

St Petersburg, Russia

THERE were no nice touches in the fifth-floor apartment. He had disposed of the curtains as soon as he moved in, throwing the gold and regally patterned imitation silk into the industrial dumpster on the street. Then he'd boarded the windows with flattened carboard boxes and gaffer tape. No one would think this was odd. Some of the apartments in the ten-storey block didn't even have windows panes; almost none had coverings.

Most things in Kirovsky were broken – its economy, its buildings, its people. One of St Petersburg's eighteen administrative districts, Kirovsky was almost completely covered in concrete. A post-apocalyptic postcard of socialism, it was a sea of ten-storey apartment blocks, all white and decaying in unison – the communist way.

Ali, the name he had chosen when he converted to Islam, hadn't had much choice when it came to renting an apartment, as the layouts, sizes and general state of disrepair of everything on offer were all about the same. But he'd been very particular about one thing: no carpet, tiles only. Hard surfaces were easier to clean. He'd eventually had to settle for linoleum, however, after he'd learned that tiles were a luxury item in Russia, only used in bathrooms and homes belonging to pop stars, politicians and mobsters.

He'd rented the apartment through an online agency for 192 euros a month. Calling himself Aleksandr Sokolov – Russia's most popular male first name and seventh-most popular surname – he'd obtained a Hotmail account with a Russian IP, then he used Google Translate to read the agent's emails and reply in Russian. He could have paid the entire six months of the lease in advance, but no one did that in Kirovsky, as everyone lived from week to week. And he didn't want to attract attention.

He'd used a no-questions-asked Russian money transfer service to pay both his bond and the first month's rent. After he'd signed, scanned and sent back the agreement, the agent had left the key inside the unlocked apartment and sent him an email. Ali had pasted the Russian text into Google Translate: *Nothing to steal, and squatters have better taste. Okay, unlocked I will leave.*

Ali had accumulated little during the four months he'd spent in the rented apartment. The unit was furnished with only two plastic chairs from an outdoor setting and a folding card table. He slept on the wood-patterned linoleum floor in the sitting room. He no longer needed blankets or sheets thanks to the warm, humid June weather generated by the summer's Baltic Sea cyclones. The doors to the two small bedrooms had never even been opened.

Ali cooked all his food in one pot and one pan and used disposable plastic cutlery. He had become particularly fond of Big Bon, a brand of Russian two-minute noodles; his favourite flavour was chicken with salsa. Everything else he owned – except for his laptop and suitcase – was kept in the oven, which he had disconnected from the power and padlocked shut after installing a latch.

He had lain low since moving in, going out only for supplies, surveillance and reconnaissance. He had studied Russian before leaving Australia and had mastered the basics well enough to get by. The locals took little notice of him anyway. He was hardly an oddity in St Petersburg, which was filled with itinerants and foreigners living there illegally. Most of them being involved in crime, the residents knew better than to ask questions or snoop.

The day before, Ali had gone down to the dock at 2 am in the morning and had burned all of his clothes except for the black long-sleeve shirt, cargo pants and black hoodie that were now neatly folded on his floor. He had also thrown some unused groceries, stationery, a well-used notebook, a heavily marked map, wire off-cuts, circuits, batteries and a soldering iron into the drum and watched them disintegrate.

Sitting on one of the two plastic chairs in his apartment, he was completely naked when he removed his necklace. He placed the chain on the card table after removing the key that he had kept on the necklace. He walked over to the makeshift safe and unlocked it.

Ali took a quick inventory of the items: two Australian passports (both genuine), two Ukrainian passports (both fake but passable), two well-worn copies of the Quran (both English translations), a plastic Chinese takeaway container filled with cash (neat stacks of euros bound by rubber bands), two prepaid mobile phones (in unopened boxes), a piece of paper bearing a name and number in black ink, a bottle of dextroamphetamine – and a bomb.

He reattached the padlock but did not put the key back on his chain, instead carrying it with him as he made his way to the bathroom. He opened the door and turned on the light, ignoring the man who was gaffer taped to the toilet as he walked in.

He would take care of himself before taking care of the traitor.

Ali lathered his legs with shaving cream from a can on the basin, took a fresh disposable razor from a bulk-buy packet beside it, and got to work. As he shaved, he used a mirror and torch to check every inch of skin, make sure he got every hair. He went over some sections of his skin four times just to be sure.

In an almost meditative state, he continued the laborious process over the rest of his body: genitals, stomach, chest, arms, using a fresh razor taken for each area.

He cursed when it came time to shave his back. 'Fucking dog,' he grunted as he turned to face the man bound to the toilet. 'You were supposed to do this.'

He didn't get a response, the gagged man having lost consciousness.

Ali did his best to shave his back, first reaching upwards. But he could only push the razor as high as the bottom of his shoulder blade. So he then reached back over his shoulder, using his opposite arm to push his elbow back and down. Stretching his triceps to their limit, he reached down almost to the bottom of his shoulder blade. Soon he reckoned he'd got it all.

He threw the razor into a plastic bag with the others, then grabbed a pair of scissors from the shelf and hacked away, first, at the hair on his head, then at the hair on his face. His beard wasn't as long as he'd have liked it to be. He'd always wanted to have a *Sunnah* beard, but he'd been told it would draw too much attention and that he should trim his beard at least once a month.

He cropped both his hair and beard as short as he could with the scissors before taking a fresh razor from the packet to finish the job. Soon his scalp was bald, shiny and white, his face clean and stubble free. Ali then shaved off his eyebrows.

Almost done. He'd left the most tedious part of the process till last. Grabbing a pair of tweezers, he shuffled towards the mirror and pushed his face so close that his breath left a small circle of fog on the glass.

One by one, he plucked out his eyelashes. Some came out easy, others stretched his eyelid like a rubber band and left a drop of blood when they finally popped out.

Ali was now completely bald, virtually every hair gone. Even if there were a couple left on his back, it wouldn't matter. He would be fully clothed and even if one fell out, it would be caught in the back of his shirt and incinerated with the rest of him.

Ali wished he could get drunk for next part. Glenn Taylor would have. The street kid from Campbelltown would have put away half a case of beer and a six-pack of Jim Beam and Cola before a job like this. But Glenn Taylor was long gone. Dead. Before that the hooligan they'd once called 'T' had been saved by Islam and reborn as Ali Muhammad. T knew it was not the most original name but he didn't care. He'd been a promising amateur boxer before his first hit of heroin, and Muhammad Ali, well, he was the greatest.

Yeah, no doubt about it, T would have got blind drunk before inflicting this type of pain on himself. But Ali was devout and did not drink. He hadn't so much as touched a drop since his conversion.

'*Bismillah*,' Ali said as he took in the strange hairless man in the mirror.

He then grabbed the pair of pliers he had left on the basin. Using his left hand to hold up his lip, he peered into the mirror, into his mouth, and identified the incisor with the cap. He briefly thought of his mum as he sighted the tooth: she'd been the one who had rushed him to the dentist after the tooth had broken in two during a sparring session at the Minto Police Boys' Club. Ali pushed away the image of her as he brought the pliers up to his face and thrust them into his mouth. He didn't want to think about his mum.

'Fuck,' he said, as he lowered the pliers and shut his mouth. He'd just realised he should have bought needle-nose pliers for this job, not the standard pliers he held in his hand. The jaws were too wide to grab an individual tooth. He considered going back to the poorly equipped hardware store in St Petersburg – but then he saw his reflection. He would stand out like a set of dog's balls now. And besides, he was on a schedule. The clock had started when he'd received the four deposits. He had to be in position in exactly twelve hours, phone in hand, ready to take the final call.

Fuck it. Two teeth instead of one. He figured the pain would be the same. So, he reopened the pliers, stuck them back in his mouth and closed them around the capped incisor and the canine next door. He pulled his right hand around the plastic handle and squeezed. He grunted as the pliers began crushing his teeth. But then he had to release them.

'Ahhh,' he exhaled as he pulled the pliers out of his mouth before turning to face the man taped to the toilet. He was conscious now.

'You were supposed to do this,' Ali screamed at him. 'That was the plan. But you're a pussy.' Ali punched him in the face.

'Watch,' he commanded. 'See my pain. My suffering is for Allah. Yours will be for nothing.'

He turned back to the mirror, lifted his lip, gripped the two teeth again with the pliers and squeezed with all his might. There was a sickening crunch. His tongue shot towards the tooth instinctively but then reeled back as a razor-sharp shard of broken tooth drew blood. Ali ignored the pain, closed his eyes and reefed. 'Arrrrrgh!' he screamed as his knees buckled.

He threw the pliers as he fell, the blood-stained tool striking a wall tile and cracking it. He'd been hit by a lightning bolt of pain, a terrific jolt of electrical excruciation that had shot into the top of his head, flashed down his entire body and finished in his heels. He had never felt pain like it. It had almost made him shit himself.

But as fast as it came it was past. Ali picked himself up off the tiles, fetched the pliers, and stood tall. He probed the two teeth with his tongue. Both loose. He stuck his hand into his mouth and gripped them between his thumb and index finger and moved them back and forth. Loose but still very much attached.

He swallowed hard, a mouthful of blood laced with the sand-like shavings of teeth going down the hatch. He put the pliers back into his mouth. This time he waggled them from side to side instead of reefing. He grunted and groaned as his hand moved back and forth. The pain was immense but he persevered. Once they were almost free, he twisted the pliers abruptly to snap the nerve and tear the flesh. He screamed, withdrew the pliers, looked down. He had the incisor, root and all, but had only broken the canine in half. He thanked Allah that it was not the other way around.

He placed a gauze pad in his mouth and bit down.

ALI used the DNA-grade chemical to wipe down the front door after he'd locked it. He was glad he'd bought the 'DNA Away', a sodium hydroxide solution made by a large American company in bulk. This was his last bottle.

He'd left the apartment completely clean, having used the solution on every surface except for the ceiling, and empty apart from the plastic chairs, card table, pot and pan, all of which he'd carefully scrubbed too.

The suitcase weighed a tonne. At least that's what ninety kilograms felt like to Ali. He was glad he'd opted for a case with wheels, not the cheaper one he'd looked at first. He'd put the hacksaw, cleaver and reciprocal saw inside after wiping them down. Then he'd put the blood-drained and bagged body parts on top of the tools. He had planned to burn Tim's

Quran, along with the four passports and mobile phone packaging, in the bathtub, but in the end he'd put them in the suitcase too, figuring it was probably some sort of sin to burn the holy book.

His own well-thumbed Quran was in the backpack he was now wearing, along with the bomb that Tim had made before he went soft, the phones, the cash and the piece of paper with the name and number. Everything else – his hair, his capped tooth, the razors, the cleaning rags, the eleven spent bottles of DNA Away, and his neck chain – was in the industrial-strength garbage bag he held in his other hand. Then he'd poured a full bottle of the DNA killer into the bag just to be sure.

Ali wheeled the suitcase to the lift, pressed the down arrow, then gave the button a wipe with a DNA Away–soaked rag as the doors creakily opened. He did the same with the 'G' button on the inside. Once he was out of the lift and on the street, he pulled one of the mobile phones from his bag, opened an encrypted application called Wickr and called the number that was on the piece of paper.

'Okay,' he said. 'I'll be there in ninety minutes.'

He took the SIM card out of the phone, snapped it with his teeth and swallowed it, then he stomped on the phone and dropped the shattered gadget into a container filled with DNA Away. He closed the lid, put the bottle into the garbage bag and tossed it all into a street bin.

Ali threw the suitcase into the Gulf of Finland. He knew there was a chance that it would be found, but it wouldn't matter. As with everything else, he'd ensured there would be no traces of DNA. On his way from the shore to the dock, his load so much lighter now, he wondered if the case had sunk all the way to Hell.

He put two bullets in the Russian gangster as soon he had handed over the gun; one in his head and one in his chest, as instructed. He let the dead man keep the cash. He wouldn't need money where he was going. Then he made his way to the next post – a public toilet. He locked the door, stripped and used the last bottle of DNA Away to coat his skin. All he could smell was the chemical as he moved on to the Church of the Saviour on Spilled Blood, St Petersburg.

To the promised land.

CHAPTER 6

Long Bay Correctional Complex, Sydney, NSW, Australia

JAX's cell was dimly lit and still cool when he returned from the yard. He scanned it for his tubs, hoping especially that his blanket had arrived, so that he could avoid another night of hypothermia.

Nothing. And in the grey daylight, the cell was even grimmer than it had been in the dark. Jax could now see all the cell's dirty little secrets. There was a splatter of blood on one of the walls. He shuddered as it triggered a flash of that day when his life had changed forever.

The mattress was even more limp and urine-stained than he'd first realised and the toilet was filthy. A pile of dead cockroaches in the corner completed the bleak picture.

Three metres by one and a half. It seemed bigger in the gloom. Eight steps by four steps.

Jax was suddenly struggling for air. *A tomb. My tomb.* Each breath he took was shorter than the last. *I'm going to die here.* He hadn't been aware that he was claustrophobic – until he'd begun hyperventilating. *Got to get out.*

He felt light-headed. Tiny lights, bright and brilliant, flashed and flickered in front of his face. He swiped at them. Then a darkness crept over him.

'Oh my,' came the voice. 'Oh, you poor boy. Oh my. This is not good. Let's see if I can help.'

Jax took a gasp of air as he turned to see a blurry figure in the doorway of his cell. The voice was soft and the words sincere, but Jax couldn't trust such things, not in here.

His vision sharpened and he saw that the voice belonged to a flushed-faced, portly older man whose black coat seemed to be topped by a band of white.

'There, there,' the man said, moving towards Jax with one arm half-raised, as though he were approaching a wounded animal.

Jax dropped his guard as the priest came nearer. Surely he could at least trust that collar?

'Here we go,' the priest said as he placed his hand on the middle of Jax's back and performed a motion somewhere between a rub and a pat. 'It's all going to be okay. Oh, you poor fella. Breathe. That's it. Nice and slow. Yes. That's it, my boy. It's not as bad as it seems. Everything is going to be okay.'

The plump hand, now rubbing with a firm, circular motion, was warm. So was the timbre in the man's voice. For a brief moment, Jax did not mind being babied by this man. His breathing slowed and the cell came back into focus.

'Yeah, righto,' he said as he gently pushed the hand away. He felt a little violated, not because the man had done anything inappropriate but because he generally avoided all physical contact – in the army, that kind of thing would have been a one-way ticket to a beating. He didn't even touch Nikki much, except when they were in bed, the whole world reduced to no more than just the two of them. He tried hard not to think about Nikki because he would never see her again. He had made sure of that by telling her in no uncertain terms that it was over. She had promised never to visit. Never to write.

'Yeah, I'm sweet. Thanks, mate. I'm all good.' Jax cleared his throat.

'Oh, don't be embarrassed,' the man said. 'Nothing wrong with having a little spell. Happens to the best of us.'

He pulled out the chair and motioned for Jax to sit.

'Come on now. Take a moment. Catch your breath and clear your head. Then we can see what I can do to help.'

Jax backed up to the chair.

The man looked around the cell. 'Not much here, is there? The usual tardiness with delivering a man's provisions.' He tutted as he took in the bare bed. 'This won't do at all.' The priest shook his head in disgust as he moved back towards the door. He waddled more than walked. He stopped and took a moment to straighten his glasses. Then he extended his index finger and leaned right in to press the red button on the face of the emergency intercom – the knock-up, as the guard had called it.

'Hello, guard?' he demanded in a voice he clearly knew how to project. 'There's a situation here needs attention. Guard?'

He released the button and gave Jax a thumbs-up. Jax watched, intrigued, as the man's bushy eyebrows shot up and, with surprising speed, he pressed the button again. 'Over,' he said, his mouth almost touching the grille. 'Sorry, I forgot to say over … Over.'

He took a step back and, with brow furrowed and index finger still out, eyeballed the knock-up like it was a poisonous snake.

The blast of static it emitted a moment later startled him. 'Blasted thing,' he said. 'Gets me every time.'

'Yes, Father,' came the bored-sounding voice, which Jax recognised as belonging to the guard named Rogers, or 'Dodge', as Marsh had called him. 'What is it this time? Over.'

The priest leaned back in, far closer than necessary, and pressed again. 'Yes, hello. You need to get down to this cell with this man's things. Right away. He's entitled to his bedding, no matter how he has sinned.'

'You forgot to say over,' came the droll reply. 'Yeah, cell number 7 – I've got the tubs here. Must have been a mix-up last night. I'll see what I can do. Don't hold yer breath.'

The priest jammed his finger back onto the button. Jax was surprised to see so much anger in his face. 'No, that won't do,' he said in a booming voice. 'Shall I remind you of our arrangement? I said "right away". RIGHT AWAY. Got that? And you forgot to say over. Over.'

Jax was curious. He hadn't planned on acquainting himself with the prison chaplain, even though the admitting officer had mentioned him in his rundown. Jax didn't pray and hadn't for years. Not since the car accident that killed his parents. That kind of thing made you realise there was no God. But, judging from the way the priest had just issued orders to the guard, it seemed he might be worth knowing.

'Uh, thanks,' Jax said. 'I'm grateful.'

'No problem,' he said with a nod, the mad glint in his eye gone. 'If nothing else, a man must have his dignity preserved in here, his human rights must be observed – as much as can be, that is. You'll get your things now, you'll see.' He was pleased with himself.

'Yeah, thanks,' Jax said again.

'And I am not going anywhere until they arrive,' the priest added.

He introduced himself as Father Martin – 'though you can call me Marty' – and took the opportunity to spruik the program he ran in the prison. After asking Jax if he'd been baptised, which he had, he invited him to attend the next 'chapel club' meeting.

'No one is going to bash you with a Bible,' the priest said when Jax replied with a shrug. 'It's not a mass. Hardly any religion at all. We just get together and hang out. A bunch of boys attend. Good boys. I think it would be a fine opportunity for you to make some friends. They can look out for you. I can look out for you.'

Jax smiled this time but still failed to commit.

The conversation was interrupted by the arrival of two guards delivering the tubs. They didn't look impressed, but they humoured the priest as he told them where to place them.

'Well, that's that, then,' Father Martin said, nodding in approval and looking to Jax again expectantly.

'Oh yeah, thanks,' Jax mumbled, careful not to give much away to the guards, who were watching on with wry interest. He turned towards the tubs, bent down to take the lid off one and busied himself looking at its contents.

He heard the three men retreat, then the guards' voices – giving the priest a hard time.

'Another convert, hey, Father?' one of them said, sarcasm dripping. 'Thought you were more of a fan of the Leb boys, though, Father. But you like this fresh little whitey too, huh? You're not fussy, I'll say that much.' Their laughter faded as they were swallowed by the wing.

Jax straightened up. It was obvious that the priest was a bit of a laughing stock, even if he did have some sway. Whatever he might be able to get out of this holy man, he was going to have to play his cards carefully.

JAX took a sandwich from the cart and returned to his cell. He was relieved that, today being Saturday, lunch was not a sit-down affair. After eating, he stretched out on his bed, which he had freshly made, with military precision, after stacking his storage tubs neatly on his shelf. Each blanket fold was spirit-level straight and each overlap exactly thirty centimetres. They called it a 'hospital fold' in the army.

The traffic outside Jax's cell was heavy. Saturday was not a work day, so most of the inmates were in the wing. Jax didn't have a job and wasn't expecting to have one any time soon. A job in a prison was a privilege, though the right to earn maybe ten dollars a day for sewing and stitching or sawing and sanding was as good as it got.

On Monday, he'd need to take note of all the men who went to work and, more importantly, those who didn't. Jax predicted that the most dangerous inmates would not have jobs – either by choice or because they'd forfeited the privilege one way or another. A job would get in the way of running an illicit prison trade, too. The guys who controlled the black market in here wouldn't get out of bed for ten dollars an hour, let alone ten dollars a day. Those at the top of the prison chain were criminal entrepreneurs with a workforce. Like Marsh. The type of men who could find a use for anybody. For Jax.

Bashed, fucked or murdered. Maybe all three …

The fearful thought returned. His unexpected ally had not only given him bedding and clothes, but also a glimmer of hope – the brief exchange had almost restored his humanity for a moment. But now that he was alone again, that glimmer was gone, that feeling was over. He knew hope was dangerous in Hell. He knew he was something less than human in here. Just an animal in cage. The cell suddenly seemed to shrink.

He resisted the urge to run and instead took a deep breath. He told himself that the panic attack was a one-time deal. He also reminded himself that nothing bad had happened … yet. He'd received nothing more than a few curious glances. But that didn't make sense, indeed only made him feel worse. He had been certain of a run-in. A 'What the fuck are you looking at?' Or a 'Have a look at this pretty boy' at the very least. He'd seen first-hand the attention that 60077, Paul Overton, had already attracted. Why had he been spared? The anticipation only added to his fear.

Jax was distracted from his thoughts by a group of men walking by his cell. He only caught a snippet of their talk before they were gone again, leaving him with only his racing mind for company. He knew he had to regain control.

He got up, took a step away from the bed and bowed briefly. Then he walked to the foot of his bed, sat on the floor and assumed a *zazen* meditation pose – legs crossed in a full lotus, his hands resting gently in his lap, his back straight and spine tall. He half-closed his eyes and felt himself begin to drift into the familiar state of detachment he was able to attain after years of practice. He'd discovered the Japanese method as a teen, after the accident, when he'd had to move into his nan's. He'd tried many things to control his anger, his hate, back then. But the Zen Buddhist mainstay of *zazen* meditation was the only thing that had ever worked.

He was interrupted by approaching footsteps: a guard, judging from the sound – Dunlop Volleys didn't echo on the lino the way the guards' boots did. The footsteps stopped outside his cell. Jax uncrossed his legs and adopted as relaxed a slouch as he could muster, relieved he'd not gone deep into the his meditation and missed the warning sound.

'Happy now?' Rogers asked from the doorway.

Jax sensed a threat, knew that what was about to happen would probably happen whatever his response. 'Sorry about the fuss. I didn't mean to bother you.'

'Well, you did,' he said. 'You and that fucking god-botherer twat.'

Rogers stepped in and shut the door behind him.

'Stand up,' he ordered.

Jax complied. He was used to orders.

'Walk over there,' he said, pointing to the corner of the cell.

Rogers then made Jax watch as he unzipped his fly and urinated all over his immaculately made bed.

THE sun had long left his room by dinnertime – but the smell hadn't. The urine had soaked right through his sheets and into the mattress. He'd been able to sponge most of it from his bedding using a soaped-up shirt but there was nothing he could do about the mattress, not now, not without the warmth of the sun.

Although it wasn't quite 6 pm Jax's cell would already have been pitch black had it not been for the fluorescent light, which, like everything else in prison, was in a cage. Dangerous things needed to be kept in cages: tigers, Jax, lights. Jax'd had no idea that so many seemingly innocuous objects were dangerous, himself included, until he'd been locked away. Until now he'd certainly never looked up at a fluorescent light and thought, *Gee, that'd make a good weapon. You could really rip a throat open with the jagged glass if you snapped it just right.* But while he could kill a man with his light – and probably another ten things in his cell if he thought about it, and he would – a globe could not dry his mattress. Or his sheets, which he couldn't hang up either, because hanging points were lethal too. He was in for another long cold night – assuming he made it back from the mess hall.

'OI!' the two vowels were shouted as loud as the man could whisper. 'Oi! Oi! You!'

No. Not me.

'Yeah, you.'

No. Please. Not here. Not now.

'Oi. Over here. Behind ya.'

Stale sweat, urine and Rexona roll-on. Jax did not have to look to know who it was. He remembered more than faces.

'Oi. Stop ignorin' me, mate.'

Jax could feel his temperature rising. He turned his attention back to the steak he could not cut. He took a deep breath, clenched his jaw and attempted it again.

'Oi,' the voice was at his ear now, and a finger was jabbing him in the rib.

The plastic knife snapped as Jax slammed it into his burnt rubber steak. He watched as the broken tip flew into the air, almost in slow motion.

'Knew it was you,' the man behind him went on. 'So, was I right? Yeah … I was. They don't go Area 51 on a good-looking fella like you. Dude like you can make some serious coin in here. They ain't going to search you after a visit. You got a missus? They won't get searched either, bra. Seriously. The screws can't touch 'em if their man ain't been done for gear. We can make bank, bro. Won't have to worry about nothing if we've got gear.'

'Gear?' said the man to Jax's left. 'Who's got gear?'

Suddenly the entire table was looking his way.

'Not me,' said the one that had been pestering Jax. 'But I would have if this stuck-up cunt had helped me out. I told him I was going to get nicked, but he didn't give a fuck.'

'Yeah, like fucked you got nicked,' said another man sitting at Jax's table. 'We aren't going to fall for that shit again. You're a fucking shifty cunt, aren't ya, Robbo?'

Robbo stood up. 'Nah, I swear on me mum,' Robbo said. 'They got it. I had enough for youse all. I'm not holding out. I swear to shit. Ask him. I tried to give it to him in the holding cell.'

Suddenly the man to Jax's right got up.

'You're a fucking snake,' he said.

'Oiiii,' a voice boomed. 'What's going on here?'

'Nah, nothing, hey,' Robbo said as he backed away from the voice that Jax thought must have belonged to a guard until he saw the inmate bearing down on his table. Jax was surprised by his size. Big voice. Little man.

'Yeah, nothing,' agreed the man on Jax's right as he retook his seat.

'You shitbags better not have gear that hasn't come from me,' said the intruder. 'Youse know the rules. Who's got it? Who brought it in?'

'Fucking him,' yelled another man as he fingered Robbo. He then pointed toward Jax. 'Or him. Heard 'em talking about it. They both came in today. Robbo's trying to pull a swifty and gyp us all again.'

'Who's this cunt?' the newcomer said as he looked at Jax.

No one answered his question.

'Fucking smartarse, hey?' he yelled at Jax.

Jax knew what was coming as soon as he saw the man's shoulder turn and his elbow drop: a left, a jab. He used his right arm to parry the punch.

Thrown off-balance, the attacker toppled onto another inmate. 'You're fucking dead, cunt,' he said to Jax as he pushed away from the hapless junkie who'd broken his fall.

Jax was now on his feet, fists raised and ready to go. Still getting to his feet, the inmate with the big mouth was a sitting duck, his head slightly turned to Jax's right. The temple was always the best target, specifically the thinnest part of the skull between the eye and the ear. A decent slap was enough to knock a person out, and from where Jax was standing – above him, balanced, with his weight loaded on his hip – he could have killed him. But even though it went against everything he'd been taught in the army, Jax wanted to fight fair. So he stood on his tiptoes with his fists up and waited for the man to get to his feet.

Jax should have retreated when he saw them rushing in: three – no, four – men, all running to back up his opponent. At this point, most people would have unclenched their fists and shown their palms. But Jax wasn't most people; he was going to go down swinging. He reloaded his right and got ready to throw but pulled the punch when the first man to arrive pulled his mate away.

Amid all the noise, Jax couldn't hear what was said, but as a child, always the kid in the corner, he had learned to lip-read a bit. He caught just one word: Marsh. And that word was enough to make them all walk away.

* * *

JAX approached the shower block, walked past the man standing at the door with his arms crossed against his barrel of a chest, a crimson scar like a flick of paint running from the top of his forehead to a chin made more prominent by his heavily tattooed neck. He nodded as Jax walked in.

Behind the brick wall were eight separate cubicles. Immediately Jax heard the muffled screams. Then he saw the blood: a red stream snaking its away across the tiles from the base of the first cubicle to the drain at the centre of the room, where it disappeared into darkness.

'Fucking stay still, ya cunt!'

Jax froze, as if the order had been issued to him.

Crack! Knuckle hitting jaw.

'I told ya.' The voice continued, and so did the hits, all bone on bone. 'Don't make this any worse.'

Rooted to the cold tiles, wearing only a towel, Jax was just six steps away from the man making the noise, and the source of the blood. As there were no doors on the cubicles, he'd have to walk straight past the commotion to get to a free faucet. He was about to turn and walk out when he remembered the man at the entrance. A lookout.

At best, Jax knew he would look weak if he walked out without taking a shower. At worst, the lookout might think he was going to get help, and stop him. The best option was to proceed, act like he hadn't heard – or seen – a thing. He'd stride through, head down, making sure he didn't slip on the wet and bloodied tiles. He didn't want to know what was happening. It wasn't his problem. He wouldn't look.

But he did look.

'Help,' came the plea, just as Jax had nearly cleared them.

Instinctively, he turned. He saw the face first: eyes desperate and full of pain. The man was bent over and being held in a headlock. His shoulder-length hair hung lank, damp. The blood was flowing from his nose and from a gash under his eye. It was 59999, the inmate with the black eye and broken nose he'd noticed at roll call that morning. Jax could hardly believe that not even twenty-four hours had passed since that first muster. It felt more like weeks.

'Fucking shut up,' said the man holding him in the headlock, a skinny thirty-something with spiderweb tattoos on his elbows and forearms. As Jax froze on the spot, the man released 59999 for a second, jerked his head up and delivered a hard jab to his face, making a sickening noise as the fist hit the already split eye. Blood sprayed onto the white tiles.

'Fuckin dog,' the skinny assailant said, inspecting his knuckles for damage.

Behind them was another man. He said nothing, only grunted and groaned as he thrust. He stood with his hands on his victim's hips, and his pelvis was a piston, moving steadily back and forth, groin clapping against buttocks. His eyes were closed. It was Marsh.

JAX moved swiftly to the last cubicle. He reckoned neither Marsh – eyes closed as he pounded – nor the man doing the holding and hitting, had seen him, so he thought he might be able to wait them out. He moved into the corner of the shower and left the taps untouched; he didn't want to turn on the water in case they came to investigate. The mate might go looking for something fresh.

Jax was terrified, but also ashamed. He had always been taught to lend a hand, to look after the weak.

Stand up to the bullies. That's what his dad had told him before he died.

Never leave anyone behind. That was the motto in the army, and the army had taught him to be brave.

Yet here he was, cowering in the corner of a cubicle as a young man was being raped. And he hated himself for it.

HE waited until he was sure they had gone before making his move. Prisoner 59999 was huddled in the cubicle, cowering, his wet hair plastered to his skull.

'Here,' Jax said, holding out an arm. 'Get up, mate. Don't let anyone else see you like this.'

'Fuck off,' came the reply. 'Just leave me alone.'

A short, lightly built guy, not much older than Jax. His face was a bloody mess. A sizeable clump of his long shaggy hair had been ripped out, revealing a chunk of reddened skull. Jax winced as he noticed blood trickling down the man's back leg.

'Nah, come on,' Jax said, still holding out his arm. 'Get up, get dry, and go to your cell.'

'I said fuck off!' And he lashed out at Jax from the ground.

Without his army medical kit, there wasn't much Jax could do anyway. All he had was his towel, his shame and his fear.

He walked out wondering when they would come for him.

CHAPTER 7

Supermax, Goulburn Correctional Centre, Goulburn, NSW, Australia

THE SERPENT, that sinister shade who shared his cell and controlled his mind, had left a puzzle for Scott Wensley, or the Professor, as the other inmates called him: a carving on the cell wall.

Wensley was rarely allowed to emerge these days. Once, maybe twice a month? He was no longer sure. In any case, he lived mainly inside his own head, which had been entirely black until the Serpent had allowed him into the light. All he knew about his body was that it, too, now belonged to the Serpent – and the thirty-three people he had devoured.

There was always some new riddle for Wensley to solve, and the Serpent knew he liked riddles. This one was strange. Arabic. But it meant nothing to Wensley. Or maybe it did. Either way he did not have time for games. He had real work to do: the P versus NP problem. He had already solved the Hodge Conjecture, one of the five greatest unanswered questions in mathematics, scrawling the solution in chalk on the prison wall during his brief time in the light.

One down. Four to go.

Wensley hoped the Serpent would give him more time now he'd proved himself. Surely he would see his genius, see how important he was. Fair enough, the Hodge Conjecture had proved elementary, but the P versus NP problem would be more challenging. The Serpent could not ignore him if he cracked that nut.

So, best press on. He never knew how much time he had. How much time the Serpent would allow him.

He shook his head when he couldn't find his chalk. 'Not again,' he yelled as he rummaged through his one and only drawer. He ignored the dead cockroaches, all in various stages of dissection – one of the Serpent's projects, and brushed past the miniature mobile phone, which he hadn't known he had but knew he couldn't use.

He remembered back to when they didn't even have chalk. After being told that pens, pencils, textas, crayons and even chalk were dangerous, he'd been forced to use his food to write with. He had experimented with soup, bananas, and mashed potato with gravy. Tomato sauce had been the best option, but he'd found that even thickly pasted ketchup would eventually dry, flake and peel. It was the Serpent who had suggested using faeces, and that, in fact, had improved his life – after the prison officers complained about the smell, the warden decided chalk wasn't so dangerous after all. A box of coloured Crayolas was then dropped through the meal slot.

'Yuck,' the Professor fumed as he pulled a maggot-infested piece of meat from his drawer and threw it on the floor. He would have put it in the bin, but he knew what the Serpent did in the bin.

'Urggghh,' he grunted, resigned to carving instead of writing with chalk. He would have to go through all the Serpent's rubbish to find the knife, but at least then he wouldn't have to worry about the chalk being rubbed out. He considered hitting the knock-up to tell the guards it was safe to clean his cell, but he decided he didn't have time to be interrupted. And he didn't want to anger the Serpent.

A sudden chill stopped him in his tracks. He realised he was naked. He looked down at his body to check for fresh self-mutilation. No bleeding. *Good.* He wouldn't have to go to the hospital. He checked for new scars. Had he just come back from the hospital? He couldn't tell, there were so many scars, but he couldn't see any fresh stitches or bandages. He was sure there would be some damage somewhere – the Serpent needed pain for his ritual – but he was confident it was nothing drastic. Not this time.

He didn't bother looking for new ink, but he did notice that his first tattoo was starting to fade. The Serpent had been little more than a voice in his head when Wensley had walked into the tattoo shop and paid \$150 to have the chaos theory equation inked on his forearm in twenty-point Helvetica: $x_{t+1} = kx_t (1 - x_t)$. The tattooist didn't even blink: Robert May's equation wasn't even in contention when it came to the weirdest tatts requested by walk-ins.

'Damn you,' Wensley said when he realised the pants he had just retrieved from a pile of clothes in a corner of the cell were wet. 'I have had enough of your games.' He took them off and went back to the pile. A stub of white rolled out from under from a sodden shirt. 'Yes. Yes, yes, yes,' he muttered as he chased it across the cell.

He didn't care that he was cold, now he had his chalk. Naked, he moved to the wall, relieved to find his equation was still there. For a moment, he'd feared the missing chalk and the Serpent's new carving meant that the ceasefire was over. A while back, he'd made the mistake of wiping off some of the Serpent's nonsense, and the Serpent had retaliated by rubbing out all of his work. The Professor had then hidden the chalk, but the Serpent started writing in excrement. Finally, the

Professor had placed the chalk in the middle of the cell, as an offering. But the Serpent hadn't wanted a gift. He'd been in a fury. Instead of using the chalk, he'd eaten it, leaving Wensley with nothing.

Thankfully, they'd agreed to a détente before the next box of Crayolas had arrived. And so far so good, although the latest carving and the hidden chalk were a concern. He was also worried what would happen if a guard found the phone.

The Serpent was up to something. The ritual was evolving.

CHAPTER 8

Long Bay Correctional Complex, Sydney, NSW, Australia

A CLICK, followed by a buzz. Instinctively, Jax pulled his hands in front of his face.

False alarm. It wasn't the door. Of course not: the door was only locked at lights-out, which was hours away; no one had to unlock the door to get to him here in the afternoon, they could just walk straight in. No, it was just the cell light going on. Jax shook his head. No wonder they kept it in a cage.

A week had passed since his admission and he still hadn't been bashed, fucked or murdered. He hadn't even been threatened. Even Robbo, the drug addict who'd harassed him, had barely said a word since the wing had been flooded with 'H' three days earlier. The unusually strong heroin had so zombified him and his addict mates that they spoke only nonsense if they spoke at all.

One had already overdosed. Jax had seen the guards wheel him out on a gurney before muster. His death was not treated as murder, even though everyone knew it had been a hot-shot. Inmate 59035 had run up a debt he couldn't pay, so they'd laced his gear with rat-kill. No one cared: his own fault, should have paid. And no one talked about how they'd got in his cell: wasn't unusual, happened all the time.

Jax had managed to stay anonymous for the best part of a week. So by now he should have felt better, safer. But calm always precedes a storm. Thunder and lightning were still coming. He could feel it in his bones.

He'd thought that nothing could scare him after Afghanistan. Just four days after arriving at Camp Hadrian, he'd been sent on a clearance patrol. Walking in front of the convoy, all he'd had to protect himself against the armour-piercing bombs that were buried all over the desert was a metal detector, no better than the kind used by a Sunday treasure hunter at Bondi Beach. From right to left and left to right he and the others swept. Painting the road, they called it.

Dicko found the first one. A bucket full of nails and ball-bearings, buried two metres off the road. Not the first place you'd look.

'Stop!' he'd yelled. 'Nobody move.'

Jax froze mid-step. Almost shat himself.

'Not another fuckin' inch,' Dicko ordered as he began pulling up a wire running out from the bomb.

Jax held his front foot off the ground and watched the dirt spurt into the air as Dicko chased the wire towards him. It ripped through the road surface, leaving a wake like a lightning bolt. Jax suspected the thunder was underneath his raised foot.

It was. He was just a step away from the trigger. A pressure plate. Made of plastic. Which, of course, his metal detector couldn't detect. The Taliban learned fast.

Thank God Dicko's shout had scared him stiff. One more step would have killed him outright. Killed them all.

'Got it,' Jax then said, before Dicko even had to ask. 'Everyone step back. Take cover.'

Now he was on his own. He had to find the trigger and disarm it. He got down on his stomach and began to clear the hard, compacted sand by prodding the ground with his knife. Then he dropped the knife and used his fingers to clear the last of the dirt and probe the plastic. He winced as he gently pulled the casing apart. Once he could see inside, he took out his wire cutters and got ready to play roulette with his life. Red or black? Click or boom?

Black ... *Click*.

It got a little easier then. Each bomb a little less terrifying. At least until Dicko stepped on a trigger before the connected bomb had been found. Though that just left Jax feeling numb, not scared.

He didn't feel fear after that. Didn't feel anything. Not until he walked into Long Bay ...

Now it was like he was on his first patrol again: hidden bombs everywhere, expecting to step on one at any moment. And this time he didn't have Dicko to save him.

WHEN it was time for dinner, he reluctantly left his cell. At the mess hall, chops, mash and vegies were plonked onto his plastic plate. All the men at his former table looked down as he walked past. The man who had attacked him stared at Jax but didn't say a word. The silence was deafening. Jax found a half-empty table at the back of the room. He nodded at the elderly man he sat across from but didn't say a word. From the corner of his eye he saw another inmate lean over and whisper into the old man's ear. He only picked up one word, and that was Marsh.

He tucked in, even though his anxiety had killed his hunger. The rest of the inmates were like vultures on carrion and he didn't want to look out of place, so he forced himself to eat, shoving roughly cut chunks of meat into his mouth, chomping and swallowing – just another animal.

The mess was awash with chatter, a low and constant hum like summer rain. But then there was a thundercrack, one voice louder than the rest. The start of the storm.

Marsh.

It was his first appearance in the mess in the week since Jax had been admitted. Jax hadn't seen him in the yard, or even coming and going in the wing – just that one time in the shower block. Jax studied him through squinted eyes, searching for some kind of hint that would explain his absence.

He was so intent on finding out what he needed to know that he let his guard down for a second. Their eyes met. It felt as though all of oxygen had suddenly been sucked from the room. Jax could hear his own pulse beating loudly in his ears.

Marsh gave him a sly smile. Jax snatched his eyes away, his vision blurring. A sour taste filled his mouth. He felt disorientated, a sudden rush of crippling heat. His vision narrowed.

He hated himself for not having the guts to look up again. He told himself he was just being smart, attempting to avoid a confrontation. But he knew he was staring at his half-eaten dinner because this place had turned him into a pussy.

When he felt the hand on his shoulder, he jumped from his seat and swung round.

'Relax, big guy.'

Not Marsh, thank fuck. But it was the co-rapist. Jax didn't need to see the spider-web tattoos on the backs of his elbows to be sure. He never forgot a face, no matter how hard he tried.

'Just letting you know I'll be paying you a visit tonight. Marshy wants me to come and talk shop. No need to go making a fuss, but, if you insist, I take me tea with plenty of sugar.'

Jax didn't react, even though he knew 'sugar' was code for sex in prison. The skinny little scumbag laughed at what he thought was a private joke as backed away.

Ignoring the filth that covered the sink, Jax filled his one and only plastic mug with water. The caged fluorescent light on his ceiling was the only source of light now that the sun had well and truly gone down. No visitors. Not yet.

Before he could even take a sip, he had to put his mug down and rush to the toilet. He wouldn't have made it if it wasn't just a couple of steps away. Everything in his cell was just a couple of steps away.

He brought up his dinner. Again. Spending every moment of the day waiting to be attacked had been making him physically ill. Last night's pea and ham soup had come up and now it was tonight's chops. The evenings were worse than the days. His cell was a death trap. There was nowhere to run, nowhere to hide. Lockdown couldn't come quickly enough. Only then would he be safe.

Fear had spread through him like a virus, first affecting his skin with a pins-and-needles-like tingle, then working its way down his throat and into his gut. Finally it seemed to enter his bones, so that he felt heavy with it. Now it was like he was being consumed from the inside out.

He wiped his mouth, flushed the toilet and gargled with the water before spitting it back into the sink. He retreated to his bed and, eyes closed, looked deep into himself for something that would help him conquer his fear. He had to; he couldn't live like this.

His thoughts were interrupted by the sound of a click followed by a buzz. A different combination. Not the light this time. He jumped to his feet.

False alarm. His door had been locked, not opened. Lockdown at last. An hour until lights-out.

Still Jax did not feel safe. Almost unwillingly, he assessed the risk of the door being breached. It was secured by a state-of-the-art electronic lock, and there was no way the door itself, a chunk of hardwood reinforced by a steel plate, could be kicked

down or jemmied open. He doubted even the 'big red key' –
the battering ram they'd used in the army – could break down
this door. Jax reckoned it would have taken a good-sized ball
of C4 to blow through it. Yet, despite its apparent strength,
he kept on staring, waiting for it to swing open. He'd been
thrown into a new world, like none he'd ever known, where
the natural laws of the universe no longer applied. And as if he
had been given the power of premonition, he was still certain
that someone was about to come barging in.

Bashed, fucked or murdered. Maybe all three. He now knew
without doubt that those seven words were no hollow warning.

Jax looked towards the knock-up on the wall opposite
his bed, right next to the door. *Useless.* In the event of an
intrusion, his path to it would be blocked. He'd have to get
past an intruder to hit the button. He could rig up a trigger that
could be activated from his bed if he had some wire and solder,
but there was no welding gear here.

Jax couldn't stop thinking about what he'd seen in the
shower block a week before. Not just thinking about it but
replaying it, over and over, an HD-quality rerun in his head.

He knew enough about torture and human nature to
understand that men often raped other men to assert dominance
rather than for pleasure. Raping a man was far more effective
than just giving him a hiding. Jax knew it wouldn't take much
more than one going-over for any man – even a tough man –
to submit to Marsh's will.

He tried not to think about what he himself would be
prepared to endure before submitting. He also tried not to read
too much into the smile on Marsh's face as he pounded away.

Suddenly Jax felt sick again: his stomach dropped, his cheeks
burned and his vision blurred. He retched. Reality was kicking
him fair and square in the guts, the weight of his situation
threatening to crush him. He struggled to breathe and it felt
like the walls were closing in. He was desperate to get out, and

now wished he had contested the charge. *You didn't do it. You couldn't have done it. Why didn't you fight?*

He hadn't contested the charge because he'd accepted the evidence. But maybe they'd faked it. Some kind of set-up.

He took a deep breath and held it in, then cleared his mind as he exhaled. They weren't coming for him. Not yet. Not tonight. He decided to try to sleep, even though the light was still on.

But then he heard the click … followed by a buzz.

IT WAS Marsh's henchmen: the big guy with the scarred face who'd been on watch and the tattooed co-rapist.

Jax shot to his feet.

'Relax, champ,' the smaller man said. 'Just here for that cuppa.' He held up his hands and showed Jax an empty pair of palms. 'See, all good,' he said. He swaggered from the shadows and into Jax's room, keeping his hands in the air, floating like a fog. But his shadow was heavy.

Following behind him, the bigger man heaved his frame into the cell, one tree-trunk-like leg after the other, then stopped directly in front of the knock-up and folded his arms.

'You have ten minutes,' came a voice from outside.

Jax looked past the intruders to the dimly lit corridor. He wasn't surprised to see Rogers.

'And don't kill him. You haven't paid for a body bag.'

The door slammed shut. Sunshine gone. Thunder and lightning inside.

'Don't listen to the Dodge,' the small man said. 'He's just taking the piss. We aren't going to kill ya. Well, not unless you don't pay. I'm Grub.' He extended a hand.

Jax didn't move. This man was not his friend. He would not shake hands with a rapist.

'Look at this tough cunt, would ya?' Grub said as he looked over his shoulder towards the other man. Then his playful smirk became a snarl. 'You simple or something? You know what's happening here, right? Marshy has been looking out for ya and you haven't paid. That's why we're here. Me and Bluey are here to collect.'

Jax knew it was no coincidence that he'd been left alone. Now it looked like the honeymoon was over. He must have had a blank look on his face, though, as Grub continued. 'Listen, cunt,' he said. 'It's simple, even for a dumb cunt like you. You pay Marsh every week and you don't get got. You pay up every Friday and you don't end up dead. Just $200 a week. Best deal you'll ever make."

Jax had money: $3612.15 in his savings account. Based on his rapid calculation, that would buy him almost 126 and a half days of not getting got. He would only have to come up with another $100,387.85 to survive his sentence – that is, if he got out on good behaviour in ten years. He could nod his head and buy himself twelve weeks of protection. But he wasn't going to do that. He knew that agreeing to pay would seal his fate. He would be declaring himself prey, not just now but forever. He would be stood over for the rest of his sentence. They would demand money he didn't have and turn him into a sex-slave when he couldn't play.

Plus, that was his money – he'd earned it. He also knew his nan was relying on it. She couldn't work anymore but still had to pay her bills. Jax helped out: his army income had always been more than enough for anything he needed – even taking into account buying stuff for Nikki – and if he could make life that little bit sweeter for his nan, he would, every time. That's what money was for, helping the people you loved. Not to line Marsh's pockets. So he didn't say anything.

'What?' Grub said. 'Nothing stashed away?'

Still not a word.

'Nup,' Grub said. 'That's okay. Say the word and we can work something out. You got a missus? A brother? How about

Mum and Dad? Surely someone is good for it? We offer a full service. Just give us an address and we will collect.'

Jax's brow furled at the mention of his Mum and Dad.

'All broke, useless cunts, too?' Grub continued. 'That's okay. Marshy is a good bloke. He'll even let you work it off. So … what'll it be? Two hundred or are we putting you to work?'

Jax replied with a forged-in-iron stare.

'Righto,' said Grub as he moved towards Jax. He was now so close that Jax could smell his sour breath. 'You,' he said as he drove his index finger into Jax's forehead, 'owe us.' He tapped Jax's forehead again. 'Get it now?' he said.

Another tap. 'How about now?'

Another tap, harder.

Jax exhaled slowly, his mind clearing.

'I'll fuck you u—'

Jax struck like a rattlesnake, snatching Grub's finger. He held it in front of his face and squeezed.

'You're fucking dea—'

Jax broke the finger before Grub had time to react, roughly jerking his wrist to the right and snapping the bone at the knuckle in one move. It sounded like a cue-ball being hit hard and was followed by a guttural cry.

'Ahhhhh! Fuuuuuck!'

Jax blanched as Grub pulled back, freeing his hand from Jax's grip, and he saw the broken finger hanging at a sickening, unnatural angle from the man's hand.

Jax stumbled back, his history of violence flashing through his mind. He told himself he'd had no choice. He recalled the image of this man holding prisoner 59999 in a headlock. He saw the tiles spray-painted with blood. Jax gritted his teeth and found his nerve.

Grub went up before he went down, the perfectly timed knee to the ribs hitting him like a car crash and lifting him off the ground. Jax waited for him to scream, but he didn't.

Couldn't. His lung had been punctured by a broken rib and he sounded like an untied balloon gushing air. It was time to deliver the knockout blow. Jax clenched his balled fist, summoned his strength.

Then everything went dark.

A PINPRICK of light appeared. Jax blinked and his vision returned.

Legs limp, his jaw screaming with pain, he looked at the big man called Bluey and suddenly realised what had happened. He'd been blindsided, hit with a sledgehammer to the face and momentarily knocked out. He was lucky to still be on his feet.

Bluey looked at him with something akin to interest as Jax made two fists and pulled them to his face. Without warning, Jax surged forward and struck first. It was his only chance.

The left jab hit Bluey in the jaw. Jax had thought about going for his abdomen, but he knew the man was too big for a strike there to have any effect. He threw another, just as quick and accurate as the first, a double left to the head. Bluey was momentarily stunned. Jax might not have had the power but he had the speed. He considered moving in and attacking what might be Bluey's only weak spot – his balls – but changed his mind when he realised it would negate his only advantage, his reach. Jax had to stay on the outside.

Yet he had to strike now, had to land something big enough to cripple his opponent while he was stunned. So he went in for the kill. Dropping his right hand to his side, he leaned back and loaded up. And then he swung, throwing the hardest right he had.

Bluey moved his head only an inch, but it was enough for Jax to miss. The punch was so powerful there was no changing its trajectory mid-flight. His fist whizzed past Bluey's chin and, as he'd thrown his entire weight into the all-or-nothing strike, the rest of him followed too. He ended up within Bluey's range, fully exposed and way too off-balance to go on the defensive.

He grimaced and braced himself for the blow. Bluey didn't need an invitation. He swivelled, loaded and fired. The left-hand rip felt like being hit head-on by a train, the blow smashing into Jax's kidneys, the pain devastating. He doubled over in agony, but Bluey kept on him, delivering another series of blows to the kidneys before hooking upwards into Jax's upper ribs. Pain bloomed and spread through Jax's body. He dropped and collapsed onto his back, the pain eclipsing everything else.

'You're fucked now, cunt,' Grub rasped. He was back on his feet.

Jax gazed up at the pair of them, looming over him. He was struggling to breathe and in pain. He wanted it to be over. Whatever fight he'd had in him had evaporated. Lying on his cell floor with the door locked and Rogers paid off, he was helpless. All he could do to defend himself was curl up into a ball. He lifted his knees to his chest and held on tight.

It didn't help.

CHAPTER 9

St Petersburg, Russia

MOST people would have thrown up, or at least gagged or placed their hand over their nose, but Kostya Volkov wasn't most people. The St Petersburg police detective had an iron gut and nerves of steel. There wasn't much he hadn't seen in his thirty-two-year career in Russia's crime capital.

Volkov had begun as a pup in 1989, during the Perestroika-era crime epidemic. Amid the social upheaval of privatisation, redistribution of property, de-militarisation and unprecedented poverty, the Russian mobster was born.

And so was Volkov.

In the early 1990s, the Tambov Gang, the Malyshev Gang and the Kazan Gang ruled the streets of St Petersburg, not with iron fists but with Kalashnikovs. Armed to the teeth with ex-military AK-47 assault rifles, they extorted, kidnapped and killed.

So Volkov had been raised on death, force-fed a diet of corpses. At least one a week. He found them strung up, shot, decapitated, chopped up, skinned, even minced. Every murder was a message, each gang wanting to prove it was the most brutal.

Hence the contents of the suitcase, washed up on the banks of the Neva River, were never going to prompt theatrics from Volkov. He looked upon the dismembered corpse like a mechanic examining parts of an engine.

The case had been found a stone's throw away from the Blagoveshchensky Bridge, first by a dog, and then by the man who'd been walking the dog. He'd made the mistake of opening it, hoping for treasure and instead receiving a lifetime's supply of nightmares.

'Has anybody else touched the suitcase?' Volkov asked the uniformed police officer who'd arrived first on the scene.

'No,' said the officer, 'only the man with the dog. The suitcase was open when we arrived. We secured the scene and called it in.'

Volkov moved in for a closer look. He saw a pair of scissors, a file and a couple of other bits and pieces on top of a pile of blood-spattered plastic bags. He couldn't be certain, but it appeared as though most of whoever this had once been was in the suitcase.

The torso had been placed in the centre of the case and the other body parts arranged around it like a macabre jigsaw. The head was stuffed in one end, face up. He didn't know what the two square chunks of meat next it were at first, but he worked it when he pressed against the plastic with a tool and saw the palm lines: hands. They'd been chopped from the arms at the wrist, and all the fingers and both thumbs had been removed. He couldn't see the missing fingers in the butcher's pile, but he figured they would be in one of the bags.

The body parts were taken back to the St Petersburg Central Intelligence Bureau, unbagged, tagged and laid out on a stainless-steel bench in the forensic centre in the shape of the original body.

'No fingers?' Volkov asked the medical examiner.

'No,' the examiner said. 'No teeth either. Well, no complete teeth anyway. Looks like a hammer was taken to his mouth. Dental records won't be much good and we won't have prints unless the fingers turn up.'

A hacksaw, a cleaver and a reciprocal saw were laid out next to the scissors, the file and the metal tube on a table beside the body. There was also a pile of white mush that had perhaps been a book.

'Any prints on the tools?' Volkov asked.

The medical examiner shook his head.

'Can we identify the victim through DNA?' Volkov asked.

'We have taken a skin sample,' the examiner said. 'We'll have the results to you soon.'

VOLKOV read the report when it was sent through.

A corruption has severed the two polynucleotides strands of the deoxyribonucleic acid. The nucleotides have also been damaged by the introduction of a foreign body. No meaningful biological information can be recovered from the provided sample.

He made a printout before storming over to the examiner. 'What the fuck does this mean?' he asked, waving the pages.

'The results were inconclusive,' the examiner explained. 'The sample was corrupted by some type of bleach product that destroyed the DNA.'

'So no DNA at all?' Volkov asked.

'Not on anything that had contact with the bleach,' the examiner said. 'But the internal organs may be uncorrupted. I've sent brain and heart samples for testing.'

The brain sample yielded some uncorrupted material, allowing the examiner to work out the victim's genetic code. Volkov struggled to believe that a man in a white coat could extract a sequence of letters like this from a drop of blood, a strand of hair or, in this case, a sliver of brain, and that such a sequence could uniquely identify an individual – dead or alive. But he didn't have to understand it; all he needed to do was feed the code into the CIB's DNA database. They'd amassed a huge amount of data over the years, taking samples from every person they questioned, including swabs of nearly every gangster in the city. He'd taken joy on those occasions in pushing the white stick with the cotton tip a little farther down the throat than usual. Volkov was pretty sure this code would belong to a member of one of St Petersburg's three major crime gangs, maybe even one of the men he had made gag.

He pasted the code into the database program on his PC, then hit search.

No match.

Volkov pondered. Maybe the victim belonged to one of the migrant gangs, of which there were plenty. Over ten percent of all crimes in St Petersburg were committed by foreigners. Ukrainian gangs, Chechen gangs, Serbian gangs, Hungarian gangs – the list went on.

Volkov pasted the same code into an international database run by the CIA, hit 'Enter'.

Match found.

The result was a surprise. The victim was *Australian*? He doubled-checked to make sure he hadn't misread the word 'Austria'. No, it was Australia.

He would have assumed the dead man was a tourist had it not been for his presence on a CIA database and the way the body had been disposed of. Tourists weren't chopped up and put into bags. The man was clearly a criminal and had died like a criminal.

Volkov put it down to a deal gone wrong. He had no reason to connect this white Australian man named Timothy Jenkins, previously convicted of theft and assault, with anything else. Let alone the church bombing that had taken place the day before, a terrorist attack that had killed 164 people. The anonymous bomber was dead. Blown to bits. A lone attacker.

Case closed.

CHAPTER 10

Supermax, Goulburn Correctional Centre, Goulburn, NSW, Australia

THE SERPENT took his hand away from the wall and placed it on his naked body. Exhaling, he shivered as he caressed his scarified skin. He closed his eyes and pushed his palm down his torso. He stopped when he found a section of unscarred skin. Opening an old wound would have been easier, but revelations were not meant to be easy. He pressed the tip of the sharpened knife into his thigh.

Nothing.

He pulled the knife back before thrusting again.

Still nothing. Not enough pain.

He reefed the knife, slicing a deep gash.

The revelation.

He began his work. Arabic. Again.

'Scorched altars burned,' he said while wondering which of the thirty-three the revelation came from.

It only took him minutes to finish.

Once he was done, he limped across his cell and hit the knock-up.

CHAPTER 11

Long Bay Correctional Complex, Sydney, NSW, Australia

JAX opened his eyes as his cell door swung inwards.

'Uhhh?' he blurted, startled by the noise and then stunned by the light, the sun a speeding comet that had just crash-landed on his face. He closed his eyes and rolled over, shielding himself from the UV blast.

'Get up,' the guard called from the corridor. 'Out in the yard for muster in ten minutes.'

'Arggh,' he exclaimed, as a pain like buckshot fired point-blank tore through his side.

He slowly lifted his heavy head and opened his eyes. *One eye.* He realised his left eye was swollen shut. He went to feel his face with his left hand but was stopped by another jolt of pain. He looked down and saw his left arm dangling like a sausage and the shoulder was at a right angle, a few inches higher than his chest. He summoned the right arm instead, lifted his hand all the way to his face and grunted when he made contact.

His cheekbone was broken.

He moved his hand higher to continue the examination, almost certain his eye socket would be smashed too. But there was no way to tell, not with the swelling, the blood-filled tissue raised an inch off his face.

'Come on,' the guard shouted. 'Get moving. Time for muster.' He poked his head into the cell. 'What are you doing on the floor. Oh fuck ...'

The guard edged into Jax's room and stood there, aghast.

'You need to go to the hospital, kid,' he said as he moved towards the knock-up. 'I'll buzz for help.'

Jax ignored the pain and tried to struggle to his feet. 'Nah,' he said. 'I'm all good. I don't need help.'

The guard pulled back from the emergency intercom.

'Righto,' he said. 'But you gotta tell me what happened. You have to tell me who did this. I can help.'

Jax could only see a big blur of blue at the door. He squinted and blinked, but couldn't focus until he wiped the fluid out of his eye. It was the hulk-like guard from the bus – Officer Turner. He seemed even bigger in the confines of the cell.

'Help?' Jax asked as he stood. He wanted to trust him. He was alone and desperate. Beaten, bruised and broken. He wanted a saviour. A protector. Even just someone to tell him it would be okay.

'Yeah, I will,' Turner said. 'Tell me who did this and I'll sort them out.'

Jax shook his head. He didn't know if this was some sort of test. Didn't know if this guard was on the take, like Rogers was.

'Nothing happened,' Jax said. 'I'm fine.'

'Marsh? Just nod if it was.'

Jax wondered if he could trust Turner. No. He had to do more than wonder. He could not let his guard down. Not even for a second. A single slip could get him killed. In here, any sign of empathy had to be treated as a red flag. The way the guard had spoken to Marsh that first day suggested he might be more friend than foe. But then again, the disdain he shown towards Marsh could have been a front, or the result of a dodgy deal gone wrong.

Jax's gut told him Turner was genuine, but he needed more than that. Prison was like no other place he knew. Every stranger was a potential enemy rather than a potential friend. Turner could easily deliver him straight back to Marsh for more if he squealed.

'I'm not going to give anyone up,' Jax said. 'That's not my style. I wouldn't do it outside and I'm not going to do it in here.'

'Good,' Turner said. 'Because dogging will get you killed. Don't trust anyone. Not even me. But seriously' – he pointed towards Jax's dangling arm – 'you need help.'

'It's only dislocated,' Jax said.

Turner gave him a look that said, 'And how would you know?'

'I had medical training in the army,' Jax shot back. 'It's not a big deal.'

'Well, you can't leave it like that. You'll need a doctor to put it back in.'

'Doesn't have to be a doctor,' Jax said. 'You still want to help?'

Turner nodded, then Jax gave him instructions.

The big guard placed his huge hand on the front of Jax's injured shoulder. 'Really? As hard as I can?' he asked uncertainly.

'Well, maybe not your hardest,' Jax replied, taking note of the guard's bulging bicep. 'Just— AHHHHHH!'

The one-inch palm punch was delivered without notice. Jax was hurled off his feet and sent flying backwards. He braced for a hard landing but relaxed as he landed on his mattress.

The pain in his shoulder was gone, the relief almost instant.

'I was about to say hit me half-hard,' Jax smiled.

'Half? That was more like a quarter.' Now Turner was doing the smiling. 'I'll get you an ice pack.'

Jax shuddered as he wondered what a full-force hit would have felt like, what the damage would be like. He suddenly realised he was a lightweight locked in a cage with heavyweights. The expression 'punching above your weight' hadn't made much sense to him when one of his army mates had used it after he'd showed off a picture of Nikki. It did now. He wasn't in the same league as men like Bluey and Turner. Or Marsh.

JAX could no longer remain anonymous. His injuries saw to that. He'd cleaned his face as best he could and put on a new set of greens. But he still attracted attention the moment he came out of his cell, felt the eyes on him as he walked down the wing.

'Have a go at this cunt,' an inmate called out, as he pointed at Jax from the other side of the corridor. 'Somebody had a good time last night.'

Jax felt a two-handed push then a whack on his back, but managed to stay upright, even as pain ricocheted through him. He fought the urge to run, scream or break down and just kept walking towards the yard, all the while bracing for another hit, his shoulders pulled up into his neck, his jaw clenched. But whoever had struck him had now moved on, absorbed into the groups of men drifting towards muster.

If he'd agreed to pay, he wouldn't be walking wounded, looking left, looking right, wondering who was going to belt him next. But he would have been spent in nine weeks, and then what? At least this way he stood a chance.

A fresh blast of sunlight hit him as he entered the yard. Then a shoulder.

Okay, a slim chance.

At least it all made sense now, Jax thought as he ducked his head and sidestepped the man that had nudged him. It all added up. Marsh had taken his nod in the holding cell as a promissory note and had been protecting him. He had put the word out that Jax was his. That nobody was to touch him.

But after last night, Jax knew he was back on the market. Up for grabs and fair game.

JAX kept his head down through muster.

'60079,' the guard eventually called.

'Present,' Jax said, lifting his head only to answer.

Standing at the back off the muster pack as usual, Jax began to move away as soon as the final number was called. He was the first back into the wing and had a clear run to his cell.

The ice pack Turner had given him earlier had thawed, the green ice inside the clear plastic sleeve now looking like a lime Slurpee left in the sun. Jax threw it into the sink and sat on his bed, dreading breakfast as much as he'd feared his first military engagement.

Arriving at the mess hall deliberately late again, Jax grabbed toast, cereal and a serving of milk and filled his plastic mug with OJ. He ignored the pain in his shoulder and carried his plate in his left hand as usual. Holding his arm up and bent at the elbow lit a fire in his shoulder socket.

The mess hall was louder than usual. Buzzing. Excitable. Jax kept his head down as he made his way to the least threatening table but zoned in on a conversation as he passed a motley-looking crew.

'They won't know what hit 'em,' one of them was saying. 'We're gonna smash 'em, boys.'

Jax overheard more tough talk after he took his seat.

'We can take them,' a man at his table said. 'They might have a few big boys, but they'll be gassed after five minutes. We'll go straight through them then.'

A riot?

'And Simmo is out,' the inmate continued.

'Really?' said another man. 'Yeah, injured,' the first man replied. 'Shanked. Owed Marsh coin.'

'You beauty,' said the other man. 'They're a one-man team. Easy beats without Simmo.'

Football. Today was Saturday. He now knew that Saturday meant footy. Inmates were allowed to use the grassed recreation yard on both Saturday and Sunday, as opposed to the caged concrete quadrangle that was only good for handball – Jax had thought it would have been perfect for cricket, if cricket bats weren't lethal. The flat green fields were ideal for rugby league.

Jax was safe for now, the entire mess hall consumed with teams and tactics.

SITTING alone on a grass hill behind one of the four full-sized football fields, freshly marked and all sporting hybrid posts that could also be used as soccer goals, Jax felt the most vulnerable he'd been since getting off the bus. After all, the fields measured 27,200 square metres, and you needed twenty guards to cover that area – not three.

The armed guard in the tower above where he sat was basically useless, as he only came out of his box four times an hour to do a quick lap around the 360-degree landing. Jax couldn't make out the exact model of his rifle, but it looked like a Ruger. Maybe a .233 carbine. Whatever it was, the weapon was no Austeyr F88, the dependable all-rounder he'd been issued in the army. The guard's old rifle would have an effective range of 150 metres at best – and an accurate range of no more than fifty metres.

Jax figured that by sitting within that fifty-metre range he would at least be protected for four minutes every hour – provided the guard was a skilled marksman. Whoever had decided on green for the inmates' uniform was either an idiot or a masochist: even Jax would have had difficulty taking a shot with the target almost perfectly camouflaged by the grass.

After a while he moved to what he'd assessed as another safe spot, at the top of the hill, the highest point of the yard. From there, he had a clear line of sight across the field, and he could sit with his back against the fence, meaning he could not be attacked from behind. He was as safe as he could be without his Austeyr.

A silhouette approached. With the sun in his eyes, Jax could only make out the man's shape and speed: short, slight, slow. Shaggy hair. He estimated the threat to be minimal. The worst of them were out on the field playing league. Still, in his current state – internal bruising, shoulder back in its socket but ligaments stretched and screaming, face a swollen mess – a gust of wind was a threat.

'How ya doing?' the man asked. 'Remember me?'

Jax thought he'd seen the last of this man: 59999. He had left him broken and bloodied on the shower-block tiles.

'Name's Johnson,' he said. 'Mind if I join?'

Jax couldn't think of a way to say no.

Johnson groaned as he kneeled, placed his right palm onto the ground to take his weight and lowered himself onto the grass gingerly, wincing as he settled in. Jax could at least relate to that – his own body was still thrumming with pain; it even hurt to breathe.

They sat in an awkward silence until Johnson eventually spoke. 'Just wanted to see if you're all right – you look pretty beat up,' he said. 'And sorry for telling you to fuck off, you know, the other day.'

'I'm sorry I didn't do more,' Jax said.

'Nah,' Johnson said. 'They would have just fucked you up too.'

'They did anyway,' Jax said, pointing towards his eye.

'So it was Marsh?' Johnson asked. 'What for?'

Jax remained silent. He had already said too much. In the sunlight, Johnson appeared older than Jax had first thought, at least thirty. Caucasian and free of bikie tats, he didn't look like he posed a threat, might even be an ally. On the other hand, he could have been sent to find out if Jax was going to snitch.

'You going to be all right?' Jax asked.

'Fuck knows,' Johnson replied. 'I've been paying them for protection for a while and everything was sweet until Marsh decided I was a dog. Too many trips to the lawyers, he says. I'm in the middle of a trial and I'm meeting with me lawyers heaps. Heaps too much, he reckons. Thinks I've been sneakin' off to talk to the cops. He couldn't beat a confession out of me, so he ...'

Jax saw an opening: Johnson offering unsolicited information. Intelligence. He needed to know what he was up against.

'So what's his deal then – Marsh's?' he asked, trying to sound casual.

'Marsh?' Johnson replied. 'Serious? You don't know? Fuck, man, everyone knows Marsh.'

Jax shrugged.

'The Gypsies, man,' Johnson said. 'He is their Sergeant at Arms. At least when he isn't locked up. He has been in and out of jail his whole life. It's a murder charge this time, so he's in for a stint. He went nuts on some poor bastard for parking him in outside a Woolworths. Clubbed him to death with a cricket bat. Dude's a fucking psycho.'

'Seems like he's a big deal in here,' Jax said.

'Fuck yeah,' Johnson said. 'He's a fucking big deal, all right. You know how it works, right?'

'I'm figuring it out,' Jax replied.

'Well, it could all change tomorrow, but for now the Gypsies are in charge. It's a numbers thing, you know? If a couple of Gypsies get released and a few more Angels get locked up, the scales will tip, but for now the Gypsies run the wing. And Marsh is the most senior Gypsy in here, so he is King Shit. But don't worry too much about who is in charge. Doesn't make much difference. All the different gangs get on for the most part and stay out of each other's way. Shit only hits the fan when they beef over business.'

'Business?' Jax asked.

'Shit yeah,' Johnson exclaimed. 'Drugs, phones, protection, hits – you name it. They make as much money in here as they do out there.'

'How much does protection cost?' Jax asked.

'Shit, you don't know? You're not paying anyone already?'

Jax did not reply.

'Fucken sort your shit out, man. They will fucking kill you, unless you can fight like a son of a bitch. You think this is as bad as it gets?' He gestured to Jax's face. 'It's not, mate. I'm only paying like fifty bucks a week. Sometimes they charge more. Sometimes they charge less. Depends who ya are and what ya got. Going rate seems to be $100.'

Jax thought about who he was and what he had. Two hundred dollars a week? He decided that they didn't want his money. They wanted something else.

IT TOOK three days for Jax to realise something: pain was king. Pain was all. For three days, he'd managed to conceal the worst of his injuries – and himself – as best as he could. Only leaving his cell when he was forced out for muster and dinner, he'd kept his head down and covered his swollen eye with shadows, angles or a hand or crooked arm. Each night, he'd perspired his way to sunrise, rolling, groaning, and at times wishing for death.

On day three, he gave up. The swelling around his eye now was two inches high and seething. A clear liquid oozed down his cheek. His eyelid was sealed shut with puss, hardened like cured Liquid Nails. The pain was immense, like he had an ice-pick lodged in his face.

He reluctantly hit the knock-up.

When it was Rogers who answered – just Jax's luck – he

almost lost his resolve then and there, but one graze of a finger over his eye made his mind up for him.

When Rogers arrived, he took one look at Jax and left, then came back with a medical form and a pen.

'Fill this out,' he said, all matter-of-fact and without the slightest hint of remorse. 'And then I'll have someone escort you to the clinic. And don't say a word. Tell 'em what happened and you're dead.'

Jax did his best with the form, though being in the throes of a fever he struggled to focus and shook so badly his writing was barely legible. He ignored all the questions about how he'd received his injuries. Another guard came and escorted him to the clinic.

The clinic had two separate entrances: one for protection inmates and one for the general population. The guard at the door checked Jax's ID card to make sure he had come in the right one. Occasionally, a protection inmate found his way into the general population area of the clinic, and sometimes a general population prisoner found his way into the protection area of the clinic. The result was usually the same: a protection prisoner dead and a general population prisoner on a murder charge.

The guard also frisked Jax for weapons and checked his form had been signed by his wing guard. With everything correct and in order, Jax walked into the waiting room and checked in with the nurse. The woman, old enough to be his grandmother, was seated safe and secure behind a glass screen. Jax handed his form through the slot and was gruffly told to take a seat. That's when he was hit by the smell.

The clinic had been doused with medical-grade cleaning products, but a foreboding odour lingered beneath that surface smell: death. That's what the addicts smelled like, Jax realised as he surveyed the half-dozen men who were waiting to be seen by a doctor. The methadone gang.

There were few appealing choices when it came to where to sit. The metal pews, painted a heavy green, were mostly occupied by the kind of men Jax would once have crossed a street to avoid. He took the closest spot, sat and concentrated on his breathing, willing himself to keep his good eye open and not fall into the deep sleep that was tugging on every corner of his mind.

And that's what he did for the next twenty-five minutes, even focusing on the bickering between the addicts to take his mind off his throbbing eye.

'You got any gear in your wing?' one asked. 'We got nuthin'. All dry. I had to smoke Buskies.'

'Buskies?' the other replied. 'What are you fucking on about?'

'Buskies! Nah, bra. You're shitting me, right? You never smoked a Buskie? Nah. Fuck off.' After a dumb silence, he resumed. 'It's Buscopan. That shit you get for stomach cramps. Tell the nurse you have crook guts. Trust me, bra, you'll be off yer tree.'

Another dumb silence.

'They're little white pills,' he said. 'Just keep 'em under your tongue and smoke 'em up on a foily when you get back to your cell. Make sure you get rid of the plastic coating and cut 'em up good. And don't eat 'em. They don't do shit if ya eat 'em, unless you have a pain in the guts. But you get mad fucked up if you smoke that shit, bra.'

Finally, after what felt like an eternity, Jax was called.

THERE were six cells inside the clinic, each like a hospital room except for the reinforced and locked steel doors, where inmates needing more than a hit of methadone, medication, or a bandage were treated. Essentially the clinic was a fully functioning hospital – and probably saw as many serious injuries as the average emergency room. *State-of-the-art and the best prison clinic in the country*, Jax recalled his admitting officer saying. At the time, Jax had thought it wasn't much to be so proud of, but he understood better now.

There were also another two cells called observation cells, whose walls and doors were completely transparent, being made of heavy-duty Perspex. One of these cells was occupied.

It was like trying not to look at a car crash. Cuffed to the bed, both his ankles and hands strapped to the metal frame by medieval-looking leather restraints, was a man – if you could call him that – whom Jax recognised immediately. Known initially in the media as Cerebral the Cannibal, Scott Wensley had subsequently gained the sinister sobriquet of the Serpent after the press learned that he had paralysed his victims with snake venom before he tortured and killed them. The police had found the correct licences for forty-four eastern brown snakes in his basement.

Jax had only been a baby when this guy had gone on his killing spree, but everyone still knew about him. Australia's most notorious serial killer, the Serpent had left Ivan Milat trailing in his wake and was surpassed statistically only by the madman Martin Bryant. After being found guilty of thirty-three murders, he'd been sentenced to life without parole and had since been locked away for eighteen years. In that time he'd completely covered himself in ink. Jax could see that every inch of the skin exposed by his white short-sleeved hospital gown was marked. Even the soles of his feet.

Father Martin was sitting by the Serpent's side. *Last rites?*

It had to be some sort of medical emergency. The Serpent was kept in Supermax, which was a jail within a jail at Goulburn. Everyone knew that. The only reason he would be in Long Bay was to be treated in the clinic, which was fully equipped, unlike the one at Goulburn, which was only had only a basic medical facility.

The Serpent was staring at him. He wanted to keep walking – but he couldn't. He was frozen stiff. He couldn't stop looking at the Serpent's eyes. For a moment he thought he could see the killer's victims, trapped in there. Those thirty-three people. But he knew it was just his mind playing tricks; the Serpent had not really taken their souls, as he claimed, by eating their brains. Still, those eyes. They were chilling. Suddenly the chains rattled and the Serpent launched himself towards Jax, as far as the restraints would allow. Jax jumped, at once forgetting what he had been thinking about, and everything else.

Jax wondered which of the criminal's alter egos the priest was talking to. Was it the genius professor or the crazy killer?

A NURSE called Laura cleaned Jax's wounds when he reached one of the treatment rooms. Blue-eyed, smiling, and smelling like sunshine and strawberries, she made him forget about the Serpent – at least for a little while. She reminded him a little of someone he loved. He didn't even mind when she used a cotton tip to clean the worst of the gunk from his closed eyelids. Pain tore through him, but he just gritted his teeth.

'You're going to need an IV,' she said to him. 'We're going to have to pump you full of antibiotics. You'll need more than tablets for this.'

'How long does the Serpent have left?' Jax asked.

'Left?' Laura said. 'Oh no, he isn't dying. He's just down here getting stitched up. He took to himself with a knife. Again. He is sent here every time he injures himself, which is a lot. You get a look at all those scars? He's sick in the head. Does it for the attention, I reckon ...'

'So why the priest?' Jax asked. 'Father Martin, right?'

'Yep, Father Marty. Uncle Marty to some. He talks to everyone. Even the Serpent. Actually, he is the only person I have ever seen speak to the Serpent. Interesting story behind it all, but yuck, I won't go near him.' She shook her head and lowered her voice. 'He really freaks me out.'

'What's he like? The chaplain, I mean, not the Serpent.'

'Marty? I dunno. He's just Uncle Marty. He's been here forever. Way before I got here. Why?'

'Oh, no reason, really. Dunno. Guess I'm just a bit suspicious of the whole "come to God" routine. Especially in here. I can't imagine he has a good strike rate.'

'Oh no, he does okay, I think,' Laura said, smiling again. 'He'd give you the shirt off his back if you asked. I've heard he even helps guys out once they leave.'

Jax zoned out as she finished cleaning him up. She was saying something about X-rays, but Jax couldn't focus. His mind kept returning to those eyes. There had been no life in them, no humanity. Jax wondered what Laura could see in his own eyes. Was there anything left in them?

The X-rays revealed Jax had a broken cheekbone and two cracked ribs. He spent the next four days in the clinic, locked away in his own hospital cell, mostly asleep. The painkillers were bliss – but the nightmares were hell. The Serpent had slithered his way into Jax's head.

CHAPTER 12

Milan, Italy

HE tied the six nine-volt batteries together with the silver gaffer tape, exactly as he had been shown. Then he soldered the wires to the terminals: the red ones to the positive terminals, the black ones to the negative.

He picked up the trigger, a modified PC joystick, and pressed the red button. 'Boom,' he shouted.

'What are you doing, dickhead,' Adam shouted back. 'Don't even muck around with that shit.'

'It's not connected to anything,' Steve said defensively. 'The bomb's in the oven, bra. Chillax.'

'Just shut the fuck up,' Adam replied. 'You're a dumb cunt. What if someone is listening, bruz?'

'As if,' Steve said. 'Nobody has a clue. Fuck me. Stop acting like you're my boss.'

Steve was glad it was almost over, as he couldn't put up with Adam for much longer. He'd been living with him for almost two years – he didn't know exactly how long because he'd stopped counting down days and looking at dates when he was released on parole. He figured they'd lived in the farmhouse for about a year and a half. A couple of hundred kilometres outside Sydney, in the middle of nowhere, completely isolated, but wanted for nothing. The Mahdi had set them up just like he'd promised. He gave them food, shelter, knowledge and, most importantly, a purpose.

The Mahdi had found Steve when he was at rock bottom. Picked him up from the floor and shown him the way. Shown him His way. Steve didn't meet Adam until he arrived at the farmhouse. He hadn't even seen him in prison, though he knew he had also done time.

They weren't supposed to talk about the past – only the future and the glory that awaited them – but they sometimes did. The Mahdi had also rescued Adam. He'd told Steve all about it one night after a few beers. Like Steve, Adam had been a nobody in prison. A nobody who got regularly pounded on by the somebodies. He had tried to hang himself in his cell with his sheets. Adam was still going to kill himself, but it was different now. Once he didn't want to live, now he hoped to die. That's what he said. And that the Mahdi had given him purpose.

Steve and Adam had flown into Italy separately, four months earlier. Using fake Irish passports rather than the genuine Australian ones they also carried, they had arrived a week apart, flying from Sydney to Heathrow and then Heathrow to Milan. Adam had arrived first and moved into the apartment, which he had found and rented through the internet, without ever meeting the agent.

It was a real shit-hole. Didn't even have carpet. All they had for furniture was a couple of plastic chairs and a table. No air-con, not even a fan to counter the July heat. They slept on the floor without blankets, but Steve didn't mind. The more he suffered in this life, the more he would be rewarded in the next. Maybe that's why he put up with Adam.

Adam thought he was smarter than Steve because he had learned to speak a bit of Italian. While Steve was teaching himself how to solder and cook chemicals, Adam had sat on the lounge listening to teach-yourself Italian tapes while looking at blueprints and maps. Steve thought learning Italian was a waste of time. Lots of people spoke English in Milan anyway.

Adam had acted like he was the boss since they'd arrived. He was the one who controlled all the cash, their big stack of euros in an empty takeaway Chinese container; he was the one who went out and bought all the supplies; and he was the one who wore the key to the oven – now a safe – around his neck. But what pissed Steve off the most was the way Adam had acted like such a big shot after his meeting with the mafia guy about buying a gun.

Steve wanted to tell Adam that he was really the one in charge. He was the one who had built the bomb – cooked up all the fertiliser, burned down the diesel – and he was the one who would press the trigger.

He would deliver them to His side.

He was also the one who had been given the secret order to kill Adam if he stepped out of line and endangered the plan. To chop him up, cover him in the DNA-killing bleach Adam had bought online, and throw him in the lake. Mahdi had told him that *he* was his favourite, the chosen one. But he wasn't allowed to tell anyone. Especially Adam.

None of this would matter soon anyway. Everything was in place and they were just waiting for the call. Well, not a call; it would be a notification that would signal the final phase: the shaving, the filing, the cleaning, then the shooting and the final blast. The resurrection.

Adam's encrypted laptop beeped and buzzed the following day.

'They are here,' Adam said. 'It's time.'

* * *

MILAN CATHEDRAL, the Duomo di Milano, was levelled nine hours later. It had taken six centuries to build it, but just the press of a button to reduce it to rubble. One hundred and twenty-three people were killed in the blast, mostly tourists.

A mafia thug was found dead the same day, shot twice: a bullet to the chest and one to the head.

CHAPTER 13

Surry Hills, Sydney, NSW, Australia

SURRY HILLS was no longer the arse-end of Sydney. Once all brothels and bums, razor-gangs and rummies, the formerly rough-and-tumble suburb had been transformed into a chic inner-city enclave. The pubs once known as duck-and-swings were now jazz bars. The iconic Aussie fish and chip shops – offering Chiko Rolls, two-dollar bags of chips and a Pacman coin-op in the corner – were now American burger bars and sushi trains. And the housos had been replaced by hipsters.

All the low-income families had been shunted down the road to Redfern, along with the druggies. Run-down terraces had been gutted and glorified. Usually only a facelift at the front – a coat of cream, the rusting wrought iron replaced and painted heritage green, the façade kept strictly Victorian. But the interiors were all millennium: steel and smoked glass.

Nikki had once dreamed of living alongside the day traders, DJs and computer engineers. Of buying a two-bedroom terrace with Riley, even a one-bedder if that was all they could afford. Of eventually getting married when he left the army and making a life there together. She'd once had lots of dreams.

Now she had none.

A gust of wind picked up a pile of leaves – the green summer canopy formed by the Moreton Bay figs and golden rain trees long gone – and sent them spiralling down the street.

Nikki sighed and sipped her coffee. This was the last time she was going to come to this café. A funky little nest with street-side tables, Boo was their favourite, and where they would come whenever he was back in town. Where they would reconnect, laughing and enjoying each other's company, and first talked of buying a terrace. Where they had fallen in love. On arrival, she'd almost ordered a large flat white with a double shot, as well as her skinny latte, the habit hard to break.

My God, she missed him. He'd been a hard nut to crack – when they'd first met, he'd had more walls around him than anyone she'd ever known before – but she'd hung in there, intrigued by this shy, handsome and serious soldier boy, and by the time she was in, she was in deep. He was the smartest guy she had ever encountered, she knew that for sure. But also sweet. Not everyone saw that side of him, she knew. Her friends thought he was a bit staid for her. But, God, she loved him. She suspected that him losing his parents so horrifically when he was young had made him wise beyond his years and much, much more sensitive than your average nineteen-year-old army boy. And the sex … well, it had been mind-blowing. Intense.

The wind whipped up again, and she felt a piece of grit blow into her eye. Great, she thought, I can't even enjoy a coffee without it turning to shit. She felt tears start to well in her eyes, and not because of the grit. Fuck! She put down her coffee and picked up her mobile phone. As she rubbed her eye, she swiped, pressed and was soon looking at Facebook, which she hadn't opened in months. She didn't bother reading any of the posts or checking the unread messages in the inbox. She just went straight to her profile, then to her relationship status. A single tear crept from the corner of her eye as she changed it from 'engaged' to 'single'. She almost hit 'It's complicated', but he'd been adamant it was over. Said it was the only way.

There, done. Time to move on.

If only it was that easy. She wiped the tear from her face after she slipped her phone back into her purse. She took one last look at the café before she left and could have sworn that for a split second she saw him there, but then her eyes refocused and she realised it was just some other guy, about his height but not him. Well, how could it have been? Stupid, she thought, as a fresh tear replaced the one she had wiped away.

She picked her way through the narrow streets, most of them chock-a-block with parked cars, back to the closest spot she'd been able to find, a couple of blocks away. It was always the way – close to impossible to find a space, only to realise it was a metred one when you finally did.

'Of course,' she muttered as she ripped the little white ticket off her windshield.

She should have known she would get a ticket: a $115 fine for overstaying the allotted hour by fourteen minutes. Fourteen fucking minutes. She scrunched up the fine and threw it onto the backseat, the ball of paper joining a ragtag collection of rubbish, clothing and sports gear – some of it his. Usually organised and unable to function unless everything in her life was in order, she hadn't cleaned her car for months. She just didn't care. Not about her car. Not about anything.

She fired her Ford Focus to life, and huffed and puffed as she was forced into a tight turn to get out; some dickhead in a Range Rover had done his best to park her in. The sadness returned as her irritation dissipated, the ticket and the arsehole in the four-wheel drive having distracted her briefly. From thinking about what she had lost.

She turned up the radio, looking for another diversion. A song came on, the singer telling his girl not to forget about him.

'Ahhhh,' she screamed as she mashed at the display, Simple Minds rapidly replaced by Top 40 trash. She turned it up to eleven, grabbed first gear and dumped the clutch. Mind numbed by the music, the all-the-way-up heat roasting her cheeks, she weaved her way through the narrow streets.

'Stupid dream anyway,' she muttered aloud to herself. 'Two million dollars and you don't even get a garage.'

An amber light at the entrance to the freeway stopped her in her tracks.

Tap! Tap!

Startled, she turned to see a man knocking on her window. Clad in black and mounted on a motorbike, he had pulled up just inches from her door. She killed the radio.

'What now?' she groaned as she wound down her window without thinking. She quickly checked she hadn't inadvertently put the hazard lights on when turning the radio off – it wouldn't have been the first time. She could almost hear Riley's voice gently scolding her. *Ni-ik!* he would say, exasperated but also laughing and shaking his head.

She suddenly remembered that it was stupid to wind the window down to a stranger, especially one whose face was concealed under a dark helmet. Was he about to reach in and grab her handbag? She reached for the window switch again, but fumbled, grabbing at the toggle for the side-mirror before finding the button she wanted and holding it down. She exhaled as the glass began to rise.

As she looked up to watch the light turn green, out of the corner of her eye she saw the man on the motorcycle throw something towards her. It sailed through the window just before it closed completely, flew past her and landed on the front passenger seat, almost as though in slow motion.

His back tyre screeched and then he was gone, just a cloud of smoke and a serving of spent rubber left behind. She was frozen with fear.

Beep! Beep!

She heard the honking, looked in her rear-view mirror and saw the angry woman gesturing wildly, but it didn't register.

Beep! Beep! Beep!

She shook her head and snapped to, jammed the accelerator and took off through the intersection and onto the highway What the hell had just happened? She told herself it was nothing. Just some random arsehole. Another weirdo. The city was full of them.

But as she sped along, just under the speed limit, she glanced towards the passenger seat.

What was it? What had he thrown?

Whatever it was, it had rolled under a pile of junk. McDonald's wrappers, coffee cups, a hoodie and a reusable green bag. And those were just the things that she could see.

Just rubbish? Most likely. That seemed right. Another arsehole in this city full of arseholes. But her heart was pounding and she was struggling to grip the steering wheel, so sweaty were her palms. She had to know.

'You've gone mad,' she said to herself as she hit the brake and worked down through the gears: five, four, three, two, one. 'Fucking crazy,' she said as she pulled into the emergency stopping lane. Cars whizzed past; the highway would not stop to help. She unbuckled her seatbelt and leaned over, began to dig through the debris.

'Damn it,' she said as she found only mess.

She started heaving items over the bucket seat and into the back: a gym bag, a jumper and a spent sundae tossed onto the rear seat. Eventually she methodically removed all of her items, one by one. Then she stared at the only object that remained: a small cylinder of lead. It looked a lot bigger than the bullets she'd seen in movies. A lot scarier too. She didn't want to touch it; she had a feeling that it might explode. But she had to. As much as she was afraid, she needed to know if it was real.

She reached over and grabbed it between her thumb and forefinger, as if less flesh touching it would help. It didn't explode and it wasn't burning, not even warm. But it was heavy and it was real. And it was terrifying. Not because of the weight, or the hardness of the metal, but because of what was written on it. Inscribed, seemingly by a proper engraver, were three letters: *J, A* and *X.*

CHAPTER 14

Long Bay Correctional Complex, Sydney, NSW, Australia

JAX lined up with the methadone gang and a handful of older inmates.

'Whatcha on?' came a scratchy voice from behind.

Jax ignored the question and kept his eyes trained on the nurse behind an enclosed counter who was checking ID and dispensing the daily doses. All medication was handed out after muster. Whether it be an aspirin or an antidepressant, prisoners requiring medication were made to collect it from this guarded counter each morning.

'Painkillers, right?' came the scratchy voice again.

Jax didn't flinch.

'Codeine? Or you on the good stuff? Tramies? Endone? Schedule eights?'

'Shut the fuck up,' Jax growled as he turned. He grabbed the man by his mullet. 'Or ...'

Jax let go, a surge of guilt slapping him in the face when what he thought was only a tug almost buckled the man. He'd been brought up better than that. He wasn't a bully. He didn't hurt people. He rarely swore. He was disciplined. Had self-control. The army had made sure of that. But it was getting harder by the day. Jax could feel himself changing. His empathy was becoming apathy.

He turned back to the front, brushing the hairs from his hand and shaking his head. He shouldn't have snapped. But at least he had shut him up.

'Tramies?' came the voice again, undeterred and louder this time. 'Fuck yeah. Tramadol. Gotta be for an eye like that. Whatta ya want? Cash? A suck?'

Jax groaned when the man poked him in his ribs. His broken ribs. Without warning, apathy morphed into anger. Still, he was no bully. He wouldn't hurt him. He would outsmart him instead.

'Just Panadol, bra,' he said, remembering how the junkies spoke in the clinic. 'Tramies? I wish. Nah, the nurse was being a bitch, wouldn't give me shit. Said it's just a bruise. Fuck, bra. I'd be smashing that shit up if I got it. Wouldn't sell it for shit. What are you getting? Anything good?' He turned to look at the man, then evoked his best Marsh impression and winked. 'Want to share?'

'Fuck off, ya queer,' came the response. 'Nah, nothing. Just some HIV shit. I've got AIDS. Herpes too.'

Jax didn't hear another word until he reached the nurse, and she handed over two tablets – one of them a tramadol.

'Fucking knew it,' the man behind him exclaimed as he glimpsed the tablet. 'Don't swallow it,' he pleaded as Jax washed the tablets down with water. 'Ah, fuck. FUCK!'

Jax showed the nurse his empty mouth.

'How about tomorrow? Tell me what ya want?'

'To be left alone,' Jax growled as he walked away. He was clear of the line and about to turn back into the wing when—

Whack!

It came from behind. Out of nowhere. Sudden and sharp. Jax dropped. He turned as he fell and saw the retreating foot. He couldn't believe it was a foot. It had felt like a scud missile.

He had been kicked in the back of the quadricep. A full-blooded roundhouse just above the back of his knee. He'd had no idea a leg blow could drop a man so fast.

Two men grabbed him from behind, one by the scruff of the neck, and lifted him off the floor, like he was child. Too taken aback to get much of a look at them, Jax tried to regain his footing, hopping on his good leg and grabbing at his bad one. The muscle was still singing.

'Spit it out,' commanded the balding man with the leathery face as he spun Jax around to face him. 'I'll have that.'

'Already gone, mate,' Jax said.

'Well, that was dumb.'

Knowing what was coming, Jax attempted to brace himself on his bad leg. He needed to know if he had a base from which to launch. His shoulder still busted, he couldn't fight two men with just one arm and one leg.

He buckled as soon as his foot hit the floor.

'Nah, you can't get out if it that easy,' the bald man growled as he caught Jax by the neck before thumping his head against the concrete wall.

Everything went dark for a split second. When Jax came to, the pain in his leg was subsiding but his head was still ringing. He attempted to size up his attackers. The bald man, not overly big but certainly hard, looked to be one of those guys that had powerful fast-twitch muscles; he wasn't much to look at, but no doubt plenty strong. The other guy was chubby and of Mediterranean appearance – Greek, Jax guessed. He hadn't seen either of them before, which meant they had just been transferred into the wing.

'I don't reckon he swallowed it,' said the bald man. 'I reckon you should take a look, Georgie.' He put his hand around Jax's neck and squeezed as the man he had called Georgie moved in.

'Open wide, cunt,' Georgie said.

When Jax refused, Georgie pincered his nostrils shut.

'That's it,' he said as Jax opened his mouth to breathe.

Jax gagged as a finger went under his tongue and then down his throat. He wanted bite Georgie's finger off, but thought the better of it, given the position was in. He would be smart, get his revenge later.

'Nothing,' Georgie said as he pulled his hand out and smacked it against Jax's face. Jax grimaced as the open palm cuffed the bottom of his wounded eye.

The bald man took over. 'Listen, cunt, we will be waiting here tomorrow. And every day after that. Here's what's going to happen. You are going to line up with your little cup of water like normal. You are going to smile at the nurse when she hands you your meds. Then you are going to pop them in your pretty little dick-sucking mouth and take a swig. After you give nursie the all-clear, you are going to walk over here, spit them out and put them straight in my pocket. Got it?'

Jax nodded.

'Old Georgie boy will put something other than his hand in your mouth if I leave with empty pockets,' he continued, before ending his sentence with a head-butt.

Darkness lapped at the edges of Jax's vision. His mind was all white noise, his ears ringing, brain a blast of static. The bald man's mouth was moving but Jax couldn't hear what he was saying. Whatever. Another threat to go with another concussion. A normal day. The blow to the head had given the room a dream-like haze. Everything had slowed and was washed in white. Suddenly, fireflies. Brilliant. Blazing white dots and dashes dancing in the fog. Jax wanted to reach out and catch one to prove to his disbelieving mind that they were real.

'Move on,' boomed a voice. 'Go on. Fuck off! Get to where you need to be or I'll write you up.'

The goons scattered as Turner rolled in like thunder.

'You right, kid?' Turner asked as he steadied Jax with a granite-like grip. 'You getting slapped around again?'

Jax cautiously put weight onto his injured leg. Just a cork. 'Yeah,' he said before correcting himself. 'No, no. Nothing like that. New blokes were just asking about the mess hall.'

'Yeah, right. You tell 'em the place hasn't changed since they were last here? Which was about three months ago.'

Jax's vision had returned to normal. The fireflies had evaporated one by one. He felt groggy but that could have been the painkillers. Senses regained, he turned his full attention to Turner. A quick study of his face told him the guard's concern was genuine. Jax hadn't seen Turner earlier when he took stock of the room. He wondered where he had been and what he had seen. His timing had been almost perfect.

'You looking out for me?' Jax said.

Turner looked Jax up and down.

'I can give you another whack if you like? How is your shoulder?'

Jax smiled. 'No, mate. Once was enough. You almost put me through the wall. I could use an ice pack, though, if you are offering.'

'No problem.'

FIFTEEN minutes later, Turner turned up at cell number 7 holding a blue ice pack and a prepacked sandwich.

'Give breakfast a miss and sort yourself out,' Turner said, handing Jax the ice pack and tossing the sandwich onto his desk. 'I'm here all day if you need me.' He pulled a bottle of water from his pocket and threw it to Jax before leaving. 'You might have to come up with a new plan, kid,' Turner said. 'The one you got ain't working.'

The guard was right. Jax was suddenly back in Afghanistan. In Operation Detonate. Not at the execution of the IED-clearing operation but at the planning of it. You had to start with intelligence. He needed information – specifically, where the bombs were, so he wouldn't step on them. He needed to embark on a reconnaissance mission. But not right now. Not yet. Not until they all came and went.

He listened for footfall as he iced his leg. So cold it felt like fire at first, the ice pack was warm by the time the rest of the inmates returned from breakfast. Jax threw the soft pack into the sink and paced around his cell as he waited for them all to leave again. His leg was warm again, the numbness almost worked out, by the time the activity outside reached a crescendo around 8.50 am, rubber squeaking, soles stamping as the inmates rushed off to work. He decided to wait another fifteen minutes to allow for stragglers, even though prisoners were military-like in their punctuality.

Jax broke his own rule when he finally stepped out of his cell for something other than muster, a meal or a medical emergency. But that was okay. His bruised and battered body was evidence that his rules weren't working. He needed new rules. Keeping his head down and himself to himself was not enough.

Still, he dropped his head as soon as he saw the man walking towards him. He didn't consider 49986, an elderly man who mostly kept to himself, to be a threat, but better safe than sorry. He didn't know the old man's name. Obviously either serving a significant sentence or a repeat offender given his number, 49986 lived in a cell on the first floor, which Jax hadn't visited. Not yet.

Once 49986 had passed, Jax lifted his head and started his cell-card search. Each cell with a resident had a cell card, which was kept in a plastic sleeve and secured to the door with a zip-tie. The door he was now looking at had two.

He read the first: *Craig Maguire. D-Block. Cell No. 9. Two-out. MIN: 50896.*

And then the second: *Desmond Green. D-Block. Cell No. 9. Two-out. MIN: 58745.*

No changes there. Jax had managed to look at all the cards on the ground floor during his comings and goings. There were seventy-two men on his floor last time he checked. He was looking for a new name. Two, in fact.

He found one of them on a cell that had previously been occupied by just one inmate: *George Charalambous. D-Block. Cell No. 19. Two-out. MIN: 59781.*

So Georgie wasn't Greek after all, but Cypriot. Jax didn't need to know his cultural heritage though, just his name. *One down. One to go.*

Jax was hoping that the other new inmate lived on the ground floor too, as he really didn't want to go up to the first floor, as the stairs were its only entrance and exit point. *Never enter a high-threat area without having at least two exit points.* That was Army 101.

But there was no sign of a new card, so, against his better judgement, he cautiously climbed the stairs. As soon as he got to the top he wished he hadn't. A kill zone. That's what they'd call it in the army. Forty doors concealing forty potentially deadly threats. And the landing area was completely open. Even the Ganjal Valley had rocks – he'd not have survived the Afghan kill zone had it not been for the body-sized boulders. Right eye firmly pressed into the soft rubber of his gunsight, he had darted from one to the next. The rocks, and some well-timed cover fire, had saved his life.

He would have never entered a high-threat area like this while he was in the army, not without a smoke grenade to conceal his movement anyway. But he wasn't in the army anymore.

He pressed on.

Jax walked across the wire-mesh floor that covered the expanse and stepped onto one of the original landings. It was riddled with concrete cancer. The first door he came to was ajar. He read the two cell cards and moved on. He'd reached the other end of the wing by the time he found the card he was looking for: *Elliott Thurling. D-Block. Cell number 67. Two-out.* The name didn't mean anything. Not yet.

By the time he walked back down the stairs, Jax had memorised the names and numbers of all 140 inmates in his wing. The elderly man, who Jax now knew was Garry Jacobs of cell number 68, MIN 49986, was holding a freshly filled buy-up bag, and gave Jax a curious glance when they crossed paths again. Jax ignored him and powered on, not stopping until he reached the guard's box.

Turner was standing at the counter, as though he had been expecting Jax.

'Nah, not ESP,' Turner said as he pointed towards an oversized old CRT monitor. 'Saw you coming. Also saw you sneaking about upstairs. You up to no good?'

'No, nothing like that,' Jax said. 'But I was wondering if you could tell me where the library is?'

'I'll do better than that,' Turner said. 'I'll take ya.'

THE library was much smaller than Jax had expected: about the size of a three-car garage. The bookshelves that lined the walls would have contained no more than a few thousand books.

Jax liked libraries. They were places of solitude. Places of silence. There were no exams and no tests. No questions. No judgements. His school library had been his refuge. No one came looking for him there. But this was like nothing like his school library. Nor his army library, which had been his second lounge room, mostly because of the lightning-fast WiFi, but also for the quiet. He was glad he wasn't here for the books.

'Can I use a computer?' Jax asked the guard who doubled as prison librarian.

'Have you got a log-on?' she replied.

Jax shook his head.

'I'll need your cell card,' she said.

Jax handed over his ID and watched as the guard battered her computer with her index finger, so hard it made the desk shake, until she had the information she was looking for.

She was much better with a pen, writing neatly on the back of Jax's ID before handing it back.

'Use this to log-in, and away you go,' she said before pointing to a row of four computers at the back of the room. They were all free.

Jax chose a computer that was facing away from both the guard and the one security camera that monitored the room. He'd resisted his urge to go to the library so far because he thought it was likely a good place to get killed. But the lack of books, computers and inmates suggested it was rarely used, and the lack of security suggested it was relatively safe. He sat down and got to it.

Username: 60079. Password: Password123.

He changed the generic password to a randomly mashed combination of letters, numbers and symbols that he committed to memory with one look. He didn't need to write it down. Jax was a little bit surprised to be confronted with a version of Windows he hadn't used since high school. At least it wasn't a Mac: they were for graphic designers and hipsters, not for soldiers.

He opened the internet browser and typed in the bald man's name.

Restricted. Access denied.

Weird. He moved on, this time typing 'George Charalambous'.

Restricted. Access denied.

He typed in his own name.

Restricted. Access denied.

He changed tack, typing in the Prime Minister's name instead. He thought his search bar had loaded as per usual, until he saw some of the search results had been censored. On a hunch he decided to search a simpler term: crime.

Restricted. Access denied.

Really? He'd figured porn sites and how-to-escape-from-prison pages would be blocked, but this was ridiculous.

Jax walked back to the counter. 'Excuse me,' he said when the guard refused to look away from her computer screen. 'Do you know what I can actually look at on the net?'

'Depends on your privileges. What's your classification?'

'Maximum security,' Jax answered.

'Oh,' she said. 'Sorry. You're shit out of luck … unless you just came here to look at fluffy ducks and sunsets. You can make an application for increased privileges if you like? There's a form online. I can also send an urgent request through if you need to search something for legal purposes. Is it about your case?'

'No,' Jax said. 'All good. I like ducks.'

He went back to the computer and clicked on the prison home page. He was deterred but not defeated when he read the long list of keywords and subject matters that would trigger the blocking software, including crimes, criminals, charges, convictions and victims. Anything relating to sex, violence and drugs was out too. Of course. He also noted that anyone convicted of a sex crime was blocked from any site that featured so much as a picture of a child.

Jax was no genius computer hacker but he was confident of coming up with a workaround. He'd learned more than enough about programming as part of the degree he'd finished the year before. He'd enrolled in the online Bachelor of Counter-terrorism Security and Intelligence three months after joining the army. He hadn't ever given any thought to becoming a spy, but enlisting had sparked an interest. Plus he'd found he was at a loose end in the evenings – he needed something to do. So using the $104 a day he earned as an army sapper to pay for the degree, he soldiered by day and studied at night. It took him just two years to earn the degree that would normally have taken six years part-time. He even finished a year in front of those enrolled full-time – or so he was told. But he'd never had reason to use spy-level hacking skills previously – never been tempted to even hack into Nikki's Facebook account, or anyone else's, for that matter.

He opened the virtual notepad as he thought about creating a program to circumnavigate the restrictions. He was scouring his mind for VPN code when he had an idea. He logged himself out of the system and typed: *Username: administrator. Password: Password123.*

He was in. Every network he had ever seen or read about was built with at least one generic log-on. He'd expected more from a prison. Then again, it was government-run – and he figured the public would rather their hard-earned cash go to schools or hospitals.

Now logged in as a prison administrator, Jax went back to the search bar and tried again. Soon he had all the details of both George and Elliott's crimes and convictions. He had been right about the pair when he had summed them up as loners. They were both hardened criminals, and violent, had enough street cred to survive in prison without protection, but they were not affiliated with any gang. Perfect. Jax could take action without fear of a third-party reprisal. He would work out the details later. Tonight.

Next he went back to his search bar and typed in Daniel Marsh's name. It took him fifteen minutes to read everything he could find, which included a confidential police file he pulled from behind a firewall. He then moved on to Grub, Bluey and the rest of the gang.

He also looked up a selection of other inmates in case there was a danger that was so far unseen. He hadn't even realised he'd started a search on the Serpent until he found himself staring at a picture of Australia's version of Hannibal Lecter. Just as he had crept into his head, so the Serpent had slithered onto his screen.

Jax was shocked by the Serpent's full story. The snippets he had picked up along the way only hinted at the true horror. At his trial, his lawyers had claimed he suffered from a severe split-personality disorder, that he wasn't one person but two: Professor Scott Wensley and the Serpent. Reports suggested the lawyers urged Wensley to contest the charges, but the Professor refused. While he claimed he couldn't remember the murders and blamed it all on the Serpent, he wasn't going to dispute the facts – he was a scientist after all.

Despite Wensley's confirmed history of schizophrenia, the prosecution had claimed he was a cold-blooded killer. They said a spectacular academic failure had prompted a breakdown first, then the killing spree. One by one, he had hunted down his critics. Revenge. Then he'd gone after his academic rivals. Envy. Both the media and public were enthralled by talk of the thirty-three murders and especially the fact that each one was said to have involved a soul-devouring ritual and that all thirty-three identities had thereby been absorbed the Professor. They couldn't wait to see who testified in court: Wensley, the Serpent or one of the thirty-three. So Wensley's no-contest plea was a disappointment. He didn't take the stand at all; in fact, he barely said a word throughout the entire trial. His silenced only fuelled further speculation.

Jax found his way into crime-scene files after reading a selection of news reports, features and commentary. He didn't look at the victim photos, as he really didn't want to be carrying images of dead people around in his head for the rest of his life. Not any more than he already had.

Instead, he started to sift through the non-verified results. Conspiracy theorists abounded, as did, disturbingly, fans of the Serpent. It looked like he had developed a cult-like following. A few more clicks and Jax found himself scanning an amateurish website, riddled with spelling mistakes and images that wouldn't load: a blog devoted to the Serpent. One of the links in the menu stood out from the others: 'Prison chaplain's plan to perform exorcism on Serpent'.

JAX stormed about his cell, pacing from one end to the other. Four steps up and four steps back. He didn't want to become like them. Like Marsh. Like the Serpent. He wasn't an animal.

Just give them the pills.

At least his conscience would be clear.

But they will never stop.

Jax wondered what his parents would think if they could see him now. If they saw him stalking around a prison cell, wondering what objects he could turn into weapons.

You're already a murderer. What does it matter?

It mattered to Jax. He still didn't know if he was a killer. In spite of all the evidence, there was something inside him that nagged at him, saying that he didn't do it, couldn't have done it. The crisis of conscience he was having about hurting a couple of criminals only added to his doubt.

They're just pills.

Perhaps he should just stick them behind his teeth as instructed, spit them out and drop them in the bald man's pocket. He was being taken off the tramadol in a couple of days anyway. They wouldn't want the antibiotics. Then maybe they would leave him alone.

But he knew they wouldn't. He knew that handing over the pills would be an open invitation to the whole prison population to abuse him. It would mark him as a soft touch.

They would keep coming, again and again and again. And not just them – but everyone.

Fight.

Jax looked up at the ceiling. Towards the light.

No, you can't.

The thought of ripping out a man's throat with a jagged piece of glass sickened him. He didn't know if he could live with the guilt. No, it was more than that. If he could do that, it would mean that he *was* capable of having killed the man in his room. Deniability due to loss of memory had a shelf life – one that Jax feared would expire the moment he justified an act of terrible violence as a means to an end and went through with it.

He stopped pacing and sat down on the bed. He would just give them the pills. He would hand them over. Unless …

THE next morning, Jax lined up with his cup of water just as he had done the day before. Today he knew what to expect. He smiled at the nurse as she handed him his meds: an antibiotic and a tramadol. He popped them into his mouth and took a swig. Then he opened wide.

'Thanks, miss,' he said. 'All down the hatch.'

He put his hands in his pockets and walked, scanning the room, looking for a guard. He couldn't see one; the only officer on duty was in the fishbowl with the nurse. He directed the bald man with his head. Towards the rear of the room, away from the mob. Jax got there first and backed into the wall, propping himself up. Now he only had to worry about what happened in front of him. Elliott and George were soon upon him, right up in his face.

'Well?' asked Elliott. 'What are you waiting for? Hand 'em over.'

Jax looked down at his pockets, still containing his hands. He waited until they were both looking down too.

And then he launched, pulling out the homemade shivs he'd hand-carved in the night from a bedspring he'd wrenched off his bed, one in each hand.

Pop! Pop!

He hit them simultaneously – right hand for the bald man, left hand for George – thrusting the sharpened bed wires into their stomachs.

Pop! Pop! Pop!

Elliott and George backed away, both holding their guts, both lost for words. Their faces were white with shock, their hands red with blood. Jax threw the shivs on the floor and walked away. He didn't care if he got caught. He wanted to get caught. The more people that knew about it the better.

CHAPTER 15

WENSLEY was relived to find his chalk. He thought he must have dropped it when the Serpent had returned. Apparently, the Serpent wasn't interested in playing chalk games because the Professor had found the white stub on the cell floor directly under the equation he had been working on when the light was taken.

The Serpent had carved more Arabic into the wall. Deeply dug and obsessively neat. Wensley figured it was important, at least to the Serpent. But he didn't have time for that now. He needed to get on with solving P versus NP and the rest of the Millennium Problems.

He felt a sharp pain in his leg when he bent down to pick up the chalk. He wasn't surprised by his nakedness or the blood-soaked bandage that was wrapped around his thigh. Another ritual, he supposed. The Serpent was a self-mutilator. He had told Wensley that pain invoked the word, and that his visions had to be earned through agony. Wensley thought it was preposterous. The Serpent hurt himself because he could no longer hurt others.

Wensley's deepest fear was auto-cannibalism. He dismissed the horrid thought and went back to his equations.

Two down, three left to solve.

P versus NP hadn't been so tough after all.

CHAPTER 16

Long Bay Correctional Complex, Sydney, NSW, Australia

THE BUY-UP form looked like a high-school exam answer sheet, the multiple-choice type that was marked by a computer. But instead of using a 2B pencil to colour in a little circle that contained A, B, C or D, Jax was using a 2B pencil to colour in a little circle that contained 1, 2, 3 or 4, and he wasn't answering multiple-choice questions about maths or science, but choosing quantities of products like; 'Shower Gel: Lynx Africa' or 'Toothpaste: Extreme Clean McLean'. With his face on the mend and movement back in both his leg and his arm, he finally found the courage to move around the jail and was visiting the D–Block recreation and leisure room for the first time.

Apparently, his act of violence had worked. More than a week had passed since Jax had stabbed Elliott and George, and neither man had given him up. They might have been thugs, but they weren't dogs. They'd both needed stitches and tetanus shots, but other than that they were okay. Jax had made sure he kept clear of their organs, stabbing away from their livers and the pancreas. He'd probably put a few holes in their small intestines, but that was a minor fix.

Jax hadn't been hauled in for the stabbing either. He'd been waiting for the knock on his door – resigned to having a couple of years added to his sentence if it meant he was left alone – but it never came. Johnson told him that another inmate had scooped up the shivs and claimed them for himself. Apparently, he was planning on trading the used weapons for drugs. There were no witnesses of course, never were.

More importantly for Jax, there were no more threats. He had been left alone. He'd even walked past George, freshly released from hospital, earlier that day. For once it was someone else looking at the floor.

He had picked the right men. They were tough enough that Jax had proved he was both dangerous and could handle himself, that he was no easy target. And no one cared enough about them to retaliate.

Up to now, Jax had taken no interest in food; if he could have done without it completely, he would have, as every trip to the mess hall was a game of Russian roulette, just another chance for someone to get him. Eating also seemed to be an admission of hope, which he thought was equally dangerous. But now, looking at this list – Mars Bars, Snickers, Tim Tams, Burger Rings, Barbecue Shapes, Twisties – he was salivating. There was real food too, things that could be eaten in between meals in his cell: cans of tuna and baked beans, noodles, bread. Apparently, he could even buy his own microwave and toaster.

Jax grabbed his pencil and scanned the form. He ignored all the products on the first page – toiletries, cleaning products and healthy food options – turned to page two: snacks. The good stuff. He ran through the list of chocolate products and stopped when he found the Snickers Bars.

He decided to start with just one. He traced the No. 1 circle with his 2B before colouring it in. Not a speck of lead went outside the circle. Perfection. He had done the same thing with multiple-choice exams at school. Taking his time colouring in, being precise and pedantic meant he finished a sixty-minute exam in thirty minutes instead of fifteen. He always stayed until the end, pretending he had just finished when the teacher yelled, 'Time: pencils down.' He made sure he never scored more than ninety percent.

He moved to the soft drinks section and was about to drop lead when his pencil was snatched from his hand and the form slapped away. He turned to face the snatcher but couldn't move, as an arm around his neck now held him in a vice.

Then Marsh came into view, strutting into the only line of sight the headlock allowed. He parked himself on the pew directly opposite. He was holding Jax's pencil. Grub walked over and handed Marsh the buy-up list.

'I'll have four of these,' Marsh said as he put a crude X in a circle. 'And four of these, these, these, these and these. Fuck me, reckon I'll have four of everything, if it's his shout. Whaddya reckon, boys?'

'Nah,' Grub said. 'Eight. Make it eight.'

'You are a simple cunt, aren't you, Grub?' Marsh said. 'How many years have you been in here? Fuck me.'

Marsh turned his attention to Jax.

'He is a special human, our Grubby,' Marsh said. 'And you think you are pretty special too, don't ya? Think you can get by without me? Think you're a fucking hard cunt because you jabbed a fat wog and a washed-up bikie with a playschool shiv. What was that fucking thing? Did you get it out of a Kinder Surprise? You still got it, Grub.'

Grub nodded.

'Well, fucken hand it over then,' Marsh said.

Grub pulled up his shirt. He had both of Jax's shivs wedged between his skin and the the elastic in the waist of his pants.

'Both?' Grub asked.

'Nah, you can keep one. Might come in handy if you get some food stuck in your teeth.'

Grub passed the shiv to Marsh.

'What is it?' Marsh asked. 'Bed wire?' He placed his finger tip on the point. 'Got to admit, it's pretty sharp,' he said, looking at the drop of blood on his finger. 'You might just be able to kill some cunt with this. Of course, you'd have to hit a vital organ. Most would go for the heart, but I'd probably go for the liver. Maybe the kidneys. It wouldn't kill straight away, but that's the point. The infection from this filthy thing would kill 'em nice and slow. Is that blood? Looks like Grubby forgot to clean it.'

'You told me not to, boss,' Grub said.

'Shut up, you idiot,' Marsh said. 'Anyway, turns out the bald fella's got AIDS. 'Wonder if this is his blood? I'm sure a smart fella like you could work out the odds. Actually, Grub, give us the other one too.'

Grub handed him the second shiv, also uncleaned and bloodied. He placed them both on the table.

'So, no,' Marsh said, 'you're not a hard cunt, and no one is scared of you. Mario Kart and Jurassic Park would have already killed you, if it wasn't for me. So, and for the second time, mind you, I went ahead and did you a favour. I put word out that you were my boy. You're only alive because of me. I would have let the useless cunts kill you had I made myself clear the first time. My fault. My bad. I made the mistake of thinking you were smart. Anyway, I am going to spell it out for you now. Make it nice and simple.'

Marsh reached into his pocket and pulled out a neatly folded piece of paper. 'All the details are here,' he said, opening up the A4 sheet. 'How to pay. When to pay. How much to pay.

'Give Bluey a hand, would ya, Grub?' Marsh said.

Grub pulled a plastic zip tie from his pocket and walked towards Jax. As he approached, Bluey swiftly and smoothly swapped the headlock for an armlock, moving with the skill of a professional wrestler as he first pulled Jax's arms behind his back and then pinned them there. Grub reach down and pulled Jax's hands together before threading and reefing the zip tie. Jax was cuffed, hands behind his back, and helpless.

He looked around for a guard. There wasn't one. The two who were patrolling the room when he arrived had disappeared.

Marsh leaned across the table, put the buy-up form on Jax's right thigh and patted the paper down. 'Now, which one do you want?' he said as he looked at the shivs. 'I'm not good at maths, but I'm pretty sure you have a fifty-fifty chance of picking the one with the AIDS. So, which will it be?'

Jax didn't respond. He was still scanning his memory bank.

Marsh reached across the table and gave Jax a backhander.

'Pick,' he said, 'or you'll get both.'

Jax nodded towards the weapon on Marsh's right.

'That's a good boy,' Marsh said as he picked up the shiv.

He growled as he jabbed the shiv through the centre of the note and into Jax's thigh. 'Hoped you picked the right one.'

Jax didn't have to hope. He knew he had picked the right one.

MARSH knew Jax wouldn't pay. Not with money. He didn't want his money. That's why he had now asked for $400 a week. Only one man had ever paid more than $400 a week for protection, and he'd been an IT millionaire. Marsh would have asked for much more than the $500 they'd agreed upon if he'd known the wife-bashing computer genius was in fact an IT *billionaire*.

Jax was no billionaire, no millionaire. Marsh knew the teenage former soldier would struggle to come up with even $100 a week, his stock standard price for protection. Jax didn't have money, but he did have value. His boyish looks, his limited criminal record, and his girl-next-door girl were worth

a lot more than protection payments. Marsh knew he didn't
have to bother with fee raises, bashings, zip ties and blades to
get what he wanted. Not when he already held the ace. But he
loved the theatrics. Prison was boring. Fucking with people was
fun. His favourite part was probably mind-fucking the newbies
in their first week. Keeping an eye on them from afar, knowing
the silent treatment was driving them insane.

Marsh wasn't ready to play his hand just yet. That would
have been too easy. And he knew he hadn't quite broken the
kid yet. Marsh enjoyed breaking people as much as making
money.

Actually, he stood corrected. His favourite part wasn't the
first week. His favourite part was the next part.

AT THE usual time, on the usual day, and on the usual phone,
Marsh logged into his TAB phone betting account.

Betting accounts, the TAB. That's how the bulk of jail
business is done. Cash is scarce in prison, a liability. Cigarettes
are only traded in movies. Bank accounts were used following
the advent of phone banking. Not for long, though: the
police soon caught on. But they had no idea about the betting
accounts. Hadn't clocked on to the fact that they were just
banks without the fees or paperwork.

The phone room was heavily graffitied, like every other
room in the prison. The phones, all ten, were bolted to the
walls. The steel partitions, also bolted to the wall, provided
only a suggestion of privacy.

There were always fights in the phone room.

'Hurry up, ya cunt. It's my turn.'

Whack!

'Are you listening in to my call?'

Whack!

'Hey, you skipped the queue. I'm next!'

Whack!

Some of the worst episodes were sparked by the calls themselves. After receiving bad news, inmates often hung up the phone and attacked the nearest person.

'I'm fucking your best friend.'

Whack!

'Your teenage daughter is pregnant.'

Whack!

'Your appeal has been denied.'

Whack!

No one had ever whacked Marsh. And he never had to queue to use the phone. No one else dared to enter the first cubicle on a Friday afternoon. That was Marsh's phone. Strictly reserved.

With his little black book sitting on the metal ledge, open and waiting, and a red pen and a black pen standing by, Marsh didn't even have to go through the prison operator to call the TAB's free 1800 number. He dialled the number himself, punched in his account number and, after a few more digits in response to prompts, he started going through the week's deposits.

'From account 34520,' the robotic female voice delivered in monotone. '$100. Deposited on Thursday. 4.12 pm. Press 1 for next transaction.'

Marsh scrolled through the numbers in his black book until he found the one the female robot had read out.

34520.
Chris Haines.
$100.
Protection Payment.

He placed a big black tick in a corresponding column, then pressed 1.

'From account 41222,' the voice said. '$68. Deposited on Thursday. 8.42 pm. Press 1 for next transaction.'

Marsh scrolled through the numbers in his black book.

41222.
Shane Budd.
$150.
Drugs.

He shook his head.

'Cunt,' he muttered.

Shane was $82 short.

When this kind of thing happened, he didn't immediately get up and whack anyone, because his bad news wasn't really his bad news. It was always someone else's bad news.

Marsh put a big red 'X' in a column next to Budd's name then used the same red pen to write $82 in the next column. Marsh couldn't spell for shit, but he had no problems with maths. Maths was money.

On he went, listening, marking and pressing buttons until the lady robot finally said, 'No more transactions. Press 9 to return to the main menu or simply hang up to log out.'

Marsh hung up the phone and looked at his list. Three red crosses. He flicked to the middle of his book and, with a delicacy he didn't look capable of, gently separated the centre page from the staples. He picked up his red pen and wrote, slowly and neatly.

Shane Budd. Touch up and collect $82. Short.
Chris Boyd. Beating and collect $50. First warning.
Charlie Smith. Nee caping and collect $200. Final warning.

He folded the paper into four and put the neat square into his pocket. He would give it to Bluey tomorrow. Jax's name was not on the list. That was one he wanted to take care of himself.

He was almost through the exit when he realised he had forgotten to pay the guard. He did an about-turn. He didn't have to tell the inmate to get off his phone, the man hanging up and scurrying away as soon as he saw Marsh coming back.

He mashed away at the keypad again, pressing after the prompts, and soon had transferred $500 into Dodge's betting account. He thought $500 was steep, told Dodge he was taking the piss, but he paid it all the same. It would be worth it. Marsh got hard just thinking about it.

HE HAD to hand it to him: the little cunt had copped it sweet. He didn't scream, squirm or beg for it to stop. He bled. But they all bled. Marsh usually got rock hard when he first saw the blood, starting with a smear of magenta on his cock. He loved the slapping sound his pelvis made when it smacked into arse.

The kid had fought. Or tried to. But there was little he could do, given Marsh and his four mates had surprised him in his sleep.

Marsh had followed Bluey, Chunk, Grub and Waz into Jax's cell after the Dodge had taken care of the cameras and the lock. Then, with a full moon providing just enough light, he'd watched as Bluey and Chunk – the biggest of the four – tip-toed their way to the head of Jax's bed.

The kid was sound asleep.

Grub and Waz had to take only a couple of steps to position themselves at Jax's feet.

Then Marsh began the silent count: one finger raised, then two and, finally, three. The four goons pounced, Bluey and Chunk grabbing an arm each, Grub and Waz a leg. They reefed Jax off the bed and flipped him face first over the shitter. The kid wriggled, screamed and tried to wrestle, but he had a man on each limb. He was pinned. No man could get out of this one.

Marsh walked up behind the kid, reached around, and shoved a rolled-up sock down his throat. He usually liked to hear them scream and beg, but not in the dead of the night. Not when the noise could carry and be heard by a guard they hadn't paid.

Marsh ripped down the kid's pants and slapped him on the cheek. He put a dollop of lube on his finger and stuck it into Jax's arse. And then he went to work.

Marsh was surprised by how well the kid took it. He swung like a bat out of hell when the boys let him go – Bluey had to knock him out again – but he copped the hard part sweet. He was a tough little cunt, no doubt about it, Marsh thought. He'd never had anyone fight this long or this hard. And he still hadn't broken the kid. He could see the fight in his eyes before Bluey knocked him out. But that was okay. He still had his ace.

Her name was Nikki.

CHAPTER 17

Birmingham, Alabama, USA

THE 16th Street Baptist Church had been reduced to rubble. The two toppled three-storey towers with their arched windows and pyramidal roofs, which had once proudly bookended the steepled entrance, were now obstacles for the swarm of rescuers wearing yellow hazmat suits. Under towers of light that had turned the night into day, cutting bright arcs in the dark, humid August night, they sifted through the shattered stones, singed wood and smashed tiles, looking for flesh and bone. For bodies.

Hudson Sami, a hulking, bear-like man with black hair and olive skin, dressed in a smart suit, stood back, well away from the heavily guarded yellow tape, and watched.

'Here,' yelled one of the yellow-clad figures. 'Got one.'

Three men, one carting a pneumatic cutting tool dubbed the 'jaws of life', rushed towards the animated worker.

'Come on,' he yelled. 'Quick.'

There was no need to rush. This was a recovery, not a rescue. Sami knew the person under the rubble was dead. They all were. No one had survived any of the other three church bombings: 67 dead in Normandy, 164 dead in St Petersburg and 123 dead in Milan. Doors locked and no way out. Anyone not killed by the explosions had been crushed by the collapsing building.

The 16th Street Baptist Church was tiny compared to the Milan Cathedral or the Church of the Saviour on Spilled Blood in St Petersburg. But Sami was sure it was part of the same series of attacks.

The head of the CIA's Office of Russian and European Analysis (OREA), Sami had sent two agents to Normandy after the first bombing, suspecting it was another lone wolf attack sponsored by ISIS. The initial reports from the French authorities had agreed with that assessment: a home-made ammonium-nitrate-based IED, between one and three attackers, and a Christian target. Unlike Al-Qaeda, which sponsored elaborate high-value attacks that were meticulously planned and coordinated by a tightly regimented command structure, ISIS was more opportunistic. It encouraged anyone and everyone to attack whenever and wherever, using whatever means they had, whether it be a bomb, a gun, a car or a knife.

Sami's agents had recovered little from the scene to either validate or refute his suspicions. Several of the victims could not be identified. The official death toll given by the French authorities was an educated guess, based on missing persons and who was believed to have been in the church at the time of the attack. Sami thought the true number might never be known, given that several bodies had been completely incinerated.

The identity of the attacker or attackers remained unknown. A canvass of the area had proved frustrating, particularly as there was no CCTV in the vicinity of the church. None of the 2890 tourists who had visited the historic town in the previous month was on a watch list of any kind or had the type of profile that suggested they might be a terrorist.

The fact that the authorities had been left to try to establish the identity of the attacker or attackers concerned Sami, because terrorists usually did that themselves, recording and posting a martyrdom video. But none had surfaced yet. And neither ISIS nor any other group had claimed responsibility for the attack.

Sami had sent his two agents back to their Paris base as soon as they'd filed their less-than-definitive report, which attributed the attack to a 'lone-wolf individual or group, either French or foreign, inspired by ISIS if not supported and financed by the Syria-based terror group'. His superiors at Langley weren't too concerned, given that no US citizens had been killed in the attack. Sami's brief was simply to monitor and report on any threats posed directly to the United States or to US interests abroad – and the Normandy attack appeared to be neither.

The St Petersburg bombing had come exactly a month later. On the twenty-fifth day of the month, just as in Normandy, the Church of the Saviour on Spilled Blood was levelled. Again a church, again a home-made ammonium-nitrate-based IED, again no survivors, again no witnesses, again no martyrdom video and again no terror group taking credit for the attack.

'What the fuck is going on?' screamed Tom Morrissey, CIA Director of Operations, from his office in Langley. 'Is this something I need to be worried about?'

Sami told him he didn't have enough intelligence to be sure.

'Well, fucking get it,' Morrissey had yelled before slamming down the phone.

Sami had sent a team of six to St Petersburg, including his best agent, a thirty-two-year-old policing prodigy he had nicknamed 'Maverick', partly because he looked like Tom Cruise but mostly because he was a dickhead like the character in *Top Gun*. Ryan Smith, as his parents had named him, put the nickname down to his good looks, of course.

But again there had been little to report on, even with Maverick on the case. While there had been a CCTV camera opposite the church, which covered the front entrance and recorded every person who entered or left on the day of the attack, Mav had advised that the footage was very poor quality and couldn't be manipulated. Sami knew that people watched enough Hollywood CSI-type crime shows to believe that any image could be run through a computer to produce a perfectly crisp high-resolution close-up of the perp, but that wasn't how it worked in real life. Very rarely could perps be ID'd from street-surveillance footage.

After going through twelve hours of film from before the bombing, Mav had been able to report only that of the 212 people who had gone into the church that day, only three had been carrying a bag big enough to conceal a bomb: a man with an oversized shoulder bag, a man with a backpack and a woman with a suitcase. Both the man with the shoulder bag and the woman with the suitcase had left the church before the blast.

Maverick sent an enlarged image of the man with the backpack to Sami.

'Is that it?' Sami enquired when the file came through. 'Just a blurry still of a man in a hood?'

'Basically,' Maverick said. 'He was picked up by another four CCTV cameras in the vicinity, but you have the best image. He knew exactly where the cameras were and knew how to avoid them.'

'What about the other man with the backpack and the woman with the suitcase? We can't rule out a remote detonation.'

'They both check out,' Maverick said. 'Clean records, clean browsing history, clean all over. We were able to identify them using an HD camera down the road. Jones and Pacman have already processed them. No explosive residue in the bags, their apartments, anywhere. We're keeping tabs on them both, but they ain't our guy – the hooded man is the perp.'

Sami, who had been at the terror coalface since 9/11, had

never seen anything like this. Not only was there no martyrdom video, but the suicide bomber had taken well-considered and preplanned steps to conceal his identity. That didn't make sense. Suicide bombers typically wanted to be known. To be celebrated as a martyr.

Why cover your head with a hood and avoid cameras when you are about to blow yourself up? Sami asked himself. He didn't have the answer. Not yet.

At least they knew the attacks were being carried out by a lone bomber. A hooded bomber with a backpack. That was something. He suggested putting out a global alert to warn the public about the threat of further attacks.

'Not a chance,' Morrissey said. 'Can you imagine the panic?'

Sami could. He'd seen the airports after 9/11, seen the Underground after the London bombings. People still gave him a nervous up-and-down whenever he boarded a plane.

The Christian world would go in meltdown if the CIA predicted more attacks on churches as part of a serial terror plot against Christianity. All the churches would end up empty, or, worse, filled with guns. There was also the risk of copycat attacks.

'And what are you doing about that madman?' Morrissey asked, referring to the Russian president. 'We can't have him starting World War III.'

'He's being briefed as we speak,' Sami said.

Not that they had any information that would dissuade the Russian president from blowing every terrorist-harbouring nation off the map.

After the third attack in three months, on Milan's cathedral, again on the twenty-fifth of the month, there was no denying that a terrorist group was targeting churches. Same home-made IED and, as Sami's team quickly established, likewise no survivors, no witnesses, no martyrdom video, no terror group claiming responsibility.

Cue the shitstorm.

Both Russia and Italy had begun making threats against several nations, including Syria, Iraq, Sudan, Iran and even North Korea. Churches began hiring armed security guards, while white-supremacist groups promised to retaliate by blowing up mosques. The United States responded by raising the national terrorism threat from Blue (guarded) to Yellow (elevated).

Nevertheless, the church attacks had still been thought of as a European problem.

Until now.

SAMI watched as the men in the hazmat suits carefully placed the bulging body bag next to the others: twelve now, neatly lined up on the pavement. There was another much longer row of body bags on the other side of the lot. They were for body parts rather than bodies. He knew he should have been feeling some sort of emotion right now, whether it be sadness or sympathy, anger or disgust, but in truth he felt nothing.

Sami had become immune to scenes like this. He wondered if feeling sorry for the guy that had to go through the bags on the other side of the lot and play mix and match with the body parts counted as an emotion. Probably not.

He pulled out his e-cigarette and took a puff. Lit up by the crime-scene floodlights, as bright as those in any baseball stadium, the white cloud of vaporised nicotine oil looked as real as cigarette smoke.

Sami had arrived at the crime scene just three hours after the blast. He'd been standing in one of the J. Edgar Hoover Building's many bunker-like rooms, recommending that the national threat level be raised to Red (severe), at a joint meeting between the CIA, the FBI and Homeland Security, when the bomb went off. It had taken just over two hours for the FBI jet, a Gulfstream G550, to fly him and the FBI counterterrorism chiefs from Washington DC to Alabama. He could see a couple of the men he'd flown in with on the other side of the tape. Now wearing their unmistakable FBI jackets – the three letters blazing bright yellow on their backs – they strutted around the scene like they owned it. Which, effectively, they did: the CIA had very little power domestically.

Sami was happy to observe from afar until Maverick arrived from Langley, Virginia, where he'd been at the time of the attack. His CIA jet had left the George Bush Center for Intelligence fourteen minutes after Sami's plane had departed Washington DC. He should have been here by now.

ANOTHER fifteen minutes passed before Maverick arrived in a blacked-out sedan.

'You have got to be kidding me,' he said as he approached. 'You're vaping? What are you, a hipster now? You gonna move to Brooklyn too?'

'It is called an electronic nicotine delivery system,' Sami said. 'Doctor's orders.' Sami had been on a non-voluntary health kick since he'd had a minor heart attack a few months prior. The vaping was new, though – after months of badgering and guilt trips from his ex-wife, he'd finally pulled the trigger and thrown his real cigarettes away.

'Yeah, right,' Mav said. 'Which doctor told you to fill your lungs with that shit? It'll still kill you, you know.'

'No, seriously,' Sami said. 'These things aren't bad for you. It's only water vapour and nicotine, none of that shit that causes cancer.'

'They said the same thing about cigarettes thirty years ago,' Mav replied. 'But I'm not complaining. Smells a whole lot better than the Camels.'

'Anyway, what took you?' Sami asked.

Mav shrugged. 'Weather.' He turned away from Sami and surveyed the scene. 'What's the count?'

Sami looked at the first row of body bags. 'At least fourteen,' he said as he handed Mav a pair of blue cotton crime scene booties. He waited for him to put them over his shoes before lifting the yellow tape. But then he faltered, and stood staring into space for ten seconds or so before whipping out his phone.

'What are you doing?' Mav asked.

'Setting a timer. We have a month to stop this from happening again.'

Thirty-one days and counting, thought Sami.

CHAPTER 18

Sydney, NSW, Australia

NIKKI did exactly as instructed. She took the three little packages and put them in a condom and knotted it, not once, but twice. Then she coated the condom in lube, squirting the clear gel all over the rubber and smearing the entire surface at least one millimetre thick.

She hadn't asked what the packages were. Each one the shape and size of a marble, they had come to her by way of a kid on a Harley Davidson, who wore a big patch on the back of his jacket that read *PROSPECT*. Tightly wrapped in brown sticky tape, the packages were slightly squishy. She had no doubt they contained powder and suspected it was heroin. But it didn't matter, she was going to do what they asked. She had no choice.

Nikki cried during the next part. Standing completely naked, one foot on the edge of the bathroom sink and the other on the tiles, she sobbed as she pushed the now packed condom into her vagina.

'Just smash it with some lube and throw it up ya safe,' the prospect had said. 'Just like whacking a tampon in.'

It wasn't. Nikki felt violated. Tears ran down her cheeks as she used her middle finger to push the package deep into her body, as far as it could go. She pulled her leg down from the bathroom sink and stood in front of the mirror, looking at herself. She didn't move for about two minutes. She was numb. Frozen. This was too shocking to be real. But real it was.

NIKKI had called the prison to book the visit, an easier process than she'd expected. All she'd had to do was tell the lady who she wanted to visit and when.

'Visiting days are Friday, Saturday, Sunday and Monday,' the woman said.

Nikki chose Friday, as instructed. It had to be Friday.

'What time?' the woman asked. 'You can either come at 8 am or 11.30 am?'

The Prospect guy hadn't told her what time. Maybe that didn't matter? She picked the later slot to avoid the peak-hour traffic.

'Okay, all booked,' the woman said. 'You will need to bring photo ID. No thongs, singlets, midriffs or excessive jewellery. You can bring a maximum of ten dollars for the vending machine. And please be aware that you may be subjected to a body search.'

Until that moment, Nikki hadn't even considered the risk of being caught. But she was too worried about Riley to consider backing out. About what would happen to him if she said no.

SHE had gone to the police after the bullet had been thrown through her car window. They'd sat her down in a room, bagged the bullet, and taken an official statement. Nikki wasn't much help.

'Did you get a number plate?' they asked.

No.

'Description of the rider?'

No.

The only fingerprints on the bullet were hers. They promised to make enquiries. She suspected they wouldn't.

But she had to call them again, frantically, a week later, after she found another bullet, on her bed. Nothing in her house had been touched aside from the back door, which had been smashed in. The bullet was almost identical to the one that had been thrown through her window and again was engraved with the name: *JAX*.

A small forensics team went through the house she rented, a three-bedroom weatherboard in suburbia, looking for prints, fibres, hair and blood. They found nothing with their brushes, combs, black powder and sticky tape that didn't belong to her or people who had legally entered her apartment.

Nikki became a nervous wreck. She packed a bag and rented a hotel room. She changed her route to work, drove with one eye on the rear-view mirror, and panicked every time she heard a loud engine, certain it was a motorbike. She thought she would be safe in the hotel, as there were cameras everywhere.

She saw the bikes before she saw the men: four of them in the underground car park. Nikki turned and started back towards the lift, but the four riders appeared from nowhere and cut her off.

'Stay calm,' the oldest of the four men said. 'We aren't here to hurt you. We're here to help you.' While the other three stayed silent, he explained that someone she loved was in a lot of trouble. That only she could help. They would kill him if she didn't do them a little favour. They would kill him if she went back to the cops. The prospect arrived at her door a few days later.

AFTER booking her visit, Nikki googled 'smuggling', 'drugs', 'jail' and 'NSW', suddenly aware that there were consequences other than death. That was soon spelled out on the screen in front of her:

NSW correctional centres prohibit certain items from entering the prison, including mobile phones, drugs, alcohol, tobacco, lighters, syringes, SIM cards, chargers, computers and offensive weapons.

    Anyone caught smuggling or trying to smuggle these items into a prison will face heavy criminal penalties.

She scanned further down the page, bile rising in her throat.

Any person who smuggles or tries to smuggle any of the following things into a prison without lawful authority will face a penalty of up to two years' imprisonment and/or a $2200 fine:

    Any of the items listed in some of the schedules under the Poisons and Therapeutic Goods Act …

Nikki took public transport to Long Bay, as instructed. She'd been told not to drive because the police conducted random searches in the streets surrounding the prison, pulling cars over and searching for drugs, but they never bothered the bus.

The ride was hell. Nikki almost had a panic attack when the bus pulled up next to a police car at a set of lights. She almost had another one when she imagined what would happen if the condom split open.

She also thought about him. About the man she loved. She'd only just resigned herself to losing him. After months of crying herself to sleep, she had made a vow to get on with her life. She would start over, never see him again. Yet here she was, packed with drugs, sitting on a bus, on her way to break that promise.

Nikki was soaked in sweet and buzzing with anxiety by the time the bus dropped her opposite the prison gates. Thankfully she was wearing all black: a knee-length skirt, a button-up long-sleeve blouse, and flats on her feet. The Prospect hadn't told her what to wear, only that she mustn't look like a slut.

As she crossed the road, she took in the scene in front of her. She'd never been to a prison before – Riley hadn't let her visit him while he awaited trial. It was as bad as she'd thought it would be, all cyclone fencing and ugly, boxy buildings. Even the grass looked dry and half-dead. She tried not to think too much about how Riley must have felt when he'd arrived here a month or so earlier. Or how he must still be feeling now.

She was ordered away from the main gate by a gruff bloke in a blue uniform. 'Visits are over there,' he barked as he pointed towards a modern building clinging to the side of the gatehouse.

The waiting room was mostly populated by prams and pregnant women, many of them teenagers. A young mother rattled a handful of coins and swore at her kid.

'Sit down, ya little shit,' she yelled. 'Your father is going to give you a fucking hiding when he sees you.'

There were a few older people too: mums, dads, brothers, sisters and wives, she guessed. They also held coins in their hands, but sat silently, looking as if they were in a funeral home. Nikki walked towards the counter.

'ID,' the woman ordered.

Nikki had it ready and waiting.

'Locker number thirty-four,' the woman said as she handed Niki a piece of paper containing a four-digit code.

'We'll call you when it's time to go in.'

'What's the locker for?' Nikki felt stupid but had to ask.

'First time, love?' the woman asked. 'Everything has to go in the locker. Your purse, phone; everything except for your coins, but no more than ten bucks.'

'Oh, okay,' Nikki said. 'Thanks.'

She pulled four coins from her purse – a two-dollar coin, a one-dollar coin, a twenty cent-coin and a ten-cent coin – before placing it in the locker. She counted the money before closing the door and keying in the code. She walked back over to the waiting area, took a seat, and waited. It was as though she was in a dream: nothing felt quite real.

She was startled by the alarm when it sounded, a school-type bell. She had no idea what it was for – a fire? An escape? Little lunch? – but everyone else did.

'Get up,' said the foul-mothed woman to her kid. 'Move it. Time to see your Dad.'

Nikki stood up and made her way to the rear of the rough line that was forming. Once it started moving, she followed the woman in front of her, trying to take it all in without breaking down and crying.

They shuffled along corridor, through four different sets of heavy doors, which clicked then buzzed open for the group. They stopped at a windowless white room.

'You,' a guard said as he pointed towards an ordinary-looking man near the front. 'Join the screening line, please.'

'You,' he continued, pointing at the woman in front of Nikki.

'Ah, fuck off,' she fired. 'Not again. This is discrimination. You cunts are always picking on me.'

The guard ignored the woman and continued down the line, singling out a young man covered in tattoos and an undernourished woman with greasy hair plastered to her head. Nikki started to panic as the guard turned back and walked towards her again.

Look normal. Look normal.

She could feel sweat beads forming on her face as he closed the gap.

Stop sweating. Think cold.

She felt her face starting to twitch as he took another step.

Smile. No, don't. Yes, do.

Too late, the guard was upon her. She could smell his cheap aftershave as he looked her up and down. Nikki was sure he would smell her fear.

'You,' he said as he pointed to the person behind Nikki. 'Over there.'

Nikki thought she might faint from relief. She let go of the breath she hadn't even realised she was holding.

Once the guard had filled his quota, Nikki and the rest of the queue went through an airport-style metal detector, down another corridor, through two more sets of security doors and then finally into an outdoor courtyard, completely enclosed by wire fencing. There, they followed a short path to another building: a red-brick block from the 1970s, covered in Aboriginal art murals. Once inside, they passed through more doors.

The whole walk had taken less than ten minutes, maybe even less than five, but to Nikki it had felt interminable. With every step, it felt as though her chest constricted and heart beat faster. Her hands were slick with sweat even though it was cool inside the building, and her breathing was shallow. She wondered whether she would be able to get through this.

For Riley, she repeated in her head with every step, like a mantra. *For Riley*. She had to do this.

Suddenly, they were in a larger room and the queue dispersed, the other visitors breaking away from the line and rushing towards four vending machines lining the far wall.

'No running,' shouted a guard, who stood behind a raised reception desk in the middle of the room.

Nikki waited patiently, watched as the other visitors pressed coins into slots then scooped up cans, chocolates and chips. When her turn came, she fed the machine her four coins, pressed a button and pulled out a packet of chicken-flavoured chips.

Clutching the bag, Nikki ignored the guards behind the desk and walked into the 'VISITS ROOM', as the sign said, a surprisingly large and open space with metal stools and tables sprouting from its polished concrete floor.

She made her way to one of the last free tables and tried to pull her stool closer to the table as she sat down, but it was fixed to the floor. She scanned the room and tried to act calm, though she felt anything but. She was terrified.

And then he walked in.

JAX did not know why he was in the visiting room or who he was about to meet. He had never had a visitor, nor had he ever wanted any. He had been firm about that.

But then he saw her.

'Nikki,' he whispered to himself. The love of his life was sitting in the corner, alone on a stool, looking pale. 'Nikki.' His heart almost broke through his chest at the sight of her, the prettiest thing he had ever seen, here in the ugliest place he had ever been.

He resisted the urged to sprint across the room, pick her up and hug her. Nikki had to know that it was over. He thought about turning around and walking out. It would kill him to do so, tear whatever was left of his heart in two, but it would be for the best. She had to forget about him. She had to hate him.

But he couldn't do it. Couldn't turn his back on that face. Those eyes.

His selfishness burned his cheeks as he walked across the room, closing the distance between them. Nikki stood up as Jax neared, opened her arms.

'Don't,' Jax said. 'I can't. You shouldn't be here.' He couldn't meet her eyes.

'What?' Nikki said, her mouth hanging open in shock at Jax's cold greeting as she sat back down heavily.

'Come on, Nik,' Jax said. 'I told you never to come here. Never. You promised. Look at this place! Look at me ...'

He pointed to his battered face but ignored the pain as he lowered himself onto the hard steel stool.

Nikki started to cry. 'Listen, just listen to me,' she said, her voice cracking. 'I—

'No, *you* listen,' Jax snapped, the shame becoming too much. 'I never wanted you to see me like this, ever! Why couldn't you just stay away?'

The look of hurt in her eyes was almost too much to bear. Jax clenched his teeth. He knew he was being cruel, but letting her believe he was still the Riley she once knew – the Riley she once loved – was even crueller. He could never be the man she loved again. Especially not after what Marsh had done to him.

'No, Riley, you listen to me, goddammit.' Nikki's blue eyes drilled into him. They were filled with fear. 'I had to come. I had to.' She inhaled sharply and her eyes darted around the room before settling back on Jax's. 'They were going to kill you if I didn't,' she whispered urgently, her voice cracking and turning into a sob as she finished speaking.

Jax's stomach turned to ice.

'Who? What are you talking about? What do you mean?'

'The Gypsies,' Nikki said, tears now streaming down her face. 'They ...' She couldn't get anything else out, as she was now hyperventilating, short, sharp gasps eating her words. 'They ...' she tried again. 'They said ... They said they would kill you.'

'Well, you should have let them,' Jax said slowly and deeply as he stood. 'I'm fucking dead anyway. Get out of here. Just go.' He slammed the table between them with both fists, causing Nikki to jump and others in the room to look over with mild interest.

Jax hadn't seen Rogers when he'd walked in. Rocked by the sight of Nikki at the corner table, he hadn't surveyed the rest of his surroundings as he usually did. In the instant her eyes had met his across the room, the whole world had been reduced to just the two of them.

'Inmate,' Rogers shouted in his most official voice as he made his way towards them. 'This is your first warning. Behave yourself or the visit is over.'

Official part out of the way, Rogers leaned in and whispered into Jax's ear, 'Do whatever she tells you to do. Take whatever she wants to give you. It's not you they are going to kill if you fuck up. It's her. There's a van waiting at the gate for her. All I have to do is say the word – and she never makes it back home, mate.'

The guard's words sucked the adrenaline from Jax's veins and replace it with acid. He sat. He opened his mouth, but no words would come out.

'Pretty girl like her,' Rogers added, grinning across the table at Nikki, who looked like she'd just been slapped. 'I'm sure they'll give her a good send-off too, mate.'

Game over. Marsh had won. He'd found Jax's one and only weak spot. Jax was now his.

Nikki stood up after Rogers backed away. 'Don't move,' she said. 'Don't you dare. I swear to God. Please, don't leave.'

Jax didn't move, not a muscle, as Nikki made her way to the bathroom, but his mind was racing. *How had they found her? How did they even know about her? What had they done to her?*

His anger flared.

I'm going to kill them. Every last one of them.

Nikki returned from the toilet, tears gone and make-up fixed, but still looking terrified. She sat back down, grabbed the packet of chips and ripped them open.

She went to grab a chip. But instead of taking a handful, she dropped something into the foil. 'Want one?' she asked as she pushed them in front of him.

Jax just looked at her, struggling to make sense of what was happening.

'Take them,' she growled. '*You know I don't like chicken.*'

Jax peered down into the packet, immediately spotting what she had dropped into it: three little brown-taped packages, each not much larger than a multi-vitamin.

'You'll have to swallow them, babe,' Nikki said softly. 'Pretend you are eating a chip. They're smaller than they look. Sorry, I should have got you a can of drink. I didn't think. They only told me to bring coins for the chips.'

Jax didn't have to think about it. It was this or Nikki's life.

He lifted the bag towards his face, then tipped his head back and tilted the packet. The weight of the packages ensured they dropped into his mouth before the chips. Two heavy balls. Too big. He spat one back into packet before he swallowed. He repeated the process twice more, wishing he had a drink. He gagged on the final package, his mouth too dry, and almost brought it back up.

Heroin in his belly. The sweetest, most loving girl he had ever known turned into a drug mule. And only a matter of hours or days till he'd be violated again. Jax's life had become a nightmare.

He looked into the eyes of the only person other than his Nan he had loved since his parents were killed. And he finally broke down. 'I'm sorry,' he blurted as the tears started streaming down his face. He tried to say something else but couldn't.

Nikki rushed around the table and pulled him into an embrace. His chest heaved in and out as he sobbed. He wanted to stop but couldn't. He tried to speak but couldn't.

'It's okay, babe,' Nikki said as she rubbed his back. 'It's not your fault. None of it. You shouldn't even be here. You didn't do it. Come on. Deep down, you know it too.'

Then she stopped rubbing. 'Why didn't you fight?' she asked, a sudden anger in her voice. 'You know you didn't do it. Why did you let them do this to you?' She freed herself from the embrace and looked at him, her eyes wild. 'Why?

Why didn't you fight? Why didn't you fight … for us?' She pushed him away roughly.

Nikki's sudden breakdown snapped Jax out of his. He grabbed her and pulled her back in close, wrapped his arms around her. She resisted him, pounding his chest with her fists before, spent, she collapsed into him and sobbed.

'I'll fix this,' he said into her ear, and kissed the top of her head. 'I'll fix this. It's over. I promise.'

CHAPTER 19

Long Bay Correctional Complex, Sydney, NSW, Australia

IT TOOK Jax the best part of a week to sort out Nikki's new accommodation and new car. On the Monday after her visit, when the buy-up sheet had arrived, Jax had ordered the weekly limit of $100 worth of items, including $60 of phone credit – enough to make the calls he needed to while Nikki did the rest on the outside. The rest was food, which he would trade for info if he could. This time, he'd been allowed to keep what he'd ordered – Marsh seemed to have lost interest in him, at least for now. Someone else had been his pet project that week, it seemed.

Marsh had told Jax he was safe after Jax had sifted through his own faeces to retrieve the balls of heroin then handed them over to him. But as Jax had sat naked on his seatless stainless-steel toilet fighting cramps and his thoughts waiting to pass the packages, something had changed in him. Something deep within him had snapped.

When he'd handed the drugs over, Jax had also agreed to pay Marsh the $400 a week for the protection he'd previously refused. Not for himself, though. He only agreed to pay Marsh to keep Nikki safe. Marsh promised she would be, at least as long as Jax continued to pay.

Jax knew he would run of money sooner or later. That did not matter. He'd only needed a week to help Nikki move on. And he didn't care what happened after that.

With Nikki's move sorted and Marsh's henchmen completely backed off, Jax even started to think that maybe he wasn't going to be killed in his sleep. But then he got the word that he was required to attend Marsh's weekly gang meeting.

Johnson had told Jax that Marsh's Saturday-morning meetings – 8.15 am sharp, straight after muster – were compulsory, so all of Marsh's goons would be there: Bluey, Grub, Chunk, Waz, Smack and Deano. The penalty for being late was a beating; the penalty for not showing up was ... well, apparently no one knew that yet, because it had never happened.

Jax approached Marsh's cell at 8.14 am. He'd learned from Johnson that the morning meetings were when Marsh would delegate the week's work: the collections, beatings, stabbings and sometimes worse. Little black book in hand, Marsh went through the list of who had paid and who had not. He then went through the payments he'd made, most to the Dodge as usual. He would then reveal the week's takings – sixty percent of which would go straight to the bikie club. The other forty percent would be divided between the group, in proportions relating to their rank. The higher the patch, the higher the pay.

Jax walked towards the cell knowing he wasn't there for any of that, though. He didn't know exactly why he had been summoned, and knew it wouldn't be for anything good. But he didn't care. Not as long as Nikki was safe. That was all that mattered. *Safe*. She had to be.

Jax said nothing as he walked into Marsh's cell. *Seven on one*. Impossible odds, even if he'd had a weapon. The cell was big enough to house up to four men – it was almost four times as large as Jax's own – but it was Marsh's and Marsh's alone. Jax looked around the room, sizing it up. In addition to the standard toilet, desk, chair, shelf unit and small shelf, he saw a sofa, a fridge, a microwave, a fifty-centimetre TV with a PlayStation II and a queen-size bed. He was also scanning for anything he could use as a weapon, but there was nothing he could kill seven men with. And nothing that would stop them killing him.

There was an envelope on the desk. Jax assured himself that the envelope had nothing to do with Nikki. Marsh wouldn't mention her until he ran out of money.

'$500 bucks a week,' Jax said. 'Is that why I'm here? You want more money. Right?'

Jax knew that Marsh didn't want his money. He'd suspected as much as soon as Johnson had told him the going rate was $100 a week. And he was certain as soon as he saw the heroin, which he had roughly weighed after sifting it from his shit: about 100 grams. Give or take. It had a street value of $100,000 – and a prison value of $300,000. Marsh couldn't care less about his measly $400 a week. Marsh wanted him to make him money. Big money.

Marsh had an intricate and well-thought-out plan. No doubt about it. But he wasn't the only one with a plan. Not anymore.

Marsh leaned back in his chair and snatched the envelope from his desk. He handed it to Jax.

'Go on,' he said. 'Rip her open. Just like a Kinder Surprise without the chocolate.' He laughed loudly, the others joining in after a moment's delay.

42 Strickland Street, Sans Souci, NSW, 2234

Jax's heart sank and his face went white.

'It's her new address, if you were wondering. She moved in there with another girl. A blonde. Not a bad little sort. Not a bad little joint either. Could do with some better locks though.'

Jax wished he had his F88 Austeyr. He could take out seven men in two seconds with it.

'Don't worry,' Marsh reassured him. 'They boys are just looking out for her. Just making sure she is safe. It's actually not the best neighbourhood. I'm a little bit disappointed in your homework.'

Marsh then told Jax what he had to do. 'Either you kill him, or I kill her.'

THE following day, just before midday, Jax stood still as he looked out the holding cage gate towards the row of heavily fortified doors on the opposite side of the concrete landing. No movement. Not yet. The door to the protection wing was firmly shut. He put his head down and paced around the three-metre-by-two-metre cage beside the visiting room, steeling himself for what he had to do. For what Marsh had ordered him to do.

The holding cages were where inmates were rounded up and kept while they awaited scheduled visits. After being escorted out of their block and down a common path to the cage by a wing officer, prisoners were required to stay in the cage until their visitor arrived. They would then be collected by a different officer and taken inside for their visit – if the visitor showed.

Prisoners also returned to the cage after a visit, before being accompanied back to their cells. Last time Jax was here, he'd been out of his mind, having just seen Nikki and swallowed the drugs. He hadn't taken much in that day, but he remembered there had been plenty of inmates there, and that tensions seemed to be running high. According to Johnson, visits tended to bring out the worst in some prisoners, reminding them what they were missing. For Jax, it had been about much more than that.

But today Jax was alone in the cage – there wasn't another soul around. It was to be expected, as visiting time on Sundays didn't start until midafternoon. The other cage, the one for protection inmates, was empty too. Jax hadn't known whether the man would be waiting. He wasn't there and Jax hadn't been told if he was definitely coming, so he'd just have to see how it played out.

Jax lifted his head when he heard the familiar buzz of an electronic lock being opened. He turned towards the protection wing and watched as the door swung open and two men – an inmate and a guard – stepped out onto the path that led to the cages. The prisoner was in front, followed by Rogers. *Of course.* Jax might have known. The inmate was the actor. The paedophile. The child rapist who had been attacked from the yard on Jax's first day. He hadn't seen him since – the prison authorities were obviously determined to avoid another such clash.

Jax felt a mix of terror and relief on seeing the man emerge and walk along the path. Terror because this meant it was happening – there'd been no hiccup, no delay. It was on. And relief because if Jax had to do this – and he did – then better it be to this kind of man, one who had committed the worst of crimes. A man the world would be better off without.

Nikki's life was worth more than that of a paedophile. That was his only justification. That and the fact that it was essentially an order, one he had to follow, just like when he'd been in the army. Thinking too much about the target was counterproductive – it was best to just get into work mode and simply get it done.

Jax flexed his muscles, pumped his fists and gritted his teeth as he watched the actor walk across the yard, head held high, well-groomed for whoever it was he thought was visiting him. Jax felt his breathing level out and everything sharpen into focus, the same feeling he used to get when on a mission. The rest of the world receded and it almost seemed to him that he was watching the scene – and himself – from a distance, his physical body a puppet he controlled.

He saw the actor stop at the first gate – the one leading to the cage where the protection unit inmates normally waited – and then Rogers come up behind him and give him a rough shove to keep him moving. He saw the actor's mouth moving, but he blocked out the sound. As Rogers escorted him to the next cage, Jax crouched down low in the wall's shadow, lying in wait. If he could use the element of surprise, he would have an advantage.

The actor kept arguing, gesticulating angrily to the guard, as they continued down the pathway. Sure enough when they arrived at the gate to Jax's cage, Rogers pulled up. The actor, busy challenging Rogers, didn't notice Jax. Rogers unlocked the gate and manhandled the actor in, closing and locking it, then disappearing in an instant.

The actor physically jumped when he turned around and saw Jax. 'Who are you?' he said. 'You shouldn't be in h—'

The actor screamed as Jax grabbed his face. Then he stumbled backwards and fell hard on his backside. 'My jaw! Fuck. Why did you do that? No. Please!'

Jax waited for the actor to stand. He wanted him to have a chance. To see it coming. But the actor stayed down, raised his arms up next to his head in surrender and began to whimper.

'Please, stop, I give up!' he squealed. 'Please. Leave me alone. What did I ever do to you?'

Jax looked at the target. He wasn't done yet. He had instructions and they were crystal clear.

Kill him or we will kill her.

Those words were ringing in his ear when he delivered the king hit. A coward punch. Hands above his head, looking at the ground, the actor didn't see it coming. Didn't even try to defend himself. The roundhouse right to the temple knocked him out cold. Left him star-fishing on the concrete.

Jax was numb. He hadn't known he was capable of inflicting so much damage, let alone capable of delivering it.

Then suddenly he was back in his own body, and the throbbing outstretched fist was his, as was the battered victim he was standing over. He took a moment to study the man, who by now was bawling and gargling like a baby. He felt a wave of deep remorse and shame wash over him, almost strong enough to unsteady him.

But maybe this guy deserved it. Jax wanted to believe he did, but who was he to decide, let alone administer justice? And the job was only half done.

How could he do the next thing?

Jax knew pretending this man was a military target was no longer enough. He didn't have it in him to play the soldier against this pathetic man before. The idea had got him this far, but it would take him no further.

The only thing that could make him kill this poor sick man was love. So he thought of Nikki. Thought of what they would do to her if he couldn't do this.

And then he raised his foot and brought it down on the actor's head.

CHAPTER 20

San Souci, Sydney, NSW, Australia

NIKKI was scampering about, back and forth, looking here, there and everywhere.

'Have you seen my keys?' she shouted. 'I can't find them anywhere.'

Ivy, her new housemate, an up-and-coming newspaper reporter, did not take her eyes off the TV: the evening news was about to start.

'No,' Ivy said. 'Didn't you, like, just get home? How can you lose them in five minutes?'

Fuck knows. All Nikki knew was that she had her Tuesday-night kickboxing class at 6.30 pm and she should have left already. She'd taken up kickboxing after her move. She knew she would never be able to take down a gang of bikies, but she thought she might feel safer knowing how to punch, elbow and kick at least one of them in the balls, a move she had been practising in the mirror.

She hadn't had a visit from the Prospect guy, the boss guy or any other bikies for that matter since she'd delivered the drugs to

Riley. He had said it would stop and it had. She'd moved house – she'd been too scared to stay in her old house on her own – got a new mobile number and not listed it, and got a new car and registered it in a business name that Riley had set up that couldn't be traced back to her. She'd followed all of Riley's instructions and here she was. She wasn't stupid, though – she knew there was no guarantee she was safe. They had tracked her down before, so they could probably do it again. If they wanted to.

But Riley had promised. And he'd never broken a promise to her before.

Still, she lived in constant fear. Her doctor said she was suffering from post-traumatic stress disorder. Nikki thought that was something only soldiers got after returning from war, but apparently she'd had it even before her run-in on the road in Surry Hills that day. The psychologist she was now seeing told her that the arrest and incarceration of 'Brad' – Riley said she should never speak his name – had already caused her serious mental anguish and stress. She'd starting taking a daily dose of a drug called fluoxetine, which just made her feel spaced out, as it the world were covered in a light fog.

Having a flatmate did more for her than the medication. So did the alarm system, the window bars and the security lights on her new privately listed rental. Actually, the lights were a bit of a nuisance. Nikki panicked every time a cat, a possum or a strong wind set them off. Riley would have known how to adjust the sensor.

'Argggh,' she exclaimed. 'Where the fuck are they?'

She started ripping her new Ikea cushions off her new Ikea lounge, having remembered that she'd sat down for a quick chat with Ivy before changing into her Lorna Jane. Ivy was glued to the news.

Adored by Australia until he was revealed to be a child molester, former star of Farmers and Daughters *Billy Briggs met a grisly*

end yesterday when he was beaten to death by a cold-blooded
killer …

Nikki dropped to the floor and looked under the lounge,
thinking she may have accidentally kicked them across the carpet.

Police have confirmed that Briggs, fifty-seven, died of head trauma
following a brutal attack at Sydney's Long Bay jail …

'Well that's a crying fucking shame,' Ivy yelled at the TV,
sarcasm dripping. 'About time he got what he deserved. What
a piece of shit!'
 After hearing two anxiety-inducing words, 'Long' and 'Bay',
Nikki tried to ignore both Ivy and the television. She never
wanted to see that place again. Not even on TV.
 The keys weren't under the lounge, so she stood up.

Serving twenty-five years after being convicted of a string of
child sex offences including rape, Briggs was found dead in a
holding cell at the infamous Sydney prison, Australia's most
feared jail. Authorities believe the actor was attacked by another
prisoner while waiting to see his wife, famous Australian actor
Viv Bishop …

Nikki tried to retrace her steps towards the front door, all the
while hearing the television but refusing to look. She told
herself she wouldn't have been stupid enough to leave them in
the lock, but she would check anyway.

Police are yet to make an arrest, and the identity of the attacker
remains unknown. Detectives are investigating a claim that a
power surge blacked out the security cameras in the yard where
Briggs was being held at the time of the attack. No witnesses
have come forward. The apparent murder of the fallen actor is

being hailed as an act of 'jailhouse justice' by the families of those assaulted by Briggs over a fourteen-year spree.

Nikki opened the front door.

'Idiot,' she shouted as she saw the keys dangling from the lock.

She pulled them out, blaming her carelessness and forgetfulness on the medication. She grabbed her gym bag and scampered out the still-open door.

'See ya,' she said. 'Back in an hour or so.'

A five-minute drive from Nikki's new house, the kickboxing gym was in an industrial area amid factories and warehouses. By the time Nikki she got there, the streets were almost deserted – Strong Arm Martial Arts Academy was one of the few businesses open after dark. Located in a warehouse that looked much the same as the others on the street, it had a metal roller-door entrance, behind which the owners made full use of the industrial space. The two commodious floors easily accommodated two full-size boxing rings, a state-of-the-art weights room, and a cardio area.

As Nikki parked then leaned into the back seat for her gym bag, she didn't notice the man in black step out from the shadows and approach her car. She'd only walked a few metres – pulling her hair into a messy ponytail as she did so – when he cut her off. It was the young bikie who'd given her the drugs.

She frantically pressed the button on the key-fob she was still holding in her hand. Her doors unlocked and the headlights turned back on. She suddenly wished she had a car alarm, one of those panic buttons. She turned to run to the car, but he grabbed her arm.

'Where you going?' he asked. 'I thought we were friends.'

'Fuck off,' Nikki said. 'Get out of my way.'

Nikki attempted to push past him, but he held her in place by her shoulders.

'I'll scream,' she said. 'Let me go or I will scream. They will be out here in a second.'

'No, they won't,' he said with a grin on his face. 'Hate to tell you, but we own this place. How do you think we found you? Got your new address? Nice place, but you have to do something about that fucking sensor light. Fucking thing goes off every time I get close.'

Nikki went limp, all the fight sucked out of her slight frame.

'What do you want?' she asked. 'What do I have to do now?'

Nikki already knew the answer. Riley's promise wasn't worth shit. He wasn't the one making the rules.

CHAPTER 21

Long Bay Correctional Complex, Sydney, NSW, Australia

JAX grabbed a buy-up sheet before going back to his cell. He'd been hoping he wouldn't have to make this order, had done everything in his power to avoid it, including killing the actor. But now, with freshly delivered drugs in his stomach, and traces of the tears he had wiped from Nikki's face still on his hands, he didn't have a choice. Nikki's second visit to Long Bay had made that clear. At least this time she'd remembered to buy a can of drink. Sunkist.

If he thought about them, he could almost feel the round packages – four this time – making their way through his digestive system. In the eight days since he had done the unthinkable in the cage, he'd barely left his cell. It was only today, after being summoned to the visits centre, that he'd finally emerged.

As he'd made his way there, a hard knot of dread had formed in the pit of his stomach, and when he'd stepped onto the path leading to the cage, he'd begun to dry-retch. Waiting in the cage had been like torture – partly because what he'd done there kept playing through his head, but also because he knew it could only be Nikki on the other side of the wall.

He just couldn't get his head around it. What had been the point of killing the actor if Marsh was not going to leave Nikki alone? And if Nikki was here, that meant they'd found her – and that he'd failed to protect her as he had promised he would. It also made it clear that they were both trapped in this drug-smuggling operation, with no escape. And, worse, it meant he was a cold-blooded killer who'd taken a man's life for nothing.

He told himself that this was Marsh's fault, as he put the buy-up sheet on his desk. All on them. They had backed him into a corner and this was the only way out. He was doing this for Nikki. To save her. He didn't care about himself.

He sat at his desk and filled out the form, this time not worrying about making outlines or colouring the circles a uniform shade of dark grey.

He started on the first page, under the heading 'Cleaning Products'.

Bleach: Easy-Off Bam. He ordered the maximum of four.

He moved down to Personal Grooming.

Nail clippers: Toe.

He ordered one.

Disposable Razors: BIC, 12 pack.

He ordered the maximum of four.

Hand and face wipes: Wet Ones, Original.

Again, he ordered the maximum.

Antiseptic: Isocol.

He ordered one.

Toothbrush: Colgate, pack of three.

He ordered one.

Dental floss: Colgate.

He ordered one.

Jax then turned to the second page.

Soft Drink: Coca-Cola, can.

He ordered two.

Pineapple Juice: Golden Circle, can.

He ordered one.

Tuna: In Spring Water, can.

He ordered one.

Chips: Smiths, Originals.

He ordered one.

He pushed the buy-up sheet to the side after filling in his personal details and authorising payment from his fast-dwindling prison account. It didn't matter. He wouldn't need money after this.

Then took out a blank piece of paper. 'Dear Nikki,' he started.

CHAPTER 22

Goulburn Correctional Centre, Goulburn, NSW, Australia

LONG past lights out, he made sure the corridor was empty before pulling out his smartphone. The prison was quiet, the thieves, rapists and murderers all tucked in. Sound asleep.

He moved to his desk but turned to his door before he sat, half-expecting a guard to be looking through the glass.

All clear.

He took a deep breath before turning the phone on. He began to worry when it didn't power up straight away. Had someone else been using it? It had been almost fully charged last time he used it. He smiled when he saw the light, the screen illuminating his face with a ghostly glow, then navigated his way to the internet and logged into his account.

Username: Mahdi_93/241. Password: Hewillrise_85/159.

He clicked on the transfer funds icon and started sending cash. He made a series of deposits, all to the same account. First $0.61, then $4.00, $9.78, and $1.42. Now he just had to wait.

He made sure his other mobile phone – a never-before-used burner – was set to silent after switching it on. Then he placed the phone on his desk, crossed his arms and stared at the screen. It soon flashed, +359 789 546 303 appearing on the screen.

'Greetings, my child,' said the Mahdi. 'I take it all is in order?' He listened to the reply. 'Good,' the Mahdi said. 'Good. My son, it is time. Now, listen carefully. You have to dispose of the seller once he gives you the gun. Make sure it is loaded when he gives it to you; if not, you will have to load it yourself. Tell him you need to make sure it works, if he asks any questions. Shoot him once in the chest and once in the head.'

He paused and listened.

'You have arranged to meet him at the Lake with the Lilies, as I directed?'

He waited for the reply.

'Well, there should be no witnesses,' he said. 'Not there. Make sure you both wear your hoods in case, and just proceed as planned. Then go directly to the target. You should be in place and ready to perform your sacred duty at exactly 7 pm your time. Is everything clear?'

He listened.

'Good,' the Mahdi said. 'I am proud of you, my boy. Proud of both of you. Remember to take the pills. They will help you in your mission. Do as I have instructed, as you have rehearsed. Leave no evidence, no trace. Call me when you have arrived at the target, ahead of the final phase. I will be expecting your call at 6.50 pm your time. Until then, *Inshallah*.'

THE phone came to life again at 3.50 am – 6.50 pm on 25 September in Sofia, Bulgaria.

Call taken, orders given, phone put away, he had to imagine the rest. The flash and the fire. The rubble and the ruin. He smiled, wide and proud. He noted but ignored his erection. The blinding flash of the detonator would be all they would see. They wouldn't see the forcefield of rushing air, the bomb sucking all the oxygen in then spitting it out, or the tsunami of shrapnel and fire, but he could see all those things now.

He imagined the sirens, the honking horns, the hazmat suits. But mostly he pictured the church, reduced to rubble.

He smiled again.

Four down.

CHAPTER 23

Long Bay Correctional Complex, Sydney, NSW, Australia

JAX waited until his door was locked before pulling out his buy-up bag, which had been delivered that morning, Friday, as expected. He'd had plenty of time to think about it since Nikki's visit – now six days ago – but he hadn't changed his mind. He was doing this for Nikki. To save her. He didn't care about himself. Or them.

He had three hours until lights-out. It would be touch and go. He stacked all the items on his top shelf, neatly, and roughly in the order in which he'd require them. He grabbed the BIC razors, the toothbrushes and the dental floss first, and moved them to his desk.

Ten minutes later, Jax was holding a precision cutting tool. Having removed the bristles from one of the three toothbrushes with a razor, he had used the same blade to make a deep groove in the plastic head. He'd then slid a fresh razor in the slot, before fastening it with tightly wound floss.

He took the Coke cans, the tuna and the chips from the shelf next. He felt both a little queasy and a little high after sculling both cans and speed-eating the chips, the caffeine, sugar and fat combining to deliver a sickly hit. He told himself he should have ordered Coke Zero and veggie chips from the Healthier Options page. Too late now.

He dumped the entire contents of the can of tuna into his bin. The stench didn't help his stomach, his room immediately smelling like a deep-sea fishing boat, and the stink would be unbearable in a few days. But he wasn't planning on being around for that.

Jax used his toothbrush blade to cut the empty Coke cans in half. He threw the top halves of the cans into the bin before heading to his sink, where he thoroughly washed the bottom halves, the tuna tin and the chip packet with warm water and soap before towelling them dry.

Next, Jax took the Isocol and the four bottles of Easy-Off Bam from his shelf and placed them alongside the cleaned and dried cans, tin and packet. He squirted a healthy serving of Isocol into the bottom of the tuna can, retrieved the lighter he'd stolen from one of the methadone gang earlier that day when he'd been out of it, and set the gel alight. The Isocol burned hot and bright, being pure ethanol, with a peak burning temperature of 1920 degrees Celsius. There was no way Jax's Isocol fire was that hot – it didn't have enough oxygen – but it was hot enough to extract hydrogen peroxide from his bleach.

Jax used his cutting tool to make a hole just below the top edge of one of his cans. He then grabbed another toothbrush from the three-pack and stuck the brushless end into the hole to make a handle. He filled the half-can up to the handle hole with Easy-Off Bam and held the can over the flame until all the liquid had evaporated. Then he took the last toothbrush from the packet and used it to sweep up the fine white powder left at the bottom of the can – pure hydrogen peroxide – into the chip packet.

Jax repeated the process until all the Easy-Off Bam was gone. It took almost all of the Isocol to burn through the four bottles of bleach. By the time he was done, his chip packet was almost a quarter full. Plenty.

The next part was relatively easy – no sculling, scoffing or singeing himself while scooping powder out of a red-hot can. He took all four packets of the Wet Ones from his shelf and placed them next to the other half Coke can. He opened the first packet of Wet Ones and began the simple but laborious task of ringing the liquid out of each towel and into the can. One by one, he twisted, turned and squeezed each of the forty towels, until he had about 150 millilitres of pure acetone.

He now had the two ingredients that, when combined, made triacetone triperoxide, or TATP. Also called 'The Mother of Satan', it's one of the most explosive molecules known to man and an explosive of choice for terrorists – it had been used in several attacks, including the London bombings in 2005. Now all Jax had to do was build his bomb.

Using the cutting tool first and then the nail clippers, Jax cut a one-inch-wide hole into the side of the toughened one-litre tin that contained the pineapple juice, poured the yellow juice straight down the sink, and rinsed out the tin as best he could, even though he knew that the juice would not react with the chemicals.

He tipped the hydrogen peroxide into the tin first – he needed all the white powder to be at the bottom – funnelling every last speck through the one-inch hole. Next he took the blades out of the remaining forty-seven BICS and snapped each one in half before feeding them all in.

Then he inserted a range of things he had been collecting since he'd decided he was going to blow them all to hell – mostly rocks taken from the yard, but also shards of glass, a handful of aluminium ring-pulls and a screw. He chucked the nail clippers in too, figuring he would never need them again. Lastly, he pushed in the four marble-sized balls that he had recovered from his own waste. He had kept them hidden in his cell since passing them, but had said he was constipated whenever Marsh asked.

He used the dregs of the Isocol to set a small fire in his trashcan. If his plan didn't work or the bomb didn't detonate, he couldn't risk a guard coming across his rubbish and exposing him before he'd have the chance to try again. He watched the little blaze burn slowly, into black dust. When it was done, he doused it with water from the sink; the slushy mix that was left could have been anything, and would probably be chucked before anyone even thought to check it.

Now all Jax had to do was pour the acetone in and shake. But he wouldn't do that yet. Not until the next day. Saturday. Not until Marsh and his boys were together, all in the same room.

'YEAH, they're out,' Jax said when Marsh approached him in the yard before muster. 'I was on the toilet all night, but all good, got them.'

'Well, what are you waiting for?' Marsh asked. 'A fucking invitation?'

'They're in my cell,' Jax said. 'I didn't think you would want me to hand them over in the open. I'll bring them to you straight after muster.'

'It's my job to think,' Marsh said, 'not yours. Bring them to me as soon as muster finishes. I'll be in my room.'

I know you will be. That all of you will be.

Jax returned to his cell after roll call and placed the pineapple tin and the half-cut Coke can on his desk. He then gave an almost imperceptible bow before sitting on the floor with his back to the cell door, his legs crossed and his hands folded in his lap. As he half-closed his eyes and began to breathe, his mind began to clear. After a few minutes, he felt light and purposeful – centred.

It was the only way to save her.

Gradually, he released himself from the *zazen* meditation, the surrounds of his cell slowly coming back into focus. He didn't bother praying for forgiveness or salvation. He'd made his choice. If there was a Hell, he'd be there soon.

JAX carefully placed the pineapple can on its side on the table, with the rough one-inch hole facing the ceiling. He held it steady with his left hand as he picked up the can of acetone with his right. He took a deep breath.

Theoretically, it shouldn't explode. Not yet. He had placed his layer of makeshift shrapnel over the hydrogen peroxide powder, but that wouldn't stop the liquid acetone from reaching it, only slow it down. Even when the two chemicals met, Jax would have about two minutes before they reacted to form TATP. And even when the hydrogen peroxide and acetone had yielded The Mother of Satan, it wouldn't explode until set off by a spark, a detonator, or friction. Well, theoretically, anyway.

Jax held as breath as he tipped the can towards the hole. But he stopped abruptly, before any liquid came out, and muttered, 'Shit.' He'd just realised he didn't know for sure what was contained in the four marble-sized balls. He'd assumed it was heroin. Was almost sure it was. But had it been cut? And with what? One of the thirty-two chemicals known to set off TATP?

He wanted to die – but not alone.

He sucked in a deep breath, gritted his teeth and winced as he tipped the can, the first drops quickly becoming a thin, steady stream.

No bang. No boom.

Jax exhaled and tipped the can a little more so that the thin stream became thicker, then pulled back a little when droplets splattered the edge of the tin. He didn't have enough to waste. The can was soon empty, the 150 millilitres or so of acetone now pooling inside the now-sealed pineapple tin. The reaction wouldn't start until he turned the tin upright.

He threw the empty half-can into his bin before taking a moment to have one last look around. At what his life had become. At why he might as well be dead. He picked up the tin, turned it upright and put it under the waistband of his shorts, his loose T-shirt hiding the bulge.

Tick, tock.

Jax stepped from his cell into the corridor. The wing was brightly lit, the spring sun streaming through the glass roof, brilliant and warm. Inmates went this way and that, some off to the yard, others going to the recreation room, a few with Saturday jobs going to work. Jax would ignore anyone that saw the bulge. He would say 'For Marsh' if they tried to stop him. He wouldn't be lying.

Tick, tock.

The acetone had started to react with the hydrogen peroxide the moment he'd picked up the tin. Jax figured he had about a minute before they combined to form TATP. He turned to his left and walked. Marsh's cell was at the far end of the wing, at the opposite end to the guard's station. About forty metres away.

Jax calculated the tin in his pants would be a fully armed bomb just as he arrived at Marsh's cell. He walked at his normal pace, doing his best not to attract attention. He was thirty metres away from Marsh's cell when he felt warmth against his skin. He must have calculated wrongly. The TATP had already formed.

Tick, tock.

Jax wanted to walk faster but couldn't, as it would shake the can, and he didn't know how much friction was required to trigger the explosion. Then wanted to walk slower, fearful he was already shaking the can too much, but he couldn't, as the tin was now too hot.

He was twenty metres from Marsh's cell.

Tick, tock.

His skin started to burn. He wanted to pull the tin out, but couldn't for fear of it exploding.

Ten metres.

Tick, tock.

His skin was sizzling by the time he arrived. As he walked through the open door, he pulled the tin from his waistband. It didn't explode.

They were all there: Bluey, Grub, Chunk, Waz, Smack and Deano – of course, they had to be – scattered around the king-size cell, waiting as Marsh flicked through his little black book.

'Pineapple juice?' Marsh asked as he looked up at Jax.

'Thought you might be thirsty,' Jax said evenly as he tossed the can to Marsh.

'What the fuck?' said Marsh as he caught the can, dropping his book as he did so.

Nothing. No bang. No boom.

'Fuck me!' Marsh said as the tin scorched his flesh and he threw it to the floor. Jax watched from the cell entrance as the goons moved in to examine the can. It started to fizz and froth, a white foam spewing from the hole.

'It's a bomb!' Grub screamed.

All together, they turned and ran for the door.

Jax closed his eyes, planted his feet, and blocked the only exit.

CHAPTER 24

Langley, Virginia, USA

SAMI felt like he was sitting at somebody else's desk. He still had an office at Langley, even though he spent at least ten months a year overseas. He'd once worked at this desk full-time, but that was almost twenty years back. Before a couple of planes had flown into a couple of buildings.

He gazed at the picture on the desk: a young man and a young woman, a toddler on each lap. He felt like he was looking at somebody else's family. Another life.

He couldn't remember the last time he had seen the twins, now teenagers. His boys didn't want to know him. He put it down partly to hormones but mostly to resentment. He had fathered by way of correspondence, all his parenting delivered over the phone from places like Paris, Beirut and Moscow. Unsurprisingly, his marriage had gone about as well as the co-parenting had.

Back in the US since the Alabama bombing, he had hoped to see his sons. But a month had now passed and they still weren't returning his calls, replying only by way of text to say that they were busy and 'Maybe next time'. He *had* wanted to be a proper father. He still wanted to be a proper father.

He was actually on okay terms with his ex these days – he hadn't cheated on her or walked out, not with or for another woman anyway. It was the CIA that had cost him his marriage and his family. Even during the two months a year he was at home, his mind was always somewhere else. Terrorists didn't take holidays, and neither did he.

Sami wondered what his desk would have looked like if Osama Bin Laden had never been born. He imagined the photograph would have been part of a series, the boys bigger in each picture, his wife sporting different hairstyles but retaining her ageless beauty, and him getting greyer and fatter while his smile grew a little wider in each frame. He wondered if he'd ever again been as happy as he was on the day of that photograph on his desk.

He turned his attention back to his laptop and hit 'Refresh'. With a touch of the key, a million or so digital trawlers called spiders were dispatched to every major news site in the world. The software, co-built by the CIA and Google, brought all the spiders back just seconds later, 1148 of them bringing news stories that contained a series of keywords including 'blast', 'bomb', 'terror', 'attack' and 'church'. Sami clicked through them. Nothing. All about the previous attacks.

Maybe it was over, the bombing of the church in Alabama the final act. With another eighty-four dead, the death toll from the four bombs had risen to 438 and the world was on the brink of war. The US had launched a series of attacks in the Middle East, using the bombings as an excuse to settle scores. Maybe the still-unknown group had already achieved its goal, whatever that was.

Sami had now been watching his screen, cycling through headlines, for close to twenty-five hours. It wasn't quite 12 pm Eastern Time, but he had been sitting at his desk since the sun had first risen on the twenty-fifth day of the month, in Kiribati, the tiny Pacific island that sits on the international date line. And it would still be the twenty-fifth day of the month somewhere in the world for another twenty-five excruciating hours. He would not know whether the attacks had finished until it was midnight in America Samoa.

Sami looked around his office, where several 'world clocks' were mounted to the walls. It was about to hit 6 pm in Paris, and most of Europe was just six hours away from being clear. It was already the twenty-sixth day of the month in some countries, including Australia and New Zealand. Even those peaceful, far-flung nations were considered potential targets because, given how little the authorities knew about the bombers – there had been no survivors, witnesses or CCTV evidence in Alabama either – every country with a church was considered to be in the blast zone.

The prayer mat caught his eye. Rolled up and jammed between two filing cabinets, the well-used rug was now covered in dust. He stood up, walked over to it and pulled it out, dusted it off. Initially, he couldn't remember that last time he'd used it, but then he remembered. It was before she had left him. Obviously, God hadn't been listening then.

'Sir,' said a young woman as she burst in without knocking. 'You're required in the War Room. Right away. It's urgent.'

The woman tried her best to ignore the prayer mat he was holding, and Sami could tell by the look on her face that she didn't know he was Islamic, even though he no longer hid his background, hadn't for years. But then again, he no longer prayed. And with a first name like Hudson – which he had chosen as soon as he was legally old enough to rid himself of Abas – her puzzlement shouldn't have been a surprise.

He pushed the prayer mat back between the filing cabinets, told himself he would pray later, knew he wouldn't.

Then he opened his drawer and pulled out a notepad. He didn't have clearance to take a computer, a phone or any electronic device capable of recording into the War Room.

He searched for a pencil – no metallic objects, including pens, were allowed.

'Sir, I can provide you with a pencil and anything else you need to take notes,' the woman said. 'We have to go. Right away.'

Sami shoved his drawer back into his desk, grabbed his jacket from the back of his chair – knowing he would need it – and followed the young lady. She was way faster than she looked, little legs pumping like engine pistons.

After the fresh pencil, notepad and his jacket had been placed on a blue tray and sent through an airport-style X-ray machine, Sami walked through the metal detector without setting it off. His side-arm, a standard issue SIG-Sauer P228 pistol, was locked away in a nearby safe and being guarded by an agent who looked more mastiff than man.

He provided the two-factor authentication needed for entry – a retina scan and a six-digit code – then the airlocked door opened and he was hit by an icy blast. It was always exactly sixteen degrees Celsius in the War Room, the optimum temperature for all the computers, of which there were dozens.

As he walked along the glass-walled hallway, Sami peered into the room to his left, a factory-sized floor full of PCs where hundreds of analysts, mostly young men and woman – the oldest he could see was barely middle-aged – stared at screens and tapped on keyboards. Sami had little idea what they were doing; he still struggled with his Android phone. He ignored the towering machines behind the glass wall to his right.

He stopped at another steel door and positioned his right eye in the cradle of another scanner after punching in a six-digit code – this one different from the last.

'Senior Special Agent and Head of the Office of Russian and European Analysis Hudson Sami entering,' an electronic voice announced.

Sami nodded before taking the last empty seat, one of twenty-four around a gargantuan table, the centrepiece of the conference room.

'Okay, that's everyone,' said Morrissey, CIA Director of Operations. 'Let's begin.'

All the walls in the room suddenly lit up: every surface, excluding the floor but including the roof, was an LCD display. The director turned and faced the screen at the head of the room and pointed at an enlarged image of a Twitter post. 'This post was picked up by one of our European social media analysts six minutes ago,' Morrissey began.

He pointed at the screen again and the Bulgarian text was replaced by English.

Oh my God. There is an earthquake. The whole building is shaking.

'The post was geolocated to Sofia, Bulgaria,' Morrissey continued. 'We have since tracked every post within a fifty-kilometre radius.'

Morrissey then pointed to the wall to his right, which displayed scores of smaller screens. 'That's a live feed of every post coming out of what we have since narrowed to a five-kilometre radius,' the director said. 'We have numerous reports of explosions, loud noises and smoke, but no confirmation of a bomb or an exact location.'

The director was interrupted by a beep.

'Sir.' A female voice came out of the speakers in the floor. 'I am about to load an Instagram post onto the main screen.'

Morrissey, and everyone else in the room, turned and waited.

The Bulgarian text then gave way to English.

St Nedelya Church is on fire. Roof has collapsed.

The picture accompanying the post showed a building half-levelled and burning.

'Get me an address,' the director shouted.

In an instant, the screen at the far end of the room brought up a Wikipedia page for the church, including its address and GPS coordinates. Morrissey began firing a series of orders at the men and woman around the table.

'Collins,' he barked, 'alert local authorities. They are still in the dark. Get emergency services to the scene.

'Jones,' he commanded, 'find our closest drone and send it in. I want a live feed ASAP.

'Stein,' he shouted, 'see what we have in the way of satellites.

'Ramirez, get the boffins to limit the live social media feed to within one kilometre of this church. Get names, addresses and profiles of anyone who posts. A full electronic sweep. I want to know everything about them.'

He continued around the room, getting to Sami last.

'How many do we have in the Bulgarian office?' Morrissey asked.

'Eight,' Sami replied.

'Get them all there now. And anyone else who's close. I want every available man on the ground. And I want you there too. Leave as soon as you contact your team.'

CHAPTER 25

Long Bay Correctional Complex, Sydney, NSW, Australia

JAX opened his eyes when he smelled the Brut 33.

'Oh, hello there. Feeling any better?' a voice boomed.

The sulphurous light was blinding. The smell of the cologne was nauseating. The voice, although gentle, was head-splitting. The sudden attack on his senses was too much. He closed his eyes and held his breath. The gloom called him back.

'Hello ... Are you awake? Hello.'

Jax lifted his arm to acknowledge Father Martin. He'd seen only a round silhouette amid the brightness, but that, along with the voice and smell, was enough to tell him it was the priest.

'Relax,' Martin said. The voice no longer reverberated painfully; Jax's ears were adjusting. 'Take your time. Boy, you really did give us all a scare, didn't you?'

Jax felt like he was floating underwater, his bones still reverberating from the effects of the now-inaudible violence. He opened his eyes again, slowly this time, admitting only a sliver of light. Still the fluorescent glare stung.

For a moment he became confused, thinking he was back in his army cot, with no one shot, no one locked up, everything as it should be. Then he felt confused by his confusion. For he never got confused.

He tried to remember what had happened. The images were foggy and vague: he saw angels, heard an alarm, felt cold hands. Nonsensical. He closed his eyes, concentrated harder and tried again, diving deeper this time, knowing that what he needed was there, if only he could access it.

Crisper images slowly began to emerge. White-washed, hazy memories were spliced with frames of complete clarity. Now he saw nurses, not angels, a heart-rate monitor rather than an alarm, defibrillation paddles instead of celestial hands.

He went back further, skipping past a dream that was definitely a dream to the previous thing he could recall. Then he watched it all in reverse. He smelled their flesh burning before he saw the fire. Then he heard the boom and saw the fear in their faces.

The bomb. It had worked. *Nikki* …

'What happened?' he asked, wondering how much the priest knew.

'Terrible thing,' Father Martin said, tut-tutting. 'Just terrible. An explosion, they say. I think they're still looking into the cause. You've been asleep for a few days. Maybe more. I thought you might not pull through. But I stayed and I prayed.'

'Am I the only one who survived?' Jax croaked, opening his eyes and looking at the chaplain.

'Oh, you don't—'

'No, I want to know. I *need* to know.'

The priest's look changed from concern to slightly alarmed.

'I'm sorry to be the one to tell you, but all the others died,' he said quietly. Then he paused.

Jax could tell he was being studied. He did his best to conceal any hint of relief.

'Except for one,' the priest said.

Pain shot up the back of Jax's neck as he jerked his head from the pillow, stunned by this last piece of information. Then his head fell back onto his pillow as he passed out.

THE CHAPLAIN was still there, eyes closed and mouth moving silently in prayer, when Jax came to again some minutes later. He almost dropped the Bible that was resting on his lap when Jax said his name.

'I've rung the bell,' the priest said nervously, 'to bring the doctor and nurse. They were expecting you to come round, though maybe not for a few more hours. Don't worry, they'll be along soon.'

Jax was pretty sure the police wouldn't be far behind them. A thought crossed his mind and he suddenly jerked his arm. *No handcuffs. Odd.*

The priest had said there was another survivor. 'Marsh,' Jax said. 'Was it Marsh?'

Father Martin took off his glasses, rubbed his eyes, then replaced his spectacles before answering. 'No. I don't know how to put this, but, well, there wasn't much left of the poor fellow to give to back to his family. McKinnon was the only survivor. The only other survivor, I should say.'

'Who?'

'McKinnon. The big ginger chap with that unfortunate scar.'

Bluey! So Nikki still wasn't safe. With Bluey alive, a revenge hit for Jax's actions would be issued and delivered swiftly, and with force.

'Where is he?' Jax asked.

'Right beside you. Behind that curtain just there. You can't talk to him, though. He's in a drug-induced coma, just like you were. You've both been through a lot.'

Jax did his best to mask his relief. *Safe. For now.*

'Terrible business,' the priest went on. 'Don't know how you got caught up in it – in the wrong place at the wrong time, hey? Some kind of bikie turf war is what they think. One of Marsh's men challenging for leadership or something like that ...' He tutted. 'You're the real victim here, son.'

Jax could barely believe what he was hearing. He went to sit up again, only to be hit by a dizzy spell that sent the room spinning.

'Best to stay still,' Father Martin said as he placed his soft hand on Jax's arm. 'You have some very serious injuries.'

Jax raised his head again, slowly this time. Only his arms, completely bandaged, weren't tucked beneath the thick white blanket that had been folded across his chest and tucked snugly into the sides of the bed. The colours and placements of all the tubes suggested he was being drip-fed morphine, blood, iron and a saline solution. The codes on the bags confirmed it.

'You have been given a second chance, my boy,' the chaplain said. 'Back from the dead, born again, just like Him.'

JAX had to drag the IV drip and monitoring machine with him. Slowly, silently he made his way to the end of his bed, his pillow stuffed under an arm. With every step, pain flashed wildly through him – his chest, his leg, his head. Gingerly, he took a few more steps, edging closer, then he drew the curtain back. The bed was empty.

He hobbled back to his own bed. He would wait. He would watch. He would not sleep.

'YOU haven't been up, have you,' a nurse said after pulling back the curtain.

'Was just testing the legs,' Jax said.

'Can't sleep, hey?' the nurse asked.

'Yeah. That's right.'

The nurse walked over to the machine behind Jax and began pressing buttons.

'Well, this should help,' she said.

'No,' Jax said. 'What did you give me?'

'WHA—' Jax couldn't even finish the word. His eyes were open but his head was still in a morphine maze. 'Is … you? I'm … Oh fuck!'

Though still not with it, he knew enough to be scared. Even in his semi-conscious state, he knew he was looking at death – a severely scarred redhead with dangerously deep blue eyes.

'Fuck …' Jax mumbled and slurred as he lashed out. 'Kill you. I'll kill you, you bastard, I will.'

Bluey put his gigantic arm on Jax's forehead, gently pushed his head back against the hospital bed pillow then pinned him there by his shoulders.

'Oi,' he said. 'Pipe down. Settle, mate. I'm not here to hurt ya. Oi. You good? You awake?'

Suddenly Jax was back from his morphine-induced dream and looking into sad eyes. He shook his head, surely still dreaming. But after blinking a few times, Bluey was still there, looking him over, though not with rage.

'Can you hear me?' Bluey asked gruffly, holding Jax down hard. 'You with me or what?'

Jax signalled in the affirmative with his eyes, unable to find the strength to nod his head.

'Mate, this is really hard for me to say,' Bluey said, sounding a little groggy himself. 'Because I've known 'em all for a long time, and a couple of them were my mates … But … you did the right thing … Marsh was a cunt. There hasn't been a night since I met him that I didn't go to sleep telling myself I would stand up to him the next day. But I never did. I couldn't find my balls and he turned me into … Seriously? What sort of man would …? Fuck, I have a boy older than you.'

Now fully alert, Jax went cold as he saw Bluey's eyes darken.

'Seriously, when you gave it to Grub,' Bluey said after a sniffle, bringing himself back from the brink. 'Gave him what he deserved. Well, I thought of my boy.'

Bluey struggled to find his next word.

'What I am trying to say is we are sweet. I'm not going to dog on ya. I'm gonna tell the cops nuthin'. And I'll tell the club it was Grub that done the bomb. You don't have to worry about your girl. She's safe. She will be safe. The club will fold now anyway. If it hasn't already.'

Bluey extended his arm. Jax hesitated before looking back at his eyes. He took Bluey's hand and shook it.

'She'll be sweet?' Jax asked. 'Do I have your word?'

'You do, mate,' Bluey said. 'And it's as good as gold.'

Bluey smiled after taking back his hand.

'Looks like they will be sending me to Goulburn,' Bluey said. 'They don't want to keep me here after what's gone down. Look me up if you're ever down that way.'

JAX became familiar with the smell of strawberries and sunshine.

'How is the pain?' Laura asked as she placed her hand on Jax's wrist to take his pulse, like she'd done almost every morning. It was only the weekends that Laura wasn't there. Mark, the weekend nurse, was a fine nurse too. But he was no Laura.

'Fine,' Jax lied. He deserved to be in more pain.

'How's the leg?' Laura asked as she pulled back the blanket.

'Yeah, heaps better,' Jax said, this time the truth.

'You know they didn't think you would ever walk again,' Laura said as she started unwrapping the bandage. 'And here you are, almost completely healed. It's nothing short of a miracle, to be honest.' She looked back up at him and smiled again. 'Father Marty agrees.'

Jax looked down as Laura unfurled the bandage, round and round, the pile of cotton thinning with every flick of her wrist. He found it almost mesmeric.

'Here comes the painful part. Ready?' she asked as she lifted the edge of the puss- and blood-soaked gauze that sat directly on the wound. The healing skin had grown into the backside of the bandage. Laura was as gentle as she could be, but even she winced as she pulled and the bandage snapped a stitch as it came away. But Jax didn't so much as flinch.

'Sorry about the stitch,' she said.

'I have way too many of 'em anyway,' Jax replied calmly. 'What's one stitch when you have 142?'

'Make that 140,' she said as the bandage tore another stitch from the wound. 'Sorry.'

She stopped grimacing when the covering was finally removed. 'It's healing nicely'.

This time Laura was doing the lying. His right upper thigh was a mess of stitches and skin grafts. Still, Jax was surprised it didn't look worse, considering it had taken four hours just for the surgeons to remove the shrapnel. From the shark-bite sized hole in his left thigh, they'd pulled out pebbles, wire, glass, tin, and bone fragments that weren't his. They didn't find any razor blades in his leg, but they did remove half a safety razor handle, a piece of aluminium and two of Marsh's teeth from Jax's face.

After redressing his leg, Laura removed the bandage around his head.

The mass of bodies rushing towards the door had shielded Jax from the worst of the blast. He was found unconscious in the corridor, with Bluey lying on top of him. The explosion had hurled him out of the cell and against the opposite wall. Marsh, Grub, Waz and Smack had been killed in the blast; Chunk and Deano had died during emergency surgery.

'Are you well enough for a visit?' Laura asked. 'Your lawyer is here.'

'Lawyer?' Jax asked.

'Yes. He's waiting in the legal rooms. Do you want to see him or should I say you aren't up to it yet?'

'Nah, I'm sweet,' Jax said, pushing away the blanket and swinging his legs to the floor.

'Really?' Laura asked as he gently pushed her hand aside. Jax smiled as he kicked away the wheelchair.

'Won't be needing that,' he said.

JAX had been expecting a visit from the police – not his lawyer. He was surprised when he hadn't found the cops beside his bed the moment he came to, firing off questions and threats. Offering him a deal. Each day he woke up expecting them to appear, start firing off questions and offering him a deal. But they never came. He figured Father Martin had been right. They'd assumed Jax had just been in the wrong place at the wrong time. So what was his lawyer doing here now? Had they finally figured out what had happened that night at the base?

He decided he didn't care. His life was already over. Nikki was safe.

Confused yet intrigued, Jax followed his escort into the legal centre. He'd expected this facility to be modern and open, like the visits building, but it was just an old sandstone cell block that he thought must have been part of the original eighteenth-century prison.

'Gallows?' Jax asked the guard as he pointed towards the old wooden stairs at the end of the small wing.

'Yep,' the guard said. 'Would you believe they are historically listed? We can't pull them down. It's all original. Even the rope they used to hang 'em is still up there. Nothing has been touched since the last bloke was dropped in 1939.'

Jax had heard rumours about this block. 'Ever heard the phantom sing?' he asked, referring to the legend of the death-row singer.

'Nah,' the guard replied. 'Not me. But all the old fellas have. More than singing too. Some real freaky shit. That's why it's a legal centre now. None of them would come in here after dark, so they had to shut it down. It was only reopened a few years ago, when they decided to put the kennel here.'

Jax didn't have to ask what that meant. Even though no one would admit it, these rooms were frequently used by informants, or dogs. Inmates met detectives here, seeking a deal, or were summoned here by detectives who had something on them. Many a 'best mate' had been given up in these rooms. Even though every prisoner swore to remain staunch – 'death to dogs' and all that – plenty of inmates became informants of one sort or another. A reduced sentence was just too good to refuse.

The meeting rooms were in fact cells. Jax looked behind an open door as he passed and saw the rusted outline of a bunk bed still on the wall. It appeared the transformation had been simple, contractors replacing the bedding with an oversized table and a pair of bench seats, both stainless steel and bolted to the floor. D-hooks welded to the tabletops provided anchor points for handcuffs. The window was new, although the holes that once held iron bars had not been filled.

Most of the rooms were occupied when Jax arrived. The inmates with access to money – cash stashed in secret bank accounts or plastic-wrapped stacks buried in their backyard – met with their lawyers every other day. Jax had heard them brag about hiring the best and most expensive firms, about loopholes, grounds for appeal and new evidence. About how their money would get them out.

Even the inmates without money frequented this part of the prison. Often facing multiple yet-to-be-heard charges, they spent days and sometimes weeks locked away with their court-appointed lawyer, trying in vain to construct a defence.

Jax stopped as an inmate walked out of a cell in front of him.

'Jax,' Johnson said, looking surprised and suddenly turning white. 'Shit. I thought you were dead. Was it you? Everyone is saying it was you?'

Jax shrugged and then looked towards the room Johnson had just left.

'Another meeting with my fucking lawyers,' Johnson said. He wished Jax a speedy recovery before a guard moved him on.

Jax looked through the open door that Johnson had exited and saw two men in cheap suits preparing to leave. One of them was putting a black notebook into his breast pocket. Few would have noticed the NSW Police insignia on the front of the notebook. Jax did. Johnson was lucky that it was only Jax. His dirty secret was safe.

The guard directed him to the only other room with an open door; the rest were shut and locked, a red light on the wall indicating they were occupied.

'Inmate Riley Jax here for Tom Clarke,' the guard announced.

Tom Clarke?

CHAPTER 26

Supermax, Goulburn Correctional Centre, Goulburn, NSW, Australia

Wensley had to hurry. He was running out of room.

Three down, two left to solve.

He feared he may never get to finish this problem, or the next one. It wouldn't be long till the Serpent pushed him out.

He was surprised to find a fresh pack of chalk. Even more surprised that it hadn't been opened. Was this a trick? Maybe. But he would take his chances. He didn't have time for games.

Yellow. Wensley always used the yellow stick first. Sunshine. Oh, how he missed it. He smiled as he pulled the virgin stick from the packet, not just because the box didn't electrocute him or explode but also because he was imagining a sunrise. He had long wanted to draw a window on his wall. A sunrise scene. Always dawn. But every time he changed his mind as soon as he thought about the inevitable retribution, the rampage and ruin. Even though he had stolen the light and left Wensley to the dark, the Serpent hated the sun.

Wensley settled for a version of Van Gogh's *Sunflowers* instead. Yellow and bright, it was the sunniest thing he could think of that wasn't the sun. But it was still a risk. He didn't think for a minute that the Serpent would like his chalk masterpiece, and feared that it might even inspire him to hack off his own ear.

Stupid. He really was losing his mind.

Wensley noticed his cell was even messier than before, which told him that the Serpent had been in a mood. The officers refused to clean his room when the Serpent was acting up. Wensley also noted some new things in his cell – books, batteries and headphones – which told him the useless priest had been here again. He shook his head. Father Martin had promised to get rid of the Serpent, not bring him gifts.

Anyway, he didn't have time for that now, although he was intrigued by the travel guide. *No. Concentrate. No time.*

He started with his sunshine stick but was interrupted by the inmate in the adjoining cell banging on the wall. 'He's not here,' he yelled back. 'This is my time, not his.' Wensley wanted nothing to do with Hammad. The terrorist next door was the Serpent's friend, not his.

But still Hammad kept banging and now he was ranting too, reciting scripture.

'Shut up!' Wensley shouted as he moved away from his drawing. 'I don't have time for this.'

He turned to another section of his wall as the noise finally ceased.

'Yes,' he said to himself, as he zeroed in on the equation before him. 'That's it!'

Four down, one left to solve.

CHAPTER 27

Long Bay Correctional Complex, Sydney, NSW, Australia

JAX was in no mood for games.

'Who are you?' Jax asked. 'And what do you want?'

No response.

The man could have been aged anywhere from thirty to fifty. His skin was smooth and wrinkle-free: no crow's feet, age spots or sags, but his short-cropped hair was salt-sprinkled and starting to recede.

Unremarkable, Jax thought. Average height. Average build. Not handsome. Not ugly. His nose wasn't big or small. His lips weren't full or flat. His jawline was neither masculine nor feminine. His eyes weren't any one colour: blues, greens and browns mixed into ambiguity. He was the type of person that could change his look with a hairstyle. Change his age with a bottle of hair dye. Bland. Anonymous. Adaptable. The type of face that people forgot. That most people forgot.

This was the third time Jax had seen this man. He'd put the second time down to chance.

Jax kept his eyes firmly on the mystery man as he slid onto the metal bench. 'You are not my lawyer,' he said.

Jax left the statement hanging. He waited for a tell. He didn't get one.

'Correct,' the man said. 'Is that all you've got?'

Jax paused. Assessed the situation. Instead of answering, he leaned back and looked under the table. 'Ah, the shoes,' he said. 'Impressive.'

To the untrained eye they looked like regular dress shoes, but Jax knew they were also steel-capped, slip-resistant and stick- and fire-proof. Jax even knew the brand – these were cop shoes, not lawyer shoes.

'So, I'm a cop?' the man asked, looking Jax dead in the eye. He was unflinching, no expression for Jax to read.

Jax looked at his suit, tailored and pure wool, before shaking his head.

The man raised his head and met Jax's eyes. 'Officer Tom Clarke,' he said. 'ASIO.'

CLARKE reached down and grabbed his briefcase. He placed it on the desk, punched in the combination code, and clicked the lock open. He quickly shuffled his way through the contents, a kaleidoscope of coloured files. After pulling out a yellow file, he slid it across the table.

'Media clippings,' Clarke said. 'I'm guessing you don't get a lot of news in here. Have a read. Might save us some time.'

Jax opened the folder and started to flick through the stack of A4 pages within. They were plain text versions of the original newspaper reports, provided by a media tracking service called Page Track.

Islamic terrorists were planning on inflicting 'maximum damage' by blowing up Australia's only nuclear reactor, police claim.

A plot to blow up the Lucas Heights nuclear reactor in Sydney was yesterday foiled when police arrested 12 men with alleged links to ISIS. In Australia's biggest ever counterterrorism operation, a joint taskforce arrested the men during a series of simultaneous dawn raids across Sydney.

Police found a Sydney street map highlighting the site of the reactor and notebooks outlining police tactics and chains of command. An unspecified amount of explosives was also seized from the home of one of the 12 men arrested in the raids. A list of material needed to make explosives was found at another address.

Jax had heard nothing about this. The military prison had been a black hole. Kept in the brig from the time of his arrest until his sentencing, he'd had no word of the outside world at all. He hadn't even been allowed visitors. He was escorted off-base by armed soldiers to his legal meetings and taken to and from court in an armour-plated Humvee. Long Bay had not been much better, the only news he got coming from other inmates, whom he did his best to avoid.

He read the next page.

The mastermind behind the Sydney reactor bomb plot can be revealed as an Australian-born Islamic extremist who was trained by ISIS.

Ali Hammad, 52, from Greenacre in southwest Sydney, received expert training in bomb-making, surveillance and espionage from high-ranking Al-Qaeda soldiers at a terrorist training camp in Syria. Travel records also show Hammad spent time in Afghanistan and Iraq.

ASIO officers suspect Hammad to be the leader of Australia's first ever ISIS terrorist cell and will allege in court that he and the other 11 men arrested as part of 'Operation Flying Fox' were acting under orders originating from Syria.

All 12 men were denied bail and are being housed in police holding cells at the NSW Police Centre, Surry Hills.

Interesting. A local cell of an international terrorist group. Radicalised Australian men, trained overseas and then sent back home to put their training into practice. This was straight out of the Terror 101 textbook. Jax looked at Clarke for a hint of what this had to do with him, but the man simply nodded as if to indicate Jax should keep on reading.

The 'Terror 12' could be just one of 'several' cells operating in Australia, according to NSW Police.

As Australia's biggest terrorism case continues in the High Court, tendered police documents allege the terror cell headed by reported mastermind Ali Hammad was just one of 'several' groups of trained militants suspected to be operating in Australia.

Hammad is alleged to have knowledge of the other cells after being personally groomed by ISIS commanders.

The frightening document written by the nation's chief intelligence-gathering organisation also claimed Australia is ripe for an attack and urged the government to pass legislation to give ASIO, the Australian Secret Intelligence Service (ASIS) and the Federal Police special powers of arrest and detention, similar to those implemented in the US after 9/11.

A spokesman for the Opposition last night dismissed the report as an overreaction. 'It's hysterical rhetoric from an organisation trying to justify its existence,' the spokesman said. 'We have not been provided with any concrete evidence that Australia is at risk of a future attack. As far as we are concerned, the Lucas Heights reactor threat was a one-off.

'Certain organisations are using recent events to extort money from taxpayers by demanding funding increases and calling for unconstitutional and unlawful special powers. It is just fearmongering. Australia is half a world away from the real threat.'

Jax remembered learning about the seemingly inextricable link between terrorism and politics in his classes. History was littered with case studies highlighting the opportunism some governments and organisations showed in the aftermath of terror events – they'd capitalise on the widespread fear in the community to push through legislation or new powers, which they'd then exploit down the line for purposes other than public security and safety. Jax wasn't overly political, but you couldn't be in the army and not take some level of interest in this stuff – it governed your life as much as your commanding officer did.

He kept reading.

Ali Hammad and the 11 other men yesterday convicted of plotting to blow up a Sydney reactor will serve their sentences in a Goulburn jail after a request to incarcerate them in a specially built facility was denied.

The Sunday Telegraph can reveal that an ASIO bid to build a terrorist-only jail was torpedoed by the government. 'We are not having a Guantanamo in Australia,' said a government spokesperson. 'No Australian citizen, no matter what their crime, is going to be thrown into a black hole and denied their basic rights – not just their rights as an Australian but their rights as a human.'

ASIO mounted a case for all 12 men – and another seven already serving time for terror-related crimes – to be isolated from not only the public but also other prisoners.

Hammad is no stranger to jail, the now convicted terrorist previously having served a two-year sentence for fraud. It is understood he met a number of his co-conspirators while serving his sentence, split between Sydney's Long Bay Jail and the Goulburn Correctional Centre.

Jax closed the file and pushed it back across the desk. He now knew why Clarke was here.

'They are all on a truck and on the way to Goulburn as we speak,' Clarke said. 'We have told the government that these terrorists can't be treated like other prisoners. That they need to be isolated, cut off from everything and everybody. But they have blocked every piece of legislation we have proposed. While we've managed to get Hammad into Supermax, his co-offenders are going to be treated just like any other maximum-security prisoners. They'll get their phone calls, their visits, their computer privileges and their jobs. I think you can see the problem.'

'You're worried they'll reactivate their cell,' Jax said.

'I'm not so much worried about it as sure of it. The only way to stop them is with complete isolation.'

Jax suspected Clarke was right. He'd studied an Al-Qaeda training manual as part of an assignment during his degree. Originally seized by British police during a raid in Manchester, the document, dubbed the 'Manchester Manual', had been translated and posted all over the internet. Lesson Eighteen was the section that dealt with incarceration, and it went into some detail, too, including how to act in subsequent court appearances, how to send covert messages, how to conduct oneself, and when and how to recruit other inmates, even guards, to the cause. ISIS had adopted such manuals and practices from Al-Qaeda.

'Are you recruiting me to go undercover?' Jax asked Clarke.

'Yes. And I want you to be recruited by them.'

'And what makes you think I'll say yes?' Jax asked, not appreciating the man's attitude – a combination of hostility and condescension – towards him.

'Well, after that trick you pulled with the homemade IED, I'd say you don't get much of a choice,' he said. 'Mate.'

* * *

'IT'S done,' Clarke said, mobile phone pressed to his ear as he walked towards his car. 'Everything went as expected.'

Clarke listened as he opened his door.

'You should already have a copy of his training plan. It's all covered in the report. We'll send him to Goulburn as per the schedule.'

Clarke kept the phone pinned to his ear as the other man checked through his emails for the report.

'Yes,' Clarke said. 'It's not long, but he is a fast learner. And it's not like he's starting from scratch. We'll have him ready.'

Clarke was still listening as he started the car, his white Toyota Camry as bland as him. 'Yes,' Clarke said. 'He'll be transferred to Goulburn too. He's already been briefed. That all?'

He hung up without saying goodbye.

Finally. Seven years in the making, Project Mnemonist was now live. He had just activated Riley Jax.

CHAPTER 28

Sofia, Bulgaria

SAMI watched as camo-clad soldiers clutching M16 assault rifles marched back and forth, outnumbering even the travellers at Sofia International Airport. The soldier who'd pulled him aside upended Sami's backpack – a prepacked overnight bag he kept in his office, which was the only thing he'd had time to grab before heading off. The soldier carelessly poured the entire contents onto a stainless-steel countertop at the end of the X-ray conveyor belt.

'Little late to be taking precautions,' Sami sniped, grumpy after the local authorities had refused to fast-track him through customs after the private CIA plane had landed and Sami had disembarked. He was being processed like any other passenger.

But he knew better than to make trouble: some southeastern European countries had been known to refuse CIA personnel entry, or to mire them in a maze of bureaucracy and paperwork before they did so, sometimes delaying them by days – and a delay was the one thing Sami could not afford. And it was understandable, under the circumstances, that the normally

beefy security presence was now on steroids. He wasn't going
to get anywhere with anything less than complete cooperation.

So he zipped his mouth and stood there patiently as the
soldier picked through the contents of his bag, and then
inspected his passport and visa again. Eventually, Sami was
given the all-clear, his passport and visa were stamped and his
backpack roughly repacked. He thanked the soldiers politely
and made his way out of the terminal and into the grey and
crisply cold afternoon.

Mav was waiting for Sami out the front, parked directly –
and illegally – in front of the main exit. When Sami reached
him, Mav got out of the car, shook his hand and popped the
trunk of the black BMW hire car. Sami threw his backpack in,
then Mav pulled a heavy black overcoat out and pressed it into
Sami's hands. 'You'll be needing this, sir. It gets cold enough
to snap your balls off here.' Sami shrugged the overcoat on and
got into the passenger seat as Mav started the engine.

Sofia would have been a ghost town had it not been for
the heavy military and police presence. The only people
Sami could see, as Mav went about breaking every road rule
in Bulgaria, were in uniform. The capital, set at the foot of
the snow-capped peaks of the Vitosha mountain range, was
undeniably beautiful. But today it was also austere – its usually
bustling population of 1.3 million residents opting to staying
indoors after 412 people had been killed the day before in the
worst terror attack in the country's history.

It was also Europe's most lethal terror attack, eclipsing the
death toll from the Beslan School Hostage crisis in Russia in
2004, when 334 people were murdered. But it wasn't the dead
Sami was interested in, it was the living. Finally, they had a
witness. Witnesses, in fact. Four.

'It's all there,' Mav said as he broke yet another road rule –
both hands off the steering wheel – and passed Sami a file. 'I
interviewed the three that could talk; the other guy is in a coma.'

Sami pulled out the first transcript and read as Maverick sped towards the CIA office in central Sofia.

Statement of Mr Yavor Dimitrov (26 September, 9 am, interviewed by Special Agent Ryan Smith and translated by Ivan Stoyanov, Second Main Directorate, Bulgarian Committee for State Security)

Smith: Hello, Mr Dimitrov, my name is Special Agent Smith and I am here on behalf of the United States of America, which, in conjunction with the Bulgarian police, is investigating the St Nedelya Church attack. I'd like to thank you for your time and would also like to reaffirm that we are speaking to you strictly as a witness and in no way suspect you had any involvement in the attack. Do you understand?

Dimitrov: I do.

Smith: And are you willing to provide me with your recollections of the moments leading up to the attack and after the attack, so as to help us identify the attackers and stop further acts of this nature?

Dimitrov: I am.

Smith: And do you swear to provide a true and accurate version of these events, to the best of your knowledge?

Dimitrov: Yes.

Smith: Sorry about all that stuff, just a formality. Can you start by telling me why you were at the church yesterday?

Dimitrov: For mass. I go to the Friday-night mass because I like to sleep in on Sunday. Sunday is the only day I don't have work, so I like to go out on Saturday night. Hit the town.

Smith: Fair enough. I understand that you exited the church just before the attack. Can you tell me why you left?

Dimitrov: Yes. I got there before the start, maybe ten minutes early. I took a seat at the back. Many of the older people have no jobs and get there very early, even at four o'clock. Anyway, *my phone rang, maybe after five minutes or so. That was embarrassing because you are supposed to have them turned off, but my boss tells me never to turn it off, so I keep it on. So I stood up, answered the phone, told my boss to hang on a moment, and went outside.*

Smith: *And you made it outside?*

Dimitrov: *Yes.*

Smith: *And what happened next?*

Dimitrov: *I spoke to my boss. I told him I'd got a good price for the apartment. He said 'Good job' and I hung up.*

Smith: *And what happened when you ended the call?*

Dimitrov: *I went to go back into the church, but the doors were closed. I thought that was strange because the doors are never closed.*

Smith: *So what did you do?*

Dimitrov: *I knocked on the door and shouted hello. And then I heard the screams.*

Smith: *Screams?*

Dimitrov: *Yes. I knew then that something was wrong, so I ran away. Not because I am a coward, but to get help. And then … boom!*

Smith: *Okay. Let's back up a bit. Did you see anyone standing near the door when you walked out? Someone who stood out?*

Dimitrov: *Yes. I'll never forget this face. And I'm sure he was the bomber.*

Smith: *What did he look like?*

Dimitrov: *He was a big man, like a bouncer. And he had no eyebrows.*

Smith: *What about the rest of his face? Was he Slavic, Caucasian, African? What colour hair? Short, long?*

Dimitrov: *White. Maybe Slavic, maybe English. Hard to say. But I am sure he had no eyebrows, no hair on his face. And he smelled strange.*

Smith: What did he smell like?
Dimitrov: Like a hospital.
Smith: Do you mean bleach?
Dimitrov: Yes. Like bleach.
Smith: Was he wearing a backpack?
Dimitrov: Maybe. I don't know.

Sami pulled out the second transcript as Maverick took a corner as if he was in a rally race. The second witness was a Mrs Petya Georgieva. Sami skipped the formalities and got straight to the meat.

Smith: When did you first notice something unusual?
Georgieva: When the priest came out. He stood at the front looking at the back of church. I turned to see what he was looking at. I saw a man with a gun and a knife coming from the back [of the church].
Smith: A gun and a knife? Are you sure? Can you describe them?
Georgieva: Yes, I'm sure. The gun was black, not silver like those cowboy guns you see in movies. And the knife was big, like a Rambo knife.
Smith: Can you describe the man? What did he look like?
Georgieva: Yes. He was a strange man. He had no hair, no hair anywhere, not even eyebrows.
Smith: And how tall was he? And can you describe his body shape?
Georgieva: I can't really say. I was only looking at his face, the gun and the knife. I would say he was of normal build. You know? Not fat, not skinny, not small, not tall.
Smith: And what happened next?
Georgieva: People saw him and started to scream. He yelled for people to shut up or he [said he] would kill the priest.
Smith: And he said this in Bulgarian?

Georgieva: Yes, but badly. He had a thick accent and confused many words. When everyone stopped screaming, he asked the priest to speak English and the priest agreed. But I couldn't hear much after that, as I was in the middle of church and they spoke softly. The man then said something to the priest and pointed to the other man.

Smith: The other man? You mean to say there was another attacker?

Georgieva: Yes. There was another man standing in front of the door at the back of the church. He looked the same, like the one with the gun and knife. He had no hair too, and wore clothes like him: a black hoodie, black pants. He had no gun or knife. But he had a bomb.

Smith: How did you know he had a bomb?

Georgieva: Because the first man said so. He yelled in English, 'Everybody shut up or he'll blow this shit up.'

Smith: He said this in English?

Georgieva: Yes.

Smith: Did you recognise the accent?

Georgieva: Yes. He spoke like he was from England. Like the bald actor from those action movies. You know? The one from The Fast and the Furious.

Smith: Jason Statham?

Georgieva: Yes.

Smith: And where was the bomb?

Georgieva: I couldn't see it, but the man at the back had a backpack so I assumed it was in there.

Smith: And what happened next?

Georgieva: My husband whispered to me to sneak out when the man wasn't looking our way. To take my son Goran into the bathroom and climb out the window. He said if the man turned round, he would make a noise and distract him.

Smith: And did you manage to get to the bathroom?

Georgieva: Yes. But the window was too high, so I just I took Goran into a cubicle and locked the door. Then I heard screaming. Then a big bang. That's all I remember. And the next thing I knew, Goran and I were in an ambulance, and a man was telling us that we had survived because the bathroom, with its tiles and pipes, had strong walls.

Smith: I am sorry about your husband. I'll come back again tomorrow to see if you remember anything else. Please think about it. Write down anything you remember, even the smallest detail could help.

Sami moved to statement number three, a much smaller file – he'd have just enough time to get through it before they arrived at the office. Again, he skipped past the introductions.

Statement of Mr Goran Georgiev, age 12 (26 September, 10 am, interviewed by Special Agent Ryan Smith and translated by Ivan Stoyanov, Second Main Directorate, Bulgarian Committee for State Security)

Smith: You don't think he sounded English? Not like Jason Statham, the guy from The Fast and the Furious?

Georgiev: No. That's what Mama thinks but she can't tell difference between anyone who speaks English. I play rugby union at school, and I watch many games on TV, especially when the World Cup is on and Bulgaria play. I think he sounded like he was a Wallaby.

Smith: Excuse me. Did you say Wallaby?

Georgiev: Yes, a Wallaby. Australian. They wear yellow jerseys and are very good. Much better than Bulgaria, but not quite as good as the All Blacks. I've heard them speak to reporters after matches, so I know how they sound.

Smith: Are you certain? He was Australian?

> *Georgiev: Yes. A Wallaby. Or maybe an All Black. The Wallabies and the All Blacks sound the same.*

Maverick's mobile phone rang as they pulled into the basement car park of the building that housed the CIA's Bulgarian bureau. It was a short conversation.

'Survivor number four is dead,' Mav said as he put down his phone.

CHAPTER 29

Goulburn Correctional Centre, Goulburn, NSW, Australia

THE BIKIE could feel the cold steel pressing against his skin as he paced around the yard, stalking his prey. He would wait until he saw him before he pulled out the weapon: an eight-inch length of concrete reinforcement bar, one end sharpened to a point, the other covered with a makeshift handle fashioned from torn bedsheets and tape.

And then he would then thrust it into flesh, and keep on stabbing until Goulburn's newest prisoner was dead.

He moved as soon as he saw his target: young, white and fresh from Long Bay. He looked around before kneeling down to pull out the shiv, making sure the only guard patrolling the yard was still on the far side of the quadrangle. Yep, and his mate was doing as he'd been told, chatting away to the guard to distract him with whatever bullshit was spilling from his mouth.

He carefully slid the weapon up his sleeve, handle first – fortunately, no one had asked why he was wearing a jumper on such a warm day. He closed his palm around the stabbing end, the two inches of steel poking out the bottom of his sleeve.

The yard was teeming, prisoners everywhere. All out soaking up the sun. He cut straight through a makeshift handball court, ruining the point, the ball hitting his leg and bouncing away from the game.

'Replay,' yelled one of the players.

His target was the fourth of the newbies who'd come through the gate. Appearing completely lost, he had worked his way into a pocket of unoccupied space about twenty metres from the entrance. The fish out of water was looking right and left, standing up on his tiptoes every so often, searching for a familiar face. Someone he knew. Being alone was dangerous.

The bikie approached from behind, unseen by the target or the guard. He opened his palm; as the shiv dropped from his sleeve, he caught it with a snap of his wrist then drew his hand back. Locked and loaded.

Whack! The shiv went straight through the target's side, punching through the flesh like a knife in jelly.

Whack! Whack! Two more, so fast the attack had not yet registered with the victim.

Whack! Whack! Whack! The victim turned and took a swing, his wild, desperate punch hitting nothing but air.

Whack! Whack! Whack! Whack! The blows kept on coming: to the stomach, liver, kidneys and back. Blood spurted from the victim's belly, painting the attacker red. He licked his lips and growled. He wasn't done yet.

Whack! Whack! Whack! The next three thrusts punched holes in the young man's neck. The second struck an artery and a geyser of blood erupted, dark crimson, from his throat.

The killer stopped and nodded. Satisfied. 'Death to dogs,' he said before he turned away.

The shiv clunked on the concrete after he'd dropped it, bouncing before landing beside a fast-spreading pool of blood.

The victim followed the shiv to the ground, collapsing to his knees and grasping at his neck.

* * *

'JOHNSON!' Jax yelled as he rushed to the young man's side. 'Help! Over here.'

Jax started jamming his fingers into the holes in a desperate attempt to stop the blood, first in the man's neck, then his torso. But he soon ran out of fingers, and Johnson bled out on the concrete and almost silently passed away.

Johnson had arrived at Goulburn only the day before. He'd told Jax he had been transferred to Goulburn for his own protection. So much for that.

OFFICIALLY, Jax had been sent to Goulburn for his own protection too. Officially, he had been moved to the prison, three hours from Sydney, to get him away from the bikies, with word getting around that he'd been responsible for the cell bombing. While he refused to go into full protective custody, he did agree to be moved to Goulburn and be housed in a wing away from the majority of the white Australian inmates. He made no objection when the prison authorities told him of their plan to move him to A-Block, the 'Lebo' block, filled mostly with men with a Middle Eastern background. They even made it sound like it was their plan, whereas Jax knew that Clarke had simply cloned the Minister for Corrections' email account and issued the order electronically.

JAX didn't even bother putting the towel around his waist, simply flung it over his shoulder and left the shower cubicle. He didn't care who saw him naked. He didn't care what they thought or what they might do.

Two inmates walked into the shower room together, jostling and play-pushing.

'Fuck you, bra,' the big untattooed one said to his smaller mate, his heavy layer of fat only partially concealing the hard-earned muscles slumbering beneath. 'I'd never fuck a trannie. Except your Mum … I'd fuck her again.'

The little fella, whose face tattoos and mullet were fighting it out in the battle of the bogan, didn't get a chance to respond.

'You think that's funny, cunt?' the big man shouted at Jax. 'You think his mum's a slut? '

Jax responded with a stare, locking eyes with the loudmouth and not breaking step. He walked straight towards the question, his answer about to become apparent. Nowadays, Jax no longer looked at the ground, but always up, at whatever was coming.

'Well …' came the backdown. 'Don't do it. Bitch gave me herpes. Lucky you can't catch it twice, ha?'

Jax said nothing, as the pair parted to let him through.

'Whatcha doing, cuz?' the smaller prisoner whispered to his mate after Jax had walked by. 'You know who that is? Fuck, bra. You coulda got us killed.'

Jax was happy he hadn't had to fight – he had seen enough blood today.

Night was descending, darkness delivering a serving of white frost; fortunately the shower block was at least ten degrees warmer than the rest of the prison. Situated a hundred kilometres from the ameliorating effects of the ocean, at 700 metres above sea level, Goulburn was a place of extremes: skin-scorching summers and soul-freezing winters. Now, in spring, the days were hot but the nights were still cold. Jax was in no hurry to return to his frigid cell.

Towel still slung over his shoulder, he walked towards one of the six basins and put his '3-in-1: Body, Face and Hair' on the countertop. He looked at the mirror, covered in condensation, and gritted his teeth before pulling his towel off his shoulder and wiping it clear.

He still barely recognised the face that stared back at him. His once straight nose was crooked from breaks, and the shrapnel from the IED had left a generous smattering of ugly scars across his cheeks, forehead and chin. It made him look older than his nineteen years. It also made him look dangerous.

He was a lot bigger now. He hadn't stepped on a scale since Clarke had started him on a combination of anabolic steroids and human growth hormone, or HGH, but he had to be well over a hundred kilograms. Jax suspected the steroids were not a standard type, given the speed at which his body had transformed.

'Building your body will be the easy part,' Clarke had predicted. 'Learning how to use it will be the challenge.'

Jax could barely bench-press eighty kilos when the training started. He could now press 160. Six reps. Four sets. Form perfect.

Clarke had arranged to have his hospital stay extended at Long Bay. Jax trained in a newly upgraded occupational therapy room that boasted a state-of-the-art gym. Even though it was ostensibly available to anyone in the clinic, on the whole Jax had had the place mostly to himself. He knew that was no coincidence. It amazed him how far ASIO's reach extended within the prison system – it seemed Clarke could get Jax anything his heart desired. Except, of course, out of there.

The 'physiotherapist' who had continued to treat Jax long after most of his injuries had healed had also been arranged by Clarke. A former commando in Australia's Special Operations Command and a decorated martial-arts expert, Dr Greg Ferris was ASIO's hand-to-hand combat trainer. He taught men and women how to maim and murder. Jax spent a couple of hours with him every day, punching, kicking, elbowing and kneeing, and learning how to defend himself.

Jax had been surprised to learn how lethal he could be without a weapon. It took just seven pounds of force to crush a man's windpipe. Ferris had warned him to be careful with that move. Deadly, he'd said. A well paced and placed slap to the ear could make a man lose his balance for hours. Ferris had warned him about that one too. Also deadly. Jax had also been surprised to learn a man's foot was a good target: all those little bones. Ferris didn't warn him about that one. Obviously not deadly.

Jax had liked Ferris. He was the only person, aside from Father Martin, he had felt comfortable around. Maybe it was because he had been a soldier too.

With the showers still blasting and steam filling the room, Jax's reflection was slowly obscured by a fresh layer of condensation. When he could see nothing more than a foggy outline of himself, he picked up his towel and wiped again. Then he stepped back, half-expecting to see his former self. But again, it was the stranger.

Riley Jax was gone. Dead. He had become one of them.

Clarke had offered to get Jax off the hook for his crimes, promising he would never be charged, let alone trialled, for the murders of Billy Briggs, Daniel Marsh, Milo Grubetski, Charlie Moran, James Warren, Paul Fitzpatrick, and Dean Spanos, should he agree to assist. But Jax rejected that offer, didn't try to avoid a probable life sentence.

'Make me one promise,' Jax had said. 'Look after Nikki. Do that and I'll do whatever you ask.'

When not in the gym, pressing and pulling, punching and pumping, Jax had sat in a legal visits room with Clarke, for at least three hours a day, taking lessons, planning and plotting, being briefed – a crash course, in other words, in becoming a spy.

Jax was surprised how much he already knew, partly from his university course – he realised it had been more on point than he'd given it credit for at the time. The rest he picked up pretty easily, inhaling the texts, files and cases he was given and easily committing them all to memory. Jax didn't even try to hide his processing and recall abilities from Clarke – what was the point?

But then he suspected he already knew. That would explain why Jax had seen him twice before he turned up at Long Bay: once at his army base and then at his trial.

IN FACT, Project Mnemonist had begun when Jax was twelve.

'What's an eidetiker?' Clarke had asked when he read the boy's medical report.

He'd soon learned that an eidetiker was a person with a photographic memory. A mnemonist. And that a doctor suspected a twelve-year-old male patient had a one-in-a-hundred-billion neurological condition that meant he would never forget a thing. Thankfully, that doctor had known that what he had on his hands was something special, and he'd brought the case to the attention of a professor friend of his. The professor, in turn, had alerted ASIO.

And so the studies had started: scans and X-rays, exams and evaluations, tests and tasks. And the twelve-year-old boy named Riley Jax was revealed not only to be mnemonist, just the fifth confirmed eidetiker in history, but also a genius with an estimated IQ of 222.

There followed a battery of psychological tests. Jax's scores for the five personality traits used by first the CIA, and subsequently ASIO, to recruit agents – openness, conscientiousness, extraversion, agreeableness and neuroticism – were smack bang on the perfect mean. They further broke down his personality and natural tendencies, and again the boy scored well – for courage, honour, flexibility, confidence, humility, amicability, subjectiveness and objectiveness. He would have achieved a perfect score for a spy, except that he had too much empathy. Still, no one at ASIO had ever seen anything like it. Nor had anyone at the CIA – Clarke had personally placed a call to Langley to check.

A board of independent experts – psychologists, neuroscientists and neurosurgeons – had been called in to review the results and verify them, and to study Jax. They'd all confirmed it: Riley Jax was exactly what ASIO thought he was – a remarkable and rare human being, a cognitive mystery. And, potentially, the perfect spy.

CLARKE had headed up the 'blank cheque' project from day one. It had been a huge opportunity for him and accelerated his career significantly. He was relatively junior for such a highly classified and unprecedented experiment – a black op – but he had made Riley Jax his obsession, so, in the end, he was the obvious choice. Project Mnemonist and Riley Jax were going to be the making of Clarke. He knew it back then and he knew it now.

Since ASIO had got involved, every moment of Jax's life had been scripted.

Jax's grandmother couldn't afford to buy him a PC or a smartphone, so ASIO arranged for her to win these items in an RSL raffle. Then they made sure a series of subliminal cues came up on the youngster's screen, via PC pop-ups, Facebook and Instagram posts and online advertisements, to spark his interest. They also went low-tech with the tried and true: strategically placed billboards, posters and people.

Jax's high-school maths teacher, who just happened to be the only high-school maths teacher he had ever had and just happened to be an ASIO agent, encouraged him.

Leaving school to join the army was ASIO's idea. Not his. Becoming a combat engineer was their idea. Not his.

Further subliminal messaging and a push from an army careers adviser – who was in fact another undercover agent – smoothed the way.

Undertaking a counterterrorism degree was their idea too. Not only that, it was also their degree. The Bachelor of Counterterrorism, Security and Intelligence, which Jax had earned by correspondence with the University of New South

Wales, was in fact an ASIO course, tailor-made for one student only. Clarke had even had agents pose as other online students for a group task.

Clarke thought the army would rid Jax of his empathy. The video games, subliminal messages and prearranged bullying had failed to do so. But Clarke was confident the army would fix that and turn Jax into the killer he needed to be. And show him the true worth of a human life: nothing.

Clarke was wrong. While Jax didn't shy away from taking a shot when they sent him to Afghanistan, he did not take a life. Not one. And while that was plausible for a bad marksman, Jax was a crack shot. He had proved himself to be as good as any sniper on the range, but he only ever hit legs, shoulders, maybe a hand, never a heart or head. This, of course, proved how good a marksman he was. And that he was no killer.

Clarke had saved Project Mnemonist by coming up with the prison plan. While finding a body had been easy, convincing his superiors to send a teenager to jail was not. They only agreed on the condition of plausible deniability. It would be his arse and his alone. But that was okay because Clarke would not fail. He never failed.

Still, he resisted gloating after Jax had killed the paedophile, knowing how much there was yet to do. And while the bombing had been another breakthrough, Jax was still far from field-ready. Clarke hadn't destroyed Jax yet. While he may have broken him, Clarke wanted him in a thousand pieces before he began the long, meticulous, precisely planned process of putting him back together.

Project Mnemonist was not due to go operational for another five years. But then twelve terrorists had tried to turn Sydney into Chernobyl. Broken would have to do.

JAX'S cell in Goulburn was bigger than the one in Long Bay, but otherwise much the same. What was significantly different was that he had a cellmate: Khalil Khadir, the youngest member of the Terror Twelve, and the inmate identified by ASIO as most likely to befriend Jax. After weeks of briefing with Clarke back at Long Bay, Jax was pretty sure he knew Khalil Khadir better than the man knew himself.

That night, Jax closed his eyes and pretended to doze off while he waited for Khalil to fall asleep. Once Khalil's breathing deepened, Jax trod softly across the cell to the young man's bunk. Rather than poking him to check he was in a deep sleep, he simply listened.

Jax was soon certain Khalil was out cold, not just because of the drug he had put in his drink, but because of the way he was breathing. The surest way of determining whether or not someone was in a state of REM was by measuring their breathing rate, and Khalil's breathing rate had decreased by twenty per cent since Jax's last count. A drop of between fourteen and twenty-four percent meant they were out. A drop of between twenty-five percent and fifty percent meant get help. A drop of fifty percent or more meant to the sleeper would soon be dead.

Jax's daily dose of medication from the prison dispensary always looked the same: six capsules – two green and white, two red and yellow, and two solid blue – but they would rarely be filled with the drug they were purported to contain. The blue ones, supposedly an over-the-counter antihistamine called fexofenadine, were in fact a blend of human growth hormone and anabolic steroids. The green and white (paracetamol) and the red and yellow (diclofenac) were filled with whatever he had requested: sometimes an upper to keep him awake, sometimes a downer to knock someone out.

Jax had laced Khalil's drinking water with a mild dose of flunitrazepam. Clarke had told him to use the contents of an entire capsule, all five milligrams of the prescription-only sleeping pill commonly known as Rohypnol, the so-called date rape drug, but Jax had only given Khalil half. He was only small, about sixty kilograms, and Jax had worried that his new cellmate might never wake up if he gave him the lot.

Jax slid across the cold floor, pushing one sock forward at a time, silently skating on the concrete. Khalil was snoring by the time he reached his box shelves, where he kept his two plastic tubs and 'buy-ups'. The cell was dark, the only sources of light a finger of moonlight coming in through the high, barred cell exterior window and the reflection of the fluorescent overhead lights in the wing, coming through the cell's small internal window. It wasn't much, as the overhead lights were only half-lit at night, but just enough to enable the guards to do their rounds.

Jax had to feel for the false front at the bottom of his shelves. He popped the magnetic lock and pulled the false front free. Then, lying on the ground, he pushed his arm into the cavity. He reached around, feeling for the item he was after, touching objects and pushing them aside. He found the small metal penlight. Arm back out, he put the penlight between his teeth as he pushed the false front back into place.

He grabbed the package that had been delivered to his cell earlier that day from underneath his mattress.

LEGAL MAIL: DO NOT OPEN: Riley James Jax, Case No. S309/2019, 171/CLR, HCA:24.

With the tiny torch still between his teeth, he opened the envelope and went through the hundred or so pages Clarke had sent under the guise of legal mail – which was the only type of mail that could not be opened by anyone other than the inmate it had been addressed to. Most of it was rubbish: fake court transcripts and fake case notes. But buried in the middle of the stack was the document Jax was looking for – an update from Clarke.

J,

An inmate named Mahmud Elias has been identified as a person of interest. Can you please investigate. Attached is his police file. I expect a full and complete report.
C.

Jax opened the file and read on:

Elias, Mahmud.
Age: 64
Country of birth: Syria
Home address: 248 Wanga Road, Greenmount, NSW
Weight: 73 kg
Height: 181 cm
Eye colour: Brown
Hair colour: Brown

Charge or charges: Unlawful Importation of Firearms; Conspiracy to Murder; Threatening or Intimidating Victims or Witnesses; Conspiracy to Escape from Lawful Custody.

Sentence: Jailed for a minimum of sixteen years and six months.

Appearance: Slightly built and standing at just over 180 cm. Of Middle Eastern descent, Mr Elias is a first-generation Australian. He migrated from Syria in 1978. He has olive skin, brown eyes and dark hair. Mr Elias is known to wear his hair short, and has stage 2 male pattern baldness. He was clean shaven at the time of his last court appearance. Mr Elias has a three-inch scar on his left knee. He also suffers from a mild form of vitiligo, which has caused minor skin spotting and discolouration on his lower left arm. Mr Elias has no tattoos. He has no known ailments, other than his skin condition, that affect his physical appearance. His teeth are slightly yellowed with tartar build-up noticeable towards the gum. He also suffers from mild gingivitis, which gives him slightly pronounced teeth due to gum recession.

Notes: Regarded by others in his community as a mufti, an authority on Islamic law. But compliant and not considered dangerous. Transferred to a maximum-security facility following a foiled escape attempt from a medium-security facility.

After reading the update, Jax stashed the bundle of pages back into the bottom of his box shelves and replaced the false front. He wouldn't need to read the file again, but he couldn't risk putting them in the bin.

'SHIT,' Khalil said. 'Shit, shit, shit.'

He swung his feet from his bed and looked at his wristwatch – a prison buy-up no-name – with an evil eye, as if it had betrayed him, then smacked his finger into its LCD screen, either to check it was working or to punish it. Jax couldn't be sure.

'What's wrong with this thing,' Khalil said. 'Stupid alarm didn't go off.'

Jax had been awake well before Khalil's alarm should have gone off at 6.15 am, just as it had every morning since Khalil had moved into the two-out cell. After realising Khalil had passed out before setting the alarm, Jax had thought of setting it, but decided against it. He thought Khalil would blame himself for forgetting to set the alarm – but blaming the cheap watch was just as good. Khalil would also blame the flu for his sore head, rather than think it was a drug-induced hangover.

Jax watched from his bed, covers on and head propped up on his pillow, as Khalil took a moment to steady himself after standing. The inmate rubbed his eyes and yawned before leaning down to pull the prayer mat from under his bed.

'Better late than never,' Khalil said to Jax.

Jax suspected this wasn't the first time Khalil had been late for his morning prayer.

Khalil unfurled his mat, blue with a white tapestry of a mosque. Half of the now grubby, once-white tassels had fallen out. Khalil's prayer mat was plain compared to others Jax had seen. Even Afghan farmers prayed on better mats. He couldn't be sure what the material was without touching it, but he was certain it was not Egyptian cotton like the one his platoon interpreter used to roll out.

Khalil positioned the mat below the cell window, got down on his knees and faced the sun. Jax had almost corrected him the first time he'd watched Khalil pray: he wanted to point out that Mecca was due west and that therefore he should be looking away from the rising sun, at least in Australia, not towards it. But an infidel like Jax was not supposed to know things about Mecca.

Jax wondered how Khalil would have reacted if he'd told him that Muslims once prayed to Jerusalem instead of Mecca, the sudden switch in the second year of the Hijra casting doubt on the validity of the entire religion. And that even though he was facing the wrong way, he was also facing the right way because while most Muslims think that God won't be listening if you are not facing Mecca, according to the Prophet Muhammad, God can be found by looking either east or west. Either way. Doesn't matter. Jax wondered exactly how much Khalil knew about Islam at all. The religion he was prepared to kill himself for.

Clarke's files told him that Khalil had only a limited and skewed understanding of Islam, imparted by a manipulative terror group leader. But Jax had no plans to give Khalil a religious lesson, today or any other day. In fact, he intended to say very little to Khalil today, just as he had done over the previous four days. He would speak only when spoken to and respond with a single word, either yes or no. Tomorrow, he would start to extend his answers to sentences, and maybe even start some conversations of his own a few days later. Little by little, he would befriend his cellmate.

Jax would not reveal his expert knowledge of Islam but he would soon show an interest – and then a burning desire to belong. He'd tell Khalil how he'd been a loner at Long Bay. Tell him he had no one left and nothing to live for.

And that's when Khalil would take him to the others. To the men he'd been asked to spy on.

Or, at least, that was the plan.

CHAPTER 30

Mexico City, Mexico

SAMI sat at his assigned desk, sweating profusely, partly because just one shitty spilt-system air-conditioning unit was attempting to cool the entire demountable and partly because he was anxious.

The results of the DNA tests were due back today. They could land in his inbox at any moment. It was the lead they'd been praying for: something that could help them identify the terror group that had killed 883 people in six attacks – in France, Russia, Italy, America, Bulgaria, and now Mexico.

Exactly a month after the blast in Bulgaria, the group by then known as the 'Church Bombers' had struck in Mexico City, at the Church of San Felipe Neri, resulting in the deaths of thirty-three people. Bald, holding a backpack and screaming '*Allahu akbar*' before detonating the bomb, the 'gringo' at the back of the church had been blown back out onto the street. The blast had claimed the lives of another twenty-eight people, sixteen killed instantly and twelve later dying from wounds. The church would have been levelled, all 186 killed, had the bomb been as powerful as the last five. Residue collected from the scene suggested an error in the chemical cooking process.

Also bald, holding a knife and a gun, and screaming '*Allahu akbar*' after his co-attacker had detonated the underpowered bomb, the gringo at the front of the church had opened fire when the explosion hadn't gone as planned. Standing over the dead priest, blood dripping from his blade, he'd shot three people dead. He would have killed more – there were another twelve rounds left in his Glock – had the Tierra Caliente drug cartel enforcer in the congregation not shot him dead, the bullets from the gold-plated and diamond-encrusted Desert Eagle handgun removing the terrorist's face.

SAMI had only ever been to Mexico on holiday. To places like Cancun and Cozumel. He had taken the twins to Acapulco just a few years back, when they still returned his calls. As an Islamic terror specialist, Sami hadn't needed to go to Mexico professionally. Not to a country that was considered too poor and not Western enough to be a target.

But now here he was, sitting in a demountable at the edge of a disused runway on a US military base shared by the DEA, FBI, DoD and CIA and guarded by the Marines – his home for last three days. He'd made only one trip out, to see the faceless body in the morgue.

He was about to call the lab – again – when his computer pinged. He looked down and saw the email he'd been waiting for.

To: Hudson Sami (Sami1@cia.gov)
From: langley.lab3@cia.gov
Subject: DNA match request 1 – Mexico City
Special Agent Sami,

Please find the details of your first DNA match request below.
Also attached are the medical report and a series of files provided
by the NSW Police in Australia.
NAME: Charlie Haddad
AGE: 22
NATIONALITY: Australian
LAST KNOWN ADDRESS: 12a Ford Street, Punchbowl,
NSW, Australia
Apologies for the delay.
Regards,
Dr Walter Creswell, CIA Chief Medical Examiner,
George Bush Center for Intelligence,
1000 Colonial Farm Road, McLean, Virginia, 22101

Sami didn't bother opening the autopsy report or the file with
the DNA code he knew he wouldn't understand. Instead, he
went straight to the file provided by the NSW Police.

Haddad, Charlie: Age 22
12a Ford Street, Punchbowl, NSW
ETHNICITY: Australian of Lebanese descent
BORN: Bankstown Hospital, NSW
HEIGHT: 179 cm
WEIGHT: 81 kg
APPEARANCE: Of average height and build. Brown eyes
and closely cropped hair. Also wears a neat beard.
DISTINGUISHING FEATURES: Full back tattoo, with a
Lebanese Cedar tree being the central feature. A cleft lip.
Charged with public nuisance and disturbing the peace.
Charged with shoplifting.
Charge with vandalism and fleeing from police.
Charged with assault with a weapon occasioning actual bodily
harm.

Sentenced to serve three years in the Minda Juvenile Justice Centre.
Charged with assault causing actual bodily harm.
Sentenced to serve a minimum of three years in Goulburn Correctional Centre.
Failed to report for parole at Bankstown Police Station.
Arrest warrant issued for breach of parole.
Location of suspect still unknown.

An Australian. A former inmate from a place called Punchbowl. Another ping.

To: Hudson Sami (Sami1@cia.gov)
From: langley.lab3@cia.gov
Subject: DNA match request 2 – Mexico City
Special Agent Sami,
Please find the details of your second DNA match request below. Also attached are the medical report and a series of files provided by the NSW Police in Australia.
NAME: Mike Evans
AGE: 21
NATIONALITY: Australian
LAST KNOWN ADDRESS: 231 Riverview Avenue, Riverview, NSW
Regards,
Dr Walter Creswell, CIA Chief Medical Examiner,
George Bush Center for Intelligence,
1000 Colonial Farm Road, McLean, Virginia, 22101

Sami opened the police file.

Mike Evans,
231 Riverview Avenue, Riverview, NSW
AGE: 21

ETHNICITY: White Caucasian
BORN: Riverview Hospital, NSW
HEIGHT: 174 cm
WEIGHT: 78 kg
DISTINGUISHING FEATURES: No known tattoos or
scars.
Charged with destruction of property.
Charged with vandalism.
Charge with assault.
Sentenced to serve two years in the Minda Juvenile Justice
Centre.
Charged with robbery.
Sentenced to serve 14 months in Goulburn Correctional Centre.
Failed to report for parole at Bankstown Police Station.
Arrest warrant issued for breach of parole.
Location of suspect still unknown.

Two Australians. Both of them former inmates, sharing both a juvenile prison and a maximum-security one, by the look of the rap sheets. Both of them failing to report for parole in the same month. Both of them then going missing – until now. One shot dead in a church and the other blown to bits, identified by half an arm.

Sami logged onto the CIA database, deciding to try his luck. He ran a couple of searches, sifting through the names of all Australian individuals involved in crimes outside Australia and in the locations of the Church Bombings since the first blast.

Bingo.

He read the file. 'Well, I'll be …' he said to himself, the CCTV footage from outside the Church of the Saviour on Spilled Blood in St Petersburg coming back to him. 'That's why there was only one of 'em …'

On the day after the St Petersburg attack, a Russian CIB officer had found a suitcase washed up on the shore of the

Neva River. Inside were the remains of an Australian, Timothy Jenkins. He'd spent time in the same correction facility as the pair of suicide bombers who'd hit the Mexican church. Jenkins' body didn't fit the profile – he had hair on his head and his eyebrows and lashes were intact – but his teeth had been smashed out, and the other identifiers matched up: age, nationality, rap sheet and failure to report for parole.

Sami picked up his phone and called Maverick.

'I hear the weather's nice in Australia this time of year,' he said.

CHAPTER 31

Goulburn Correctional Centre, Goulburn, NSW, Australia

'HEY, Riley,' Khalil shouted across the yard, 'over here. *Yalla, yalla.*'

Jax pretended to look surprised as the invitation he had spent every minute of every day working towards finally arrived.

'Yeah, come on, bro,' Khalil called out again. 'It's all sweet. Come and meet 'em.'

Jax had played the part of the ready-to-be-radicalised man perfectly. Appearing anxious and alienated, insecure and impressionable, dependent and dejected, he'd gradually and systematically put on show all the personality traits that terrorists look for in a recruit. He'd read the textbook, and ensured he was a textbook target.

'Hey, man,' Khalil said as Jax neared. 'Come meet my brothers. This is the Sheik.'

Jax moved forward and took the hand of Abbas Bashir, a self-appointed sheik with loose links to a Sydney mosque and the man suspected to have assumed leadership of the Terror Twelve now that Hammad was isolated in Supermax. Jax had been tasked with confirming this appointment, as well as identifying the role of every member of the cell.

'*As-salamu alaykum*,' Jax said as he shook Bashir's hand. 'Ah, damn it. I stuffed that up, right?'

'*Alaykum as-salam*, my brother,' Bashir replied. 'No, not at all. The effort flatters me. Please call me Bashir.'

Bashir was wearing a white *taqiyah*, or skull cap. Not just any white *taqiyah*, Jax noted, but the one he had been gifted when he'd been anointed Chief Recruiter, Al-Qaeda, Southeast Asia Station. The small tear at the base and the red stain were a give-away. Abu Bakar, Osama Bin Laden's deputy, had personally placed the Islamic hat on Bashir's head following a training camp in Malaysia, or so his ASIO file said.

Bashir turned to Khalil.

'You make a fine teacher, my brother,' Bashir said. 'You have kept this talent hidden from us, no?'

Since being sentenced to serve twenty years in jail – the second-longest of the sentences dished out to the Terror Twelve – Bashir hadn't altered his appearance. He still wore a long beard without a moustache and kept his hair, under the *taqiyah*, short. He studied Jax momentarily before continuing the conversation in Arabic, this time asking if he was fluent.

'Uh?' Jax replied. 'You talking to me?'

Bashir looked at Khalil. 'Maybe you are not so good a teacher?' He laughed. 'But "Peace be upon you" is a fine start.'

He smiled at Jax. 'Sorry for making a joke.' Please join us, *habibi*. Khalil has told us much about you. Any *habib* to Khalil is a *habib* to us all. Now meet all my *habibis*.'

Bashir took his eyes from Jax and looked towards Fasin Halim. Short and stocky, a powerful-looking man, Halim did not wear the skull cap or a beard like Bashir. 'Good to meet you, mate,' he said. Years of working on construction sites had made him sound as Aussie as a sausage sizzle. 'Please let me know if you ever need anything.'

If only it were that simple.

Halim, Halim and Halim Construction Company (HHHCC) had an estimated wealth of $730 million. ASIO had seized almost $30 million worth of cash and assets when they'd arrested the Twelve, but the other $700 million remained unaccounted for. So ASIO had followed a trail, an elaborate network of shell companies and offshore accounts, all the way to Lebanon. But there it had stopped dead, at a company registered in Beirut, Kol Khara Ya Kalb. Which in English was: 'Eat Shit You Dog'.

So another of Jax's tasks was to find the missing millions. He was to establish trust and work himself into the group, become Fasin Halim's friend. He knew Halim was materialistic, and he'd seen that without his cash he had started to slide down in the group's pecking order. Clearly, he needed something that would make him more important than the rest, help restore his status. Jax would talk to him, find out what he needed, what he wanted. And then he would deliver it – with the help of ASIO of course. Then Jax, quite naturally – he was in prison, after all – would ask that any payments be transferred electronically from Halim's account to his own secret account. That would reconnect ASIO with the money trail, which would in turn lead to Halim's millions. And without his money, the cell was done.

'And this is Mahmud,' Khalil now said. 'He has been in here for many years and knows everyone.'

Jax took note of ASIO's mystery man.

Finally, Jax was introduced to 'soldiers' Adam and Kyle Kent. Jax didn't bother with Arabic this time, knowing the Australian-born and raised brothers did not speak a word of the language. He also knew that they had only recently been reunited. Originally, as part of a half-baked plan to split the terror cell, Kyle had been housed in a different wing of the prison, along with another six members of the Terror Twelve. The government was attempting to appease ASIO, which had recommended isolation for every member of the Twelve, by putting their leader in

Supermax and splitting the remaining eleven across two prison blocks. But Kyle had recently been moved into Adam's block after his lawyer had successfully appealed to have them closer together on compassionate grounds. Halim attempted to follow suit by making an appeal to have his two brothers, Kazem and Mahir, moved over to his block. While ASIO did not fight to keep the Kent brothers separated because they were considered bottom-of-the-rung soldiers, it drew the line at this and successfully blocked Halim's appeal.

Following the introductions, Khalil put an arm around Jax and took him off to the side. 'Told ya it would be sweet,' he said. 'And don't listen to what anyone else says, they are top blokes. They'll look after you.'

Jax heard Fasin speaking in the background, in Arabic.

'I don't trust him,' Fasin was saying. 'I don't care what Khalil says.'

'Believe me, he is sweet,' Khalil called back to the group in Arabic.

Bashir intervened, also speaking Arabic: 'He and only He can decide if this man is worthy. Our merciful Lord will guide us. If this man does good deeds and is a believer, his efforts will not be ignored. Nor will they if he is a disbeliever, the fires of Hell his eternal damnation. Allah the almighty will decide if he joins our mission.'

'All of you, shut up,' Mahmud said in Arabic. 'Silence. No more. Not even in Arabic. We speak of nothing in the open. We can only talk of the mission during meetings.'

They all nodded, except for the Kent brothers and Jax, who, despite looking dumbfounded, had understood every word.

'What's going on?' he asked Khalil. 'Did I do something wrong?'

CHAPTER 32

Canberra, Australia

THE rising sun had set fire to the water, which blazed red, orange and yellow, all the blue hiding under a sheet of glass. With no whisper of wind, the surface of Lake Burley Griffin had turned into a mirror. An early-morning rower glided across the fiery surface, leaving a wake of spitting embers.

Sami looked out the window of the speeding sedan, a Holden Commodore, admiring the view. Everything had been so bleak back in the US. He couldn't remember a darker fall, everything cold, colourless and dying. But here, half a world away, everything burned bright. The heavy tint on the black Commonwealth car did little to dull the colours, the blues and greens almost as spectacular as the auburn flame thrown by the sun. He felt a flush of hope.

'How long until we get into the city?' he asked the driver.

'This is the city, mate. Welcome to Canberra.'

Sami pushed himself off the back seat, leaned forward and peered out the front windscreen.

'That's a city?' he asked.

'You betcha, mate. Capital of Australia.'

Sami was on his way to brief his Australian counterparts. Of course he would share any intelligence that wasn't classified and any intelligence that indicated a direct and immediate threat to Australia. But in truth, it was simply a courtesy call and he planned to mainly shake hands, smile and answer most of their questions – and he was certain they would have many – with 'Sorry, that's classified.'

As a spy, Sami wasn't supposed to trust anyone, but he allowed himself to do so now and again – he was never one for rules. And while he knew that might be seen as a flaw, he liked to think of it as a strength. But Sami's trust had to be earned, and this was his first trip to Australia. He had never dealt with ASIO before.

'Behave yourself once we're in there,' he cautioned Mav. 'You might not like it, but this is their country and we are just visiting. As far as they know, we are here to help.'

Working with an ally could be difficult. While he could simply ignore the laws of a country with which the US had no official agreement, in a place like Australia he and Mav were supposed to adhere to the local rules. Apparently, Australia had a long list of don'ts when it came to dealing with suspected terrorists: sleep deprivation, waterboarding, electrocution and even heavy-metal music were among the most fucking definitely do not. He'd had plenty of time to plough through ASIO protocols as he flew from Mexico City to Los Angeles, Los Angeles to Sydney and, finally, Sydney to Canberra. Twenty-nine hours in total.

Mav sighed, and rolled his eyes.

'I'm serious,' said Sami. 'You don't tell them anything without checking with me first. You certainly don't start giving out orders.'

Mav sighed again but gave a small nod of acceptance. 'Yeah, boss, got it.'

The government car made its way through a number of checkpoints and finally dropped them in front of the Ben Chifley Building, where they'd been told someone would be waiting for them. Although its sleek, curved design was certainly striking, Sami noted it was postage-stamp sized compared with their headquarters back home.

Wanting to lighten the mood after his pep talk, Sami looked around, then turned to Mav. 'Look out for kangaroos!' he said, laughing. 'Though I don't think they're just jumping around cities, to be fair.'

Mav looked unimpressed by his attempt at humour. *Always too cool for school, that Mav*, Sami thought.

The chief of the Oceanic Bureau, CIA Agent Ford Roberts, was waiting for them in the foyer. Bald, sun-beaten and slightly hunched, he stood in front of the two-factor-authenticated security gates, looking like he was in desperate need of a chair.

'Is that Rupert Murdoch?' Maverick joked, loudly.

'Shhh!' Sami said, choking back a laugh. 'You'll get us both deported.'

The CIA had only a token base in Australia – its only real interest there was in monitoring Chinese criminals who used Australia as an offshore bank. Sami suspected Roberts had been sent to Canberra as part of a retirement plan. Judging from his tan, he probably spent most of his days sitting on the beach. Sami suspected that Agent Roberts would be about as much help as the Australians would be on the Church Bombings. Unless he needed a beach towel.

CLARKE sat alone in the briefing room, a glass of water next to his colour-coded files. The red file on top was labelled 'Project Mnemonist'. He'd been holed up in the Ben Chifley Building for the last two days, grabbing sleep here and there, just an hour or two on the office couch when he could no longer read the words on his computer screen.

The CIA revelation that at least two of the Church Bombers were Australian had thrown him into the forefront of the world's biggest international terrorism investigation, a geopolitical shitstorm that already had planet Earth on the brink of a world war. A clusterfuck that could cost him his job.

'Who the fuck are they?' the Director of ASIO, one of the few men in the world to know the Mexico bombers were Australian, had demanded. 'How and why? Why are we hearing this from the CIA? Who are these blokes and why have I never heard of them? And what about the rest of them? Another nine? Fuck me. How could we not know about any of this? How could you not know about any of this? Just what the fuck is it that you have been doing for the last two years? For fuck's sake. FUCK! I'm not going to cop a bullet for this. You'd better fuck off and find me some answers if you want to keep your job. FUCK! Get something, anything, before the Yanks get here. Don't make us all look as fucking stupid as you.'

Clarke and his team, two of them now on the way up to join him in the conference room, had scrambled, pulling files, hitting the phones and writing reports. He was quite satisfied with what they had put together, all of it now in the files stacked neatly in front of him, meticulously in order. Starting a briefing with paper files was a time-honoured tradition at ASIO and had once been the way a whole investigation was handled. Although nowadays most of the info was stored digitally, people still tended to like old-school when it came to initial briefings. There was something more tangible about details when you were holding them in your hand.

One file contained complete and thorough histories of each of the dead Australian bombers: police records, court transcripts, school reports and employment histories, even their hobbies, political leanings and favourite foods. Clarke's guys had conducted over a dozen phone interviews with associates of each man in under twenty-four hours.

A thicker file contained a comprehensive geopolitical study and profile of the unknown terror group. The extraordinary attempts taken to mask the identities of the attackers were believed to be part of a well-considered ploy to sow confusion and spread blame. The mastermind behind the movement wanted as wide a range of countries as possible to come under suspicion, so that the inevitable retaliatory attacks on countries known to harbour terrorists – Iran, Saudi Arabia, Syria, Sudan, Cameroon and Malaysia – would spark further retaliation and, in turn, a global conflict.

The military power of each of the attacked nations was noted: America (third-largest army in the world), Russian Federation (fifth), Mexico (seventeenth), France (twenty-second) and Italy (twenty-eighth). The only one of the targeted countries without the ability to inflict catastrophic damage on another nation was Bulgaria, with an army of just 33,000. It was an anomaly, but not enough to nullify the theory. Russia, the United States, Italy and France had cordial relations, but would act independently, without consensus or approval, and possibly in haste, each determined to take their own revenge, show their own strength. The terrorists' endgame, the theory predicted, was a global caliphate, with Saudi Arabia, Iran and Malaysia spearheading an Islamic alliance that would in turn declare war on the Christian world.

A third file contained an analysis of every known terror group in the world: ideologies, methodologies, histories, resources, reach, and all known links to Australia and Australians. At the last minute, the team of in-house statisticians had even managed to assign each group a probability rating based on a specially formulated equation to indicate how likely it was that they were responsible for the attacks.

The final file, marked 'Suspects', was thick and contained a comprehensive list of Australians who could have been the other nine suicide bombers, based on scouring the database for criminals released on parole who matched three or more of the identifiers the three known bombers shared. It was, of course, possible that the other bombers were not Australian and that they were dealing with an international terror cell – perhaps the Aussies had only been involved in the Mexico City attack and Timothy Jenkins turning up in pieces in a suitcase was completely unrelated, but Clarke didn't think so. Another list in this last file consisted of the names of potential masterminds – whoever the hell was running the show.

SAMI was embarrassed by his own files: plain manila folders covered in scribbles – phone numbers, doodles, random notes – that were also dog-eared, dirty and, more concerningly, thin.

Following the introductions, the Australian agent with the obsessively ordered and enviably thick files – Agent Clarke, he said – took the floor with an equally annoying swagger. 'I'm not going to pretend we know anything you don't,' the Aussie said as his PowerPoint presentation started. 'I am sure there isn't much a small nation like Australia can tell the CIA. So, let me save you some time by skipping through the obvious.'

The Aussie pointed his remote at the screen and hit fast forward. Sami gasped as he saw headings, facts and figures flash across the screen. He saw enough to realise he needed to see more. Here were things he didn't know, things he needed to know. He had to refrain from standing up and asking the Aussie to stop and explain, the embarrassment it would have caused the CIA keeping him reluctantly connected to his seat.

Agent Clarke eventually paused to sum up the hundred or so files that he had excruciatingly flown through. Sami tried his best to look nonplussed when Clarke suggested the ultimate aim of the group was to force Iran, Saudi Arabia and Malaysia to create an Islamic superpower that would declare war on the West. Start a religious fight to the death. World War III. The Apocalypse.

Sami suddenly realised just how fucked up the CIA had become. They were over-resourced. All the cash that had been thrown at them post-9/11 had turned them into a ten-thousand-piece jigsaw, with agents everywhere, all occupying roles that were utterly specific and tightly defined. With each one focused on his or her own niche, they had lost sight of the big picture. Sami had been blinkered by his brief, which was Europe, just as the agents in Asia and the Middle East had been blinkered by theirs. Neither had looked up and noticed the matching pieces, which the simplest of moves could then have put together. The keeping of secrets in CIA departments was only outdone by the lack of cooperation between the fellow law-enforcement agencies that also investigated terrorism: the FBI and Homeland Security, the CIA's best of frenemies. ASIO might have been small, but apparently it was cohesive.

'A copy of all of this material will be made available to you should you want it,' Clarke said, noticing the gruff American's agitated interest. 'But for now, let's get to the important stuff. Who it is and how to stop them.'

Clarke hit his remote and brought up a mugshot of the first identified dead bomber. 'Let's start with Charlie Haddad,' he said, then provided a detailed history of the dead Australian. He did the same for Mike Evans and Tim Jenkins.

'The thing that links them all, other than two of them being dead Islamic jihadis, is Goulburn jail,' Clarke said. 'All three were incarcerated in that prison and we suspect that's where they were all radicalised and recruited.' He gave them the numbers. 'We've been able to locate all but forty of the 16,000 or so individuals who have been released from Goulburn jail over the last five years. If we assume that the other nine dead terrorists come from this forty, that leaves us with thirty-one suspects for future attacks.'

Clarke handed out the files, each agent in the room getting a folder full of names, photos and rap sheets.

'Operation Roam is already underway,' Clarke said. 'Our national law-enforcement agencies are searching for every name on that list. Some are most likely dead, some have probably committed further crimes and gone on the run, and some will have joined the homeless population of 116,000. We hope to have our list significantly narrowed soon.'

Sami, who had swept his files from his desk when no one was looking and returned them to his bag, stood up. 'And how about the recruiters?' he asked. 'Do you have an idea of who is behind all of this?'

'Yes,' Clarke said. 'Give me a sec ...' He grabbed his remote and started flicking through the slides. He stopped when he found the picture of Ali Hammad. 'This fifty-two-year-old man is the leader of an ISIS-trained cell that has been operating in Australia,' he said. 'He and another eleven men would have blown up a nuclear reactor in Sydney had we not caught them. Hammad is currently serving a life sentence in isolation in Supermax, within Goulburn jail. The other eleven are also in Goulburn jail, serving a range of sentences from two to twenty-five years.'

'Two years for trying to blow up a nuclear reactor?' Maverick blurted out. 'Are you shitting me? They all should have got the needle.'

'Welcome to Australia, Special Agent Smith,' Clarke said. 'A country renowned for surf, sun and soft sentencing. We haven't strung anyone up for at least fifty years.'

Sami interrupted. 'So, this Ali Hammad, is he our guy?'

'We have no direct evidence to suggest he or any of the others are involved in the Church Bombings,' Clarke answered. 'But until two days ago we weren't looking for it. While we have no hard evidence yet, there is plenty to go on.'

Clarke then revealed that eight of the twelve men had served time in Goulburn jail before their current sentence. Of those eight, at least four were radicalised during that period of incarceration. 'And all three of the dead bombers would have served time with at least one of the twelve,' Clarke said.

He then went on to explain that the Goulburn group had both the means and the skills to orchestrate such an attack. 'They've had the training, they have the knowledge, they have the motivation and they have the financial clout,' Clarke continued. 'If ISIS isn't directly involved, it is certainly the inspiration.'

Clarke clicked to a picture of Fasin Halim. 'This is the man we suspect is financing the operation. He and his two younger brothers, also part of the twelve, have an estimated combined worth of more than $700 million. We were only able to locate a portion of their wealth when we arrested them.'

He clicked his remote again. 'Abbas Bashir provides religious counsel to the group and is an expert when it comes to radicalisation. They call him the Sheik.'

Another click. 'Mahmud Elias. He was already in custody when the twelve were arrested and was not officially part of the reactor plot. But an asset recently flagged that he is associated with the twelve, and that information has proven particularly valuable: Mahmud served time with all three of the Church Bombers who have been identified. He once shared a cell with Mike Evans.'

Sami finally gave in to his urge and jumped out of his seat. 'Well, what are we waiting for?' Sami shouted. 'Let's go and get them.'

Clarke shook his head. 'It's not that simple.' He then explained that there would be no black sites, torture or even questioning anyone without a warrant. 'Even if we were granted a warrant to question them, they would be released back into the general prison population afterwards. We are prohibited from putting them into isolation. And you all know what will happen if we start asking questions and can't put them into a black hole when we are done.'

Sami did. *Boom!* They would activate all their assets and blow up the entire cell. All remaining targets would be attacked at once. The only way you could question one of them was if you had all of them locked away in cages, blindfolded and gagged. He suddenly longed for Guantanamo.

'This is bullshit,' Maverick said, slamming his fist into the desk. 'What sort of country is this? Do you guys want to be responsible for the next hundred people they kill? What is it today? The thirty-first? We only have twenty-five days until the next attack. Get your president on the phone and make him change the goddamn laws. Or is he a fucking terrorist too?'

'Special Agent Smith!' Sami said in his most official voice. 'Sit down. Enough.'

He turned towards Clarke. 'I'm sorry for my colleague's outburst, but he does have a point. Is there any way we can change whatever it is that is stopping us from pulling all these guys out of the prison and placing them on a suitable site? Do you have a line to the Prime Minister?'

Clarke explained that not even the Prime Minister could change the law, that any proposed amendment had to be presented to parliament and passed by both the lower house and the upper house before being sent on to the Governor-General for royal assent.

'We have already submitted our proposal to the Minister for Defence,' Clarke said. 'But it will take time that we don't have, and the amendments will almost certainly be blocked.'

'So, what's the plan then? Is there one?' Sami asked.

Clarke clicked his remote again, bringing up a picture of young man. Blue eyes, blond hair.

'Meet Riley Jax.'

CHAPTER 33

Goulburn Jail, Goulburn, NSW, Australia

CLARKE wasn't himself. Pale and clammy, eyes glazed and slightly red, he looked like he hadn't slept for a week. He barely appeared to be paying attention when Jax delivered his latest report, verbally, in one of Goulburn jail's legal visiting rooms.

'The vitiligo has extended to his right arm,' Jax said. 'His gingivitis has also worsened from mild to what I would say is severe.'

Clarke showed little interest.

'I believe Mahmud is not only an associate but part of their hierarchy,' Jax continued. 'He was third in line when it came to the introductions. While, according to Islamic custom, that may have been because of his age, a subsequent exchange led me to believe it was more about his standing in the group. Speaking in Arabic, he cut over the top of the group and issued an order, which was obeyed. They were all subservient to the demand, if not to him.'

Clarke didn't look up from the notepad he was scrawling on. 'Good,' he said. 'What about the others?'

'Khalil thinks I am his mate,' Jax said. 'He trusts me and has become the facilitator you predicted he would be. I believe

Bashir is the group's recruiter and that he is in the process of recruiting me. Based on standard M.O., he is currently in the first phase: offering protection and companionship, showing kindness; he has made no attempt to make me subservient yet or spoken about a conversion to Islam. His profile matches that of an extremist. He uses religious rhetoric to reinforce or condemn behaviours within the group. He often misquotes the Quran, on purpose I believe, to manipulate others and align them to him and his agenda. I have heard him recite several inciteful verses, all known to be used by extremists.'

Jax had to stop to make sure Clarke was actually listening, as there hadn't been a nod or raised brow from the agent to acknowledge anything he had said.

'Continue,' Clarke said.

'That Halim ...' Jax went on. 'I was going to say he is proving a problem, but, really, he is probably the most telling of the lot. He doesn't like me one bit. He has told the others not to trust me, but I think it is more about him than me. He is unsure of his place, maybe having a crack at me just to see if the others will act on his advice. And they haven't. They've dismissed him. I don't believe he is their 3IC from what I have seen, but I haven't even collected enough observational data to establish a baseline. Given his personality profile and what I have observed, I believe there could be an opportunity to turn Halim down the track. I would suggest that we come up with a strategy to further alienate him from the group. A few more knocks to his ego. That sort of thing.'

Again, Jax waited for an acknowledgement. Nothing was forthcoming, so he forged on. 'They have no idea that I understand Arabic,' he said. 'And they've been talking about a "mission".'

He peered at Clarke. Pupils not dilated. Brows not raised. Not a single physiological sign of interest. His mind was elsewhere.

'I've been privy to most of the group's conversations in the yard and also in the mess hall,' Jax persevered. 'But we have two big holes. I have no idea what goes on in their prayer meetings and they have also been gathering in the Kent brothers' cell ...'

'Go on ...' Finally, a sign a life from Clarke.

'I haven't been here long enough to establish whether the meetings are scheduled or organised on a whim, but I know they have congregated in that cell at least three times since I arrived. Given that they all share cells with outsiders, it does make sense for them to meet in the only cell occupied by two of their guys when they want to talk shop. I could probably push Khalil for information?'

Clarke shook his head as he reached for his briefcase. 'No need,' he said. 'We'll just listen to them instead.' He opened his briefcase and pulled out an oversized plastic ziplock bag containing smaller ziplock bags holding what looked like electrical cords. Clarke opened the large bag and pulled out one of the smaller ones. Jax could now see it was a mobile phone. Tiny. About the size of a credit card, only thicker. The electrical cord was its charger. Jax looked back to the bigger bag and counted another six, all individually bagged: phone and charger.

'Damn,' Jax said as he snatched the bag from Clarke and unsnapped the ziplock. 'It looks like a kid's toy.'

'All plastic, too,' Clarke said.

'Is it some sort of specially made spy phone? I can't give them anything that I can't explain. Are these on the market?

'Yes. You can get them from eBay. In fact, we bought them on eBay. Sixty bucks each after we were given a discount for buying in bulk.'

Jax passed the phone from hand to hand, estimating its weight. *About 20 grams.* 'Perfect,' he said. 'Give me six weeks and they will all have one. I'll get the first one to Khalil next week, after visits day.'

Clarke was shaking his head again. 'We need to get them all in there now,' he said. 'We need them speaking on them this week.'

Jax almost thought Clarke was joking, but Clarke did not tell jokes.

'Seven phones at once?' Jax said. 'Are you mad? How am I supposed to explain how I all of sudden got seven phones into a maximum-security prison? How many of those things do you reckon you can fit up your arse?' He pointed at the little phones with their not-so-little chargers. 'How about you bend over and we will find out?' Jax said. 'Get all seven up there and I will deliver all of them this week.'

Clarke said nothing, responding with only a cold stare. Jax took a moment to think. *Was he being unreasonable? Could he get this done? No. Not a chance.* He had to build a cover story. How he'd got them and from who. That took time.

Clarke spoke. Finally. Firmly. 'I am not going to demonstrate, but a standard-size male rectum will quite comfortably accommodate two of these bags. So it would be quite plausible to say that you already had one phone and that your supplier will bring in two a week for the next three weeks. I'll give you twenty-one days.'

Stress. Clarke had hidden it well until now. 'I'll take that as a yes then,' Clarke said. 'Seven mobile phones delivered to seven men in twenty-one days.'

Seven phones delivered to seven men?

Jax had assumed one of the phones was for him, as there were seven phones and only six targets in his wing. He thought Clarke might have made a mistake, but he knew men like Clarke didn't make mistakes.

'Seriously?' Jax exclaimed when Clarke told him that the seventh phone was to be delivered to Hammad. 'How am I meant to get into Supermax?'

Clarke told him how. Then he pulled out another item, something he was not intending to give Jax, but a standard bit of kit he always carried.

Jax furled his brow. 'This wasn't part of the plan,' he protested.

And it hadn't been. Not until Jax had told Clarke about the weekly meetings.

Jax was now certain something was going on. Clarke had always been cautious and methodical. They had meticulously mapped out the operation. Spent months working on scenarios, probabilities and outcomes. Yet now all of that appeared to have been thrown out the window. Someone had hit fast-forward. Pressed 'panic'.

'Clarke,' Jax said sternly. 'What's going on? What do you know? Has something happened? Is something going to happen?'

'No.'

CHAPTER 34

Canberra, ACT, Australia

CLARKE's eyes darted between the road and the police scanner as he changed the channel. Again. There was nothing worth listening to. Only petty crime and misdemeanours. He moved onto the encrypted channel and began listening to an undercover surveillance operation after failing to find a raid.

He was about forty kilometres away from Goulburn, hurtling towards Canberra, when he switched the scanner off. Usually he never switched the scanner off. He then switched the radio on and found some music. He *never* listened to music. But Clarke needed to clear his head.

Clarke didn't like doubt. It was a feeling he wasn't used to. Clarke was always certain. He planned and plotted. Took his time. He didn't like changing his plans, because his plans were always right. And he certainly didn't like changing the best and most thought-out plan he had ever produced. His masterpiece. Yet he'd now been forced to change the plan that would make or break him three times. Sure, the first change was his own fault. He'd been wrong and it had to be done. But the other changes had been forced upon him because of politics and pressure. Because of terrorism. Suddenly nothing else mattered.

Clarke wished they had left him and his plan alone. He would have given them Jax as soon as he was ready. He would have created and delivered the perfect spy, as per his original schedule and as per the plan. But now he didn't know if he could, because he had been forced to activate his asset – *his* asset – before he was ready. Initially he'd been excited about activating Jax, at least when it was just a surveillance side-project. But the current assignment was no side-project. It was *the* project. And stopping the bombs was more important than his project.

Yet he resented that they were putting all his hard work at risk for this – for anything. Even if they succeeded in stopping the bombs, he would not be able to use their meddling as an excuse if Project Mnemonist failed. It would still be all on him.

No. Project Mnemonist would not fail. He would catch the terrorists and get back to his plan. But first he had to deal with the CIA.

He turned off the music.

'Call Ronin,' he told his phone.

The man picked up after the first ring. 'Yes, sir.'

'Where are they?' Clarke asked.

'Holed up in the hotel. We have both eyes and ears on them. The surveillance equipment was deployed in their rooms as requested.'

'What about their phones?' Clarke asked.

'Negative, sir. They are CIA encrypted, as you predicted.'

'Any visitors?' Clarke asked.

'Just Agent Roberts,' came the reply.

'Okay, get a team ready,' Clarke said. 'I'm scheduled to meet them in the hotel lobby in forty minutes. I want their rooms turned inside out. Take note of every item and make duplicates of all physical files, but, whatever you do, don't touch their laptops. Aside from the encryptions, I would also suspect some sort of silent alarm.'

'Orders received loud and clear,' the man said.

'And get the tech team to compress whatever audio has been recorded and send it to me now,' Clarke said.

'Yes, sir,' the man said.

Clarke hung up.

SAMI was in the hotel lobby alone.

'Where's Agent Smith?' Clarke asked.

The American looked up from his broadsheet. 'It will just be me and you, Agent Clarke,' Sami said. 'Thought it best to keep Mav in his cage. Please take a seat. Would you like some coffee?'

Clarke shook his head. 'No, let's get to it,' he said. 'I trust you have already received my report?'

'Indeed,' Sami said. 'Both timely and thorough. Your asset is already proving his worth.'

Clarke posed the question in the form of a blank stare.

'The phones,' Sami said. 'Seven in seven days? We would have blown the entire operation with our haste had he not only seen the flaw in a joint CIA/ASIO plan but also had the courage to tell a man as intimidating as you he was wrong. Are you sure we should be keeping him in the dark? I was surprised to find that even we have a file on this kid, and from what I've read you may be keeping your best player on the bench.'

Clarke was about to ask – and then he remembered he'd placed the call to Langley himself. 'You've been keeping tabs on him?' Clarke asked.

'Excuse me,' Sami said as he looked down at his phone. 'Just have to reply to this.'

After he'd fired off a quick text, he looked back up at Clarke. 'Oh, not me,' he said. 'But, yes, we have. You didn't think the CIA would simply dismiss a one-in-a-hundred-billion chance did you? Ever met Agent Roberts? Bald, tanned, looks like he needs a good lie down?'

Clarke nodded.

'Well, turns out he was here for more than the sun,' Sami said.

Clarke suddenly felt violated. Jax was his. Like a son. What else did they know? Not just about Jax, but about him ... He suddenly felt compelled to explain himself.

'Probably not the best idea. I need him focused on tasks without the added pressure of outcomes.' Clarke was surprised by his unmeasured and almost emotional outburst. *Twenty-four days until the next bomb. Tick, tock. All on you, kid.*

'Good,' Sami said as he nodded. 'Finally, some honesty. And I understand. Managing an asset is never easy. And managing an asset as unique as this, well ...'

Clarke felt the shift before he saw it, the hairs on his neck standing up just as the agent changed his expression.

'But I am not one to be fucked with,' Sami said as he leaned in. 'You're not the first to mistake my good nature for a weakness.'

Clarke hadn't noticed how big this man was until now. His kind eyes suddenly became killer. Oh, how stupid he'd been to underestimate an American Arab who worked for the CIA.

'Mav has already taken down two of your guys,' he said, 'It will soon be four unless I call him off. Do we have an understanding?'

Clarke nodded.

Sami fired off a text as Clarke pulled out his phone.

'Stand down,' he said after hitting redial.

'I'll be going for my afternoon walk now,' Sami said. 'I expect my room to be clean when I get back. I also expect full cooperation from this point on.'

CHAPTER 35

Goulburn Correctional Centre, Goulburn, NSW, Australia

JAX counted again, both breaths and seconds.

He kicked off his blanket, pivoted and placed both his bare feet on the concrete floor. It no longer felt like ice; summer was beckoning, Hell-frozen-over starting to thaw. He walked to his box shelves, just like he did every night after lights-out, only a little earlier on this unusually bright evening. Not needing to bend over or lie on the floor to find what he needed, he simply grabbed the kettle from the top shelf.

Behind him Khalil stirred.

Jax turned his head and saw his cellmate reposition the brick-like prison pillow under his head. He returned his attention to the kettle, all good to go. He didn't need the torch tonight, a steady stream of silver moonlight eating into the gloom. Holding the plastic kettle in his right hand – a generic Chinese piece of rubbish that had cost him $80 through the buy-up – he popped the lid and fished out a plastic bag from the cool water.

Again, Khalil stirred.

Jax glanced at his cellmate, who'd rolled over in his sleep. He placed the still-open kettle on his bedside table and jumped back into bed with the plastic bag after shaking off the water.

He pulled the zip-lock apart and removed both the mobile phone and its charger from the bag. He was still in awe of how small the phone was. Measuring just 71.8 x 23.6 x 13 millimetres, the Zanco Fly Phone weighed just twenty-one grams. And it was completely plastic, all the electronics made with a conductive polymer that negated the need for metal. It was like the phone had been designed with metal detectors and concealment in mind. For criminals. For terrorists.

Jax thought he was going to be given some speciality ASIO kit when they'd told him their plan. He imagined they had their very own Q from James Bond – a bespectacled technology whiz in a laboratory somewhere, testing tech that was fifty years away from hitting a shelf. And then they gave him a Chinese-built burner that they'd bought online for $60. Maybe Q had become a mass marketer.

He plugged in the charger and connected the midget mobile to the power socket next to his bed.

Beep! Beep! As soon as he flicked the switch on the wall socket, the LCD screen on the phone turned bright green as it barked twice, a noise that seemed too big for a phone so small.

'What the fuck?' said Khalil. 'What was that?'

He lifted his head from his pillow and turned towards Jax.

'Is that a phone?' Khalil said. 'Serious? You got a phone?'

Jax attempted to hide the phone between his legs, both his shock and the attempt to conceal the phone fake. This was all part of the plan.

'What are you talking about?' Jax said. 'You must have been dreaming. Go back to sleep.'

'Nah, bullshit,' Khalil said. 'You got a phone. Give me a look.'

Khalil jumped to his feet. He was as solid as a rock, completely balanced, no wobbles. Jax hadn't drugged Khalil that night, hadn't given him the full dose of Rohypnol that he was now giving him most nights, the half-dose no longer enough now that Khalil had built up a tolerance to the drug. Tonight he hadn't given him anything at all. Sure, he'd counted Khalil's breaths as usual, but this time it was to make sure he was awake.

'Yeah, alright,' Jax said. 'But don't tell anyone I got it. You aren't going to dog on me, right?'

'No way, man,' Khalil said. 'You are my bro.'

Jax again faked reluctance as he sheepishly pulled the phone from between his legs and handed it to Khalil.

'Fuck, man,' Khalil said, surprised. 'How small is it, bro? This is mad, hey? Fucking tiny. Sweet.'

'One of my old army mates is into stuff like this,' Jax said. 'He is into all his gadgets. It's so small that he forgot he had it in his pocket when he came in.'

'How?' Khalil asked. 'What about the metal detectors?'

'All plastic, bro,' Jax said.

'Fucking awesome,' Khalil said. 'How did you get it?'

'I took it,' Jax said. 'Said if he got busted on the way out he would end up in here with me.'

'Sweet, bro. Reckon you can get any more?'

Jax was certain he could. In fact, he already had more: another six in the secret compartment under his shelf, rather than in the kettle, the hiding spot he wanted Khalil to see. All bugged and ready to record, with an agent at the other end, already assigned to listen in full-time.

HALIM couldn't see what all the fuss was about. Why was Bashir so interested in bringing this Aussie in? This fucking infidel. It would have made sense to him if this Riley Jax only had a year left to run on his sentence. Then they could give him a bomb and send him to die. Better him than one of their own. God could decide if he was a true believer or not.

But Bashir had made Jax a project. Made him his pet. Halim refused to even admit it to himself, but he was jealous. He hadn't been a soldier, he didn't know how to make bombs, and he couldn't obtain mobile phones. All Halim had was money, which he'd been reminded of the day before when Bashir told him he had to pay Jax for the phones. Apparently Jax had a phone! And a mate who could get more. Halim had been furious when Bashir had told him he wouldn't be getting one of the first two, which were coming the following week. He was paying for them, but Mahmud would get his first.

Halim felt like a piece of shit.

He'd once been able to use his money in a way that made people think he was important. In fact, he had become accustomed to always being the most popular man in the room. He would never let anyone pay, always buying the drinks, the dinners, and sometimes, if he really wanted to show off, the restaurant. He liked the way people looked at him when his chauffeur dropped him off at the mosque in his Mercedes-Benz AMG S-63, when they saw the twenty-four-carat gold around his neck and the Rolex on his wrist, when he rolled out his $50,000-dollar prayer mat. He looked important, and that made him feel important.

But in here, Halim wore green like everyone else. He dressed the same as the drug addicts, the thieves and the filthy homosexuals. The same as the infidel. He hated how the cheap material felt against his skin, but most of all he hated how it made him look. Normal. Just like everyone else. He had asked if he could have custom-made clothes sent in. He would have them made green of course, but they would be cut from the finest material and tailor-made to fit, not synthetic and saggy. When they flat-out rejected his request, he appealed, through his lawyer. This time he said he was allergic to the fibres in the synthetic blend and required custom-made clothes on medical grounds. The sons of bitches asked for proof. He saw the prison doctor but he was also a son of a bitch, refusing to make a false report, no matter how much cash Halim offered. They'd even rejected his bid to have orthopaedic shoes for his genuinely bad feet brought in, telling him to wear inserts instead.

So Halim wore the same clothes as everyone else, and that made him feel ordinary, and this newcomer, this Jax, made it worse. Bashir thought Jax was special, and he was getting all the attention. But not for long. Not if Halim could help it.

Halim told the others he was feeling ill and could not go to prayer group that morning. He told them he would pray in his cell. But he didn't. Instead, he stood in the wing. Waiting. Watching.

He made his move as soon as Jax was gone. Summoned by a guard, the infidel had left the wing. Jax would say it was for another meeting with his lawyer. That is what he had said when Halim had asked yesterday. Halim didn't believe him, but Bashir did. Bashir also said the phones would be okay. Nothing to worry about.

So Halim's opinion was worth the same as his money in prison. Nothing.

Halim casually walked down the corridor swinging his toiletry bag. He looked like he was just on his way to the shower room. But then, after checking nobody was looking, he sidestepped through the open door of Jax and Khalil's cell, then closed it behind him. He couldn't lock it of course, but nobody would see what he was doing unless they looked through the small window.

Halim went straight for the kettle. Khalil had told him that was where Jax hid his phone. He popped the lid and smiled when he saw the plastic bag in the water. The infidel must be stupid after all, not changing his hiding spot after showing it to Khalil. He unzipped the bag and pulled out the phone after putting the kettle down. He left the charger in the plastic bag, figuring the battery would be full.

He mashed at the tiny keys with his fat fingers.

Beep! Beep!

He jumped when the phone barked, almost throwing it away.

'*Sharmoet,*' he cursed in Arabic. Thank Allah a guard wasn't walking past the cell. He'd be sent to join Hammad in Supermax if they found him with a phone. He looked down at the glowing green screen once he was certain no one had heard.

He went straight to the infidel's text messages.

Nothing.

He had either received none or deleted them all.

Suspicious.

He then went to the call log.

Nothing.

He had either received none, made none or deleted all records of calls.

Even more suspicious.

Unfortunately, he would need more than an empty phone log to convince Bashir that Jax was a traitor. Or maybe it was Mahmud he had to convince. Halim wasn't even sure who the leader was anymore. He would need more than suspicion for either of them to let him slit the infidel's throat.

So Halim searched the cell, looking under the blankets, the mattress, the bed.

Nothing.

He went through Jax's box shelves. Just food and toiletries. He looked in his tubs – clothes in the first, legal papers in the other two. After flicking through the printouts – they looked legit to him – he pushed the last tub back onto the shelf.

Nothing.

'*Eire-fik,*' he muttered. And he lashed out, kicking the bottom of the shelves. On hearing a clunk, he looked down.

A panel had opened, revealing a cavity. He bent down, and smiled when he saw the stash.

THE DOCTOR took one look at Jax's leg and told him he was good to go.

'All done?' Jax asked.

'Yep,' he said. 'Nasty scar but you've made a full recovery. I won't need to see you again.'

The guard escorted Jax back to the wing.

'Thanks, mate,' Jax said after the guard cracked the electronic lock and let him back into the block. He was surprised to be back so quick.

Jax headed back to his cell, wondering what he should do next. What information he could get. And then his stomach dropped when he saw his cell door.

He'd left it wide open, but now it was closed. Khalil wouldn't be back from prayer group yet. And the guards only closed the doors when they wanted to lock someone in. Jax's stomach dropped even further when he peered through the porthole-sized window in his door.

Someone was lying on his floor. Clad in green, obviously an inmate, the mystery man had his arm stuck under Jax's shelf unit. The front panel was lying on the floor next to Jax's torch and the phones. Jax couldn't see who it was, but it didn't matter – he was already dead.

He pushed the door open as quietly as he could before creeping into the cell. The intruder had his arm deep in the cavity, fishing for the items at the back. Jax closed the door as quietly as he had opened it. Even though he couldn't see the intruder's face, the stocky frame, hairy arms and bald patch identified the man as Halim. That made him feel slightly better about what he had to do, as the cash-man had been a problem even before now.

Jax took a moment to plan Halim's death. It had to be quick. It had to be quiet. It had to look natural.

He rehearsed it all in his head. He was ready to execute.

Jax flung himself to the floor, flopping on the ground parallel to Halim. He would have dropped an elbow on the way down, but he had to make sure they found Halim's body unmarked. Jax then hooked his right arm under Halim's head as the shocked intruder tensed and attempted to turn. He covered Halim's mouth before he could scream. With Halim's head locked tightly between his palm and his bicep, Jax rolled him back and, before he even got a chance to squirm, locked him up with his legs. He had spent just as much time on the mat with Ferris learning Brazilian jujitsu wrestling moves as he had on his feet rehearsing Gojo Ryu karate strikes. Jax made sure to apply only enough pressure to hold him. Not enough to bruise him.

'Shhhh,' Jax whispered as Halim tried to scream over the top of his hand. 'Stop fighting. I'll make sure there is no pain.'

Jax tightened his grip, both with his legs and his arm, before rolling a quarter-turn to get his free arm access to the cavity under his shelf. Halim resumed his fight, attempting to kick, shake and bite his way out as Jax felt for the pills.

'Shhhh,' Jax whispered again. 'It will be quick. Painless. I promise.'

Jax heard a metallic clink as he knocked into the mint-tin that contained his pills. He pulled it out and, one-handed, opened the flip-lid with his thumb. He applied a little more pressure, attempting to still Halim – one buck would be enough to send the pills all over the room – as he tipped the pills gently onto the floor.

The capsule Jax needed was red and yellow, but there were ten pills that colour and only two of the ten contained the heart-attack inducing and completely untraceable poison called oleander. He reached over and grabbed the closest red and yellow pill before lifting it into his line of sight. He struggled to focus amid a fresh fight from Halim, but managed a smile when he saw the little black letter on the pill casing was a D.

D for death.

Jax now needed to get the pill into Halim's mouth without allowing him to scream. Holding the pill between his ring finger and his palm, Jax used his index finger and thumb to pincer Halim's nostrils shut. He started fighting for air.

Halim was turning blue when Jax finally removed his hands from both his mouth and his nose. Halim gasped and gulped, not even noticing the pill go down his throat. Jax had thrown it down his pharynx as soon as he'd drawn his first desperate breath. Jax quickly shut Halim's mouth again before he could scream. The rest happened fast: first Halim fighting, next Halim fitting, and then Halim dying.

Jax toyed with the idea of dragging Halim to the bathroom after finding his toiletry bag, but he was quick to dismiss the idea – the man was too heavy, the bathroom too far away, and the risk of being seen too high. Instead he left Halim where he was, putting the kettle next to his body after re-hiding his contraband and replacing the false front.

The guards wouldn't be able to work out why Halim had been in Jax and Khalil's room making himself a cup of tea when he had the heart attack, nor would they care. Jax had overheard Bashir telling Halim not to steal Jax's phone, so he'd be angry that Halim had gone against his orders. He would also be happy that Jax had thought fast, removing the phone from Halim's stiff hand and hiding it before alerting the guard. Halim was dead but the phone deal wasn't.

Jax delivered the first two phones at the end of that week.

CHAPTER 36

Federal Highway, Collector, NSW, Australia

CLARKE saw something up ahead. Smoke. Still, he continued at the same speed, his Camry purring along at 3000 rpm. He could soon see that the smoke was coming from cars. Two of them. A crash. His eyes darted from the road to the scanner as he flicked through the channels. Nothing. All petty crime, misdemeanours and a boring surveillance operation that hadn't turned into a raid like he had hoped. He was about to be the first on scene.

He was about a hundred metres away when he knew it was serious. One car, a Nissan SUV, was in the ditch, the other, some crap Korean compact, on the shoulder. A Kia, he confirmed as he got closer. Or what was left of one anyway. He saw the woman when he was about fifty metres away. Bloodied, she was staggering up the bank. As Clarke powered past, she was on the side of the road with her hand out.

Clarke knew he was different. That not stopping to help an injured lady was not normal. Especially when he had medical training. He didn't know if it was bad wiring that had made him this way or the job. The things he had seen. The things he had done. He didn't do anything to be cruel intentionally. He just wasn't interested in anything that wasn't part of his plan. And he didn't have time to stop: he had to get his package to Turner at the drop point.

'ETA twenty minutes,' Clarke barked into his hand-held radio.

Halim's death had been a blow. No doubt. It was Halim who was going to pay for the phones. The transaction would have led them to his money. To the cell's money. To the people with the bombs. But Jax had done exactly the right thing by eliminating him. In fact, he had done outstandingly well: few would have been able to execute an untraceable kill on the spur of the moment and thereby save the entire operation. The kid had serious talent.

Clarke had to stop himself from smiling when he delivered the news to the Director. While Halim's death was a setback in the Church Bombing case, it was a milestone for Project Mnemonist. Clarke's plan for Jax was working. Prison had turned him into the killer he had to be. His empathy had been crushed.

'I've instructed him to supply the phones on credit,' Clarke said. 'We will get ears on them and then worry about the money trail.'

Jax had since put four of the seven phones into circulation. As expected, the first of them had gone to Bashir and the second had gone to the new player in town, Mahmud. The second pair of phones, delivered a week later – the day before – had only just been activated. It had taken a day for them to be smuggled across the prison and delivered to the remaining Halim brothers: Kazem and Mahir.

Perhaps Halim's brothers were now in charge of the money. That might be the reason they got the phones ahead of the Kent brothers. But Clarke suspected that there wouldn't be a transaction to trace until any transfer of responsibility was authorised by Hammad, who was locked away in Supermax. And Hammad was not due to get his phone until the following week, on the twenty-first. That might mean they'd have just four days to stop the attack.

The phones had already provided them with plenty. Nothing direct, no talk of targets or times, but a series of calls made by both Bashir and Mahmud that confirmed they were involved in a plot. Still, Clarke needed more. Much more. And time was running out.

He arrived at the drop zone a minute ahead of his ETA with the scanner, the keys and the plastic screwdriver, all CIA kit. This cooperating thing was working out okay.

CHAPTER 37

THE CAMERAS would be taken care of. Jax didn't know who would do that or how; he knew only that he had an hour. The CCTV would not be recording between 2 am and 3 am, instead showing a loop of the previous hour. No one would notice the glitch. Not when every hour after lights-out looked the same: inmates asleep, locked away for the night. The only thing that ever changed on the monitors was the time stamp.

Jax was fully dressed and standing behind his cell door. He pressed the light on his watch, a cheap digital prison buy-up job, and looked at the time.

2.01 am.

He'd now been standing behind the door for eleven minutes. Khalil was sound asleep. Jax didn't count his breaths to check if he was out like usual. After giving him a double dose of Rohypnol, Jax simply checked that he was still breathing.

Jax had also taken a pill before lights-out, a green and white capsule containing five milligrams of dextroamphetamine. With the plan in place and everything scheduled and set to go, he couldn't risk falling asleep, so he'd swallowed what was essentially a shot of speed.

Jax looked at his watch again, the tiny orange light on the left-hand side of the screen barely lighting up the last number.

2.02 am.

Jax suddenly felt a flush, a wave of heat hitting him like a truck. He could feel the beads of sweat pooling under his arms and on his back, his face burning hot with anger. He wanted to scream but couldn't, wanted to bang on the wall but couldn't. He'd been relatively calm when he'd taken up his post twelve minutes earlier, but as every minute ticked by he became more and more agitated. Now he was three minutes late and stuck in a traffic jam. He knew it could clear at any moment, but feared it wouldn't. He lit up his watch again.

2.04 am.

Bluey, his new ally from Marsh's gang – who, as anticipated, had also been moved to Goulburn – had agreed and sworn he would hit the knock-up at exactly 2 am. Jax hadn't told him why or what was on the line, he'd just stressed that it needed to be done. This was the only part of the plan that had worried Jax. He hated relying on others, always had, but he couldn't think of a way to do this on his own that didn't involve killing the guard. That fact that he even considered killing the guard made him realise he was now like most of the inmates in this place – a killer. He also realised he had barely thought about Halim since murdering him.

With the cameras taken care of, his keys cut and the Kent brothers drugged, the only thing between him and planting the bug was the guard. The irony that the only man he trusted to be the decoy also happened to be a man he had tried to kill wasn't lost on him.

2.05 am.

He was now regretting his decision. Bluey must have fallen asleep or decided to stand him up. Jax considered a Plan B.

Maybe he would have to kill the guard. Maybe he should have just planted the bug during the day. Walked into the open cell when the brothers were out and got to work. No. Anyone could have walked in. And a camera loop wouldn't have worked with corridor traffic.

His eyebrows shot high when he heard a door open. *The guard.* He was coming. Bluey had come through. He listened. *Fast. Loud.* The guard wasn't running but he was in a hurry. He waited for the footfall to pass his cell.

Jax had under a minute. Bluey would probably occupy the guard longer, but he couldn't take the risk. He placed the black plastic electronic key, or fob as Clarke had called it – which had arrived in a package along with an RF scanner and electronic key cutter – in front of the black pad beside his door. His lock snapped back, sounding like a thundercrack in the dead of the night. He pushed the door open, closed it, and then waved the card over the pad at the front of his door. Another crack. Jax winced as his cell snapped shut.

It took him exactly twelve seconds to get to Cell No. 16. He put the black key fob into his pocket and pulled out a second fob, coloured red. Only then did he notice the adjacent cell door. He had casually stopped in front of Cell No. 16 earlier that day and bent down to tie his shoelace. Then he'd pressed the button on the radio frequency scanner in his pocket, the tiny box picking up the nearest device emitting a 315 megahertz signal and copying the code. He'd then gone back to his room and used the same device to transfer the code onto the red FOB key. He'd thought it had all worked perfectly.

But maybe not.

The electronic keypad for Cell No. 16 was mounted directly next to the one for Cell No. 17. There was a significant possibility that the RF scanner had cloned a key for Cell No. 17 instead of 16; he figured he had a fifty-fifty chance of his key working.

He held his breath as he waved the fob in front of the pad. *Click.*

He exhaled as he entered Cell No. 16 and locked the door behind him.

Adam and Kyle were dead to the world, one of them even snoring loudly. The slow-release sedative he'd slipped into their drinks at dinner had well and truly kicked in. Jax stood still and listened, waiting until he heard the guard return to his office, Bluey having told him it was a false alarm. After he heard the office door close, he waited another five minutes. The guard was back in his box, watching TV. He was clear. Good to go.

Jax dragged the closest set of box shelves from the wall and slid it towards the centre of the cell, the hardwood scraping on the concrete, until it was directly under the light. He then pulled a series of items from his pockets and lined them on the top of the shelving unit: a screwdriver, a torch, a self-tapping screw, and a two-in-one video and sound recording device.

The screwdriver, which had also arrived in the care package, was made entirely of plastic. It looked like something a 3D printer had spat out, but it was as hard as steel, as was the self-tapping screw.

He had made a slight modification to his pen torch earlier, covering and sealing the bulb with a piece of red film from a Skittles packet. Cell No. 16 was much closer to the guard's office than his own cell. The red light would be bright enough light for him to do the job, but not for the guard to notice should he look away from his TV.

Jax climbed onto the shelves and used his screwdriver to remove the light covering – a long metal grille and then, inside that, a long sheet of plastic – that protected the fluorescent tube underneath. He lowered himself back to the ground and used the self-tapping screw to drill a peephole into the plastic. Then he fixed the camera onto the underside of the covering, lens positioned over the peephole, before climbing back up and screwing it all in place again. Shelf unit returned, tools back in his pockets, he was done. But now he had to wait. Again.

Bluey wasn't late this time, pressing the knock-up at 2.30 am on the dot.

'Fucking bullshit,' the guard swore as he stomped his way down the corridor. 'Better be something wrong with you this time.'

Jax waited for the guard's footfall to clear the Kents' cell before he made his move. He darted his way down the corridor and made it back to his own cell without being spotted. Bluey had done his job keeping the fuming guard occupied. Again.

Jax didn't sleep that night. Couldn't. Dosed up on dextroamphetamine, he tossed and turned and stared at the ceiling. He wondered what he would have done if Bluey hadn't come through. Would he have killed the guard?

THE FOUR-INCH-THICK glass disappeared into the wall cavity after the guard in the box nodded and pressed the button to activate the sliding door. Jax gave the officer a wave before placing his hands back on the trolley. He was soon standing in a place where no one would ever want to be: the Goulburn Supermax, the most secure jail in Australia.

Jax had studied the blueprints Clarke had sent him via legal post. He had to admit that the set-up was impressive and – given what he was planning to do – intimidating. Especially now that the mission had been rescheduled – the day before, Jax had received word from Clarke via Turner that the delivery of a phone to Hammad in the Supermax had to take place the following day.

Officially called the High Risk Management Correctional Centre, the Supermax was a jail within a jail. Seventy-five cells. All one-out. All no way out. This was where the country's worst prisoners were held: the mass murderers, the serial killers and the terrorists. With the unit sitting on a third-of-a-square-kilometre plot in the northwestern corner of the Goulburn jail complex, the inmates might have had a nice view of the historic town – had it not been for the impenetrable and windowless white masonry walls lined with five-metre-high fences lashed with razor-wire.

The facility had more cameras then the rest of the prison combined, Jax knew. They looked in and out. They looked down. They even looked up, a camera in the yard watching the sky for any approaches from the air – a helicopter arriving to scoop up an inmate, for example.

Jax thought about the Serpent as he pushed his empty serving trolley along the corridor. This was where he lived, his lair a three-metre-by-two-metre cell with a completely see-through glass front. Jax hoped he wasn't home. He hoped he had been dragged off to court to have his 338-year sentence extended to 358 years. Or, even better, that he was back in Sydney, in the Long Bay hospital, dying – no, already dead.

JAX looked on as a kitchen hand, a prisoner he didn't know, loaded the meals onto the trolley: foil trays with white cardboard lids that had all been numbered with a thick red texta. Earlier that week, he'd been surprised, even slightly suspicious, when Turner, the guard from Long Bay, had suddenly arrived in Goulburn and informed Jax that he was being given a new job, the long-time Supermax server, Benny, having suddenly fallen ill. Jax hoped the virus ASIO had given Benny wasn't serious.

'They're all in order,' the kitchen hand said. 'No. 1 goes to Cell No. 1, No. 2 to Cell No. 2 and so she goes. Nothing to it … But whatever you do, don't fuck it up. We'll never hear the end of it if one of the Leb cunts ends up with a tray full of bacon.'

The kitchen hand pointed towards the now fully packed trolley. Jax had fifty-eight meals to deliver. Jax wondered if the kitchen hand was in on the plan.

'Got it?'

'Don't give the Leb cunts bacon, right?' Jax said. 'Got it.'

No. Surely not. Not unless ASIO hired racist scumbags.

Jax stopped his trolley and applied the footbrake in front of Cell No. 1. With both the wall and the door made of an unbreakable glass-like, ballistic-grade polycarbonate, the inmate could not hide. Neither could Jax.

A man stood on the other side of the door, bald on top but with the horseshoe of long hair around the sides of his skull gathered into a ponytail.

'Where's Benny?' he demanded. Who are you? I don't know you.'

Jax kneeled down and pulled the first meal from the trolley. He couldn't tell what it was, given the mix of aromas coming from the trolley: beef, chicken, lamb, fish – it was just one meaty mash-up.

'I don't know you,' the elderly man with the ponytail repeated. Then he started to scream as Jax slid his meal through the slot in the door. 'Chief,' he yelled, seeking the assistance of a guard, his moist, fleshy lips poking through the small circular sound holes peppering the glass. 'Chief! Quick! They're trying to kill me again. Quick!'

He opened the box that now contained his food and snatched his meal. 'No way,' he shouted as he ripped off the lid and emptied the contents onto the floor, pea and ham soup splattering on the concrete. 'Youse won't get me. I'm onto youse. Chief, quick! They're trying to get me. Youse won't get me. You'll see.'

He then put the foil container on his head and mashed the pliable aluminium until it hugged his skull.

'Can't get me now,' he said, proudly wearing his foil-cap, leftover soup streaming down his face. 'Ha! Fuck off. Your brain laser won't work.'

The man turned and walked to his bed. Jax shuddered to think what crimes this man had committed to end up in

Supermax. Clearly mentally deranged, he must have been deemed too violent to keep in a psychiatric institute. Being crazy was not a defence against Supermax, which, with a psychiatrist on staff, was legally allowed to house such inmates.

Jax shook his head and moved to the next cell. 'Hey, what happened to my dinner?' came the question from the cell as he walked away. 'Benny. Hey, Benny. Whydya throw it on the floor. Ah! Me soup!'

Thankfully, that response was a one-off, and the majority of inmates just ignored him as he delivered their meals. One after another, he pulled the containers from the trolley and shoved them through the slot without incident or interaction – some of the inmates were sleeping, some reading, two shitting and one masturbating, the obese man in Cell No. 5 not even breaking his stroke as Jax pushed his meal through the door. Jax didn't respond to the two men who wanted to converse: one challenging him to a fistfight and the other threatening to cut his head off if his steak wasn't medium to well done. He would have dismissed the threat had he not recognised the man who had issued it: George Carpenter had decapitated three prostitutes.

JAX LOOKED down at the trolley. Only two meals to go. One of the foil containers had an orange sticker on the side: HALAL. He looked at the lid: Cell No. 75. Almost there.

He stopped in front of Cell No. 74 and, as he bent down to pick up his penultimate delivery, he noticed a strange smell. Something was off. He thought it was the food – until he looked into the cell.

Jax turned away as soon as he saw the filth on the floor: rotten food, rubbish, soiled clothes, insects dead and alive – fruit flies were buzzing around a pile of faeces. He wanted to grab the trolley and keep going but he couldn't; he didn't want to attract attention by denying an inmate dinner.

So he stretched the tray as far away from himself as possible while leaning his head back and holding his nose with his other hand. He fumbled as he tried to push the meal into the slot, which was barely bigger than the package he was trying to deliver. As he released it, he sensed something moving inside the cell.

Jax buckled as soon as he saw the Serpent. Already leaning back to distance himself from the air holes, he went weak at the knees and fell on his arse when he saw all the blood.

Oh no …

He didn't want to look again. He knew what he'd seen. But some primal instinct twisted his neck back round and forced his eyes to focus on the mutilated man. On the Serpent.

Jax heaved a little in his mouth, the sight of the Serpent hacking through his own arm, combined with the stench, making him physically sick.

That image would stay with him forever.

Of course, he'd heard about self-mutilation – apparently it was disturbingly common in all jails – but he had always imagined bruises, burns and shallow razor-blade cuts, not what would soon be an amputation if the Serpent didn't stop. Completely naked and standing in a pile of filth, he was ringbarking his forearm with what appeared to be a butter knife.

Jax didn't want to look again. He'd seen enough, too much. But his watering eyes swung back to the car crash that was the Serpent as soon as he'd swallowed.

The look on the Serpent's face was worse than the blood. Blank. Sawing away, knife now so deep it must have been hitting bone, he was expressionless, blank: eyes dead, mouth closed, not a hint of pain.

Jax looked harder. No, not blank. The Serpent was smiling.

Jax no longer even felt sick. Just scared. He wanted to run. To get up off the floor and go. Screw the meals. Screw the phone.

But something told him he needed to stay.

The Serpent suddenly stopped sawing. And then he turned.

Jax didn't realise he had stood up again until he became aware he was walking towards the plastic glass. Towards the Serpent. The madman was mesmerising.

Part of Jax wanted desperately to turn away, but another part of him couldn't. The Serpent seemed to ooze some kind of ominous pheromone that drew Jax in.

On his part, Jax realised, his interest was more than morbid fascination. The Serpent was a riddle. He was unexplained. Unsolved – crazy was too convenient for Jax. And he wanted to solve the Serpent as much as he wanted to solve himself.

Jax stopped an inch away from the cell. It was only then he saw the erection. Arms by his side, his bulging scarified muscles covered only by tattoos and smeared blood, the Serpent was aroused and standing like a statue. He was staring at Jax.

Those eyes. Again. Cold. Dead. Crazy. Crowded.

The Serpent's smile widened just before he turned away. He was pleased to have an audience, Jax thought. A witness to his ritual. Serial killers always crave attention, so the isolation and anonymity of prison are the biggest punishments of all. Maybe that's why he'd cut himself. For attention.

Jax was wrong. He winced as the Serpent plunged his right index finger into the open wound on his left forearm. There was no explanation for this. Or so Jax thought – until the Serpent turned blood into finger paint.

He lifted his right hand towards the adjacent wall. On its surface was a mural of madness, a canvas of crazy. Jax had never seen anything like it. The wall was completely covered in graffiti. Maps, charts and equations. Arabic and Armenian. Dodgy doodles and detailed drawings. Genius and gibberish. Most of the marks had been made with chalk – blue, yellow and white – but the wall had also been scratched and incised, smeared with shit and splattered with blood.

In the middle of this mess five large numerals had been etched into the concrete.

'Nine,' the Serpent said as he traced the first of the numbers with blood.

'Three,' he said, moving to the second numeral.

He returned to the ink-well in his arm, sticking both his index and middle fingers in this time for a bigger serve.

'Two,' the Serpent continued as he methodically turned another numeral red.

He whispered as he worked. Jax could see his lips moving, but he couldn't hear him properly again until the Serpent, fingers dripping with blood, shouted out the next number. 'Four.' It was bingo for the bonkers.

The neatness of the numbers unnerved Jax. Crazy was slashing and scratching. Jagged edges and all out of control. Not precision.

'One,' the Serpent said before stepping back to study his work. *93241.*

The five numerals were dead centre in the middle of the wall. Viewing the whole wall now that the Serpent had backed away, Jax noted that the only significant space left on the chaotic canvas was a patch of clean concrete below the freshly bloodied numbers. It stood out like a beacon.

The Serpent turned.

The Serpent charged.

Jax reeled away from the glass. He pulled his hands into fists even though he knew he was standing behind a bulletproof barrier. He was almost disappointed when he realised the Serpent was after him – he didn't even merit a glance. The Serpent smashed his bloodied hand into the knock-up, which was a crazy thing for a crazy person to do, then placed his hands on his head and sat on the cell floor.

The alarm was silent but it rang inside Jax's head all the same. It snapped him back to reality. To the cart. To Cell No. 75.

To the meal which was actually a mobile phone. He had to hurry, as the wing could be locked down in moments. He dragged himself away.

Hammad was clothed, cleanly shaved and, thankfully, not bleeding. Jax had been expecting another monster, but the inmate thanked him politely as he pushed the meal that wasn't a meal through the slot of the final cell door.

The Emergency Unit was storming into Supermax as Jax left. Four of them, wearing gas masks and body armour and moving more like soldiers than prison guards. The man at the head of the line would be the one to crack the cell; the second man would fire in the tear gas.

Jax stood to one side as they whipped past him. The last man in the line brandished a baton behind his shield. Meanwhile a pale man in a white coat waited on the other side of the door, behind a gurney that was armed with an arsenal of restraints. He was shaking.

JAX stared at his ceiling and waited for lights-out. Day done, head on his pillow, his mind was racing.

What was going on?

Jax suspected Clarke was keeping something from him. But he didn't push him for answers because he knew he wouldn't get any. Clarke was a very deliberate man, seemingly always in control, and he wasn't going to tell Jax anything that he didn't want him to know. Not unless Jax had leverage.

Jax had considered his options during his second meeting with Clarke. Pleading would not work. Neither would reason. His only play was to issue a threat. Jax knew he had leverage. He could deny Clarke his service. Refuse to deliver the final phones. But he also knew that Clarke would know it was a hollow threat.

Whatever was going on, and Jax had several theories, was not good. Every scenario he came up had the same outcome: people dead.

Jax was aware, though, that no matter what the crisis, Clarke's role was to save lives. Or at least try. And even if Clarke miscalculated and took a quiet threat seriously — almost a zero chance given all the personality profiling — there still wasn't any great likelihood that Jax would get to the truth.

If he were in Clarke's position, Jax told himself, he would have anticipated such a threat and already developed a sound and convincing explanation for the situation. And Clarke would have done that too.

So Jax said nothing. He listened, nodded and then did what needed to be done.

Now, with all the phones delivered, the listening device installed, and his head on his pillow, he could feel himself bracing for impact. He didn't know what was coming, but he knew it was coming. And soon.

CHAPTER 38

Goulburn Correctional Centre, Goulburn, NSW, Australia

'GO,' Clarke barked into his two-way radio.

And with that they stormed in.

Dressed from head to toe in black, wearing body armour and balaclavas, the ASIO attack dogs were let off their leash. Divided into 'bricks' – groups of two for this mission – the unit of eight powered its way into the darkness. As their night-vision googles, or NVGs, turned the wing into fifty shades of fluorescent green, the first brick peeled off from the unit and darted left.

'Brick One in position,' said the soldier standing on the left-hand side of the door. The soldier on the right said nothing: mouth shut and finger on the trigger.

'Affirmative,' said the leader of Brick Two, not breaking step or changing speed as he became the new leader of the rolling train.

Clarke sat in a blacked-out van monitoring an array of LCD screens covering every inch of internal space inside the stripped-out Ford Transit. His eyes darted from one live feed to the next, taking in the eight individual feeds coming from the helmet cameras on top of the soldiers' heads.

'Brick Two in position,' came the next transmission, the former leader now standing in front of another cell door with his partner.

'Affirmative,' said the leader of Brick Three.

His Colt M4A1 assault rifle swaying from left to right as he charged, the new leader kept his finger on the trigger, even though the slightest press would send fifteen rounds into the dark.

He pressed on, his NVG lighting the way. Just. Despite the public perception – movies and video games were to blame – NVGs were still a terrible piece of kit. Even with cutting-edge military technology – at least ten years away from being copied by the Chinese and sold on eBay for forty bucks – the world through NVG still looked like a rave: a green laser pulsing through a smoke machine.

And the goggles were useless without a light source. Thankfully, that was not an issue here, the wing's glass ceiling allowing enough moonlight through for the NGVs to do their job.

'Brick Three in position,' he said a moment later when he and his partner reached the cell door.

'Affirmative,' said the leader of Brick Four.

Six of his screens now still, Clarke focused on the movement. His final brick.

'Brick Four in position,' came the call.

Clarke ran his eyes across all of the screens quickly. He was amazed that they were all so still. No bobbing up and down, no nervous looking around. He turned to another monitor, where a series of biometric indicators flashing across the screen confirmed what he was thinking: that these men were freaks. Not one of the eight men had a heart rate above sixty; they might as well have been asleep. He shook his head in amazement.

Recruited by ASIO from the Australian Special Forces (Special Operations Command, or SOC), they'd been told only that their country needed them for a highly classified six-month assignment. Their units thought they'd been sent to undergo a new kind of survival training in the New Guinea Highlands. But, in fact, they'd never left New South Wales.

Clarke called his special-forces hit squad 'the Ronin', the Japanese word for former Samurai turned hitmen for hire. All clad in black and wearing balaclavas, they were indistinguishable – simply anonymous parts of a well-oiled machine, which Clarke controlled.

He put down the radio that he used to talk to the Ronin and picked up the one that connected him to command. 'All in place,' he said. 'I repeat: Ronin in place. Do we have permission to proceed?'

A sharp squelch of static followed by a voice: 'Ronin are good to go.'

Clarke picked up the other radio and issued the order: 'Ronin are green.'

JAX was on his feet and in a defensive stance he'd learned in his combat training within seconds of his cell door bursting open. The snap of the lock had jolted him awake and he'd reacted without pause. As his eyes adjusted to the dark, he could make out a shape in the small amount of moonlight coming through the open cell door. He'd been waiting for something like this for three nights. Since he'd delivered the last of the phones.

'Fuck,' he exclaimed, as he was suddenly blinded by a blast of light. He knew immediately that whoever was behind the intrusion was both military trained and equipped. While a standard LED torch produced about 100 lumens, some military flashlights could put out 4000 lumens – enough to set fire to paper. Still unable to open his eyes, he knew he had been hit with the fire-starting type. He also knew the light would be attached to an assault rifle, strapped to its barrel, which would now be aimed at the middle of his forehead.

'What the—'

His question was cut off by the intruder, a hard hand suddenly smothering his mouth. The man wore a tactical glove – Jax could feel the toughened plastic on the fingertips.

Army. Infantry.

He resisted his animalistic urge to fight. The man was only using enough force to subdue him and wasn't trying to hurt him.

With the flashlight now lowered, Jax was able to open his eyes. He blinked hard, still temporarily blinded by the earlier scorching. He wanted to see his attacker's face, search it for more information.

Gradually the spots of light in his eyes dimmed, details emerged and the scene began to take shape. The man was wearing black and his face was covered by a balaclava. Jax's eyes were drawn to his outstretched arm, the one that wasn't holding him down. It was raised high and pulled into a fist.

Jax nodded.

The man then unclenched his fist, opened his hand and pressed his index finger to the tip of his thumb, forming a circle: OK.

Jax nodded again, raised his own hand, made a fist and extended his thumb.

Now it was the man in the balaclava nodding, acknowledging that Jax had just given him the military hand signal for 'I understand'.

He made a final hand signal after removing his hand from Jax's mouth.

Hold.

Jax gave him another thumbs-up.

Eyes fast adjusting to the dark, Jax saw that the man was carrying a Colt M4A1 assault rifle and was night-vision equipped, his googles flipped up and sitting on the top of his head. He also saw the other man, dressed in black, carrying a Colt M4A1, and standing over the top of Khalil.

The man over Jax turned towards his partner. Towards Khalil. Moving like lightning, the men in black had Khalil gagged and bound before he even woke up. Jax remained silent and still as they peeled him off the bed and whisked him towards the door. Khalil could do nothing to resist except groan. The man that Jax had been conversing with in military sign language stopped and turned just before leaving the cell.

He nodded at Jax.

Jax nodded back.

And then they were gone.

Click!

Jax jumped, the sound of the lock snapping shut startling him even though he'd expected it. He looked around his cell: dark, quiet and empty. Like nothing had just happened. The whole episode, from door-opening to door-shutting had taken sixteen seconds. Jax hadn't even realised he'd been counting, but he also knew he was right. Sixteen seconds. Bound, gagged and gone. In and out.

In sixteen seconds? They weren't just military. They were Special Forces. They were SOC. The brand of NGVs and the types of weapons they had on them confirmed his suspicion. While regular army used Steyr AUGs, the SOCs opted for the M4, a US weapon and America's response to the game-changing AK-47.

Jax was sure that Khalil wouldn't be the only one they'd taken – they would have grabbed all of the Terror Twelve, minus one after Halim's sudden heart attack, plus newcomer Mahmud the Mufti.

Jax estimated there would have been a battle group of eight in the wing, operating in bricks, two men for each cell. There would have been another battle group conducting a simultaneous raid in the other block, of a size Jax couldn't estimate because he didn't know how the inmates were arranged in their cells. No doubt they had also sent a team into Supermax, Hammad being the ultimate prize.

Jax wondered who had brought them undone.

Was it Bashir, the shady Sheik perhaps talking of the plot while using his contraband mobile phone?

Was it Hammad, as he ordered the cell into action from Supermax?

Was its Khalil, the simpleton maybe shooting his mouth off during a meeting in the Kent brothers' cell?

Or was it none of them?

Clarke had looked completely frazzled that last time they'd spoken. To the point of recklessness, even. Jax wouldn't be surprised if the prisoners were being sped towards an abandoned warehouse with hoods over their heads. He really didn't know what Clarke was capable of.

CHAPTER 39

SAMI and Mav had been watching them for three days. The fitted-out milk van was fully equipped, but not the most comfortable place to hole up. They slept in shifts, but didn't exit the vehicle – it had an operational fridge and microwave, though the food supplied wasn't exactly gourmet. The less said about the cassette toilet, the better. It had been a while since Sami had done this kind of gruelling surveillance work himself – he was more used to sitting behind a desk in a bureau. He'd never take the coffee machine in the office for granted again.

The four men who were living in the rented unit they were staking out had done very little in the last seventy-two hours. Aside from a group visit to the local mosque for prayer, only two of them had left the building.

An ASIO agent had followed the first of the suspects to an electronics store, a hidden camera recording the man as he purchased a radio frequency transmitter and its matching receiver. A second ASIO spook picked up the tail and followed him as he drove his rusted Toyota, registered to a construction company owned by the Halims, to a different electronics store in another suburb. There, he bought a roll of speaker wire. A third agent followed him as he made a third stop, at another electronics store, where he bought a soldering iron, fuses, switches and parts.

He could have been making a stereo. But the fact that he travelled to three different stores when all the components were available at the first store suggested he was making something else.

A bomb.

A separate team had followed the second suspect. An agent had sat at the opposite end of the carriage of train, eyes on the target for the entire trip to the city. He remained seated when the suspect got up.

'Target alighting the train,' he whispered into the microphone attached to the underside of his collar.

The five other agents on the train, all on separate carriages, disembarked with the target at St James Station, a small but busy underground stop near Sydney's centre.

'Got him,' the agent taking lead of the trail said.

Sami wasn't leaving anything to chance. Witnessing first-hand the efficiency of Clarke and his team, he'd had something of a wake-up call. Now, he was operating with a level of focus and precision he hadn't experienced for years, if not a decade. There was no way he and Mav were going to be the weak link.

Sami immediately passed the coordinates of St James Station to the drone operator who was on standby. On loan from the US, the state-of-the-art military drone was on the suspect almost as fast the sunlight, its million-dollar camera picking him up the moment he emerged from the station and set foot on the street. Even though the drone flew at an altitude of 20,000 feet, the image it provided was so good that Sami felt like he could reach out and touch the top of the target's head.

Six separate feeds were being delivered to Sami and Mav in the van by the time the target reached St Mary's Cathedral, the drone pictures still the clearest. Sami watched as the suspect cased the historic cathedral. To any passer-by, he probably looked as if he were simply admiring the church, standing out the front with his paper and pen, making a sketch then taking some pictures.

But it was clear to Sami that wasn't what he was doing. The phone call he'd made to an inmate at Goulburn jail revealed he was using his pen and paper to list exit points and count the crowd, while the pictures would likely be used to identify points of vulnerability in the cathedral's structure.

AFTER that, while tempted to make an immediate move, both Sami and Clarke had agreed they needed to watch, listen and learn – just a little longer.

Now, Sami was almost certain these were their men. The information they had gathered, much of it resulting from the work of an intriguing inside asset named Riley Jax, suggested there were going to be two more attacks. One this month, on 25 November, and another the following month, on 25 December. That made sense. A Christmas Day finale. No better date to put an exclamation mark on the biggest attack on Christian Churches since the Holy Wars.

The four men in the flat, paid for by an already convicted terrorist named Halim, had all spent time in Goulburn jail. That made sense too.

So Sami was almost certain that he had his men. Ideally, he preferred to be completely certain, and doubts remained. While confident they were set to scoop up a cell – plotters and soldiers alike – he couldn't be sure it was the entire cell. But now, in the early hours of 24 November, 'fairly certain' would have to suffice.

It was on.

'Copy,' Sami said when Clarke informed him that the extraction was done and the raid was to commence.

Sami put down the radio, gave Mav a nod and spoke into the microphone to the commander of the NSW Police Special Protection Group (SPG), who was waiting on the ground with his team.

'We are green,' Sami said.

The SPG was unleashed.

ASIO was required by law to use the NSW Police unit for public arrests. Though the SPG weren't as highly trained as Clarke's commandos, Sami was impressed nonetheless. He and Mav watched the body-cam footage from their van as the spear of the SPG battle-group stormed towards the terrorists' apartment block. The battering ram known as the 'big red key' made easy work of the entrance door, and the team moved swiftly and smoothly up the stairs, everything seemingly going like clockwork.

Sami heard the explosion before his screens went dead, a thundering blast. He dived to the floor, pulling Mav with him, as the two-tonne van rocked back and forth in the shockwaves and shrapnel fell from the sky, a hailstorm of smashed glass and shattered bricks.

When the aerial assault ceased, Sami pulled his hands from his head and got up on his knees.

'You right?' he asked Mav, who had a look on his face like he'd just had the smug knocked right out of him.

'Yeah, yeah, I'm fine,' he replied, rising gingerly.

Sami reefed open the van door and stumbled onto the sidewalk. Mav tumbled out after him. The apartment they had been looking at for the last three days was gone. So were the ones under it, above it and next to it. Flames licked the shell that remained.

CHAPTER 40

Goulburn Correctional Centre, Goulburn, NSW, Australia

The guard burst into Jax's open cell. 'Visit,' he barked.

Finally, Jax thought. He'd been expecting a visit from Clarke since the day before. Following the 2 am extraction, he'd sat alone on his bed in the dark, waiting for an explanation. He'd had then watched the sun rise, figuring answers would come with the morning. They didn't.

Jax had gone to muster and listened hard, not for the numbers that were being called, but the ones that weren't. The wing was suddenly down five men. The guard either didn't notice or knew that they were gone. Either way, there was no explanation.

He passed the day in the gym and then went back to his solitary cell after dinner and watched the sun set, the night bringing only darkness – no mail, no messages. He barely slept, tossed and turned, a million scenarios running through his head.

But now a guard was here. 'Come on,' he urged Jax. 'Let's go.'

Jax looked at his watch before getting to his feet.
10 am, 25 NOV.

BRIEFCASE closed, arms folded and wearing a smile, Clarke was already in the room when he arrived. The transformation in Clarke's face was remarkable: his eyes were clear, his skin flushed with a healthy daub of pink, and there were none of the previous physiological signs of stress. Jax did note, however, that Clarke appeared to have been particularly busy: his crushed clothing, face stubble and scent of body odour smothered by too much deodorant were sure signs that the agent had not been home.

'Good news, I take it?' Jax asked as he sat down.

'Yes,' Clarke replied.

Jax listened and Clarke spoke, the agent telling him the Terror Twelve were the group behind the six international attacks known as the Church Bombings. That a joint CIA/ASIO task force had tracked and destroyed the Terror Twelve's two remaining cells and moved all surviving members of the organisation to a secure location for questioning.

Jax had a million questions. So much didn't yet make sense. Not without all the details.

But he knew better than to ask.

JUST after lights-out, he made sure the corridor was empty then pulled out his smartphone. The prison was quiet, not yet asleep. But that didn't matter. Not now. He wasn't a suspect. They had the men responsible.

Or so they thought.

He smiled, delighted with himself. He tapped his way across the screen.

Username: mahdi_93/241. Password: Hewillrise_85/159.

He raised his brows when he was denied. Wrong password. He was so excited that he'd been typing too fast. The prospect of the live feed had his heart racing and his stomach full of scampering bugs. His hands were shaking. He took a deep breath and this time used only his index finger to type.

Username: Mahdi_93/241. Password: Hewillrise_85/159.

A capped M, not an uncapped m. Got it.

He would not be denied. Not now. Not ever. Only the disbelievers would be denied. He would be the first to touch His outstretched hand.

He opened his internet browser and logged into a fake but secure WhatsApp account created specifically for that night. He had already activated the cell, sending the deposits: $0.61, $4.04, $5.55 and $9.82. He'd also given them their instructions when they called: where to obtain the gun, what to do with the seller and, finally, what time they needed to be in place to make the final call.

His burner phone flashed at 10 pm +44 7346 984 325 appearing on the screen. It was 11 am, 25 November, in Salisbury, England.

'Greetings, my child,' said the Mahdi. 'Are you in place?'

He listened to the reply.

'Good,' the Mahdi said. 'Good. And how about the phone? Are you all set to record?'

The Mahdi smiled when he got his reply.

'Excellent,' the Mahdi said. 'I am proud of you, my son. Proud of both of you. Now do as I have instructed. Everything exactly to plan. I will be watching, as will He. You go with God. You do this for His glory.'

This time the Mahdi would not have to imagine the rest. He had instructed one of the former Goulburn jail inmates to record the attack on his mobile phone and live-stream it on another WhatsApp account – the world would see it unfold through the eyes of the attacker wearing the bomb and guarding the door at the back of the cathedral. The Mahdi had been too cautious to attempt anything like this during the first six attacks, but now, following the recent developments, he felt it was a risk he could take.

The Mahdi had suspected that the Goulburn link would be exposed. Having established that both Charlie Haddad and Mike Evans had been inmates there, the investigators would probably also work out that the dead Australian found decapitated in a suitcase in Russia was part of the St Petersburg plot. Three of the attackers coming from the same place was too much of a coincidence.

So, knowing that the prison would be put under surveillance and swarming with spies, he'd enacted his backup plan. He'd instructed Mahmud, his co-conspirator and recruiter, to lead the copycats on – to plant the idea with the freshly convicted terrorists, still hungry for jihad, and give them the blueprint. He knew that would get them talking about the plot, in meetings and on their ASIO-issued mobile phones, make them the obvious suspects. And all had gone to plan – the dummy cell even blowing themselves up as ordered.

The Mahdi could take more risks now, as the men in custody would be blamed for whatever came next. Their denials would mean nothing. The authorities would assume the cell was still running autonomously. The only one who knew what was really going on was Mahmud, and he would die before saying a word. In fact, he would kill himself as soon as he got the chance.

And even if the authorities thought the mastermind was still at large, which wasn't likely, they couldn't look any harder at the jail than they already had. They'd given it their all – bugs, phones, secret agents – and he was still there. And now, for the first time, he was about to witness the terror he'd sown, the carnage and the deaths, the glory of his plan.

He smiled when he heard the screams. He smiled even wider when he saw the blood. But he frowned when his screen turned to static, as the feed went dead following a flash.

Again, he was forced to imagine the rest. The ruin and the rubble. The buried bodies. The honking horns and the hazmat suits.

Maybe he would have them set up a camera outside for the next one. For the last one. For the one that would bring Him back.

He smiled before turning off his phone.

Seven down.

CHAPTER 41

Goulburn Correctional Centre, Goulburn, NSW, Australia

THIS time, Clarke was not alone. Jax was not surprised. If the word going around in the wing was true, there'd been another terror attack on a church. Despite the fact that the last time Clarke had visited, he'd told Jax that the terror cell behind the church bombings were now under lock and key.

Somewhere along the line, someone had seriously stuffed up.

'This is Special Agent Hudson Sami from the CIA,' Clarke said, not looking up from his files as Jax entered the room. 'Please take a seat. We have a lot to get through.' Clarke looked briefly at the CIA agent. 'Shall I start?' he asked.

'Shoot,' the American replied.

Clarke turned his attention to Jax. 'We were wrong,' he said. 'We now have reason to believe that the mastermind behind the church bombings is still at large. That he is still here. Still in this jail. And you now have twenty-nine days to help us work out who he is.'

'What makes you think there's still a link to this place?' Jax asked. 'Maybe it's two cells, operating independently, and you've just shut the local cell down. Honestly, I did find it a stretch to think that a coordinated global attack could have been masterminded by that mob. They're too busy bickering over their own pecking order to get something that big underway.'

Both men were silent.

'It's time we levelled with you,' the American agent said. 'It was a mistake not to do so sooner.'

Clarke looked as though he was about to react – argue or shout or put the CIA man in his place. But then he just shrugged and nodded. Then he put his hand on top of a thick blue file on the desk and pushed it towards Jax.

Jax silently opened the file and began reading. He spent the next fifteen minutes learning about the three dead Australian terrorists. Two had been killed in a botched attack in Mexico and one had been found butchered in a suitcase in St Petersburg. The file contained their complete histories: police records, court transcripts, school reports, employment histories, hobbies, political leanings, favourite foods – the lot.

Jax shoved the bundle aside when he was finished.

Clarke slid a second folder to him. 'The attacks, everything we know,' he said.

Jax spent almost two hours reading the documents in the second folder. Most of it was new to him. Finally, he had all details of the church bombings: where, when and how. He examined the facts more closely than the presumptions.

He held his tongue as he pushed the blue folder back; he would not comment. Not yet.

Clarke immediately exchanged the file for a green folder.

Jax spent almost half an hour poring over the documents inside, which amounted to a detailed analysis of all the world's known terror groups. Jax was especially interested in ASIO's assessment of which groups were most likely to be conducting the Church Bombings.

The green folder was followed by a yellow one containing information on twenty-seven former Goulburn inmates who were still at large. It took Jax about twenty minutes to go through it. By then he had some ideas on how he could narrow the list down.

Clarke finally slid Jax a black folder, a compendium of all the evidence collected on the Terror Twelve. Included in the file were transcripts from the calls made on the contraband mobile phones and conversations picked up by the bug in the Kent brothers' cell. There were also detailed reports on operations called 'Watch', 'Extract' and 'Apprehend'.

'What you won't find in any of the reports was what happened yesterday,' Sami said after Jax had turned and read the last page in the final folder. 'As you've heard, there was another attack. Another 351 killed when a bomb was detonated inside Salisbury Cathedral in the UK.'

The specifics were news to Jax. Though the prison grapevine was hardy, it wasn't usually entirely accurate, nor rich with subtleties.

'The Magna Carta?' Jax asked.

'Gone,' Sami said. 'Burnt to a crisp.'

'So what do you need from me?' Jax asked.

'We need you to find out who's behind this, son,' Sami said. 'I have read all your files and I reckon these guys from ASIO should be the ones—'

Sami bit his lip as Clarke's fist slammed into the table. Sami gave Clarke a meaningful look before turning back to face Jax.

'We need everyone we can on this, and from what I have read about you, you could be our best shot. I think you can do a lot more than deliver phones and install bugs. Am I right?'

Jax nodded.

'So, whaddya need?' Sami asked. 'Say the word and it's yours.'

Jax rattled off a list: a laptop, an internet connection, an iPhone, a bag of blank electronic keys and a file on every Goulburn inmate.

JAX found the laptop in his cell. It had been left in the cavity behind the false front in his shelves, along with everything else he'd requested.

Muster over, he had the whole day ahead of him. His twenty-nine-day countdown started now.

He surveyed the cell. All Khalil's possessions had been removed – his toaster taken, his food and toiletries tossed. The Quran he'd kept on his bedside table was no longer there, neither was the prayer mat, usually rolled up and leaning against the end of the bed. His box shelves were empty and the bed he'd been dragged from had been remade perfectly.

The site of the bed had made Jax inexplicably sad. He wondered what people would think if he ever admitted that a convicted terrorist had become a friend.

But neither Khalil nor anyone else would be returning to this cell. Sami had pulled whatever strings the CIA pull to make sure Jax had the room to himself, at least for the next twenty-nine days, so he wouldn't have to worry about sleeping pills and secrets. Alone in his cell, Jax was tempted to pull out his laptop and make a start. But he didn't. Couldn't. Not during the day. Not with his cell door unlocked. A guard could pay an unscheduled visit at any time. An inmate could walk in. Being caught with a laptop was worse than being caught with a weapon. He'd end up in Supermax with the Serpent.

He would have to wait until lights-out. He did, however, sneak a peek at the inmate files using the iPhone, and a peek was all he needed.

THE SOON-to-be-summer sun battered the yard. A heat haze hovered above the asphalt, the empty chalk-drawn handball courts. The metal bench seats were also deserted, threatening a well-done rump for any inmate stupid enough to sit on the sizzling surface.

Jax walked towards the sun as soon as he entered the yard. His belly full after his lunch of two ham-and-cheese sandwiches, vegemite crackers and an orange juice, he squinted as he walked across the concrete, only stopping when he reached the cyclone fence.

He turned away from the sun and looked back into the yard, then climbed on a tabletop to get an elevated view. Happy with his vantage point, he nodded. With the sun at his back, he could see all of them, the entire yard. But they couldn't see him.

Jax had learned about silhouettes while conducting a joint operation with the Navy. They'd shown him how to make a 60,000-tonne battleship disappear using nothing but the sky and the sun. While he couldn't make himself vanish, he could use the sun to make himself unrecognisable. Just a black outline. And that's what he was now. No one in the yard would detect him spying and studying. No one in the yard would know they were a suspect.

Jax started scanning the crowd. Going from left to right, he gave every inmate present a once-over: name, age, crime, sentence, social media profiles and posts. He matched the files he'd just devoured to the faces, then compared them to the profile he'd started building: male, aged thirty or over; intelligent, idealistic, resourceful, charismatic, egocentric, pathological, messianic, megalomaniacal.

Most of the prisoners were standing in groups. Searching for shade, they'd congregated under trees, awnings and in the shadows cast by buildings. There was only one inmate sitting in the sun. Alone and looking at his feet, he was appeared to be in a world of his own. *Matt McAuliffe, eighteen. Drink driving. Eight months. No prior convictions.*

Jax crossed McAuliffe off his list of suspects, which he had now narrowed down to twenty-one. Jax had been able to rule out almost eighty-five percent of the yard on his first sweep, based on his profiling. But twenty-one was still twenty too many. There was only one mastermind.

Jax turned back to his left and started a fresh scan in a bid to further narrow the field. This time he would not be looking at their files. He would be looking at them. Concentrating on the twenty-one who still matched his suspect profile, he would study them closely: their mannerisms, group dynamics, gestures, posture. If a picture was worth a thousand words, then an action was worth a million. The files couldn't tell him everything. He had to observe to truly determine things like megalomania, egocentricity and charisma. And once he'd narrowed the list further – by the next day, he hoped – he would go even deeper, hovering behind his targets to not only watch but also listen. Then, finally, he would interact – his behaviour tightly scripted and his questions carefully crafted.

Jax was almost through his second sweep when he saw that the kid called McAuliffe was no longer alone, and no longer in the sun either. Four Samoans, ranging from big to fucking huge were standing over the first-time offender.

Jax sprang from his tabletop and onto his feet. *Don't do it. Don't get involved. It's not your fight.*

He knew the smart move would be to back up, to turn the other way and go back to studying the inmates. He couldn't afford to draw attention to himself. Not now. Not with just twenty-nine days to find the mastermind. The Samoans would most likely come after him if he intervened. They might even try to kill him.

Jax wasn't scared of death – sometimes he wished for it – but dying right now would be selfish. They wouldn't just be killing him, they would be murdering the hundreds he had been entrusted to save. He turned round, retraced his steps. But then ...

'Fuck it,' he snarled.

He couldn't help himself. The skinny kid reminded him of somebody he used to know. A scared kid who was bashed, raped and made to murder. A kid no one helped.

Jax started sizing them up as soon as he took his first step. He played out the worst-case scenario in his head, in which the biggest of the gang went straight for Jax's throat and the remaining three then piled in, jumping Jax and beating him to a pulp. In the best-case scenario, the gang backed down on the mere threat of Jax's involvement. Not likely, he knew.

By the time he neared the group, Jax had run through a dozen scenarios in between the worst and the best. He knew which one he wanted to trigger.

His plan went out the window when the smallest of the group made a move before Jax had even reached them, kicking the still-seated kid straight in the face. Jax took two explosive steps and launched himself off his left foot. With his right knee thrust towards the heavens and dragging him into the sky, he was three feet above the ground when he started cocking his kick.

He struck the smallest Samoan on the side of his leg, just above his knee, Jax's weight and speed combining with gravity to deliver a perfectly timed sidekick with the force of a car crash. The sound of the bone breaking was horrifying, as was the screaming that followed when the floored giant saw the razor-sharp point of his broken fibula sticking through his skin.

Jax was appalled, not by the damage he'd done, but by the way he felt: satisfied. The feeling he'd experienced when his right foot had landed exactly where he'd intended, and struck with even more force than he'd thought he could generate, had been something akin to elation. He wondered what he had become.

The part of him that didn't like the steroid-induced strength and black-ops-level hand-to-hand combat skills struggled with the part of him that did. Doing the hurting was of course better than being hurt. Being the bully was better than being bullied. Strong was better than weak. And right now wasn't the time for a crisis of conscience – he had another three Samoans to fight.

Jax pulled his fists to his face as he swivelled to confront the remaining men. He was relieved to find they were all standing exactly as they had been, huddled in a group around the kid. They obviously hadn't served in the military. Had never heard of flanking or attacking in an offensive horseshoe. Nevertheless, by the looks of them – big, powerful and showing no sign of fear, they had never lost a fight.

Jax was about to change that.

Returning to his original plan, he took out meanest-looking motherfucker first, using a *hiraken*, a punch made with the fingers bent at the middle knuckles in a claw-like form. The blow to the trachea crushed the man's windpipe and ruptured his thyroid gland. Jax suspected he may have also severed his vocal cord given that he didn't scream. Instead, he just fell to the ground and gurgled.

Now facing left after throwing his right hand, Jax was in the perfect position to attack the man behind him. He transferred all the weight loaded onto his left leg into a devastating roundhouse kick, his leg whipping through the air and straightening to create tearing torque just before his foot smashed into the Samoan's hip. Jax continued to drive the kick even after hitting bone.

The Samoan's legs stayed still as his torso twisted.

Pop!

With his hip ripped clean off his femur, the Samoan became a human corkscrew, his upper body twisting away from his legs before he crashed to the ground with his toes up and his belly down.

Jax loaded his right fist and swivelled to face his final foe.

'Nah, bro,' said the only Samoan still standing. 'I'm sweet, hey. I've got nothing against you, bro.'

With his hands in the air, palms facing forward, the Samoan retreated.

'It's sweet as, bro,' he said before turning and running off.

Jax ignored the three injured men, two screaming and one gurgling, and moved towards the kid. McAuliffe was still sitting on the ground, covered in blood and holding his nose.

'Come on,' Jax said as he helped him up. 'Quick. We gotta go.' He hadn't even considered the screws, his rage rendering him uncharacteristically careless. But so far, so good.

He led McAuliffe away from the broken bodies to a bench seat away from what was now a crime scene.

'Give me a look,' Jax said as he pulled the kid's hand away from his face.

The blood began to leak, then flow fast.

'Shit,' said Jax, pinching the boy's nostrils shut. 'Tip your head back,' said he told him.

The kid complied.

'That's it. We'll have it stopped in no time.'

McAuliffe started to sob.

'What did they want?' Jax asked, hoping the conversation would distract the kid from the pain. 'I got flogged for two hundred bucks down at Long Bay.'

'Don't know,' the kid said through the sobs. 'I told 'em to eat a dick when they asked me something about a betting account.'

Jax's eyes lit up. He was suddenly desperate to get back to his cell.

JAX didn't bother getting under his sheet; he just lay on top of his military-style bedding, all inch-perfect folds and hospital corners, as he waited for lights-out. His mind had been racing since his chat with the kid.

He'd been excited at first. It was a light-bulb moment. A lead.

But then he'd got angry. Pissed off that he'd been denied the chance to stop the last bomb. Until the day before, Jax had thought he was simply collecting evidence. He couldn't stop an attack because he hadn't known there was an attack to stop. He could possibly have saved them had Clarke told him the truth. But he hadn't.

Clarke had not trusted him. Yet he'd never lied to Clarke. And he'd done everything he had asked.

He wondered what else Clarke had lied about.

Click!

It was suddenly dark. Lights-out. Almost time.

He just had to wait for the guard to finish his patrol. Propped up against his pillow, Jax listened for the echo of footsteps.

The guard soon came and went.

Jax went to his hiding hole and returned to his bed with the iPhone. Blanket pulled over his head to smother the light, he logged into his old Yahoo account. He ignored the 1301 unread messages and got straight to work, thumbs skipping across the glass, text fast filling the screen. He'd decided to contact Sami – not Clarke.

To: Sami1@cia.gov
From: jumpingjaxflash@yahoo.com.au
Subject: Information Request
Special Agent Sami,
Can you please go through the suspect list and find out if any of them have betting accounts? I need to get hold of a transaction list for each account, going back at least a year. I also need the same records for Mike Evans, Charlie Haddad and Tim Jenkins.
R.J.

It was only 10 pm so there was still a chance of getting a reply. He decided he would wait up, all night if he had to. But for that he needed help. He retrieved two green and white pills from his secret safe then got back into his bed, under his blanket. And there he sat, phone in hand, checking his email every ten minutes until 6.57 am.

To: *jumpingjaxflash@yahoo.com.au*
Cc: *tom.clarke@ASIO.gov.au*
From: *Sami1@cia.gov*
Subject: *RE: Information Request*
Done. *Files attached. All 27 had at least one betting account. Reply when you can.*
H.

Jax opened the attachment and began looking through the files. A former inmate named Gordon Mailer had one online betting account. Jax flicked straight past his transaction history after he saw that the account had not been used since the day he'd been released. He moved on to the next name.

His reading was abruptly interrupted when the lock on his door snapped open. He threw the phone between his legs and pulled the blanket off his head. He was expecting to find a guard standing in his cell but the door was still closed. He heard a muffled conversation, just outside his cell.

He didn't have long. He sprang from his sheets, dived onto the floor, yanked the false front off the shelf unit and threw the phone into the hole before slapping the front back on.

'What the fuck are you doing?' the guard asked, suddenly standing in front of him.

'What the fuck does it look like? Oh, that's right. A fat bastard like you wouldn't know what a push-up is.'

The guard laughed.

'Yeah, righto,' he said. 'I left myself open for that one. Get to muster, ya funny cunt.'

Jax had a horrifying thought while he was standing in the morning sun waiting for his number to be called. He realised he had not switched off the phone. He wondered what the factory set ringtone was, and, more importantly, how loud it was. Surely, they wouldn't call him?

They didn't, thank God. There were no missed calls when he broke his 'not before lights-out' rule to check his phone after breakfast. Nor were there any later that night when he switched it back on.

HIS HEAD back under his blanket, his face lit by the glow of the screen, Jax started going through the other files summarising the betting accounts. Not taking notes felt a little awkward. He'd never needed to write anything down, as everything was saved in his head, but he had made it a habit. Not wanting to look out of place, he was always armed with paper and pen. He also pretended to read his notes whenever someone was watching.

Jax logged back into his email account when he was done and sent Sami another note.

To: Sami1@cia.gov
From: jumpingjaxflash@yahoo.com.au
Subject: MEETING
Special Agent Sami,
I need to see you tomorrow. It's urgent.
R.J.

Jax slept soundly for the first time in weeks. He even managed to get the Serpent out of his head.

CHAPTER 42

Ben Chifley Building, Canberra, NSW, Australia

IN a room way too modern and clean to be a torture chamber, Clarke circled Mahmud with a freshly purchased pair of pliers.

'He's enjoying this way too much,' Sami said to Mav as the pair watched through one-sided mirror glass.

A personal call from the President of the United States had convinced the Australian Prime Minister to allow a 'light working over'. After receiving advice from his cabinet, Prime Minister Taylor had used the *National Secrets Act* to both make the strenuous interrogation of terror suspects legal and also ensure the amendment was never made public.

Clarke had driven himself to Bunnings for some DIY torture shopping. He'd headed straight for the tool shop and picked up an angle grinder.

'We're not cutting hands off,' Sami said when he saw Clarke's loot.

Clarke ignored Sami and continued unpacking the rest of his purchases.

* * *

KHALIL had broken fast. As soon as he saw the hose and the towel.

'Yes,' he answered, Sami asking the questions after Clarke had insisted on doing the slapping.

'The cathedral. Yes. Bashir was going to blow it up. That was the first target.'

Sami pushed him on the second. 'What did they plan on blowing up next?'

'I don't know,' Khalil said.

Clarke turned on the hose.

'No, please,' he begged. 'I'm speaking the truth. Bashir and Mahmud were fighting about it. Bashir wanted to go back to the nuclear reactor. He was adamant we had to finish what we'd started. He wanted to show everyone that we had not failed. But Mahmud wouldn't let him. He said it had to be the same as the rest of the attacks or no one would believe it was us. He said we had to attack churches if we wanted to take credit for the rest. He said we would become the most famous mujahideen in the world.'

After that, they'd all broken one after another, like dominoes falling. To Sami's surprise, even Hammad, the so-called mastermind of the group, had squealed as soon as he saw all the power tools, which had been splattered with red corn syrup – Mav's special touch.

'It was Mahmud's plan,' he'd said. 'All I did was approve it. I was just going to take the credit.'

THE only one who put up a fight was Mahmud. The one Clarke was circling now, Bunnings pliers in hand.

'We are responsible for all the church attacks,' Mahmud continued. 'We are not copycats. Tell the world, it was us.'

Jax's email arrived just in time for Sami to save Mahmud's fingernails.

'We have to go,' said Sami. 'Now.'

Clarke reluctantly dropped the pliers.

CHAPTER 43

Goulburn Correctional Centre, Goulburn, NSW, Australia

JAX began writing as soon as Sami handed him the pen.

> *Stuart James*
> *25 May*
> *04:00:02 Deposit +$0.61*
> *04:00:09 Deposit +$4.19*
> *04:00:15 Deposit +$5.09*
> *04:00:22 Deposit +$6.13*

He printed as neatly as he could. Names first.

> *Timothy Jenkins*
> *25 June*
> *02:59:58 Deposit +$0.61*
> *03:00:04 Deposit +$4.03*
> *03:00:11 Deposit +$5.26*
> *03:00:16 Deposit +$7.72*

Followed by the date.

> *Adam Wright*
> *25 July*
> *04:00:00 Deposit +$0.61*
> *04:00:05 Deposit +$4.05*
> *04:00:11 Deposit +$5.28*
> *04:00:16 Deposit +$1.45*

Then the betting account transaction, beginning with the time.

> *Omar Amir*
> *25 August*
> *11:00:10 Deposit +$0.61*
> *11:00:14 Deposit +$4.32*
> *11:00:19 Deposit +$4.46*
> *11:00:24 Deposit +$1.59*

The nature of the transaction next, all deposits.

> *Jamal Ahmad*
> *25 September*
> *03:00:14 Deposit +$0.61*
> *03:00:20 Deposit +$4.00*
> *03:00:25 Deposit +$9.78*
> *03:00:34 Deposit +$1.42*

And finally, the amount – not a single transaction was over ten dollars.

> *Charlie Haddad*
> *25 October*
> *12:00:00 Deposit +$0.61*
> *12:00:04 Deposit +$4.11*

12:00:09 Deposit +$8.50
12:00:21 Deposit +$8.40

Four transactions for each name, all made in rapid succession.

Ben Wilson
25 November
06:00:18 Deposit +$0.61
06:00:25 Deposit +$4.04
06:00:31 Deposit +$5.55
06:00:36 Deposit +$9.82

Jax picked up the paper after making his final entry. He then stood, walked around the table and placed it in front of Clarke and Sami.

'What do you see?' Jax said, standing behind them and pointing at the page.

'Names and betting account deposits,' Clarke said. 'All on the twenty-fifth. All on days of the attack.'

'Well, the twenty-fifth in Australia anyway,' Jax said. 'It was still the twenty-fourth in most parts of the globe. What else?'

'Charlie Haddad.' Clarke said. 'He received four deposits on what would have been the twenty-fourth in Mexico, at about' – he counted some numbers on his fingers – '8 pm.'

'It was exactly 8 pm in Mexico,' Jax said. 'What else do you see?'

Clarke ran his finger down the list.

'The first deposit in every instance is sixty-one cents,' Clarke said.

'Why?' Jax asked.

Clarke squinted as he studied, before throwing up his hands. 'Fucked if I know,' he muttered.

'Phone numbers,' Sami interrupted, 'fucking phone numbers.' Sami snatched the paper from the table and jumped out of his seat. 'YES!' he yelped. 'Phone numbers. The sixty-one cents is a country code: +61 – Australia.'

'Correct,' Jax said. 'Someone used the betting account system to send each terror cell a phone number at what would have been 8 pm on the twenty-fourth in their time zone.'

Sami started slapping Jax on the back.

'Good work, kid,' Sami exclaimed. 'You're a goddamn genius.'

'Not really,' Jax said modestly. 'It's something only an inmate would know – sorry, that only an Australian inmate would know. Betting accounts are used like banks in our prisons. It's the financial system behind the jails' secret economy. You missed it because you didn't know to look.'

Jax noticed Clarke hadn't said much.

'It's ingenious,' Jax continued, trying to get through to Clarke. 'A series of deposits, so small that not even the betting agency would take note. Whoever made those deposits was anonymously telling their operatives that they need to contact him – and is supplying the number to do it. Each of the numbers is different. Each call was no doubt made to a burner phone, and probably from a burner phone.'

Jax looked at Clarke. 'Well?'

'Sorry, I'm just thinking it through,' Clarke said. 'Tracing the calls will give us a general location for where the calls were received. Depending on the network, that tower could be a hundred kilometres away from where the call was actually taken or made. Let's assume the records say the calls were received in the Goulburn region. Let's go even further and pretend we can get an exact location – Goulburn jail. That only confirms what we already know. That the man we are looking for is an inmate. We'll learn something we didn't know if the calls have been received somewhere else. But ... it isn't about the calls that have been made already – it's about the call that is going to be made.' Then Clarke smiled, from ear to ear.

'Yes,' Jax said. 'If we monitor the betting accounts, we'll get his new number.'

Clarke looked towards Sami.

'One call and I'll have the combined resources of the CIA, the NSA, the FBI and Homeland Security tracking every betting account in the world. Hell, I'll even put a call in to NASA. How about the hardware?'

Clarke nodded. 'We'll be able to locate him to the nearest centimetre as soon as he turns the thing on,' Clarke said. 'We'll have him in zip-ties and a hood five minutes after he makes the call. But that call won't be made until the twenty-fourth or maybe even the twenty-fifth. That'll leave us just twelve hours or less to get the location out of him … We can't sit on our hands until then.'

'No,' Sami said. 'We can't.' He looked towards Jax. 'Got any ideas?' he asked.

JAX was now racing the clock.

Twenty-six days and counting …

He had to do more than just wait. He couldn't sit around until the twenty-fifth, doing nothing until the deposits were made. Waiting for the bombers to make their final call. Nor could he rely on Clarke and Sami to force a confession from the mastermind once he'd been identified through triangulation. No matter what they did to him – pulling fingernails, chopping toes – he'd only have to hold out for a day at most. Then *boom!* Game over.

Jax had to work out a way to give them more time, even if it was just an extra day.

He suspected the Christmas Day attack would be the finale. It made sense to end a religious reign of terror on the most celebrated religious day of the year. And as the finale, the attack would no doubt be bigger and bolder. Something spectacular.

But more of a world-ender than showstopper. A war-starter, at least.

Back in his cell after the meeting, Jax pulled up the latest press update from Sami on his phone. The appetite for war was building, Churches were empty and clergy were fighting among themselves. The Pope was calling for calm and demanding peace. But the rest of the Vatican, pushed by the all-powerful South American diocese, was calling for a holy war. The Crusades, version 2.0.

According to the CIA, the United States would have already declared war on every enemy state in the Middle East had it not been for the Australian revelation. America had formed an official alliance with Russia, France, Italy and Mexico in the immediate aftermath of the Mexico attack. But it had hit pause on talks and plans as soon as the Australian link was revealed. Still, the US government was still firmly holding the remote, finger itching to press play.

President Forrester, a devout Christian elected largely thanks to the size and power of the American Bible Belt, had begun talks with Russia immediately after the Alabama bombing. The attack on America gave him the legitimacy he needed to make a friend of a foe. It also gave him the opportunity to do what no American President had been able to do: take control of the Middle East. Finally. And for good.

With Russia and all of the former Soviet states joining America and all of its allies to form the biggest international army ever assembled, Forrester would have both the might and the justification to invade, occupy and install a pro-American government in every Middle Eastern state. Fundamentalism would be crushed, Islam would be censored and they would have the oil. All of it.

Nobody outside America and Australia knew the truth about the attacks. The identities of the three known attackers had been kept classified. A state secret. Aside from the US President and Secretary of State, the head of the CIA and the Australian Prime Minster, the only others who knew were the ones who had to know.

After reading the update, Jax stowed his phone and spent the day in the yard. He watched and listened. Narrowed his list of suspects as much as he could.

TWENTY-five days and counting…

Jax spent the next day attempting to rank the names that were left on his list. He would never be able to get to all of them, so he would start with the most likely and work his way back. He sat up in bed that night studying target number 1: Eli Said, a convicted car thief who'd run Australia's biggest car rebirthing operation before his arrest.

Jax didn't sleep until he'd thought up a way in. He googled things like *What's the difference between a big block and a small block?*, *351 Windsor v. 351 Cleveland*, and *What's an Eleanor?*

TWENTY-four days …

Jax made contact with Said. Armed with the knowledge that Said was an American muscle-car collector, Jax began bragging about having a 1969 Ford Mustang Mach 1 Fastback while eating his lunch. Said, within earshot, took the bait.

Jax spent that night on his laptop, googling *Chevrolet, classic car restorations, engine builders* and similar terms.

TWENTY-three days …

With their shared passion established, Jax spent the next day in the yard telling Said why the 69 Mustang was better than the 69 Camaro. He then spent the night in his cell wondering how he could get him talking about anything other than cars before Christmas.

He also began studying target number 2, Sam Baz, a convicted arms dealer with known ties to ISIS. Jax spent the night on his laptop, searching *Canterbury-Bankstown Junior Rugby League, St Johns JRL, Roosters RL ...*

TWENTY-two days ...

Jax appealed to Baz's ego. He pretended to recognise him in the yard.

'Hey, you used to play for St Johns,' he said. 'You were that gun centre. You played a bit for the Roosters too, right? Man, you should be playing in the NRL.' Jax had found all the team lists and year books on the internet.

'Yeah, man,' Baz said. 'You see me play?'

Jax said his older brother had played against Baz. He named the rival team and some of its stars. He also revealed that he had played against Baz's younger brother, whom he also declared a gun. He could have named every player in both his alleged team and the brother's team had he been asked. He could have even told Baz all the scores.

Jax spent the afternoon in the rec room talking cars again with Said, this time recommending spray painters and engine builders, all of whom Said knew and some of whom he had even used.

TWENTY-one days ...

Jax had talked and read about nothing but cars and football for days. But it was too slow. It would be weeks before he could ask a question that wasn't about horsepower or tackling techniques without risking his cover. And these were just two of the names on his list. There were still another nine.

Jax racked his brain as he heaved weights during his morning workout at the packed gym, ignoring the banter of the other inmates mostly working out in groups of three or four. As he focused on coming up with another way of narrowing his list, he wasn't even counting his reps. Bench-pressing 160 kilograms, he moved the weight like he was lifting only the bar.

The phone … It was more an idea than a revelation. He realised that instead of tracking people he could track phones. The man he was looking for would be taking the call he was waiting for on a brand-new phone. A burner. It wouldn't take him long to find out which inmates – or guards – were selling phones. And it wouldn't take long to make them tell him who they were selling them to.

Jax paused his train of thought when the weight he was lifting suddenly became heavy and he realised he was just about maxed out. But then he decided he would push himself today, go for another two lifts.

One … He only just got it up and down. He dug his toes into the ground and arched his back as he prepared for his final lift. He took a deep breath as he prepared to push—

And then everything went black.

CHAPTER 44

Goulburn Correctional Centre, Goulburn, NSW, Australia

BLEACH and Brut 33. Jax knew he was in the hospital before he even opened his eyes. He also knew that Father Martin was sitting by his side.

'Last rites?' Jax asked.

Startled, the priest threw the Bible he'd been reading into the air.

'Oh my,' he said as he sprang from his chair and tried to catch it.

'Oh dear,' he said as he caught it, juggled it then dropped it.

He almost fell over as he reached down.

'You're awake,' he said as he rose. 'Oh boy, did you just give me a scare.'

Jax looked at the chaplain, his chubby cheeks flushed red, appearance almost comical, and chuckled. The light laugh caused heavy pain.

'Ahh,' Jax groaned, a blazing piano suddenly pressing on his chest, crushing and burning at the same time. 'What the—?'

He began to hyperventilate.

'Relax,' Martin said, reaching out and placing his soft hand on Jax's forehead. 'Shhh. Take a long, slow breath. That's it. Good. Now gently let it out.'

He lifted his hand from Jax's head and placed it on his arm.

'You have broken some ribs,' the priest said as he gently patted. 'You need to take it easy.'

Jax gritted his teeth and swallowed the pain. 'What happened?' he asked.

Martin told Jax that he had been attacked in the gym. Hit in the head with a dumbbell, or at least that was the surgeon's guess, given the size and the shape of the piece of skull he'd had to remove. Immediately knocked out by the blow, Jax had then dropped the weight he was lifting – 160 kilograms – onto his sternum. The priest told him he was lucky that none of the five ribs that were broken had punctured his lung. But not so lucky that they didn't have to replace his sternum with steel.

'You may have some more explaining to do when you go through the metal detectors,' Father Martin said, after also telling Jax about the steel plate in his head. 'But aside from that, you will be fine. It could be a lot worse. The surgeon was astounded that your brain wasn't damaged. He only induced the coma because of the pain.'

'Coma?' Jax gasped. 'How long was I out?'

'That doesn't matter,' the priest said. 'You don't need to worry. Ju—'

'No! How long?' Jax interrupted. 'I need to know.'

'I'm not sure,' Martin said. 'A couple of weeks. Two, maybe three.'

Jax ignored the pain as he sprang forward and grabbed for Martin's wrist. For his watch.

'The date,' Jax barked. 'What's the fucking date, you imbecile?'

Father Martin stood up and backed away. As the colour suddenly drained from his usually rosy cheeks, he remained silent, simply staring at Jax, with his mouth agape.

'Sorry,' Jax said as he slumped back onto his pillow, 'I wasn't ... Sorry, I just need to know the date.'

The chaplain did not need to look at his watch.

'The twenty-fourth of December,' he said quietly, before turning and walking off. 'Merry Christmas,' he said, without a hint of joy, as he pushed his way through the double doors and left the hospital wing, his elegant leather-soled shoes clicking softly on the linoleum.

One day and counting....

JAX ripped the tangle of wires from his chest.

'Fuck,' he said as the ECG next to his bed wailed. An alarm.

He mashed at the face of the machine, pressing all the buttons, trying to turn it off. It only got louder. He then backhanded the screaming box, sending it to the ground before ripping out his IV. Blood spurted from his wrist and sprayed the blue divider that was drawn shut. Jax pressed against the wound as he swung his legs off the bed, but he had to let go of his bleeding wrist to push himself up and off the bed. And that's when he saw the guard. The man mountain. The Hulk. Turner.

'What are you doing?' Turner asked as he bent down and punched a four-digit code into the screaming machine.

Silence.

Jax considered pushing past the guard, but thought the better of it, Turner being too big, too strong and Jax all busted and broken.

'Easy,' Turner said. 'Relax. Back up. You need to rest.'

'I can't,' Jax said. 'I'm fine. I need to get back to my cell.'

'Why?' Turner asked. 'Have you worked it out? Do you know who it is?'

Jax froze. The adrenaline was sucked from his veins and replaced with ice. And then he smiled. He was right. Turner was an agent.

'Are you—' Jax stopped himself. He had to be smarter than that. He could be wrong. He could blow his cover. He could also end up in a loony bin.

Turner looked left and then right. Coast clear.

'Yes,' he said softly. 'Who do you think cleaned out your cell after the bomb? All that evidence didn't magically remove itself. I have been checking on you every day and then giving them updates. Now, tell me what you know? What were you going to report before this happened? Can you remember?'

Jax could. He remembered everything up to the moment when the world went black. He thought it was strange that he could remember so much, crystal clear and in detail, after having his skull crushed, but still couldn't remember shooting a man dead in his room. But now wasn't the time for such thoughts.

One day and counting …

Jax told Turner about his list. About his eleven suspects. Told him he had been talking to Said and Baz, but only about fast cars and football.

'I was also going to start tracking phones,' Jax continued. 'But it's too late for that now.' It was clear they hadn't found the man behind the blasts, as Turner wouldn't have asked him if they had.

'Do we know anything about the target?' Jax asked. 'Where and what they are going to attack?'

Turner shook his head.

'I've got to get out of here,' Jax said. 'Gotta get back to the wing.'

'Why?' Turner asked. 'It's too late. What are you going to do?'

'I don't know,' Jax said. 'But I can't do nothing.'

Turner nodded. 'I'll have it arranged,' he said.

Later, as he was leaving the hospital, Jax crossed paths with the little Samoan he had king-hit, who was in a wheelchair with his leg still in a full cast. He smiled when he saw Jax.

'He fucked you up good, hey, bro,' the Samoan said, and then laughed.

At least Jax now knew who had put him in the hospital. That was one less mystery to solve.

It's sweet as, bro, I've got nothing against you, bro.

Yeah, right.

ONE day and counting …

With the sun setting on 24 December, Jax desperately needed to do something. He would never forgive himself if he didn't at least try to help and another church was blown to bits.

So he got down on his knees and put his hands on the floor.

'Arg—' He choked back an exclamation of agony. Hit by a lightning bolt to the heart, his chest suddenly ablaze, he wanted to scream. But he didn't. He couldn't. Not without being busted. Or sent back to the hospital.

He gritted his teeth and ignored the pain as he dropped his belly to the floor and slid towards the shelf unit. He pulled the false front off quickly and removed and extracted his pill container. He put the blue capsules – his steroids – and the red and yellow capsules – an assortment of uppers and poisons – to one side then sifted through the remainder, all green and white imitations of Panadol, and separated the painkillers from the sleepers. He put one of the pills stamped PK in his mouth and the rest with same marking into his pocket. Everything else went back into the container and back under the shelf. Then he took out the phone and laptop.

Back on his bed, sheet over his head, he connected his laptop to the internet and opened Google. He had no idea where to start. As if mesmerised by the flashing cursor in the empty search box, he just sat staring at the screen for ten minutes.

Realising he had swallowed a full dose of the heroin-like drug called oxycodone, Jax shook himself out of his opioid-induced stupor. But he still didn't know where to start. What could he possibly do on his computer to stop a mass killing?

Think. Think. Think.

There had to be something.

Use common sense. Simplify the complex. Point A to point B.

It no longer made sense to try to find the mastermind. The man behind the bomb would soon be in custody. He would be zip-tied, hooded and dragged out of the prison by a posse of balaclava-wearing, assault-rifle-carrying former SOC soldiers. Jax didn't have to find the mastermind because he already had. Jax had found him when he found the phone numbers in the betting accounts.

Point A to B. You need to get to B.

B. What was B?

Think. Think. Think.

The bomb. The target. The location.

Still he no idea where to start.

Think. Think. Think.

It was obvious. He had to start at *A*. He blamed the oxycodone for his stupidity. He began to type. First, he searched for the Church of Saint Étienne in Rouvray, France. His screen was soon teeming with text. Thousands of results, many coming from untrusted sources. Fake news. He went back to his search bar and refined his search to verified sources only – reports and documents posted by government bodies, recognised news outfits and individuals in possession of a big blue tick.

There were still pages and pages of results. He skipped over the paid hits, and then he read. Page after page, site after site, Jax consumed it all: facts, theories, opinions and analysis. Two news articles piqued his interest. A former DSGI agent named Pierre Caron was quoted in both reports. He tapped in another search and soon had every quote and every comment that the former French spy had made about the Normandy attack – newspaper articles, blogs, Instagram and Facebooks posts, even emails after he hacked into Pierre's Gmail. It was interesting and there was lots that Jax didn't know, but nothing he could use to predict the location of the next attack. Still, he hadn't been expecting to find a magic wand. Not yet.

He broadened his search to include unverified sources, but, before hitting enter, added an additional search restriction. The geo command limited his search results to only posts, pages and articles about the church attack that had been uploaded in Normandy. He added another command to limit the results further, to those uploaded on day of the attack. Jax then spent about thirty minutes scrolling through first-hand witness pictures and posts and checking the EXIF data on each of the pictures to make sure the GPS coordinates and the time stamp were accurate. Finding the metadata was simple: just a right click, unless they had been posted on Instagram, in which case he had to use a reverse search command to reinstate the EXIF data – the social media platform had added an automatic stripping function when it found out that hitmen were using their app.

He then used another command to do a deep dive into the witnesses who spiked his interest. To check if they had offered more details in chats, private posts, messages or emails. Thank God for Google Translate – almost all of it was in French, and Jax knew only the basics of the language.

He didn't find his smoking gun, but, again, he hadn't expected to. He wasn't going to find a pattern by looking at just one stitch. But he also wasn't going to find a pattern unless he knew every detail of every stitch – and that included details that everyone, including the CIA, the DSGI, MI6 and ASIO, had missed.

So far, the only actionable pattern they had was that all the targets were churches. That left them with 37 million potential targets for the next attack. He needed to do better than that. He knew he could do better than that.

Jax cleared his search bar and started the series of searches again, but this time zoning in on the Church of the Saviour on Spilled Blood. Jax spotted a link between it and the Church of Saint Étienne during his first cyber-sweep. An obvious connection. So obvious he assumed it would be shared only by the first two attacks. But he thought it was worth checking.

He opened a new browser tab, typed in 'Milan Cathedral', and included the search term 'terror attack', along with another filter excluding all recent results.

He was rewarded with 218 results. He clicked on the Wikipedia entry at the top.

1889 Milan Cathedral bombing
    On February 4, 1889, an explosive device secreted in a casket killed an Italian politician and two members of his family in the …

Just like the Church of Saint Étienne and the Church on Spilled Blood, Milan Cathedral had been the scene of a previous terror attack. Just two years before Tsar Alexander II was killed in front of the Church on Spilled Blood by the world's first suicide bomber, an Italian minister was killed by a bomb that had been planted in his father's coffin. The Church of Saint Étienne had been terrorised by a gunman in 1903.

Three out of three. He started a new search.

1963 16th Street Baptist Church bombing, Birmingham, Alabama – Wikipedia.
    The 16th Street Baptist Church bombing was an act of white supremacist terrorism which occurred at the African-American 16th Street Baptist Church in Birmingham, Alabama, on Sunday, September 15, 1963.

Four out of four soon became five out of five. Then six out of six. And, finally, after learning the Archbishop of Salisbury had

had his throat slit in a politically motivated attack in 1884, he had seven out of seven.

Jax could now narrow down the number of potential targets from every church in the world to only those churches that had previously been attacked. He figured there wouldn't be many. Ten, maybe twenty.

He was wrong.

There were hundreds. So many he didn't bother counting. There was no way they could organise and deploy sufficient personnel to stake out all of the churches. Not in twenty-four hours. There was also little chance of convincing the churches to shut their doors on Christmas Day on the word of an Australian inmate.

Think. Think. Think.

There had to be a pattern within the pattern.

Jax jumped when the electronic lock to his cell door snapped shut.

No way.

He pulled the sheet from over his head and looked around. 'Shit,' he said softly into the dark.

He couldn't believe it was already lights–out. He checked his laptop to make sure. *Thu 10:00 pm*. That made it mid-afternoon in Europe – 3 pm – and Christmas Eve morning in the United States. Time had flown – Jax had been under his blanket for almost five hours. He now had just five hours until the first of the four deposits would be made if the next attack was in Europe and only eleven hours until the deposits were made if the terror cell was in America.

Think. Think. Think.

He went back to Google and searched.

Eventually he found the hit he wanted. He clicked on the link and was then looking at a list of every terror attack in history. He scanned it carefully. Then he opened Excel, checked the list was in chronological order and numbered them all accordingly.

1. *The Gunpowder Plot, England, 1605.*

He stopped reading the list when he got to: *114. The 16th Street Baptist Church Bombing, USA, 1963.*

Next he narrowed the list down to only the recently attacked churches.

10. *Salisbury Cathedral, England, 1884*

13. *Milan Cathedral, Italy, 1889*

15. *Church on Spilled Blood, Russia, 1891*

19. *Church of San Felipe Neri, Mexico, 1895*

28. *St Nedelya Church, Bulgaria, 1902*

29. *Church of Saint Étienne, France, 1903*

114. *16th Street Baptist Church, USA, 1963*

He then studied the numbers: *10, 13, 15, 19, 28, 29, 114.* Not so much the numbers but their relationships to each other. He looked for patterns. More specifically, sequences. Using algebraic rules, he first looked for an arithmetic sequence. There wasn't one. Then a geometric sequence. Nothing. Then a Fibonaccian sequence. No. Then a triangular sequence. No again. Then a prime sequence. No, no, no. And finally, a factorial sequence. Nope.

He then listed the churches in the order of the recent attacks.

29. *Church of Saint Étienne, France, 1903*

15. *Church on Spilled Blood, Russia, 1891*

13. *Milan Cathedral, Italy, 1889*

114. *16th Street Baptist Church, USA, 1963*

28. *St Nedelya Church, Bulgaria, 1902*

19. *Church of San Felipe Neri, Mexico, 1895*

10. *Salisbury Cathedral, England, 1884*

Jax studied the new numbers: *29, 15, 13, 114, 28, 19, 10.*
Again, he attempted to find a pattern using every sequence
used in modern mathematics. Again, he came up with nothing.
But he wouldn't quit. He couldn't quit.

Going back to the master file of all terror attacks, he made
another list, consisting of only churches that had been attacked,
the first of which was Salisbury Cathedral.

1. *Salisbury Cathedral, England, 1884*
2. *Milan Cathedral, Italy, 1889*
3. *Church on Spilled Blood, Russia, 1891*
4. *Cologne Cathedral, Germany, 1893*
5. *Church of San Felipe Neri, Mexico, 1895*
6. *Church of Saint Séverin, France, 1897*
7. *Ávila Cathedral, Spain, 1899*
8. *St Nedelya Church, Bulgaria, 1902*
9. *Church of Saint Étienne, France, 1903*
10. *Cathedral of the Holy Spirit, Istanbul, Turkey, 1905*

...

41. *16th Street Baptist Church, USA, 1963*

...

He then deleted the churches that had not been attacked this year.

1. *Salisbury Cathedral, England, 1884*
2. *Milan Cathedral, Italy, 1889*
3. *Church on Spilled Blood, Russia, 1891*
5. *Church of San Felipe Neri, Mexico, 1895*
8. *St Nedelya Church, Bulgaria, 1902*
9. *Church of Saint Étienne, France, 1903*
41. *16th Street Baptist Church, USA, 1963*

He could already see it. He wouldn't need Fibonaccian or
factorials. All he had to do was reorder the list, once again

arranging them in the order in which they had been attacked this year.

9. Church of Saint Étienne, France, 1903
3. Church on Spilled Blood, Russia, 1891
2. Milan Cathedral, Italy, 1889
41. 16th Street Baptist Church, USA, 1963

And there it was: *93241*, the first four attacks formed the five numbers that had been embossed in blood on the mural of madness. The Serpent. It was the number the serial killer had carved into both his wall and Jax's brain. A sudden rush of adrenaline caused Jax's hands to shake. He took a deep breath and tried to calm himself before looking down at the rest of his list.

8. St Nedelya Church, Bulgaria, 1902
5. Church of San Felipe Neri, Mexico, 1895
1. Salisbury Cathedral, England, 1884

Had he seen 851 on the Serpent's wall? Whatever came after 851, the next numeral or numerals, would reveal the location of the next attack.

He already knew he hadn't seen the number. His mind didn't hide things. Couldn't hide things. He remembered everything. No matter how much dirt he tried to shovel over things he didn't want to remember – like what he'd done to the actor in the holding cage, what had happened in his cell with Marsh, Nikki's face at his sentencing hearing, waking up to the body on his army barracks floor – his recall was as vivid as if he were watching the scenes unfold on a high-definition screen. He would know if he had seen 851 on the Serpent's wall.

He went back to the scene anyway.

93241.

Made bold by blood, the numbers were the centrepiece of whatever it was that the Serpent was creating on that wall. There was cursive script above, carved and hard to see, and the section of the wall closest to Jax was a chaotic crowd of chalk: blue, yellow and white. It was stroked and scratched with letters big, small and tiny, in styles ranging from computer-perfect print to kindergarten scribble. There were languages he recognised, some he didn't and some that might not exist. Food scraps and shit had been smeared across quotes and equations; star charts and maps were buried beneath.

He couldn't see the numbers he was looking for, but that didn't mean they weren't there. They could be scrawled in a corner. Hidden on a sunflower stem in the almost perfectly reproduced chalk Van Gogh. He couldn't make out what was on the far end of the wall, although there the colours seemed grouped and ordered and the text less chaotic, almost neat.

There was also the blank space. The beacon ...

But the Serpent? He suddenly asked himself a question.

What could the Serpent have to do with this?

He couldn't be the mastermind. Or could he?

No. No fucking way.

As well as the fact that the Serpent had zero contact with the outside world – no phone calls, no visits, no letters, nothing – Jax found it hard to believe that even the most radicalised, extremist, death-wishing jihadi would be stupid enough to go into a partnership with the Serpent, a sick psychopath with no grip on reality.

But 93241 ...

Jax kept on asking himself questions.

Was the Serpent smart enough to pull it off?

Of course. He was a certified genius. But he also ate brains, shat on his floor and carved equations into the soles of his feet.

No. Zero chance. Couldn't be him.

But 93241 ...

All of Jax's interrogations of the facts before him led him back to the same conclusion. It couldn't be the Serpent. He didn't have the opportunity, the resources, the access or the mental competence to orchestrate such an intricate plot.

But still, Jax couldn't explain why that number was on his wall. Or why the Serpent had been slithering around in his head.

Jax had to see what other numbers were on his wall. He had to check if *851* was there, and if it was, what numbers followed it.

There was only one way to find out ...

JAX doubted the wisdom of pressing the knock-up the moment he'd done it. What was he going to say if his hunch was wrong? Or if it wasn't Turner. It had been over twelve hours since Jax had seen him in the hospital. And the guards worked twelve-hour shifts at most.

'Phew,' Jax said when Turner entered his cell. 'For a moment there I thought I was going to end up back in the hospital.'

'Lucky the rostered-on guard got called home for an emergency,' Turner said with a chuckle. 'Whatcha need, buddy?'

Jax handed Turner an RF scanner.

'I need to get into Supermax,' he said. 'Can you scan the keycodes?'

Turner nodded.

'Can you disable the cameras?' Jax asked.

'For an hour at most,' Turner said.

'That will do,' Jax said. Then he handed Turner a fistful of pills.

CHAPTER 45

Goulburn Correctional Centre, Goulburn, NSW, Australia

TURNER had taken care of the cameras and the Supermax screw, but Jax knew there was nothing he could do to stop a guard from happening upon him while he made his way from his wing to the Supermax wing. He would have a hard time explaining why he was out of his cell, and a hell of a time explaining the torch and the seven electronic keys he was carrying.

With lives on the line and the prospect of a nuclear war, he needed to mitigate that risk. Jax had pulled up the prison blueprints supplied by Clarke before pressing the knock-up. And as well as having Turner scan the RF frequencies to the four doors he needed to open to gain access to Supermax, he'd also got him to scan a broom closet, a mains room and a plant room. He was now holding those three keys, ready to dive through the nearest door and take cover if he heard as much as a footfall.

With the three in-case-of-emergency FOBs unused, Jax breathed a little easier as he reached the entrance to Supermax, although, given where he was standing was also known as the Gates of Hell, he probably should have been hyperventilating.

He swapped the three electronic keys he had been holding for the four he had in his pocket. Then he looked down, picked out the key marked 'D1' – short for Door 1 – and waved it in front of the electronic pad. And … Open Sesame! … Supermax.

As per his training, Jax crouched and duckwalked his way through the open door. He had no reason to doubt Turner, and was sure he had done what he'd asked, but he nevertheless wanted to minimise his exposure to the guard's box – which in Supermax was actually a round dome with a 360-degree view.

Jax turned, sat and put his back against the guard's box when he arrived. Now would be the time to check his weapon – if he had one. Now would also be the time to call in his position, let his team know he was locked, loaded and ready to go. But he did not have a team. Not anymore. He was one-out and all alone.

He listened carefully but heard no movement. If Turner had not been successful, the mission was over. Jax couldn't fight an armed man in his condition and win, no matter how skilled he was in hand-to-hand contact. He slowly moved towards the doorway into the dome, staying below the half-sphere of clear perspex the guard should be periodically gazing through to ensure all was in order. He rounded the final bend and closed in on the door.

He slowly stood up until his eyeline was level with the glass. Peering through, he could see a disposable coffee cup and a half-eaten sandwich on the desk. And, beyond them, the guard, slumped over the desk, having the deepest kip of his life.

Jax stood tall and exhaled, the butterflies that had been fluttering about in his stomach leaving with the spent breath. He looked down into his hand and pulled out the key marked 'D2'. He walked over to the next door: blast-proof and four inches thick. Suddenly the butterflies were back, no longer fluttering, the winged creatures scratching and clawing as they rushed down his throat, stealing his air as they burrowed their way back to his belly.

The four-inch glass wasn't there to keep him out, but to keep them in. Them. The monsters. He wanted to turn around, his brain urging him to take flight. But he fought off the instinct to run and held the key up against the entry pad.

Now there was just one barrier between him and the beasts. Between him and the Serpent.

'Fuck it,' he said.

Jax was a monster too.

Bring it on.

The hairs on the back of his neck stood up as soon as he stepped into Supermax. The overhead fluorescents that had lit the corridors when he had delivered the meals were off. A series of red lights lining the corridor provided the only illumination, little more than a bloody glow that did nothing more than colour the darkness red.

Jax looked into the first cell as he silently moved past it, but he couldn't see past the glass. He prayed that the paranoid inmate was fast asleep, that he wouldn't suddenly start screaming about brain-lasers or whatever his conspiracy du jour was.

No amount of noise would disturb the guard – he'd be knocked out for a few more hours based on the dose Turner had given him – but any outburst would likely wake the rest of the wing up. Including the Serpent.

Jax relaxed a little after he got past the first cell without incident. He relaxed even more when he got past the second, third and fourth cells, all of them dark and silent. But the tension returned as he approached Cell No. 5. He relaxed again when looked into the glass and saw only his red-washed reflection, not a man masturbating.

Supermax was asleep. Thank God.

With every step bringing him closer to the Serpent, Jax mentally ran through what was ahead. As always, he had a

Plan A, a Plan B, a Plan C ... hell, he even a Plan Z. The plan he liked best was the one where he didn't even have to use his final key, the one marked 'SC' for Serpent Cell. He was hoping to be able to point his flashlight straight through the glass and find his final number: preferably in big neon lights.

But he didn't like his chances. The numbers – the eight, the five, the one and whatever followed – which Jax believed were the key to the location of the final attack, could be scratched into the wall in tiny script, or concealed in God knew what kind of bodily fluid.

He was almost resigned to having to enter the cell, so his next best scenario had the Serpent asleep, and staying asleep: he'd go in, find the numbers fast, and get out, the Serpent none the wiser.

Jax's least favourite plan was the one where he had to fight the Serpent. In his worst-case scenario, the Serpent was standing on the other side of the glass, naked, erect and waiting for him. In this imaginary but very likely hell, he then had to fight the Serpent, the 140-kilo behemoth they said had once taken down an entire squadron of riot police. And Jax was in no condition to fight, not with five broken ribs and a still not fully fused plate in his skull. He prayed he could leave the fighting, the arresting and the interrogating to the experts. He was only there for the writing on the wall.

Jax smelled Cell No. 74 long before he saw it: the stale, musty scent fast becoming a full-blown stink. He breathed through his mouth as he walked past Cell No. 73. And then he stopped breathing all together.

He turned and looked hard when he finally reached the Serpent's lair.

Nothing.

He couldn't see a thing. The Serpent's cell looked the same as every other cell in the dark: no blood, no shit, no Serpent.

Nothing but black. Jax took a big gulp of air and then wished he hadn't, the stink now so bad he could taste it.

He looked down at his torch, made sure it was pointing at the ground, then winced as he went for the button, as if he were about to flick the switch on a fireworks show. While there were no sparklers, poppers or waterfalls, the sudden rush of bright made him flinch all the same.

He suddenly felt eyes upon him. And not just any eyes, but big yellow eyes with black slits. His mind had turned the Serpent into a real-life monster. He imagined the Serpent sitting on his bed, tongue slithering and fangs out. He lifted his head and looked into the darkness, towards the corner. To where the bed was. He couldn't see a thing, everything still black.

Jax raised his torch, the spotlight jumping from his feet and skipping into the cell. The trail of blood the Serpent had left on his way to the knock-up was still there, although now smeared and partly obscured by trash. He raised the torch a little higher and to the right. He stopped when he saw the shit-stained sheet dangling from the end of the Serpent's bed.

He swung the spotlight back to his feet. What was he thinking? He was about to shine a light straight into the Serpent's face. About to wake him up. He could not do anything that could potentially wake the Serpent up. No noise, and certainly no flashlight in the face.

That's if he is asleep …

He supposed he would soon find out.

Holding the torch as if it was a dart, positioned between his index finger and thumb, he shone it on the left-hand side wall and examined it. It was utter madness: equations, star charts, and a Picasso freshly painted in blood. There were plenty of numbers scribbled and scrawled into the mess, but not the numbers he was looking for.

On the section of wall closest to where he stood, Jax had no problem making out even the smallest of scratches – with only a foot to travel, his torch threw a tight, bright, tennis-ball-sized spotlight onto the concrete. But soon, only a couple of metres over, the tennis ball had blown out to beachball size, blurry and dim.

Jax could just make out the numbers in the middle of the wall: 93241. He could also see the cursive carving he had noted before. Maybe Arabic. Then again, with the light barely reaching that far into the dark, it could have just as easily been gibberish. He would have to get closer to find out.

Time to switch to his next best plan.

Here we go. In and out. Serpent none the wiser.

Jax knew how fine the line was between the second-best scenario and the worst.

He pulled out the key he'd been hoping he wouldn't have to use. He had to stop himself from shining his torch towards the bed. He hated not knowing.

Here goes …

He swiped the fob in front of the keypad.

Beep. Beep.

An electronic acknowledgement.

Then, *snap*, the lock opening.

Fuck.

He quickly fumbled for the button on his torch.

Fuck.

He found it, killed the light.

Fuck.

He took a breath and told himself to calm down. The noise hadn't been loud: something like a text message alert at half-volume. And the speaker was on his side of the glass. Not the Serpent's. He looked into the dark.

Nothing. Black. No movement. All good.

He pushed on the glass and eased into the cell. Into the Serpent's lair.

JAX had to summon all his strength to stop himself from throwing up. He'd thought the smell was bad on the other side of the glass, and it was, but nothing like this. Death: that's what this was. The smell of death. Rot, decay, carrion.

Jax was standing in the dark, door shut behind him but not locked, alone in a Supermax cell with the Serpent. And he didn't know if the world's worst serial killer was asleep or awake. Out like a light or watching him, fangs out and ready to strike.

Jax suspected his mind had given the Serpent yellow eyes, a forked tongue and now fangs to make him more monstrous than human. Jax himself was now a monster. He did not deny it. Maybe he was just like the Serpent: once a genius, now a killer. He shivered as he drew the comparison. And that shiver told him was *not* like the Serpent. Not yet.

Beep. Beep.

An electronic acknowledgement.

Then snap, the lock closing.

Fuck.

Jax tensed and waited. The blow would come soon. At any moment. Springing from the dark, the Serpent would strike.

Jax wanted to flick the torch on and wave it about. To yell, 'Here I am ... Let's go!' But he wouldn't stand a chance. Not injured. His only play was to cower in the dark and pray the Serpent was asleep – or, even better, not here. Oh, he would feel stupid if he survived, only to find out the Serpent was back in Long Bay. But stupid was better than dead.

The blow did not come. He waited some more. Still standing. He listened hard. He might get in a lucky blow if he struck first. He would be forced to try if he heard a sound that suggested the Serpent was here and anything other than asleep.

Yet he heard nothing but his own heart, which was beating too hard, too fast. He breathed deeply but quietly, slowing his heart and quietening his mind. Then he moved and ... stepped on something slippery. Maybe shit. Maybe piss. Maybe blood. Maybe all three.

Maybe something worse.

He resisted the urge to find out, pointing the torch towards the wall instead of the floor as he switched it back on.

Jax decided to start in the far corner and work his way back to the middle. Eyes just inches from the wall, he went from top to bottom, reading every word and studying every symbol. It was mostly madness, but there was also genius. Carved, painted and written over the top of a noughts and crosses series that must have featured all of his thirty-three personalities was the solution to P versus NP, one of mathematics' greatest unsolved problems. Incredible. The Serpent, or somebody inside him, had also answered the previously unsolved Hodge Conjecture.

But Jax hadn't found his solution. The bomb-stomping, life-saving, war-averting number he needed. He slowly worked his way back to the middle. To the number he already knew, with the addition of a colon between the 3 and 2.

93:241

Up close, Jax saw that the blood had not merely been smeared into the grooves, but layered on. There were multiple coats, now dried and flaking

The amount of blood in the grooves told Jax that the numbers had been on the Serpent's wall for a long time. Since at least before the 16th Street Baptist Church had been bombed. So he had written the 41 on the wall – the number that represented the 16th Street Baptist Church – before the attack. That meant he'd either planned, known about or predicted the attack.

And then there was the colon. An intriguing addition, it had not been on the wall last time he was here. At first Jax thought they may have been random blood splatter. But there was nothing random about the two perfectly rounded holes under the blood. With the colon, the numbers looked like ... Jax stopped himself from presuming. *Facts. Evidence. Get on with it.*

Even if he was right, it would not tell him anything about the next attack, so he moved on. Moved up. To the cursive script, most certainly Arabic and most certainly connected to the numbers. Sharing real estate, and of a similar size to the numerals, the script above the numbers had also been carved and was also coated in blood.

Same size. Same space. Same treatment.

It was most definitely connected. And so was the new writing – also Arabic – written under the numbers.

Same size. Same space. Same treatment.

The wall had been filled. This was the final piece. It could have been his number. But while he had learned to speak Arabic, he couldn't read it or write it. Clarke should have given him books and not just audio tapes. Not that it mattered. Not with his memory.

Jax took a step back so that he could get a clear view of the writing and translate it later.

And that was when he felt the Serpent's breath on the back of his neck.

Jax repositioned his torch as he spun around. He'd been holding it like a pen as he studied the wall, but the one-inch-wide tube of metal was firmly in the middle of his fist by the time he completed his turn, a ready-made weapon as well as a light. And when Jax brought his metal-laden fist up to his chin, the bulb was just three inches away from the Serpent.

FACE to face, toe to toe, only a slither of light between them. Jax began to circle as the Serpent remained statue-still.

Rising onto the balls of his feet, fists ready to fire, Jax waited for the Serpent to strike. He would hit after he made the monster miss, then use his speed and the Serpent's momentum to turn his superior strength into a weakness.

But the Serpent, fully clothed but no less terrifying, did not move.

The anticipation was harder than any hit.

'You need to leave,' the Serpent whispered into the dark. 'Please. Go. He will be back soon.'

What the fuck? Nah ...

Jax raised his torch. Not far. Just enough to light up the Serpent's eyes.

Nah ...

Not yellow. No black slits.

Jax looked harder.

No death. No rage. No thirty-three souls. They were not the same eyes he had seen in the clinic. Or in this cell. These eyes were sad eyes. They were desperate eyes. They were defeated eyes – like eyes Jax had seen in Afghanistan after a swap deal with the Taliban.

Hostage eyes.

'Please,' the Serpent continued. 'You shouldn't be here. Leave. Now. Before it is too late.'

Jax could not believe what he was seeing. What he was hearing. And now saying: 'Professor Wensley?'

'For now,' Wensley said. 'But he could be back any moment. I can't stop him. You really have to leave. Please. I beg you.'

This hadn't been in any of Jax's plans.

'Not until you tell me what this means.' Jax lit up the wall.

'Means?' the Professor said. 'Nothing, something, everything, who knows? He is a lunatic. And so are you. Leave. Please. Too many already. I don't want any more. Please. Before he takes you too.'

'851,' Jax said urgently. 'Does 851 mean anything to you? Have you seen it written anywhere? 851 followed by another two numbers?'

Wensley began blinking. An involuntary twitch of the eyelids.

'He's almost here. Last chance. Please. GO!'

Jax took a step back when Wensley stopped blinking. His eyes were no longer sad, desperate or defeated, they were deathly.

Fuck this ...

Jax didn't believe in any of this, but Wensley did. And if Wensley said the Serpent was coming, then Jax was leaving. He had what he needed in his head. He kept both his eye and the flashlight on Wensley as he backed towards the door. The Professor had still not moved when Jax let the darkness swallow him, taking one last look as he swung the torch away from the madman and towards the electronic lock.

Beep. Beep.

An electronic acknowledgement.

Then snap, the lock opening. But there was more.

The sound of feet slapping hard against the floor. The sound of the Serpent.

Fuck.

Jax dropped the torch and heaved at the heavy door. He saw yellow eyes and fangs again, as he slipped through the opening. While he might have been imagining the teeth, the terror was real.

The Serpent was two steps away.

With one foot in the corridor and one still in the cell, Jax pulled the door with one hand and reached back for the external keypad with the other.

One step away ...

Beep. Beep.

The Serpent went crashing into the door just as the lock snapped the cell shut. Jax waited for the tantrum. For the banging, bashing and shouting. Instead the Serpent disappeared into the darkness. All Jax could see was his torch. It had rolled into the middle of the cell and it lit up the Serpent's hand as he bent to picked it up.

Jax watched as the light beam slashed its way through the dark then the Serpent lit up his centrepiece, the group of numbers.

'And he shall rise!' the Serpent roared.

Then he turned off the torch – and vanished.

CHAPTER 46

THE Mahdi had a hell of a time trying to separate the SIM from the plastic card that it came in. He always struggled with this part.

'Oh my,' he said as he pressed a little too forcefully and his thumb sent the SIM high into the air.

He got down on his hands and knees and scoured the floor.

'There you are,' he said when he found it.

Eventually, he got it into the fresh burner phone.

'There,' he said, tray replaced and phone turned on.

Christmas night, long past lights out, the prison silent, everyone asleep. The Mahdi beamed a broad smile as he logged on. It was finally time.

Username: Mahdi_93/241. Password: Hewillrise_85/159.

He clicked on 'Account details' and then 'Transfer funds', keyed in all the details and moved down to 'Send'.

But he didn't click. Not yet. He wanted to savour the moment. The anticipation was the best part.

Now.

He hit 'Enter' and made the first deposit: sixty-one cents. And then, as quick as he could, he made the next three. He took a deep breath before clicking his way to the 'Transaction history' page. He knew he'd got it right, but only a fool wouldn't check.

25 December
04:00:00 Withdrawal −$0.61
04:00:06 Withdrawal −$4.80
04:00:13 Withdrawal −$0.19
04:00:16 Withdrawal −$4.58

He checked the numbers against his prepaid $20 SIM card. Correct. He looked at the silver Seiko strapped to his wrist.
   Tick, tock.

'WE'VE intercepted the first transaction,' a clad-in-black ASIO tech said as he turned away from his computer screen. 'Sixty-one cents. I repeat: sixty-one. The first two digits of the number are six and one.'

'Do we have a name? Clarke yelled. 'A location?'

'The betting account is registered to Walid Salim. But we don't have a location. He's using a VPN, so we don't even know what country he's in.'

Sami turned and walked to the back of the truck. The command vehicle was part of a convoy parked in the reception area of the prison, which had been deserted since dusk. He talked into the walkie-talkie he'd been strangling since the operation began.

'Get me everything you can on an Australian male named Walid Salim,' he ordered. Then he paused as the tech belted out the next three numbers.

'Travel records first,' Sami continued. 'We need a location. And photos.'

WALID read out the final three numbers as Chris punched them into the brand-new mobile phone.

'Er … eight?' Chris asked after hitting the keypad twice.

'Yes,' Walid roared, 'the last number is eight. Are you fucking retarded? Can't you remember three numbers?'

'I was just checking,' Chris said as he punched in the final digit.

'Give it here,' Walid said, dipping his head towards the phone. 'Hand it over.' He ignored the shaking hand that passed him the handset. Too late to get rid of him now, he thought.

The phone was already ringing as he raised it to his ear.

'THE number is active,' the ASIO tech said. 'Tracking is up. We are now live.'

Clarke grabbed his radio. 'Samurai to Ronin One. Tracking is live. I repeat, tracking is live. Stand by for orders.'

'Ronin One to Samurai. Copy. Standing by.'

The flashing green circle that had suddenly appeared on Clarke's screen covered the entire map. Clarke turned to the technician. 'Isn't that thing supposed to be a dot?'

'We've only just begun triangulating the signal, sir,' the technician replied. 'It will get smaller as we close in.'

Clarke remained hunched over the screen, watching the circle slowly shrink. Right then it was a green beach-ball bouncing over the entire prison, and the phone could have been anywhere in the jail.

'Come on!' Clarke rode the circle like a racehorse. On-off, on-off, the ball returned again and again to the screen, getting a little smaller with every bounce.

Clarke picked up the radio when the circle was half its original size and positioned on the right-hand side of his screen.

'Samurai to Ronin One,' Clarke barked. 'Move to the Echo Gate. I repeat, move to the Echo Gate and wait for further orders.'

'Ronin One to Samurai,' the call came back. 'Copy. We are on the move.'

JAX locked his cell then grabbed his iPhone and laptop. Back on his bed and connected, he went straight to his search bar. He typed in 'And he shall rise 93:241' and pressed enter. The screen filled. Jax clicked on the first result.

And he shall rise on the day he was born, scorched altars, numbering his resurrection, burned. 93:241
Jesus Will Return with Imam Mahdi: The Return of Jesus in Islam
Muslim scholars, irrespective of their denominations, are quite unanimous that upon the reappearance of Imam Mahdi (may God hasten his reappearance), Prophet Jesus will also descend to Earth from the heavens. During that time, Jesus and Imam Mahdi will spread peace and justice on earth and the earth will attain unprecedented peace, justice and welfare. Jesus will be like the minister for Imam Mahdi and his main mission will be to correct the dogma of Trinity and to clarify his humane personality and servitude to God.

The Islamic doctrine of the descent of Jesus to Earth is derived from two Ayah in the Quran and many hadith which are narrated by both Shi'a and Sunni narrators.

'And when Allah said: O Jesus! I will take you and raise you to Myself and clear you of those who disbelieve, and I will make those who follow you superior to those who disbelieve till the Day of Resurrection. Then you (Believers and disbelievers) will return to Me and I will judge between you in the matter in which you used to dispute. And he shall rise on the day he was born, scorched altars, numbering his resurrection, burned.'
93:241

Jax was pretty sure what the number of the resurrection would turn out to be. He hastily banged a new search into Google and clicked on the first result.

> *The number 8 is very significant, such that it is used seventy-three times in the Bible. It is the symbol of resurrection and regeneration. In Bible numerology, 8 means new beginning; it denotes 'a new order or creation, and man's true "born again" event when he is resurrected from the dead into eternal life'.*

The madman behind the attacks had turned a Quranic verse into an action plan. He believed he could resurrect Christ by destroying eight scorched altars – in the form of eight previously attacked churches.

But where was the eighth church?

THE BEAST was waiting for him. Rather than reflect the sun, the black blast-proof steel of the Cadillac XT6 seemed to devour it.

'Good morning, Mr President,' said Agent Neil Wallace as he stood by the open door, wearing shades as black as his suit.

The President did not even acknowledge Wallace, the senior US Secret Service agent in charge of the protective detail for the presidential motorcade. He never did.

'Merry Christmas,' the First Lady said with a smile as she followed President Forrester into the plush tan leather of the oversized back seat. 'Make sure you take time out to call that beautiful wife of yours. Her name is June, right?'

Wallace confirmed his wife's name and said he would comply, before closing the door. 'Package is secure,' he said, directing his voice into the small radio receiver on his lapel.

The President and the First Lady were now sealed in an airtight chamber with their own oxygen supply and protected by almost 10,000 kilograms of ballistic armour. The Cadillac

looked similar to all the other Presidential limousines Wallace
had seen during his eighteen years on the job: big, black, and
bulletproof. But the Beast was far superior to its predecessors.
Capable of withstanding a biological attack, the 6.7-metre-long
vehicle could deploy a smokescreen, cover the road with an oil
slick, and shoot canisters of tear gas. Wallace had never had to
order the use of any of these defensive measures, and hoped he
never would.

Wallace nodded as he walked past the next vehicle in
the convoy, today totalling twenty-eight cars. Sometimes
there could be as many as forty vehicles accompanying the
Presidential vehicle, but this was a low-threat route.

The head of the President's personal security detail responded
with a thumbs-up from the front passenger seat of the SUV
called the 'Halfback', a Chevrolet Suburban jam-packed with
would-be first responders and their FN P90 submachine guns.
Wallace worked his way down the line, giving vehicles that
included decoy limousines, sweepers and an intelligence truck
a final check before reaching the end, where he climbed into a
truck-sized van and approached a wall of LCD computer screens.

He gave them a once-over before picking up a radio.
'Roadrunner to Overwatch,' he said. 'Are you in position?' He
heard the rotor blades before he heard the reply.

'Overwatch in position,' said the helicopter pilot.

Wallace responded then picked up the radio that was
connected to every vehicle in the convoy. 'Operation
Stagecoach is a go,' he said. 'Roll out. ETA to delivery: twenty-
eight minutes.'

THE GREEN circle had halved in size again, the ball now
bouncing over a single prison block.

'Samurai to Ronin One,' Clarke barked. 'Move through
Echo Gate and proceed to Block Bravo. I repeat, move to
Block Bravo and wait for further orders.'

'Ronin One to Samurai,' the soldier said, 'Copy. We are on the move.'

Organised as a single brick of four for this operation, the Ronin burst through the door beside the East Gate of Goulburn prison. Dressed in full operational night gear – head to toe in black with body armour, balaclavas and tactical gloves – they charged across the birdcage and took cover behind a wall, two of them standing on each side of a steel gate.

Ronin One issued a series of orders via hand signals and the gate began to open, a technician remotely flicking the switch.

One. Two. Three!

Ronin One swung his Colt M4A1 assault rifle around the corner and provided cover for Ronins Three and Four as they sprinted across the freshly opened space to take the far flank. Watching through his holographic gun-sight, Ronin One waited until they were in position before ordering Ronin Two to the near flank. With the corridor taken and secure, they jammed their rifle butts into their shoulders and stormed along the passageway. They stopped when they reached a double set of steel doors.

'Ronin One to Samurai. We have reached checkpoint Delta Block.'

Clarke swore as he stared in astonishment at the screen. The green ball had finally became a dot. But it was now on the other side of Delta Block.

'Copy,' the soldier said when he was given the coordinates.

'GREETINGS, my child,' said the Mahdi, phone pressed firmly to his ear. 'Is all in place?'

He listened to the reply.

'Good,' he said. 'I am proud of you, my son. Proud of both of you. Hold on a second.'

The Mahdi thought he'd heard a noise. Something outside his door. He placed the phone under his leg to hide the glow and listened hard.

Just his imagination. What had begun as nothing more than a mild concern following the raid on the Terror Twelve had turned into paranoia. The text message he had received from the Serpent about the interloper was a problem that would have to be solved. And soon.

'You there?' the Mahdi asked. 'Good. Now, do as I have instructed. Do everything else exactly as we have planned. Remember: you fall so He can rise. He will call you *Shahid* and reward you with paradise. Remember that He selected you for this mission. The most important mission. The final mission.'

The Mahdi ended the call and placed the phone in his pocket. He then reached into his drawer and pulled out a knife. The sharpened steel edge of the blade glistened silver as it caught the moonlight, but the Mahdi was seeing only red.

WALID turned off the phone and placed it in the bag with the bomb. He had practised destroying phones back on the farm in Australia, but the Mahdi had told him it wasn't required for this mission. The final mission. That news had pleased him because he had not been looking forward to eating the SIM card. They'd also been told they didn't have to shave or cover themselves with tracksuit pants and hoods – also a relief, as it was hot now, even though it was winter. He and Chris both wore collared shirts and cargo pants.

'You see that guy,' Chris asked as they walked east along a sparsely populated city street. 'He was looking at us.'

'No he wasn't,' Walid said. 'You're just being paranoid.'

'Nah, they're on to us,' Chris said. 'I don't think we sh—'

'Shut up,' Walid said. 'We are almost there. Just shut up and do your job. You know what is going to happen if you don't. Say one more word. Go on. I dare you. I'll do you right here.'

Chris held his tongue.

Walid reached into his pocket, pulled out a white plastic pill container and opened it. 'Here, take a few more of these,' he said as he pushed the container towards Chris. 'They'll sort you out.'

He tipped the contents into Chris's outstretched palm. Chris shoved the pills into his mouth and swallowed.

'We are almost there,' Walid reassured him as he pointed toward a box-like block of concrete that stood adjacent to a bell tower and soaring triangle of glass topped with a crystal crucifix.

'WHAT?!' Clarke yelled. He pointed to his screen. 'No, that can't be right … can it?'

But it was. The green ball was moving.

JAX didn't have to go back far to find the memory he needed: of the Arabic text on the Serpent's wall. What he did need to know was how to type Arabic into a QWERTY keyboard. It didn't take him long to find an image of an Arabic keyboard on the internet. One at a time, he pulled the Arabic letters from his head and found them on the Arabic keyboard he'd also memorised. Having changed the language settings in Microsoft Word to Arabic, he then found the corresponding key on his QWERTY keyboard.

He soon had the entire passage on his screen. He copied the chunk of text from Word and pasted it into Google Translate. And, like magic, the impenetrable Arabic became English.

He will rise with the Mahdi, redeemer of all religions: Twelfth Imam and high priest, to defeat the al-masih ad-dajjal and rid the world of evil. Together they will rule the righteous dominion.

Jax copied the translation and pasted it into his search bar. He knew exactly what he was looking for: an English translation of the Quran, with chapter and verse. 'Come on,' he muttered under his breath as he waited for the results to load.

Then suddenly he sat bolt upright, startled by what he was sure was a distant footstep ...

WALLACE studied the screens: live traffic cameras, helmet cams, vehicles cams and a live feed being beamed down from Overwatch. Facial recognition software was being used to scan the people in the crowd.

'Sector Two is clear,' came the call from Sweeper One, the forward-deployed motorbike unit, giving the green light for the motorcade to proceed.

'We are green,' Wallace relayed to the other units. 'ETA to delivery is twenty-four minutes.'

RONIN One threw his hand in the air and drew a fist, the command freezing the rest of his unit statue-still. He kept his hand raised while Clarke delivered the latest order.

'Target is on the move,' the soldier said after acknowledging the command. 'Proceed to checkpoint Alpha Block. I repeat, new order is to proceed to Alpha.'

JAX turned towards his door and looked hard into the dark, listened closely. The footstep became footsteps. *A guard*. Had to be a guard. *Maybe a random cell check?*

Jax ignored the search results, which had now loaded, and closed his laptop. He turned off his phone. He thought about putting it to sleep instead, but the thought of it waking up while the guard was looking through his window forced his hand.

He pulled up his covers, lay his head on his pillow. He would pretend to be asleep. He closed his eyes, but his ears remained wide open.

The footsteps grew louder.

Not a guard. Those weren't the chunky rubber soles of the guards' boots. *Not a random cell check*. The footsteps were the sound of leather striking concrete. *So, not an inmate either.* And the footsteps were getting louder.

Click!

WALID was furious with himself for giving Chris too many pills. His mate was no longer being a chicken shit, but the sweat was just as bad. Maybe worse. Chris was soaked in his own perspiration by the time they reached the intersection. All the lengths they had gone to to blend in, and now he was wringing wet. Standing out like dog's balls. And as if the sweat wasn't bad enough, Chris began twitching, his head repeatedly jerking to the left as they crossed the wide city street that led to the park in front of the church.

Officially it was called a cathedral, but Chris called it a church. Cathedrals were supposed to have spires and gargoyles. Not a crystal crucifix.

A healthy crowd had gathered. Walid hoped Chris would not be freaked out by all the news crews and their cameras.

JAX saw the blade first: four inches long and stainless steel. Razor sharp. It was no prison-made shiv, but a hunting knife. And the man holding it was a hunter.

Jax had just had time to leap from the bed and position himself on the wall adjacent to the outward-opening door after the electronic mechanism had alerted him to the intruder. He realised he was still holding his phone as the hand holding the knife followed the blade into the cell. He sure was glad he'd turned it off.

Then his stomach dropped as he sensed a familiar scent. *No. Surely not.* But it was. As with sights and sounds, Jax did not forget smells. The overpowering cologne was unmistakable; it even swamped the smell of the freshly bleached floor.

Jax held himself hard against the wall, completely still. It was pitch dark and he had the advantage of surprise: no doubt the intruder was expecting him to be asleep, an easy kill. It would take him a moment or two to realise that Jax was not in his cot, and a moment was all Jax needed.

Yet he had to hold fire, resist the urge to strike, make sure the intruder was in front of him so he could attack his back. He didn't know if the man could use the knife and he didn't want to find out.

Jax held his breath as the intruder took another step and he momentarily closed his eyes, somehow thinking it would make him invisible should the intruder decide to look anywhere other than straight at the bed. *Don't look left. Don't look left.* Then he heaved a deep, silent breath, opened his eyes and prepared to spring forward. *What the—?*

The intruder was gone. Vanished.

An instant later, the mystery was solved as a 4000-lumen blast of light smashed Jax in the face. *Army. Infantry.* Blinded, he didn't see the soldier who grabbed him and spun him round before putting him in an excruciating, vice-like arm lock. Nor did he see the soldier who zip-tied his hands or the one who gagged him before hooding his head.

Jax did not resist, because he figured they weren't here for him.

Then one of them knocked him out with a thundering blow to the back of the head.

'SHUFFLE,' Wallace barked into his radio as the Presidential motorcade hurtled down the highway. The veteran Secret Service agent watched his screen as the convoy performed a shell-game shuffle at ninety kilometres an hour. Like a street performer moving cups to hide a pea, the President's limousine and its two replicas dodged, darted and swapped positions. And then they did it all again.

'Package is in place,' the call came over the radio when the Beast settled on the predetermined place in the queue.

'Copy,' Wallace said. 'ETA to delivery is sixteen minutes.'

THE HOOD came off first, then the gag.

'Ahhh,' Jax cried as the gaffer tape that was stuck to his face removed both hair and skin. His instinct was to berate the solider standing in front of him but he resisted the urge. He'd had time to calm down a little after coming to as he was being carried out of the wing like a hog-tied prize pig. He'd also had time to access the situation.

Then a soldier ripped off the other man's hood.

'You!' Clarke screamed as Father Martin's face was revealed. 'You are fucking kidding me, right?'

Jax had known it was Martin the moment he smelled the cologne. The Brut 33. And he would have known earlier if Clarke had given him access to all the intelligence, instead of keeping him in the dark.

Clarke turned to Jax and stared daggers. As if it was his fault.

Oh fuck you. Are you serious? Jax stared back at Clarke. His mind was playing back the memory of Martin visiting the Serpent in the clinic, spitting out snippets of conversations: 'Actually, he is the only person I have ever seen speak to the Serpent. Interesting story behind it all …' and 'I've heard he even helps guys out once they leave.' Then the Dodge's comment: 'Another convert, hey, Father … Thought you were more of a fan of the Leb boys, though, Father.' And he recalled the headline 'Prison chaplain's plan to perform exorcism on Serpent'. He hadn't bothered to read the story because he'd known nothing of the plot then. In fact, he hadn't known anything until they'd shoved a bunch of files in front of his face in the wake of the Salisbury attack. And with what Jax now suspected was only selected intelligence, they'd given him only thirty days to work it out, twenty of which he'd ended up spending in a coma.

He suddenly hated the Australian agent almost as much as the unlikely mass murderer in front of him. Killer of 1234 people.

Abruptly, a clean-cut man wearing a black suit pushed Clarke aside and ripped off the priest's gag. 'Where is the next attack?' he demanded in a thick American accent – East Coast, Jax thought. 'When?'

Jax was surprised that Martin didn't so much as grunt as a layer of skin was removed with the tape. But not surprised when he shook his head and laughed.

'Too late,' Martin said. 'Boom! It's done. "And from the ashes He will rise."'

The American shattered the chaplain's nose with a textbook right cross.

'Mav!' yelled Sami as he emerged from a shadowy corner of the truck.

Martin's guttural laugh filled the room.

Sami pulled Mav away from the priest as his nose began to gush blood.

Jax knew the CIA would have no problem with violence, given the urgency of the situation, but Mav had hit the perp so hard he'd almost knocked him out.

Jax studied the chaplain again. A clergy collar. The perfect red herring. The intelligence services would naturally have been looking for a Muslim. No doubt they'd done a background check on Martin – they'd have gone through every person who had access to the prison – but they probably hadn't dug very deep.

They were all staring at Martin now, looking for some sort of read. Some sort of indication of what might force him to divulge the details of the final attack.

'Hit me if you like,' the clergyman said, breaking the silence. 'Make me bleed some more. I will savour the pain, for it will be short.'

'Would you like me to attend to your nose?' Sami asked.

Martin shook his head after looking at the large digital clock located next to the computer screens.

'No thanks,' he said. 'He will heal me in five minutes.'

'Five minutes?' Sami said with urgency. 'Five minutes?'

Martin looked back towards the clock.

'Closer to four now,' he said.

Jax was about to speak when Clarke hurled himself towards the priest. He threw a brutal right hook straight into the chaplain's ribs. Martin grunted before attempting to stand, struggling against the restraints that kept him pinned to the seat.

'I am the Mahdi,' he boomed, his chubby cheeks wobbling with fury. 'Uniter of all religions. Ruler of all dominion. I am the one who will bring Him back. Jesus will rise and I will be standing by HIS side!'

'Want to bet?' Jax said as he jumped to his feet.

He turned to Sami. 'Give me a computer,' he demanded. 'Now!'

JAX didn't even have to click on the link to get his result; the number was in the preview.

QURAN, SURAH 85, AYAH 159: *He will rise with the Mahdi, redeemer of all religion: Twelfth Imam and high priest, to defeat the ...*

And there were the numbers:

85:159

And there was his number:

59

The target was the fifty-ninth church on his list. The Cathedral Church of St Andrew, Hawaii.

Behind him, Sami yanked his phone from his pocket and began mashing at the screen, ignoring Clarke's puzzled inquiries.

'Agent Sami,' he snapped. 'ID CIA444323. Put me through to the head of the Secret Service. Fucking now!'

Jax looked at Martin. The tough man who'd hardly flinched as his gag was removed was gone. The whimpering fool frightened by the intercom was back.

'ETA to delivery: two minutes,' Wallace declared after Sweeper One cleared the final stretch of road. Wallace returned to the screens that showed the end of the line: Honolulu's Cathedral Church of St Andrew.

Since being elected seven years earlier, the President had spent every Christmas in Hawaii with his family, partly to avoid the chill of an East Coast winter and partly to escape, at least for a while, the madness of the mainland. But he'd still insisted on attending a public Christmas Day church service despite Agent Wallace's recommendation that he opt for the ceremony held at the Marine Corps base.

'Y'all want me to spend Christmas morning in a soldiers' shack,' the devout Christian had roared. 'Find me a proper church.'

And that's why Wallace was once again sitting in the back of a truck scanning the faces of the hundreds of people crowded in front of the cathedral, hoping to get a glimpse of the President.

The red light on the emergency phone suddenly flashed. Wallace snatched the black phone from its cradle and slammed it against his ear. Two mug shots flashed up on his priority screen as the caller introduced himself. The facial recognition software automatically went to work.

WALID could not see the procession from where he stood, but the buzz among the crowd told him the first car had been spotted.

'Now,' he said to Chris. 'It's time.' The pair had waited at the back of the throng as instructed, but now began to push their way to the front. As they advanced, Walid looked at Chris and knew why the Mahdi had instructed them to make a bomb with dual triggers.

'Focus!' Walid ordered. 'This is our moment. This is what it has all been for.'

The instruction seemed to snap Chris out of his stupor.

Walid led the way as the pair moved towards the cathedral. He imagined he was playing soccer as he sidestepped his way past the spectators at the back of the throng. 'Excuse me,' he said repeatedly. Soon the throng was so dense he had to imagine he was playing rugby instead of soccer, using his shoulders and his weight to forge a path. It would have been so much easier had they staked out a position at sunrise, but the Mahdi had been explicit in his instructions.

Still, they eventually got to where they needed to be. Exactly where they needed to be. The President would be well within range.

'Come on then,' Chris said. 'Give me my trigger.'

'No, not yet. Not until he pulls up. Until the car stops. How many times do you need to be told?'

Walid was now perspiring too. Nothing like Chris, but he could feel the sweat beginning to pool around his armpits. He watched as the lead car in the procession passed, quickly followed by another car that looked exactly the same, and then another. Walid thought the little American flags on the cars' aerials looked strange. Stiff. They didn't seem wave about like a flag should.

He turned away from the procession and looked up to the sky when he heard the helicopter. The Mahdi had said nothing about a helicopter. Oh well. It wouldn't matter. Nothing could stop them. Not now.

The Presidential limousine was in sight. Not the two decoys – they had already passed – but the one they called the

Beast. The one that carried President Forrester. Salim moved his right hand into his pocket in anticipation of handing the first trigger to Chris – not that he expected it would be pressed. More likely the one in his left pocket would detonate the bomb. The glory would be all his. He smiled as he thought of the rewards that awaited him.

When the President's limousine came to a sudden halt, stopping on a dime, Walid thought of a Formula One car – a McLaren or a Red Bull pulling up in the pits at Albert Park during the Australian Grand Prix. He drew a depth breath and withdrew the trigger from his pocket. 'Chris,' he was forced to mutter to get the idiot's attention. Discreetly, he transferred the palm-sized trigger into Chris's hand. 'Not until he is out,' Walid warned.

He looked at his mate and waited to be acknowledged. But, just then, Chris's head exploded like a watermelon.

Chunks of brain slapped Walid in the face. Only then did the sound of the bullet reach his ears.

The helicopter hovered directly overhead. Walid did not have to look up to know the sniper's rifle was now aimed at his head.

'Freeze!' screamed a soldier on the ground as a swiftly formed battle group stormed his way.

But Walid only followed orders from one man.

He was dead the moment he made his move.

EPILOGUE

Goulburn Correctional Centre, Goulburn, NSW, Australia

JAX walked into the visits room and was surprised to find only Sami sitting behind the steel desk and a satellite phone sitting on top.

'Where's Clarke?' Jax asked.

'This doesn't concern him. Take a seat, kid.'

The absence set off an inner alarm. This solo visit from Sami, along with his terse dismissal of Clarke, seemed almost sinister. There was mischief in this mystery, Jax felt sure, but solving the riddle would have to wait. He glanced at the padded black travel case Sami guarded with his right hand before sitting down.

'Sorry for leaving you in the dark, but it has been a busy couple of days,' Sami said. 'I hope Clarke's thugs were a little less bruisy when they escorted you back to your cell.'

'Going home?' Jax said as he gestured towards the military-style Ogio duffle bag on the floor. Jax knew the brand and model because he'd once had one just like it.

'Soon,' Sami said as he heaved the bag onto the tabletop. 'But I think you will find this a little more interesting than my underwear.'

Jax suddenly felt like a kid at Christmas. *Answers: the ultimate gift.* He'd spent the two days since the foiled attack attempting to fill in the dots. Trying to work out the whys more than the hows. He'd done the best he could without his phone and laptop – which had not been in his cell when he was unceremoniously returned before morning muster – but this was a ten-thousand-piece jigsaw with a thousand missing pieces.

Sami began working on the padlock. It was nothing like the padlock Jax'd had on his Ogio. In fact, it was nothing like any padlock Jax had ever seen. Sami held the mobile-phone-sized lock in his left hand and moved his right hand towards what appeared to be an LCD screen. The lock chirped: an electronic acknowledgement, after Sami had pressed the fleshy pad of his index finger against the black glass-like surface. Then the steel cable that bound the oversized and steel-strengthened zip end sprang free after Sami punched a six-digit code into a number pad that had appeared on the LCD screen.

'Double authentication?' Jax mused out loud.

'Triple, in fact,' Sami said. 'It has also collected my DNA.'

'A bit excessive for a bag that could be ripped apart with a knife,' Jax said as he pointed towards the nylon blend.

'I'd agree, if it wasn't carbon-fibre reinforced and lead-lined,' Sami smiled. The agent chuckled as he knocked on the soft-looking material, which turned out to be rock-hard. 'CIA special order.'

Sami then unzipped and unclipped the bag and reached into it. His hand emerged clutching a plastic ziplocked bag marked 'Evidence'. Through the clear plastic Jax could see a framed photograph of Imam Zuhdi, an Islamic cleric he'd learned about while studying for his counterterrorism degree.

'It was hanging above the chaplain's desk in his home office,' Sami said as he pushed the opened package across the table.

'Zuhdi,' Jax said. 'Founder of the Islamic Reform Movement and suspected terrorist.' As he picked up the bagged photo for a closer look, he noticed the signed message: *Mahdi, my friend. Turns out we are not so different. He shall rise. Zuhdi.*

Sami then revealed that Father Martin had met Imam Zudhi at a religious conference six years earlier.

'That in itself is no smoking gun,' Sami said as he reached back into the bag. 'But this is.'

He pushed another ziplocked bag across the table, this one holding a leather-bound notebook.

'His diary,' Sami confirmed. 'The self-incriminating musings of a madman.'

Jax stared at the bag with wide eyes.

'Go on,' Sami said. 'It has already been put through every forensic exam known to man. And some only known to the CIA.'

Jax unzipped the bag, removed the diary and began reading.

It had been Zuhdi, founder of the Islamic Reform Movement, who had first told Martin that Muslims believed in Jesus, that the Quran predicted His return – and that it would be a religious man called the Mahdi who would bring Him back. A diary entry recorded the priest's response:

Mahdi. Almost what they call me. Marty, Mahdi. Uncanny. Could it be? I always believed I was destined for great things.

Jax was soon turning pages like it was an action thriller.

Martin's interest in Islam had been piqued, and it soon became an obsession. He sought out Mahmud, a mufti before he was convicted of recruiting for both Al-Qaeda and ISIS, for advice. Mahmud showed him what had been left to interpretation and what was sacrosanct. He told him Surah 93,

Ayah 241 was most certainly the word of God, or Allah, as he now correctly called Him: *The High Priest. The uniter of all religions. The Mahdi.* And eventually he convinced the priest that he, Martin, was the incarnation of that Twelfth Imam, ruler of the final dominion.

Zuhdi had shown him his destiny and Mahmud had confirmed it, Martin wrote. He was Allah's soldier, put on this earth to unite all people under the one and only Allah. He would destroy the *Al-Masih ad-Dajjal* (the anti-Christ), which he and Mahmud had decided was the most powerful figure in Christendom, the Pope. Corruption, false testimony, sacrilege – they were a disgrace to the man they had put up on the cross. The Mahdi would show Christians the truth by bringing Him back. Jesus was the only one who could tear up the Christian scriptures, that self-serving propaganda the Church said was indestructible – even though every Pope in history had claimed the authority to change the Holy Missal.

One vitriolic diary entry alluded to Martin being 'stood down'.

'He was defrocked?' Jax asked.

'Yes,' Sami said. 'There were allegations of paedophilia, which were of course covered up by the Church, which was why he was able to work in the prison system as an unpaid chaplain. He continued to wear the clerical collar in defiance of the decision.'

Jax went back to the diary, which detailed Martin's meetings with Mahmud. He had told Martin that only his *shahids*, or martyrs, could know his true identity. Mahmud promised there would be plenty of *shahids*, and that he would do the recruiting. Prison was fertile ground.

In return, all Martin had to do was find the cash to fund their holy war, which Mahmud already knew he had – Martin had told him about his inheritance, the $17 million, sitting in a bank account, earning interest and still untouched.

He shall rise. Increasingly, the diary was punctuated by this proclamation – the one Jax had found on the Serpent's wall.

'So, what was the Serpent's role?' Jax asked as he placed the diary back inside the plastic ziplock bag.

Sami shrugged. 'It's unclear. We can't get anything out of that madman, but we suspect he helped Martin find the targets and work out the sequencing. There is a certain genius in all this that we can't ascribe to the chaplain. What we do know for sure is that the Serpent tipped him off about you.'

Sami detailed the rest of the evidence gathered by the joint ASIO/CIA operation since the foiled attack. Jax found the payments Father Martin had been making to the guard called 'Dodge' particularly interesting.

THE SATELLITE phone in the centre of the table began to ring.

'Right on time,' Sami said before picking up.

'Hello,' Sami said. 'Yes, sir. I will put him on.'

Sami was wearing a big, cheeky smile as he passed Jax the phone.

Jax would have assumed it was Clarke had it not been for Sami's 'This does not concern him' comment earlier.

'Hello,' Jax said into the receiver, still puzzled.

'Am I speaking with Riley Jax?' asked the man on the other end of the line. An American. A Texan, by the sound of it.

'Yes,' Jax said. 'This is Jax.'

'Well, son, this is President Forrester here, and you just saved my life. I am sure Agent Sami will fill you in on all the details, but I wanted to get in first and thank you. I was fixin' to tell the whole damn world everythang, but, gosh, that just ain't gonna be possible after having a little look at your file.'

'I understand, sir,' Jax said, barely suppressing his astonishment to be talking directly to the leader of the Western world. 'I wouldn't expect you to acknowledge a criminal.'

The President laughed loudly. 'Ah, bless your heart. No, son, I can't acknowledge you because, well, shoot, having a secret agent without a secret is about as good to me as tits on a bull. Anyway, son, I'm offering you a job. How'd you feel about coming over and working for good ol' Uncle Sam?'

'Mr President,' Jax said. 'I am serving a ten-year sentence in a maximum-security jail. I don't think—'

'Oh, don't go worrying yourself about that,' the President cut in. 'We know all about it. And all about you. We even know some things about you that you don't know. A little something about a big something you've been trying to figure out. A big damn dirty secret is what it is. But not for long. Not if you come work for me. All ya gotta do is say the word.'

Jax was utterly dumbfounded. He looked at Sami, who was grinning ear to ear.

'So, whaddya say, kid?'